MAPS

Maps

Nuruddin Farah

PANTHEON BOOKS NEW YORK

Note: In names and words from Somali and Arabic, the letter *x* is used to represent the guttural *h* sound similar to the one in *loch* and *ach*—not the *ks* sound we are used to in *axe*.

First American Edition

Copyright © 1986 by Nuruddin Farah.

All rights reserved under International and Pan-American Copyright Conventions. Published in the United States by Pantheon Books, a division of Random House, Inc., New York. Originally published in Great Britain by Pan Books, Ltd., in 1986.

Library of Congress Cataloging-in-Publication Data

Farah, Nuruddin, 1945–
Maps.

(Pantheon modern writers)
I. Title. II. Series.
[PR9396.9.F3M3   1987]   823   87-43050
ISBN 0-394-56325-5
ISBN 0-394-75548-0 (pbk.)

Manufactured in the United States of America

CHAPTER ONE

[1]

You sit, in contemplative posture, your features agonized and your expressions pained; you sit for hours and hours and hours, sleepless, looking into darkness, hearing a small snore coming from the room next to yours. And you conjure a past: a past in which you see a horse drop its rider; a past in which you discern a bird breaking out of its shell so it will fly into the heavens of freedom. Out of the same past emerges a man wrapped in a mantle with unpatched holes, each hole large as a window – and each window large as the secret to which you cling as though it were the only soul you possessed. And you question, you challenge every thought which crosses your mind.

Yes. You are a question to yourself. It is true. You've become a question to all those who meet you, those who know you, those who have any dealings with you. You doubt, at times, if you exist outside your own thoughts, outside your own head, Misra's or your own. It appears as though you were a creature given birth to by notions formulated in heads, a creature brought into being by ideas; as though you were not a child born with the fortune or misfortune of its stars, a child bearing a name, breathing just like anybody else, a child whose activities were justifiably part of a people's past and present experience. You exist, you think, the way the heavenly bodies exist, for although one does extend one's finger and point at the heavens, one knows, yes that's the word, one *knows* that that is not the heavens. Unless . . . unless there are, in a sense, as many heavens as there are thinking beings; unless there are as many heavens as there are pointing fingers.

At times, when your uncle speaks about you, in your presence, referring to you in the third person and, on occasion, even taking the liberty of speaking on your behalf, you wonder if your existence is readily differentiable from creatures of fiction whom habit has taught one to talk of as if they were one's closest of friends – creatures of fiction with whose manner of speech; reactions to situations; conditions of being; and with whose likes and dislikes one's folk-tradition has made one familiar. From your limited knowledge of literature, you feel you are a blood relation of some of the names which come to mind, leap to the tongue at the thought of a young boy whose name is Askar and whose prodigious imagination is capable of wealthy signs of precocity – because you are this young boy!

As you sit contemplatively, your mind journeys to a region where there were solid and prominent shadows which lived on behalf of *others* who had years before ceased to exist as beings. As you sit, your eyes open into themselves, the way blind people's eyes tend to. Then you become numb of soul: in other words, you are not yourself – not quite yourself anyway. The journey takes you through numerous doorways and you are enabled to call back to memory events which occurred long before you were a being yourself. Your travel leads you through forests without any clearing, to stone steps too numerous to count, although when you reach the highest point, your exhaustion disappears the instant you see an old man, grey as his advanced years, negotiate the steps too. You remember now, that in the wake of the old man there was a girl, barely seven, following the old man as a goat follows a butcher, knowing what knives of destiny await it.

And you ... !

You! You who had lain in wait, unwashed, you who had lain unattended to at birth. Yes, you lay in wait as though in ambush until a woman who wasn't expecting that you existed walked into the dark room in which you had been from the second you were born. You were a mess. You were a most terrible sight. The woman who found you described the chill of that dark room as a tomb. To her, the air suggested the dampness of a mortuary. You cried at her approaching and wouldn't be calmed until she dipped you in the bathtub she had filled with warm water. Then she fed you on a draught of goat's milk. Did anyone ever tell you what you looked like when the woman discovered you that dusk some eighteen years or so ago? No?

You wore on your head a hat of blood which made you look like a masked clown. And around your neck there were finger-stains, perhaps your mother's. (Nobody knows to this day whether she tried to kill you or no.) You displayed a nervous strain and you began to relax only when embraced either by another person or dipped in warm water. When you didn't cry, you searched, with your hands up in the air, for someone to touch.

When day broke, once the woman had shared the secret of her find with a few of the other neighbours, the men took over and they prepared your mother for burial. Alone with you, Misra noticed that your eyes were full of mistrust. They focused on her, they stared at her hands suspiciously! Your eyes, she would say years later, journeyed through her, they journeyed beyond her, they travelled to a past of unfulfilled dreams: in short, your stare made her feel inadequate. There was an element of self-consciousness in the small thing I had found, she said. It was so self-conscious it moved its hands as though it would wipe away the mess it had been in; it moved its eyes, when not staring at me, she continued, as though to apologize for its shortcomings. And what eyes! What hands!

It was not long before you tasted in Misra a motherliness which reabsorbed you, a motherliness in whose tight, warm embrace you felt joyous one second, miserable the following instant. Again, you would try to make contact and when she did her best to return it, you would appear startled and ready to withdraw, you would shun any contact with her completely and move away. She helped you minimize life's discomforts. She groaned with you when you moaned constipatedly; she helped you relieve yourself by fondling you, touching you and by telling you sweet stories, addressing you, although you were a tiny little mess of a thing, as 'my man', 'my darlingest man', or any such endearments which would make you feel wanted, loved and pampered.

In her company, you were ecstatic – there was no other word for it. Yes, you were visibly ecstatic. And you were noisy. You displayed your pleasures with the pomp and show one associates with the paranoid among kings. But then you could be quiet in her embrace too, reflective and thoughtful – so thoughtful that some of the neighbours couldn't believe their eyes, watching you pensively quiet, your eyes bright with visions only you could see. It was when she wasn't there, when you missed her presence, when you couldn't smell her maternal odour, it was then that you cried and you put your soul into crying, appearing as though possessed, looking satanically agitated and devilishly messy. Upon returning from wherever she had gone, she would dip you wholly in water, scrub you and wash you with the same devotion as she might have used when cleaning the floor of her room. The community of relations decided that Misra, the woman who once was a servant, would 'mother' you. One thing ought to be said here – you were the one who made the choice the community of relations had to approve of; you, who were barely a week old. And Misra agrees with this statement. So, begrudgingly, would Uncle Qorrax in Kallafo.

When agitated, you stretched out your hands in front of you like a blind man in search of landmarks and if you touched someone other than Misra, you burst instantly into the wildest and most furious convulsive cry. But if Misra were there, you fell silent, you would touch her and then touch yourself. It seemed to her that you could discover yourself only in her. 'By touching me, he knows he is there,' she once confided in a man you were later to refer to as Aw-Adan.

There was something maternal about the cosmos Misra introduced you to from the day it was decided you were her charge, from the moment she could call you, in the privacy of the room allotted to the two of you, whatever endearments she mustered in her language. But to her you were most often 'my man' or variations thereof – especially whenever you wet yourself; especially when washing you, touching and squeezing your manhood or wiping, rather roughly, your anus. Occasionally, however, she would gently spank you on the bottom and address you differently. But she always remained maternal, just like the cosmos, giving and giving. 'While,' she said to you, 'man is the child receiving into himself the cosmos itself, the cosmos grows larger, like a hole, the more she gives.' Admittedly this was something impenetrable to your own comprehension. To you, whether what she said made sense or no, she *was* the cosmos. She was the one that took you away from 'yourself', as it were, she was the one who took you back into the world-of-the-womb and of innocence, and washed you clean in the water of a new life and a new christening, to produce in you the correct etches of a young self, with no pained memories, replacing your missing parents with her abundant self which she offered generously to you – her newly rediscovered child! And you?

[2]

To Misra, you existed first and foremost in the weird stare: you were, to her, your eyes, which, once they found her, focused on her guilt – her self! She caught the look you cast in her direction the way a clumsy child grabs a ball and she framed the stare in the memory of her photographic brain. She developed it, printed it in different colours, each of which expressed her mood. She was sure, for instance, that you saw her the way she was: a miserable woman, with no child and no friends; a woman who, that dusk – would you believe it? – menstruated right in front of you, under that most powerful stare of yours. She saw, in that look of yours, her father, whom she saw last when she was barely five.

'Annoy a child and you'll discover the adult in him,' she would repeat, believing it to be a proverb. 'Please an adult with gifts and the child therein re-emerges.' And she annoyed you, she pleased you, and she was sufficiently patient to watch the adult in you come out and display itself. Not only did she see her father in you but also the child in herself: she saw a different terrain of land, and she heard a different language spoken and she watched, on the screen of her past, a number of pictures replayed as though they were real and as painful as yesterday. She sought her childhood in you and she hid her most treasured secrets which she was willing to impart to you and you alone. In you, too, she saw a princess, barely five, a pretty princess surrounded with servants and well-wishers, one who could have anything she pleased and who was loved by her mother, but not so much by her father because she was a girl and wouldn't inherit his title – wouldn't continue his line. A princess!

To you, too, although you were too small to understand, she told secrets about your parents no one else was ready to tell you. She told you why your mother had been hiding in the room where she had found the two of you and why she died in a quiet secretive way. She also whispered in your ears things about your father, who had died a few months before your birth, in mysterious circumstances, in a prison, for his ideals. Your mother took refuge in a room tucked away in the back yard of a rich man's house and it was in there that she gave birth to you – in hiding.

Possibly you would have died of the chill you were exposed to, if Misra hadn't walked in accidentally. Fortunately for you, anyway, Misra had found the room in which you were, a most convenient place to hide from Aw-Adan, who had been pestering her with advances she didn't wish to return in like manner. The room had been open and she stumbled into it, closing the door immediately behind her. She didn't realize until later that you and your mother were there: you alive and your mother dead. Hers would have to remain the only evidence one has and one has to take her word for it. She would insist that she didn't know until later who your father was. Why she waited until she had washed and fed you and mothered you – these are things of which she refuses to speak. At any rate, by the time the community of relations had been informed of your existence and your mother's death, some sixteen or so hours had gone past, and it was during this time that you and Misra had become acquainted and that she made sure no one else set eyes on you. Of course, no one dared challenge her statement. As a matter of fact, it was thought very wise that you were kept an untalked-about secret, considering whose son you were; so no one outside the immediate family knew about you for a long time. It was for this reason that your mother's corpse was buried in haste and secretly too, your mother who left behind her no trace save yourself – you who were assigned to Misra as a ward, or some said as if you were her child. You were the whisper to be softly spoken. Your name was to become two syllables no one uttered openly, which meant that not only were there no Koranic blessings said in either of your ears to welcome you to this world but your presence here in this universe was not at all celebrated. You did not exist as far as many were concerned; nor did you have any identity as the country's bureaucracy required. Askar! The letter 's' in your name was gently said so as to arouse no suspicions; whereas the 'k' was held in the cosiness of a tongue couched in the unspoken secrets of a sound. As-kar! It was the 'r' which rolled like a cow in the hot sand after half-a-day's grazing. Askar!

The point of you was that, in small and large ways, you determined what Misra's life would be like the moment you took it over. From the moment you 'took her life over', her personality underwent a considerable change. She became a mother to you. She began walking with a slight stoop and her hip, as though ready to carry you, protruded to the side. She no longer saw as much of Aw-Adan, the priest, as she used to, a priest who used to teach her, on a daily basis, a few suras of the Koran and in whom she was slightly interested. That interest deteriorated with the passage of the days and finally petered out the way light fades when there is no more paraffin in the lamp. The point of you was that, in small and large ways, Misra, now that you were hers, saw her own childhood 'as a category cradled in a bed of memories, one of which was nurtured in thoughts which alienated the child in her'. She had had a 'fatherless' child herself and the child had died a few months before you were born. She was sad she had had to feed you on a bottle; she was sad she couldn't suckle you, offer you her own milk, her soul. Her own child had been eighteen months when he died and she had only just weaned him. Very often, in the secret chambers of her unuttered thoughts, there would cross an idea: that she probably had some milk of motherhood in her. And she would bare her breasts and make you suck them; you would turn away and refuse to be suckled and she would cry and cry and be miserable. Your crying would provide the unsung half of the chorus. She would promise you and promise herself never to try to breast-feed you again. Although she did, again and again. The question nobody is in a privileged enough position to answer, is whether or not your mother suckled you just before she died. You are in no position to confirm that. But Misra is 'obsessed' with the thought that you were breast-fed by her. When pressed, she would insist, 'I know, I know for sure that she did.'

Your father existed for you in a photograph of him you saw, in which he stands behind an army tank, green as the backdrop in the picture, and you were told that he had 'liberated' the tank, while fighting for the Western Somali Liberation Movement, of which he remained an active member until his last second, brave as the stories narrated about him. Your mother existed for you in a suckle you do not even recall and there is nobody to dispute Misra's theory that your mother actually suckled you. One thing is very clear. You did not inherit from her any treasures; if anything, she bequeathed to you only a journal and stories told you in snippets by others. And what did you bequeath to Misra? There is a photograph taken when you were very, very small; there is a hand, most definitely yours, stretched outwards, away from your own body, searching for *another* hand — most probably hers, a hand to touch, a hand to help and to give assurances. Also, there is one of the pictures which she still has and which has survived all the turmoil of wars and travel and displace-ments, a picture in which you are alone, in a bathtub, half-standing and playfully splashing in the joy of the water's soapy foaminess. In the photograph, there is a hand of a woman — Misra's most likely — a hand reaching out to make contact with yours but which accidentally 'hovers', like a hawk, over your private parts — which the hand doesn't quite touch! And there is, in the picture, a patch of a stain, dark as blood, a stain which your eyes fall on and which you stare at.

But most important of all, you bequeathed to Misra the look in your eye when she walked in that evening, running away from Aw-Adan's lusty attentions. At times, she saw you reproduce a look which she associated with what she could remember of her own father; and at others, she saw another which she identified as her son's — before he was taken ill and died.

It was a great pity, she thought, that there was no maternal milk she could offer to you, her young charge. But there was plenty of her and she gave it: she kept you warm by tucking you between her breasts, she held you close to her body so she could sense your movements, so she might attend to you whenever you stirred: you shared a bed, the two of you, and she smelled of your urine precisely in the same way you smelled of her sweat: upon your body were printed impressions of her fingerprints, the previous night's moisture: yours and hers.

She nourished you, not only on food paid for by a community of relations, but on a body of opinion totally her own. With you, young as you were, needy and self-sufficient as an infant, she could choose to be herself – she could walk about in front of you in the nude if she wanted to, or could invite Aw-Adan to share, with the two of you, the small bed which creaked when they made love, a bed onto whose sagged middle you rolled, sandwiched as you were between them. When awake, and if you were the only person in the room, Misra spoke *at* you, saying whatever it was that she had intended to, talking about the things which bothered or pleased her. But there was something she did only in your or Aw-Adan's presence. She spoke Amharic. She cursed people in her language. To her, it didn't matter whether you understood it or not. What mattered to her was the look in your eyes, the look of surprise or incomprehension; a look which took her back to the first encounter: yours and hers.

Because of her relations with you, and because you were so attached to her, Misra's status in the community became a controversial topic. To many members of the community, she was but that 'maidservant who came from somewhere else, up north' and they treated her despicably, looking down upon her and calling her all sorts of things. It was said that her name wasn't even Misra. However, no one bothered to check the source of the rumour. No one took the trouble to reach the bottom of the mystery. But who was she really? To you, she was the cosmos and hers was the body of ideas upon which your growing mind nourished. It didn't matter in the least whether she came from upper Ethiopia or not, neither did it matter in the least if she had been abducted by a warrior from one of the clans north of yours when she was seven. Maidservant or no, she meant the world to you. Also, you believed that no one knew her as well as you did, no one needed her as much as you and nobody studied the changes in her moods as often as you. In short, you missed her immensely when she wasn't with you. And so, with a self-abandon many began to associate with you, you cried and cried until she was brought to you. With a similar self-surrender, you displayed the pleasure of her company. Which was what made some say that she had bewitched you.

She taught you how best you should make use of your own body. She helped you learn to wash it, she assisted you in watching it grow, like the day's shadow, from the shortest to the longest purposelessness of an hour; she familiarized you with the limitations of your own body. When it came to your soul, when it came to how to help your brain develop, she said she couldn't trust herself to deal with that satisfactorily. Not then, anyway. Was this why she went and sought Aw-Adan's help?

Aw-Adan and you didn't take to each other right from your first encounter. You didn't like the way he out-stared you, nor did you like him when Misra paid him all her attention, leaving you more or less to yourself. He commented on the look in your eyes: a look he described as 'wicked and satanic'. To defend you, she described the look in your eyes as 'adulted'. Aw-Adan did not appear at all convinced. Then she went on to say, 'To have met death when not quite a being, perhaps this explains why he exists primarily in the look in his eyes. Perhaps his stars have conferred upon him the fortune of holding simultaneously multiple citizenships of different kingdoms: that of the living and that of the dead; not to mention that of being an infant and an adult at the same time.' Disappointed with her explanation, Aw-Adan went away, promising he would never see her again.

But he came back. He was in love with her – or so she believed. And as usual, he couldn't resist commenting upon the fact that she had organized her life around you: you were 'her time' as he put it; for she awoke, first thing in the morning, not to say her prayers but to attend to your needs. And what was she to you? To you, said Aw-Adan, she was your 'space': you moved about her body in the manner an insect crawls up a wall, even-legged, sure-footed and confident. And he continued, 'Allah is the space and time of all Muslims, but not to you, Misra, Askar is.' He didn't see anything wrong in what he said. But then how could he? He was jealous.

In the unEdenic universe into which you were cast by your stars, you were not content, like any intelligent being, with the small world of darkness you opened your eyes on. You behaved as though you had to find and *touch* the world outside of yourself, and this you did in order to be reassured of a given continuity. 'He behaves,' said Misra to Aw-Adan, her confidant, one night when the three of you were in bed and the priest was not in his foulest of moods, 'Askar behaves as if he feels lost unless his outstretched hands bring back to his acute senses the reassuring message that I am *touchably* there. He cannot imagine a world without my reassuring self.'

'What am I to do then? Suggest something,' said Aw-Adan.

'Be as accommodating to me as I am to him,' she said.

'You are insane,' he said.

'And you jealous,' she said.

'You are never alone,' complained Aw-Adan, who wanted her to himself. 'I see you with him all the time, so much so that I see him even when he isn't there. You smell of his urine and at times I too smell of it and it upsets me gravely. Why can't we just marry, you and I? He isn't yours but with God's help, we can make one of our own, together, you and I. Come to me alone – both of body and of spirit – and let our bodies join, without Askar's odour and cries.'

'I cannot,' she said. 'I am his – in body and spirit too. And no one else's. I can be yours or somebody else's only in sin. Yes, only in sin. Imagine – you, a man of God at that!'

And she burst into tears.

And Aw-Adan stirred.

And you woke up and cried.

[4]

To make the picture more complete, one must talk about your paternal uncle, namely Uncle Qorrax. The truth is, he too had designs on Misra and you suspected he had his way with her many times. It was no secret that you didn't like Uncle Qorrax or his numerous wives: numerous because he divorced and married such a number of them that you lost count of how many there were at any given time, and at times you weren't sure to whom he was married – until one day a woman you nicknamed 'Shahrawello' arrived on the scene and she *stayed* (as Sheherezade of the *Thousand and One Nights* did). But neither did you like his children.

He was a ruthless man, your uncle was, and you were understandably frightened of him. You often remember him beating one of his wives or one of his children. Naturally, you didn't take his apparent little kindnesses nor did you accept the gentle hand he invariably extended to you. You shunned any bodily contact with him. It was said you cried a great deal if he so much as touched you, although he never gave you a beating and could hardly have justified himself in scolding you. You were an orphan and you had a 'stare' with which to protect yourself. He didn't want the 'stare' focused on him, his wives or his children.

When you were a little older and in Mogadiscio, living in the more enlightened world of Uncle Hilaal and Salaado, you began to reason thus: you didn't like Uncle Qorrax's children because they behaved as children always do, no more, no less; they insisted on owning toys if they were boys, or on making dolls and dressing them if they were girls. His sons enjoyed being rough with one another, they took sadistic pleasure in annoying or hurting one another, whereas his daughters busied themselves nursing or breast-feeding dolls or clothing bones, not as though they were women caring for infants with broken hearts but as though they were little girls. In retrospect, you would admit there was a part of you which admired these girls when they jumped ropes, challenged the boys, or took part in daredevil games – not when they chanted childish rhymes which small girls always did at any rate. And you admired the boys, from a distance anyway, when they dislodged fatal shots from catapults, cutting short the life of a gecko climbing up a wall or a lizard basking in the sun. It was the life-giving and life-taking aspects of their activities which interested you.

You once said to Misra that if there was anything you shared with adults, it was the visceral dislike of children's babble or the infantile rattle of their mechanical contrivances and the noise of their demands, 'I want this', 'I want that'. You concluded your remarks to the surprise of those listening to you (there was a woman neighbour, married to an invalid, a man who lay on his back all the time, suffering from some spinal complaint you had no name for), by saying, 'When will children stop wanting, when will they *be*, when will they do a job, as Karin's husband says, when will they accomplish something – not as children but as *beings*?'

She commented, 'But you are an adult.'

Karin agreed, 'He is. Surely.'

What you didn't say, although it crossed your mind, was that you *were* an adult, and, for whatever it was worth, you believed you were *present* at your birth. But no one said anything. Perhaps because you knew that when windows of bedrooms closed on the sleeping lids of children's heads nodding with drowsiness; when their snores filled the empty spaces of the rooms they were in; when their tongues tasted of the staleness of slumber in their mouths; when their parents surrendered themselves to their dreams, pushing out of their way the daylight inhibitions of who enjoyed the company of whom, in bed; when thoughts were unharnessed and allowed to roam freely in the open spaces of the uncensored mind: it was then, you knew, that Misra and you could tell each other stories no one else was listening to. And in the privacy of the late hour, in the secrecy of the night's darkness, you could afford to allow the adult in you to emerge and express adult thoughts, just as Misra could permit the child in her to express its mind.

And then the two of you would gossip. Like adults, you would exchange secrets each had gathered during the previous day, you would condemn and pass judgements. You would talk about people, talk about Shahrawello whose daily blood-letting of Qorrax was said to have kept him in good check. You also gossiped meanly and unpardonably about a neighbour's son who ate ten times as much as you and who, at four-and-a-half, didn't utter a single word save 'food'; a boy who weighed 'a ton' and whose open mouth had to be stuffed with victuals of one sort or another. You nicknamed him 'Monster' following your overhearing his mother say, 'Oh Lord, why have you made me give birth to a monster?' Misra would feign interest in hearing you tell the story but suddenly her features would change expression, suggesting you were overdoing it, and she would say, 'That's enough, Askar', and would immediately change the subject to something less trivial, less controversial; or she would tell you a story until your breathing was slow, then shallow, as if you were wading through a pond where the water was muddy and knee-high. Misra was an expert at handling your moods. And she was different from your uncle's wives. As mothers, these were generally indulgent for the first two or three years. Then they became ruthlessly rigid with their children, who were expected to behave according to strict codes and norms of behaviour with which they had not been made familiar. You imagined these women to be in season all the time, what with their constant loss of temper with their children and their caning them whenever they didn't leave the room the moment they were instructed to do so.

Misra would say, 'To these women, when in their best moods, children are like passing royalty. Don't you notice how everything comes to a standstill when they totter past them and how they are admired?'

And you asked, 'But why do people love children?'

'Some because they can afford to lavish a moment's indulgence on a child that didn't keep them awake the previous night; some because they see angels in the infants they spy and marvel at God's generosity; some because they have no children themselves and envy those who are thus blessed. There are as many reasons why adults admire children as there are adults who admire them.'

'And why is it that they don't like me?' you said.

She answered, 'Because you are no child. That's why.'

In your mind, the memory door opened and you saw visiting relatives of Uncle Qorrax's and they were giving his children cash with which to buy sweets or footballs; you also saw that these same relatives caned them if they caught them misbehaving in public. But when it came to you, they asked after your health, although they did so with extreme caution, speaking articulately to Misra in the manner of one who was talking to a foreigner who didn't understand the nuances of one's language. And these relations never took liberties with you, no, they didn't. You wondered if it was 'guilt' that made them act the way they did, 'guilt' that made them look away when you 'stared'. Or were they uneasy because yours was the 'stare' of a parentless child?

'I want you to think of it like this,' said Misra to you one night. 'You are a blind man and I am your stick, and it is I who leads you into the centre of human activities. Your appearance makes everyone fall silent, it makes them lower the volume of their chatter. And you too become conscious and you interpret their silence as a ploy to exclude you, and you feel you're being watched and that you're being denied entry into their world. From then on, you hold on to the stick, both as guide and protector. Since you cannot sense sympathy in their silences, you think it is hate. You, the blind man, and I, the stick. And together we pierce the sore – that's their conscience.'

You said, 'No wonder they don't like me!'

Again, Misra changed the subject to less demanding topics, topics that were less burdensome than the notions of 'guilt' or 'conscience'. And she lulled you to and led you to sleep: gently, slowly, with a voice that changed rhythms and a lullaby sung in a language that wasn't your own. Some of the tales she told you had plenty of blood in them, there was no denying that. In a couple of these, there were even human-eating types – with Dhegdheer dying not and the heavens raining not! On occasion, she would give, in outline, the moral of the tale before she narrated it to you, and at times she would let you retell it so you had the opportunity of offering your own interpretation. Years later, you discovered (it was Karin who gave you the information) that Misra used to have these tales told to her when you were away from the compound so she could feed your fantasies on them when you returned. Admittedly, this endeared her to you.

Unlike Uncle Qorrax's children, you never stole things from anyone. You mentioned your needs – and Misra met them. If she couldn't, she told you why. And she trained you not to value money or

15

possessions. Also, no visiting relation unfolded secretly onto your outstretched palm a coin a parent might not have given you. Uncle Qorrax's children, you knew, stole from their father. They conspired to do so – one of them would keep an eye on him, say, when he was in the lavatory and the others would rummage his pockets and take away a small sum that he wouldn't notice and share it among themselves. Often, they timed it so it coincided with the arrival of nomads, who had come to buy provisions from his shop, pitching their tents in their compound, when there was a great deal of movement. They knew he dared not put embarrassing questions to these guest-clients. His sons knew he would never offer them or their mothers anything they could do without. It was his 'public' persona that insisted on being generous at times. He could be kind to his children and wives when 'others' were there; he could even be generous. When alone with them, he was a miser. So, they stole from him when he wasn't there.

Misra had a public and a private persona too. She was warmer and kinder when alone with you, calling you all kinds of endearments, sharing with you secrets no other soul knew about. And in any case, you needn't have stolen anything from Misra or from yourself. It was when she wore the mask of the public persona that you 'stole' from her time a few moments of tenderness which you exchanged surreptitiously.

And when Misra was in season and therefore nervous, you were entrusted to Karin, who was equally kind, equally generous – and who treated you, not as a child, but as a grandchild. Because you were two generations apart, Karin indulged you in a way which didn't meet Misra's patent of approval. The two women were the best of friends – the one with an ailing husband who had lain on his back for years and who was confined to a mattress on the floor from where he saw, whenever he looked up at the ceiling, a portrait of Ernest Bevin; the other, a woman who, by virtue of her foreignness, felt she had access to the Somali cosmos – if there is anything like that – only through you. Karin baby-minded for her. Likewise, when she was indisposed, Misra looked after the old man. Conveniently for the three of you, Karin and her husband's compound lay between yours and Uncle Qorrax's. And so you were content to go from one compound to the other without ever needing to touch the fringes of the third – namely Qorrax's.

But Qorrax called at yours when he chose, preferably when you began breathing shallowly through your nose, almost asleep. He would wait until your dream had taken you to a watery destination – where it was moist, green and all your own – your Eden. Then he would come into bed with Misra.

Oh, how you hated him!

[5]

On the other hand, you loved Uncle Hilaal and his wife, Salaado, directly you met them. The flow of their warmth was comforting – sweet as spring water. And everything either of them did or said, once you gave it a thought, appeared as necessary as the blood of life. You loved Hilaal and Salaado, you loved the sea and you loved Mogadiscio.

You began writing letters to Misra a few months after your arrival in Mogadiscio. But you never finished writing even one single letter, suspecting, rightly, that she wouldn't be able to read Somali although she spoke it well enough. You were most distressed when you learnt that there never was a mail service through the official channels between Somalia and Ethiopia. Uncle Hilaal told you that letters had to be sent to other destinations, preferably via a European rechannelling system, like letters between a person living in apartheid South Africa and another in black Africa or a correspondence between one person residing in Syria and the other in Israel. So, apart from the wall of separation the Somali orthography raised between the two of you, there was also the official Ethiopian line of thinking, which was inimical to any communication taking place between Somalis living on either side of the *de facto* border between Ethiopia and Somalia. There were, indeed, rumours to the effect that a number of people suspected of holding Somali sympathies had been summarily executed, some were said to be still in jails serving sentences a military tribunal passed on them. You couldn't vouch for the truth of all that you heard, but you heard reports in which a man entered the Ogaden on foot, one day, and was apprehended. In his holdall, they found letters said to have been written by one member of the Western Somali Liberation Front to another. The man was sentenced to death, there being no question in the mind of the tribunal that he was a saboteur.

You began most of your letters with the standard greetings and then penned something like this: 'Perhaps you don't remember me any more and perhaps you do. But I am the Askar who, for years, was strapped to your body, was almost one with it. I am sorry I've been beastly and haven't written . . . but!' And so on and so forth. In them, you spoke lovingly of Hilaal and Salaado, describing them as kindhearted, enlightened and highly educated. However, you were sad, you said, because they didn't have 'a festivity of goings-on' as in Uncle Qorrax's compound, where there were many people, relatives and others, who came, who called and were entertained and where one felt one was a member of a community. 'Here,' you went on in one of those unposted and unfinished letters, 'it appears as though it were a great virtue to be self-sufficient – and Uncle Hilaal and Salaado are. And I am the child they've been awaiting all these years. I am a godsend to them, although I am sure this isn't the right way of putting it since they both strike one, at first, as not being at all religious. They lavish their love on me. And this matters greatly to me.'

And you boasted of your material acquisitions. For example, a watch 'that circulates with my blood, one that stops if I don't wear it somewhere on my person'. And a radio which 'is on all day and night, entertaining us with the latest songs'. Not to forget the room 'that is all mine and on whose walls I have mirrors and maps, the one to reflect my visage, showing me whether or not I've grown a beard after so many disastrous beginnings – including, do you remember? my saying that if Karin's menopausal hair-on-the-chin was "manlier" than mine then it was high time I did something about it; the other, i e. the maps which give me the distance in scales of kilometrage – the distance that is between you and me. Which is to say that we are a million minutes apart, your "anatomy" and mine'. Again, you boasted of the learning you acquired and spoke commendably of Cusmaan, whom Hilaal and Salaado had engaged as your tutor. You showed off by asking Misra if she knew how far the sun was from the earth.

You were happy. You missed Misra. Evidently. Or, to put it differently, you missed her body's warmth and the odour of her sweat – which was natural. Salaado was a cosmopolitan woman, she smelt of perfumes and her clothes smelt of mothballs, her nails of varnish, her shoes of polish. It was Hilaal who reminded you of Misra – his was the natural body odour. And he was fatter and liked to make bodily contact, just like Misra!

There was one essential fact which you never mentioned, not even in those unposted, unfinished letters – that Hilaal cooked all the meals, and Salaado drove their only car and everything was in her name, bank accounts, land deeds, literally everything. He drove, yes, but only when necessary. And she was a terrible cook. And neither did you translate into Somali one of Uncle Hilaal's favourite phrases: 'Sooner or later, sex'.

They were wonderful: calm when you were caught in a storm of your own making; comforting whenever you were in some form of discomfort; providing space when that was what you needed desperately; trusting of you and of one another and of your need of each other, giving, forgiving and loving all the time. You were your own person and your life was your own and you could do with it what you pleased. And they? They were at your service, they were there to help you if it was their assistance you sought; they were there to let you go if that was what you wished. For example, there was that time in Hargeisa, where Salaado and you were holidaying – you had earned a vacation by doing well in your eighth-grade examination – when Hilaal sent you a letter you've preserved till this day. Here is the body of the letter:

My dearest Askar,
I am indeed disturbed by your behaviour, disturbed and bothered by what Salaado refers to as your most depressive state of mind to date. And what do you mean by saying that you haven't become 'a man' so you can sit 'in a Mogadiscio of comforts, eat a mountainful of spaghetti while my peers in the Ogaden starve to death or shed their blood in order to liberate it from Ethiopian hands'? Do I also understand that you wish to straighten out 'this question about my own birth'?

Now, first point first. A man, indeed. Are you 'a man'? One day, I would like you to define what or who is a 'man'. Can one describe oneself as a man when one cannot make a viable contribution to the struggle of one's people; when one is not as educated and as aware of the world's politics as one's enemy is; when one is not yet fifteen; when all the evidence of one's being a man comprises of one's height and a few hairs grown on the chin? Who will you kill, your enemy or yourself? And what's wrong with eating well and not being a refugee, which you might have been if you weren't my sister, Arla's, son and if Salaado and I weren't doing well financially. And pray don't talk ill of the UNHCR people, whether in Geneva, Mogadiscio or here, in this, or any other continent: they're not statisticians obsessed with abstracted numbers and charts of starvation and malnutrition. Of course, they have to ascertain how many refugees there are and how much money they can raise and how many calories an African child can cope with. It is the tone I don't like, eating 'a mountainful of spaghetti', etc. Indeed! Askar, one must be grateful for the little mercies in life. One must be thankful to the dedicated souls, serving in these camps under very hard conditions (for them), while they wait for a donor to donate the food and medicines – making sure (and this is very, very difficult) that the local mafia doesn't misappropriate them.

I confess, it pains me to remember the number of times you, Salaado and I have spoken about and analysed the seeds of your sense of 'guilt'. Salaado's telegraphic message suggests it to be as bad as the days following the tragic weekend when, overnight and in a coup de grace, the Ogaden was wrung out of Somali hands and 'returned' to Ethiopia's claw-hammer. Now what's this that I hear, that you were salvaged from the corpse of your mother? Is there anyone who can substantiate that with some evidence? Your mother lived long enough to have scribbled something in her journal. That means that she died after you were born, especially if we take into account Misra's statement which agrees with this claim of mine.

To think, at your age, when you're in Hargeisa for a holidaying trip, that your thoughts are still obsessed with some obscure facts relating to your birth. This disturbs Salaado – it perturbs me. Salaado tells me that you want to return to Kallafo in order to have this question answered once and for all. That is not the same thing as joining the Western Somali Liberation Front, I take it? But Salaado is under the impression that for you, the two are one and the same thing. Now what do you want to do? Of course, you can do both and we have no objection to your deciding to return to the Ogaden as a recruited member of the Front (which we all support) and when there, do your research into your beginnings. You tell us what you want and we'll give you our opinion.

Forgive me, but I've never held the view – nor has Salaado – that, since there are many able-bodied men and women in the Ogaden who can shoot a gun, kill an 'Amxaar' in a scuffle and, if need be, confront the lion in the den, a youngster like you mustn't go. No. 'Somebody' must go. But who is this 'somebody'? If every father, mother, relation said, 'No, not my son, let someone else join the Front', then you know where we'll end up? The view Salaado and I hold, is that since you'll prove to be excellent material as a researcher, as a writer of articles and as one who can impart enlightened opinion about the cause, why not 'eat mountainfuls of spaghetti while others die' and why not, when doing so, complete your education.

Should you insist that you wish to re-enter the Ogaden without touching Mogadiscio, then I am afraid that neither Salaado nor I can do anything about it. All we can suggest that we offer is help. But I plead to you not to depart without at least letting Salaado know. If you inform me by return post that you're definitely leaving, then I'll make arrangements for more money to be transferred to Hargeisa, care of a bank.

If we're to believe that you 'stared' at Misra when she found you and Arla, my sister, then you were at least a day old. For sight, my dear Askar, is a door which does not open instantly in the newly born. What I mean is, that it takes longer than a few minutes for a baby just born to develop the knack to look, let alone 'stare'. Be that as it is. But the fact that it shrouds your beginnings in mysteries preponderant as the babies born in the epic traditions of Africa, Europe and Asia – this fact does interest me greatly. Did you sprout like a plant out of the earth? Were you born in nine months, in three or seven?

In other words, do you share your temperament with the likes of Sunjata or Mwendo, both being characters in Africa's epic traditions? For example, it is said that Sunjata was an adult when he was three. Mwendo, in the traditions told about him, is said to have chosen to be delivered, not through the womb, but through a middle finger. There are other epic children who took a day to be conceived and born and yet others required a hundred and fifty years to be born at all. Now why did this 'epic child' wait for a hundred and fifty years? Because he made the unusual (I almost said, rational) request not to use as his exit (or was it his entrance) the very organ which his mother employed as her urinary passage. Another feature common among epic children is that they are all born bearing arms. And you, Askar, you're armed by name, aren't you?

Again, this is nothing unique to epic traditions of peoples. The world's religions produce 'miracle' children. Can you imagine an Adam, a grown man, standing naked, with leaves of innocence covering his uff, when God pulls at his ribs and says to him, 'I am sorry but it won't take a second, I assure you, and it won't give you any pain either. Now look. Here. A woman, an Eve, created from one of your ribs'? I am sure you've heard of heroes given birth to by mountains or rivers or fishes or for that matter other animals. It seems to me that these myths make the same point again and again: that the 'person' thus born contains within him or her a characteristic peculiar to gods. Well. Where do we go from here?

All is doubt.

Are you or are you not an 'epic' child of the modern times? Do we know what the weather was like the moment you were born? Yes, we do. Your mother, in her scrawls, tells us that the sky was dark with clouds and that a heavy storm broke on her head as she fainted with the pains of labour and the heavens brightened with those thunderous downpours. But you didn't take shorter than a month to be conceived and born, or seven hundred years. And there was no eclipse of the moon or the sun. I've read and reread your mother's journal for clues. I am afraid it appears that you completed your nine months.

21

Please think things over. And please do not do anything rash. We will miss you greatly if you go — but we understand. Rest assured that we'll not stand in your way if you wish to return to your beginnings.
Much, much love.
Yours ever,
Uncle Hilaal.

CHAPTER TWO

[1]

Misra never said to me that I existed for her only in my look. What she said was that she could see in my stare an itch of intelligence – that's all. She said she had found it commendable that I could meet death face to face and that I could outstare the Archangel of Death. For, in my stare, there was my survival and in my survival, perhaps 'a world's' – mine and hers. I remember how often she held me close to herself, and how, lamenting or plaintive, she would whisper into my ears, endearments the like of which I am not likely to hear ever again. One of these endearments, I recall, was, 'My dearest, my little world'! She would then lapse into Amharic, her mother-tongue, and, showering me with kisses, she would utter more of such endearments I wouldn't understand. Then she would end them with the one she most often employed when teasing me or giving me a wash, one which, if translated, would mean, 'my little man'!

As a child, curious as the questions he puts to the adults, I asked Misra if a dead woman, that is my mother, could've given birth to a living thing like me. 'You were born early in the evening,' Misra said, 'sharing a moment's life with a falling star. You were cast into darkness, both of you, although the star dropped into extinction while you existed in the dark. No. You didn't kill your mother.' She concluded her remarks and again held me closer to herself. 'Besides, your mother breast-fed you and that, for me, is the reason why you wouldn't take to other women's milk, wet-nurses who offered to help. Your mother, how could she breast-feed you unless she survived giving birth to you – tell me, how?'

And yet, I overheard her, one day, say to Aw-Adan that when she came upon me and encountered my stare, she thought that it appeared to her as though I had made myself, as though I was my own creation. 'You should've seen how self-conscious he was. You wouldn't think a little dirty thing would take self-pride in touching his body admiringly the way he was doing. He was like a sculptor whose hands were caressing a self-portrait, an artist whose eyes lit up with self-adulation. A dirty little thing, a self-conscious little thing, but one for whom there was no world other than the one in his little head. And I said to myself, yes, I said to myself...!

It feels like yesterday, the day I was born; and it feels as if I were there, as though I were my own midwife. Misra's recounting of what I was like, what I did, coupled with what she was like, what she was doing – these encase me like a womb and I try unsuccessfully to break loose. It is hard to accept or reject when you are told things about yourself as a child. You haven't the authority to refute them, nor are you easily convinced. Besides, no two persons would agree as to what you looked like or what you did. Does that mean that everybody expresses himself or herself uniquely? Or that everyone is unique and nothing can be expressed correctly?

It is absurd, if you want to know my opinion, absurd because I know of no birth like mine. The hour of my birth, the zodiac's reading, the place of birth, the position of the stars, my mother's death after she had given birth to me, my father's dying a day before I was born – do each of these contribute, in small ways, towards turning the act of my birth into a unique event? And let me not forget Misra – how could I? Misra who eventually tucked me into the oozy warmth between her breasts (she was a very large woman and I, a tiny little thing), so much so I became a third breast; Misra who, on account of my bronchial squeamishness, engulfed me in the same wrapping as her breasts – a wrapping as cosily couched as a brassiere; Misra who, as the night progressed towards daylight, would shed me the way a tree sheds a ripe fruit and who would roll over on her back and away from the wrapping which had covered us both, and I would find myself somewhere between her opened legs this time, as though I was a third leg.

Misra told me, again and again, the details of the day and hour she had found me. And I know what she was wearing that day and with whom she had been. She came into the room I had been in, she elegant-looking and I an ugly mess and nearly dead. I became, immediately she saw me, the centre of her focus. And she picked me up – she, whose hands were life to me. From the instant she lifted me and held me to herself (thus dirtying the brown dress she was wearing), I was a living being and I began to exist. I was dirty, yes; I was nameless, yes; but I existed the second she touched me. Did I stare at her? I do not know. However, my look might have been similar to a blind man's stare, one whose eyes see nothing other than what is inside them. Can I simply say that she brought me into existence?

No one received news of my existence until a day later. For she chose to keep me as her secret find. She held me close to herself, having washed me clean; she held me to herself, warm as a secret one doesn't wish to disclose. I remained nameless for a day and no one accounted for me. She then confided in Aw-Adan. He came and whispered a devotion in my ears; he told his beads in secretive whispers to the Almighty. That same day I was 'delivered' into the hands of a world, in which a storm stirred and awoke the dead ghosts. My mother was given name and burial, too; for my father, a prayer was spoken and I was named 'Askar'. Perhaps that is when I began to mean something else to Misra. Or is that an absurd statement to make? Until I was sent to school – or rather, until I met the larger world which consisted of a large number of children – I called Misra 'Mother'.

What survived my real mother was 'memory', not I. People were, in a general sense, kinder and more generous to me, because my parents had died and I was an orphan. People said kind things about my parents, while they gave their counsel, gratis of course, to Misra, telling her how best to take care of me and how best to raise me, so I would be a monument of remembrance to them. Some looked disfavourably upon my calling Misra 'Mother' and took the first opportunity to correct that. Others didn't bother and argued that in time I would know she wasn't my mother. As I grew older and met more and more of these people, I decided I would refrain from calling Misra anything until we were in the privacy of our room, so she could address me, or I her, however each liked. It was during this period that I asked Misra if she remembered anything about her own childhood. She answered that the only thing she could recall was that she wasn't allowed any of the things she wanted to do and she longed to grow old enough so she could be herself. I asked, 'As a child you weren't yourself, do you mean?'

She said, 'Childhood may best be described as a condition of becoming someone else when with adults, and yourself when alone or with other children; it is difficult getting used to either. I mean, it is difficult getting used to the idea that, although you've been given clothes bought specifically for you, the choice when and why to wear them or whether you would remain without them is not your own.'

I remember, I was six then. And I remember thinking about 'nakedness'. In those days, whenever I saw someone naked, I could think of two things – beds and baths. One day I saw Misra and Aw-Adan naked. They were near a bed all right, but they were not in it, nor were they having their baths. I wondered if the choice to remain undressed could be an adult's, too. A child, this I knew for certain, was allowed to roam about in the house or even in the street, totally unclothed. Although 'who' the child was mattered a great deal too. If you were the child of one of those people who couldn't afford to buy clothes for themselves, let alone for their children – well, one could understand and sympathize, couldn't one? With this, and many other related and unrelated thoughts in my mind, I formulated a question in my head, a question which, in a roundabout way, had something to do with 'nakedness' and which, in so far as I was concerned, directly had to do with my seeing Aw-Adan, the priest, and Misra, naked, although then they weren't in bed but near it. I asked Misra what their 'relationship' was.

To Misra, the question, 'What's this person's relationship to me?' meant nothing more and nothing less than, 'Who is this person?' – which in turn meant, 'Is he an uncle or an aunt or a cousin?' To her, the fabric of Somali society was basically incestuous and you had a glimpse into the mind of a Somali if you knew to whom he or she was related by blood or by marriage. Neither she nor Aw-Adan was born Somali and I suspect she knew that I had been aware of that and therefore she must have sensed that no amount of tapestrying her woven story with patterns of her own inventions would have convinced me as the truth might have – life's most excellent embroidery. She smiled sweetly, silently and looked away as though looking for an answer. She might have been inventing a genealogical tree whose branches and roots supplied a pedigree of the appropriate answers to my question. But I doubted very much if she was the type of woman who could lose herself in the eternity of a search for who she was – for she knew who she was.

When I insisted she respond to my question, she said, simply and plainly, as though she were speaking the words for the first time ever, 'Aw-Adan? He is a man.'

For a moment or two, she sought and sat under the cool shade of the generic term 'The Tree of Man' – and smiled triumphantly. I was sure she was under the wrong impression that she had dealt with my question satisfactorily. Then I asked, 'What about Uncle Qorrax? Is he a man too?'

She was most singularly exposed, like an isolated eucalyptus tree a lightning had struck. She sat motionless, speechless, looking away from me, embarrassed.

I didn't like Uncle Qorrax. It was no secret I didn't like him. I was barely three days old when I made that abundantly clear to everybody, including himself. The story is told how he arranged to make a formal call on his nephew – that is me – how he had asked that I be washed with a scented soap which he had provided for that very purpose, how he had sent ahead of himself his youngest wife so she would help Misra with the arrangements and be present when he was introduced to me.

He came dressed in his best – a silk sarong he hadn't worn until that day, a most colourful *cimaama* to go with it and a Baravaan hat. Also, he wore his patent-leather shoes and his favourite socks. He left his compound predicting that I would like him. He added, 'I am determined to make him like me'. He said so to Shahrawello. I doubt it if she told him how ludicrous he looked, calling on his nephew not even three days old, dressed as though he were visiting a king. But what good would her speaking her mind have done her or anyone else? She stood aside, letting him go past her, and chuckled to herself as he took his long strides. After he had gone, I believe there was an improvised gathering and each of them commented on how absurd this all was, some laughed until their ribs ached. Anyway, Shahrawello is reported to have said that a man is not his clothes but that 'a child inherits its mother's hates and loves'. And she bet her life, if anyone was willing to bet a coin of the smallest denomination, that the young one wouldn't like his uncle.

I was asleep when he entered. He was angry at Misra, accusing her of disobedience, scolding her for not having prepared me for the occasion. And he made unnecessary noises so I would wake up. I wouldn't. Not until Misra went out of the room to cry outside. I heard her crying and I awoke. I looked this and that way. No Misra. And who was this – a man awkwardly dressed with top hat and all, ugly, thin and tall? What's more, I was lying on my back, helpless, like a beetle on its spine, and my hands, however many times I raised them, returned to me empty – empty of Misra and full of vacant air. Then I heard Uncle's ugly voice, thin and yet sharp, piercing, cutting me in two halves. And I cried a furious cry, so heinous that he froze where he was, frightened at the thought that I might harm myself. When he came nearer me, I cried louder and with vengeance and no one could silence me until Misra returned. Once she was back in the room, you could sense that my cry wasn't as fierce as it had been. All she had to do was to lay a finger on any part of my body and I fell quiet. But my body remained nervous and there was something agitated in the atmosphere until Uncle Qorrax was out of the room. I began to relax when I could no longer hear his ugly voice.

That I burst into tears immediately he walked into the room I had been in – this entered the lore of the traditions told in my uncle's compound. Obviously, it made him very uneasy. But there was little he could do to me, or about me. His position as a respected member of the community dictated that he treat me with apparent kindness, and that he provide for me, someone else to take my mother's place. Misra, until then, was not a *bona fide* member of the compound. It appears she became one, especially, when I chose her – chose her in preference to all the other women who had been tried on me, one after the other, a dozen or so women into whose open arms I was dropped. I cried with vigour whenever Misra wasn't there. In the end, the community of relations approved of my choice. But not my uncle. Not until a year later.

To reduce the tension, my uncle decided to earmark a fenced mud hut with its separate entrance for our own use. That way, he wouldn't encounter us when going into or out of his compound, of which he was the unchallenged master. One could tell if he was or wasn't there – when he was there, we wouldn't hear anything except his terrible voice, giving instructions to or shouting at somebody. Often, we would also hear the help-help cry of a wife or a child being beaten. When he wasn't there, the compound and its residents wore an air of festivity, and women and children exchanged gossip and wicked jokes about him, or men like him, and neighbours visited and were entertained. But we were excluded from the joys and sadnesses of the compound. We had our life to lead and a compound which was all our own, Misra and I. We lived the way we saw fit. At least, until nightfall. And then Uncle came.

He came after nightfall and made his claims on Misra. It was one thing to make a political (that is public) statement by being kind to her and myself, it was another to give something for nothing. He didn't confound issues – he would hire another woman in her place and dispense with her services unless she offered herself to him. I learnt later that she did. She said it was so she would be allowed to be with me. Misra suffered the humiliation of sleeping with him so she could be with me. I don't know what I might have said if I had known. Things do look different from this height (now I am a grown-up and a man myself!), from this distance; besides, one tends to indulge oneself until the end of one's days, talking until daylight, about the possible alternatives and compromises of a complicated situation such as this. But were there other avenues, other alternatives, other possible compromises that she could've struck with Uncle Qorrax?

She thought Aw-Adan might have become one healthy alternative – if I had liked him. But I didn't. Looking back on it now, I think the reasons why I disliked Aw-Adan were different – different in that Misra and he had a world of their own, a language of their own, and so when they lapsed into it or chose to dwell in the secretive universe of its nuances and expressions and gestures, I felt totally excluded. I was afraid they would either take me away from the Somali-speaking world or deny me my Misra, who had been for me the end-all and the cosmos of my affections.

It is hard to admit it, but I suppose I was a vulnerable child, much more vulnerable than anyone suspected. Aw-Adan nicknamed me 'Misra's nightingale'. I didn't understand his meaning until years later. For a long time, I took him to mean that I sang Misra's love-names. He didn't mean that at all. He meant that only Misra was allowed to enter my freehold space, the freehold territory which I had acquired for myself.

It is true that only Misra had access to the freehold kingdom of which I was the undisputed lord. And since I held Uncle Qorrax, his wives and his children in total awe and at bay, it appeared there were only Misra and Karin whose civilized company I kept. Nor did I like playing with the children of the neighbourhood when I grew up a little bigger, because they remained infantile, fighting over the ownership of toys, dolls and balls. I took pride in my being self-sufficient and came to no grief so long as I knew either Misra or Karin was in my view or earshot. At night, dreams kept me busy; during the day, if Misra was otherwise occupied with one of life's many chores that needed attending to, I sought the companionship of my imagination. It was only when Misra was short-tempered (this happened when she was in season), or when she beat me because she was short-tempered (because she was in season) – it was only then that I knew I was an only child and an orphan. And Misra couldn't bear the stare-of-the-orphan. And she would dispatch me off for the day to Karin's compound – Karin who was, to me, like a grandmother: gentle as one, generous as one.

I am sure it is appropriate that I address myself to the question: was there ever any time that I remember liking Uncle Qorrax? Was there a period I remember having a soft spot for the man who paid all my expenses, the man who was my father's brother?

I was fond of adults' shoes, as many children are, when I was an infant, and I recall the pleasant thought of owning such good and colourfully patterned shoes as Uncle Qorrax crossing my mind. It used to give me immense happiness to touch them whenever I crawled near them. It used to make me sad when I was not allowed to put them in my mouth or lick them. But when the phase of loving adults' shoes was passed, I ceased going to him or being friendly with him.

I think that the patterns of his shoes appealed to my sense of the aesthetic, since their designs reminded me of some of the calligraphic images I had seen painted on doors to the palaces my dreams had taken me to but which I had never entered. After all, *The Arabian Nights* were full of such gates with such motifs and such colourful designs. The truth was that I admired them even when I was a little older and loved their bright colours. Although, when he asked me once what my favourite colour was, I surprised him by saying that I preferred earthen to neon – knowing full well what that meant. This decided for him – as a present for the Ciid festivities, he didn't buy for me a pair of shoes with bright colours and patterns as he had intended – instead, he got me maps. And he called to deliver them in broad daylight. He came dressed as though in mourning. Misra inquired if somebody had died. He was in a foul mood. He said, 'Someone will die, somebody will.'

Misra looked unhappy that day and the following. If only she paid attention to my comments that someone always dies, that someone is born when another dies and that we are affected by death or birth if we know, are close to, or love the persons concerned.

'What on earth are you talking about?' she said.

I said, 'Of death.'

[4]

Death-as-topic-for-discussion was taboo in our house and no one was allowed to speak of it or mention the Archangel's name in my presence. It was of life we were to talk, the blood and vitality of life that is the essence of one's being. Even the past, when clothed in garments of death or mourning, was a forbidden subject, for it was feared that this past might eventually lead to the names of my dead parents, to the fact that I knew next to nothing about my mother or my father.

There were epidemics, there was a drought, and the earth lay lifeless, treeless, dead, growing nothing, causing things to decay and metal to rest – and we weren't allowed to talk about death. Whispers. Conspiracies. With the night falling secretly and Uncle Qorrax crawling into bed with us and making love to Misra – the cycle of life and death, the circle ending where it began – the flow of menstruation, of death ascertained – and we weren't to talk of death. Not even when Misra was helped to abort, not even when a calendar was brought into the compound and when circles in green were neatly drawn round the safe days and nights. An ovum lives for less than thirty-six hours, sperm for about twenty-four. Yes, only one, maximum two days in each cycle. And we weren't to talk of death.

Not until I came to Mogadiscio during the 1977 war in the Horn of Africa, not until then was the discretion about death completely disregarded and only then could 'death' occur in my vocabulary in the manner it occurs in the thoughts of a spinster who's been robbed by it. I recall saying to Uncle Hilaal, who helped me loosen up and with whom I could comfortably talk easily, that 'death' was to me simply a metaphor of 'absence'; and God was a 'presence'. My uncle's stare was long but also difficult to interpret. He was silent for a while, then, sighing, he mumbled something which I took to be the syllables of Misra's name.

Mis-ra!

Then I repeated to my uncle the story of how I asked Misra to explain what it is that happens when death visits its victims.

'The heart stops functioning,' she said.

'Nothing else happens?' I inquired.

'That is death. The heart's stopping,' she explained.

'And the rest of the body?'

'It rigidifies as a result.'

'Like . . . like Aw-Adan's leg? Wooden like Aw-Adan's leg, is that what happens? Lifeless and unbending . . . like Aw-Adan's leg?'

I had never seen Misra as angry as she was on that day. She wouldn't speak for hours. And in the body of my fantasies there took place something interesting: I remembered how fast the third leg (the wooden leg, that is) was dropped and how fast another between his legs came to raise its head, jerkily, slowly and nervously; and how the whole place drowned in the sighing endearments of Misra who called him . . . yes him of all people . . . 'my man, my man, my man'!

Then suddenly I remembered something – a question I had meant to put to somebody, any adult, I didn't care to whom. Misra happened to be angry, yes, but I felt she would answer it if I asked. So I did just that. 'And the soul?' I said.

Most definitely, she had forgotten what we were talking about before she fell silent and into a dudgeon dark with rage. 'What about the soul?' she said, lost in the zigzaggy mazes of bewilderment. 'What about it?'

'What happens to the soul when somebody dies?' I said.

She was silent for a while – silent in a naked way, if I may put it thus, and she took her time gathering her ideas like an elegant robe around her, her hands busy touching and caressing her face, levelling and smoothing the bumps and the roughness her anger with me had brought about, and a thought crossed my mind (my thoughts as usual began to outrun me): what do monkeys pick when they pick at each other's head? Lice? Or something else? Or nothing at all? I thought I would wait for the right moment to question her on this.

She cleared her throat. I knew she was ready to speak. I sat up, waiting. In the meanwhile, I could see her repeating to herself something in mumbles. I was sure she was quoting either the Koran or Aw-Adan. She said, 'The soul is the stir in one, for one stirs not when dead.'

I was disappointed. She wondered why. I told her.

'And what do you want me to tell you?' she said, unhappy.

I was disappointed her answer was brief and had ended, in a sentence, long before I was aware she had begun. What I wanted her to do was to talk about death in as much detail as was possible for a seven-year-old like myself to understand. I needn't have reminded her that I had encountered death before, in the look of my mother, in the rigidity of her body. I needn't have reminded her that, in so far as she was concerned, I had made myself, that I was my own creation and that upon me was bestowed, by myself of course, everything other mortals wished for in their dreams.

'So?' I challenged.

She appeared dazed. Could it be because she could not recall telling me herself that when she first encountered my undiluted stare she thought that 'I had made myself and had been my own creation!'?

There may have been other reasons. But she stared at me as though the world had shrunk to the ground beneath her weighty body and as though any memory of her would disappear with it too and she would die. Anyway, she was silent for a long, long, time. However, this silence was different from the previous silences in that she appeared frightened, afraid of my stare. And so she pulled at her dress, nervous.

I said, 'Death takes many forms in my head. Generally, it is donned all in white, robed in an Archangel's garment into whose many-pocketed garment is dropped the day's harvest of souls. I wonder if my mother and father's souls ended up in the same pocket, just like a beloved wife is buried in the same tomb as her husband or a child its mother if they all die together. I wonder if I would have a soul to speak of had I died at birth – I instead of my mother.'

Flabbergasted, she could only stare at me. And I continued: 'I was ready to be born but it appears my mother was ready to die. Maybe I would have died if she hadn't. And I suspect it wouldn't be I telling this story, I suspect, as a matter of fact, the story wouldn't be the same, not the subject matter. My death wouldn't have earned me an obituary and my life wouldn't have engaged anybody's time and energy. You see, death ends all talk. From then on, death rules. Or, if you please, God.'

Again, she stared at me in disbelief. She asked after the appropriate pause: 'How old are you, Askar?'

I replied, 'I am seven.'

'I might as well ask myself if Satan is older,' she said.

'I am sorry?'

'Oh, never mind,' she said.

Before long, she was herself again, mothering me, requesting that I bow down and subject my clothes for inspection, reminding me at one and the same time that I was very young, capable of 'accidents', unforeseen things, and that put her in control of the situation again and she was saying that I should change my clothes, etc., etc., etc. But: woe to me if she were in season. Then – well, that's another story.

[5]

The sight of blood didn't repel or frighten me. That of water, however small or large its body, attracted me. Water comforted me and I fell silent when in it, as though in reverence to its god. I splashed in it so that its crystals, clear as silver and just as lovely, flew up in the air, winged, like my imagination, until these balls of magic beauty were recalled back to the body from whence they had sprung. I could never determine my relationship with water. Not until I met my mother's brother, who told me that water had the same sort of satanic fascination for my mother, Arla. She had endangered her own life so many times that in the end, he decided to teach her to swim. She was the only woman who knew how to swim, it being uncommon in Somalia for women to learn. Water, she had explained to him, gave her the mobility and space her fantasies required, and she used to begrudge the water in the ocean its moods of calm or rage, the water in the river the determination to return 'home' in vaporous form or end in the bigger ocean.

I asked myself often if this is what I remember of my foetal existence – water. It was total bliss, I said to Uncle Hilaal one day. He was happy to hear that. He said – and I am not certain if he was quoting from something he read – that the first water is indubitably the best, it is heavenly bliss. There is no other expression for such a feeling.

So, in depthless water, my beginning. It was water ushered me into where I am, water that made me the human that I am, water that gave me foetal warmth – and a great deal more. Water was my mirror and I watched my reflections in it, reflections at which I smiled and which grew waves – waves dark as shadows – when I dipped my hand in. I was fond of drinking from the very spot across which my shadow fell. The water never tasted as good, in my cupped hands, from any other place.

In depthless water, too, it was I saw my future. I had it read by Misra who was exceptionally gifted in this sort of line – reading one's future in the waves of water or in the quiver of meat or in a pool of blood. Water in a container or blood in another, the blood of a slaughtered beast, lying untouched where it had fallen and remaining there until it was empty of running, i.e. living, blood. But was it for religious or health sentiments that this was done? Misra didn't know. Anyway, she knew how to read the future in the quiver of meat. The intestines, the fats, the entrails – every piece or slice of meat was, to her, like a palm to a fortune-teller and she read it. I was certain no other child had as much fun as I. Definitely not any of Uncle Qorrax's children. They were beaten in the morning, in the afternoon or in the evenings by their tyrannical father, by Aw-Adan who was their (and later became my) teacher, or their mothers or a visiting relation. Not I. I was Misra's property.

And Misra would bathe me. She oiled my body with care. I crouched in the *baaf*, my eyes half-closed, in concentration and anxiety, waiting for the water to descend from a great height. I would shake, I would shiver, as though the cold water was hot and had burnt me – my arms moving in all directions as though they might take off in flight. A second and a third scooping of the water would ensure that my body was sufficiently wet for her to soap it. At times, when standing, I held on to her shoulders, lest I fell forward. My eyes remained closed, however, until I heard her say that I could open them. It was she who determined when this was to occur. As part of the ritual, she insisted that I blow my nose. For this purpose she would place her open left palm directly under my chin and with her right hand's index finger and thumb squeezing the nose as I exhaled. Now where was I given these baths? Right inside our mud hut; or in the yard, if it was day, under the tree planted the very day I was born. That she had hers in the privacy of a closed door and all by herself was something I associated with her being an adult. Children had no *cawra*, whether boys or girls, they could walk about naked, displaying their *uff* until they became grown up. Anyway, after the bath, another joy.

She would oil my body a second time – tickling me as she did so, touching my *uff* and squeezing it. She made me laugh, made me happy. Then she prepared a meal for the two of us to eat, and when I was good, as a treat, she boiled milk and sugared it for me and I drank it warm. Playfully, I refused to lick away my moustache of milk and she would tease me and we would have great fun, laughing, chasing each other under the bed or behind it. Suddenly, her voice changed. No more drinking of water lest I wet the bed which she and I shared. 'What have you in your bladder?' and she would tickle me. 'Why does it leak?' And the nipping, as she pinched my *uff*, would make me laugh.

Water: I associate with joy; blood: not so much with pain as with lost tempers and beatings. But I associate something else with blood – future as read by Misra. Once I even made a pun – my future is in my blood. The funny thing was Uncle Qorrax misunderstood it as meaning that my destiny was the destiny of the family of which he was head. Well, I didn't correct him. We had a laugh, Misra and I. The poor man did not know that she had read my future in blood.

As for water. Have you ever watched a storm of rain? Imagine this:

every drop of rain is escorted by an angel who keeps it company until it touches the earth, the angels who make certain that seasons change for the better when it rains, that people prosper, the dry brown grass turns green, dust into mud – and human beings pray in thankful offerings, slaughtering beasts for their carnivorous tables – and Misra is thus enabled to tell a future – which is past.

For Misra, and therefore for me too, everything had a past, a present, and a future. The earth had its history, the sun its life, the moon its pattern of behaviour. Blood. Sand. Dry leaves, dry twigs. Papers, yellow with age and roaming the open spaces, riding the dust and the wind – everything told of a future. One had to know to read it. Or so said Misra.

And stones had faces, spiders souls, serpents ideas, lizards intelligence. Human beings are not the only living and thinking beings. Rivers have memories, she said. They remember where they've come from, they have allegiance to the people in whose country they rise. The wind recalls whom it has met in its journeys across the vast deserts, it exchanges greetings with some, turning an unhearing ear to the salutations reaching it from others. A reed possesses a mind of its own and holds steadfastly to this, even if, at times, the wind makes it go dizzy, lose its head and balance as it somersaults over rocks, sandbanks, etc. The earth draws strength from the sky, the sky from the earth – and the living from the dead. The history of the earth can be read in its eclipses, that of the sun from its being partially or completely obscured by the shadow of another body – the earth or the moon.

I continue, since I have heard her recite the 'Ode to Nature' so many times: a child is to its mother what the sun is to the moon; what the heavens are to earth. Yes, I'm quoting her. The mother is what the moon is to the sun; what the earth to the heavens. A mother receiving little, giving a great deal. It makes a mother take delight in the giving and the child (or man) in the receiving. The shock is greater when one learns one must give – not always receive. A shock so great, it is like falling suddenly and unexpectedly from a great height, onto the lap of death. Amen! The living draw strength from the dead, don't they? And those who are asleep receive sustenance from those who are awake. Amen! And remember – the Prophet has said that men are asleep. It's only at their death that they are awoken. Amen!

[6]

She looked like a corpse when asleep – motionless, with her hands folded together across her chest, her eyes closed and hardly a snort, or even a sound, issuing from her nostrils. But I told myself she needn't have worried, when all others die, she won't, I would say to myself. So long as I lived, she would too. Either in me, or she would live a life independent from mine. And I would watch her stir, then rise, as though from the dead, every morning, after I had been awake for hours. She would dust her dress and walk away – as if she had woken from the dead, from her own grave. Every morning, the same thing. At times, she would take a nap in the afternoon. And Aw-Adan would come and he would pull up a chair by her head, and sitting quietly, would read a selection of suras from the Koran, as though she were dead and he were reading a devotion or two over her. If she didn't look like a corpse, I would turn her into one, I said to her one day.

'But why?' she asked, disturbed.

'Or I would kill you. So you would be a corpse like my mother.'

'Kill me? Why? But what have I done?'

I found it extremely difficult to explain myself. Of course, I wasn't going to 'kill her' because I had hated her, far from it, far from it. What I meant was, that only in death could she and I be united – only in death, her death, could she and I be related, only then would I somehow feel as though we were a mother and her son. And then, and only then, would I find myself, alone and existing and real – yes, an individual with needs of his own – no longer an extension of a maternal hand whose touch quietened the childish cry in one.

And then I asked, 'Is it possible that death took me for my mother, is it, Misra? Please answer me honestly. For this is something I ask myself often and I don't know what to think or say.'

She shook her head and said she didn't think death would mistake one person for another. It was all to do with whether one's time in this world was up and in any case, she went on, it is only under exceptional circumstances that a person's lifetime in this world is extended. And she told me the story of the man to whom an angel appeared and said that he, the man, was to die in a year to the day, having had his time which had been up extended in view of the good things he had been doing. Although grateful, the man admitted that one year wasn't probably enough for him to finish all the things he had begun and besides, what is a year but three-hundred-and-sixty-

37

five days and what is life but these incalculable mysteries, mysteries that remain unrevealed to one, mysteries that descend on one like grains of sand from the sky. I would've preferred it, said the man to the angel, had you not come to tell me when death would call on me – whether in an hour, a day, say, or even a year. The angel said he had been given instructions to do so and he left the man saying no more. For three-hundred-and-sixty-five days and nights, the man spent every second of his life in this world praying and he spent every cent he had on some charitable cause or other and he did not sin either in thought or deed. A year later to the day, the angel, robed all in white, appeared before the man, and all he said was, 'You've been dead for a year. If one were to extend your life in this world by another year, one wonders if you will live. Why pray day and night? Why spend every cent you have on charities for the needy? Do you think God created you only to pray? Live. Live, we recommend. Live like a human.' And the angel left the man in similar agony. The man *lived* for a year. He overate, he gave not a cent to godly causes, but prayed enough so as to placate his own conscience. When next the angel called on him, the man was prepared to receive the news of his death for he was still in pain, burdened with the knowledge that he would die in less than a year. The angel, it came to pass, turned up two years later and his only comment was that the man had the making of a human who sinned and knew he had. That man, or so the stories tell us, lived to be a hundred-and-fifteen years before another angel knocked on his door.

'But what was exceptional in the man's life?' I said.

'He was like every other human being, I think. And death could've mistaken him for another person. He was weak and didn't know the meaning of life, didn't know why God created him,' she said. 'Like most of us.'

It didn't make much sense to me and I wondered if Aw-Adan had told her a story whose details she had half-forgotten. I asked her, after a long pause, if this was so.

As usual, she was unwilling to admit there were gaps in the story she had told me. So she changed the subject. She said that we could play hide-and-seek until I fell asleep.

She hid; I sought her out.

Did I, in the act of looking, bring into being a world in which there existed not only Misra but many other persons as well? Did I, as a result of this my stare, bring into existence a life of memories in which I am not the rememberer but the remembered? I – who did surrender myself wholly to Misra and her world; I – who existed in a look I myself couldn't have seen or known of; I – who had lived in a universe dark as a photographer's room, a universe developing into identifiable beings, some in duplicate, others in as many copies as one wanted. A look? Or a touch?

For me, life began in her hands and it was *in* her touch that I began to exist. Not in the savage stare which was so primitive it penetrated to the depth of her guilt, a savage stare which stirred in her soul a selfless desire to give and give and give and therefore *be*, exist only in the giving. Is this why I touched her whenever the chance presented itself to me? And is this why her physical absence upset me greatly when I was tiny – because I couldn't reprint, on the screen of my undeveloped memory, my image of her in as many copies as I wanted? Anyway, my life was in her hands and she could do what she wanted with it and she did very well by it. Yes, by all accounts, she satisfied my uncles and aunts and other relations and was able to obtain their approval – although there were secrets between her and myself, secrets to which no other person had access. These secrets comprised things we did together, she and I; they consisted of games we played in our room when darkness fell and the silence of night engulfed all and everything and we went under the bedcovers and she told me stories or taught me things she wasn't supposed to. These secrets included the fact that I knew everything she did. For example, one of my uncles used to come and knock on the small window of our room after midnight and Misra would get out of bed and wash and prepare and wait for a second knock. At times she would open the door and he would enter and make love to her on the floor or she would follow him to another place. Often, I pretended as if I were asleep. But at times I would cry so violently I would spoil the night for them, she would get back into bed with me and would calm me down, hold me between her breasts and would whisper something in a serious tone – either, 'I hope you'll learn to be on your own like all other children of your age'; or, her eyes misted with tears of anguish, she would say, 'I will kill you unless you behave yourself. I'll strangle you – so as to live my own life.' Then she would place her index and middle fingers on her closed eyes and the fingers would rest there, as though they were the holes of a flute. And she would continue: 'I will kill you or I will kill myself.' I would cry more furiously and would wet myself in the enraged frenzy of a pervasive self-expression, and her tears would drip on me. She would lift me up, disregarding the mess of my moisture and the fact that she was dressed in her most elegant dress, and she would rock me to silence. She would place me within her reach, either on the floor or on a stool. If she moved away from me, if her hand didn't lay on me, she knew I would burst into another convulsive cry and would also vomit or cough or do both. After a long bath, I would sit up and, as though nothing had occurred, would play. And she would hide and I would look out for her in the dark or lighted sections of the room. When neighbours or relations who had overheard my tumultuous cries the previous night asked after me the following morning, Misra, generous and loving, would not speak of the inconveniences I had caused her, nor would she speak of the visitor who had called after midnight. We would look at each other and share a grin or a smile, depending on our respective moods. But neither would talk of our common secret. When nervous, she would rise from where she had been sitting and look away. I would smile to myself triumphantly, knowing that I had her whole life in the power of my mouth and I could do what I wanted with it.

I'll admit that many things are confused in my memory. My head, I feel sometimes, will explode with the intensity of the anecdotes I remember – events which in all likelihood didn't take place, not, at any rate, as I remember them. One thing which I definitely recall, with the clarity of a daylight occurrence, is how 'responsible' Misra felt regarding me, my body and my thoughts. She was responsible for me in the same way as the dweller of a certain place takes upon himself or herself most things that happen in it, so much so that water shortages or power-cuts and similar anomalies are explained away as personal shortcomings. If I had a cold, if my stomach ran or if I spoke unduly rudely to anyone, Misra explained – she justified or interceded for me or she would say that she would take the beating on herself. If taken ill, she would explain why my constitution had weakened or why I wasn't as healthy and strong as I used to be. But when not in public, she would complain to me directly or grumble or mumble, within my hearing, as though she were talking to herself. 'It is in your element to be mean,' she would accuse me. 'Why, you know I am a foreigner here and that if you fall ill, your people will say it is because I haven't taken good care of your food. You also know that, when you do well, the credit is not mine but your people's, that is your [Somali] nation whose identity I do not share. Why must you make my life a misery?'

But there are many things of which I am not sure. For instance, I'm not sure who said this: 'Your look was smooth – like pebbles in a stream'. Misra herself? Will someone tell me what it means – in concrete terms? Please? Will *you* tell me? Will *you* explain? *You* who sit in judgement over me. Will somebody? Yes?

CHAPTER THREE

And he was running and running, he was breathing hard and running. But he didn't know why he was running, nor did he know what he was fleeing from. He ran, blind with fright; he ran senselessly. And he couldn't define the purpose of his running – but neither could he stop. He crossed nearly three-quarters of a large forest and wouldn't stop even when he saw that he had entered a clearing littered with discarded dolls of which he hardly took any notice. He couldn't tell how many hours it had taken him to get to where he was or whether he had been running in circles.

Dawn was beginning to break.

And something up in the heavens, luminous and small, attracted his attention. He asked himself, could it be possible – Venus at dawn? But he heard a noise and he turned – a woman who was thin and dark was standing in front of him, a woman who resembled Misra and yet who wasn't Misra for she introduced herself when he approached her not as Misra but Ummat; and he made as if to speak, he started saying 'I am . . .', but left the sentence unfinished. Misra offered to be his guide. She promised she would answer his questions, all his questions. And it was to be so. Most people they met along the way had their bodies tattooed with their identities: that is name, nationality and address. Some had engraved on their skins the reason why they had become who they were when living and others had printed on their foreheads or backs their national flags or insignia. There was a man on whose chest was tattooed the Somali flag with three points of the star missing and Misra explained to Askar why. They also met a man carrying a placard on which was written the words 'a martyr from the Ogaden'. Askar thought he had seen the man before. Then he turned to face her so he could ask if she too had known him. Alas! She was not there any more, not only was she not there, but she wasn't in his memory either. She had disappeared completely and he now asked himself, was it possible that his 'I am . . .' addressed to Misra was not, after all, incomplete? And he was Misra? In his mind, he removed the dots denoting the incomplete nature of the statement and spoke it again. He heard himself say 'I am', and the echo returned to him a sound which he found to be meaningful.

Now he looked up to see if 'Venus' too had vanished. Here he wasn't totally disappointed – but in a peculiar way curiously reflective. He felt awkward, like when you cannot name something you know, when the combination of letters in your mouth will not match the sound your lips are willing to make. It was not 'Venus', he decided in his Edenic impression. It was a species, looking rather like a spider, large and colourful – a spider as huge as the dreamscape he had been treading, a spider which had managed to weave from out of that small belly, out of that tiny body, a web so complex, a trap so long, one would be lost in it. The spider ascended the ladder of lengths of its innards.

Now he moved away, convinced that he had to do just that. And he walked. After half an hour, he came upon a river about to break at the banks. Undisturbed, he sat under a tree and contemplated while waiting. But what was he waiting for? He didn't know. He sat, waiting; he sat, burdened with a Thomist's questioning of the self: he told himself he knew what purpose rivers served – to irrigate and help grow food in the form of fruits, vegetables, etc.; but what did man's existence serve, or whom? To worship God? To study God through nature? Why was *he* born? For some unforeseeable reason related to the thought that had just crossed his mind, Askar remembered the story of a man who challenged everything, a man who contested that 'even mirrors didn't reflect the true identity of things and persons'. The man was bald – but he chose to refuse to see his baldness, although people confirmed what the mirror reflected, or rather what it saw. People said that he was insane, they argued, how could anyone contend that what people saw and mirrors confirmed wasn't true? Months later, the man went insane. Would Askar in the end go mad questioning things, challenging received opinions?

Finally, he was standing in front of a huge portal with the letter *A* boldly printed on it. He remembered that, perhaps in a previous life, he had seen that portal before and he had been turned away from it by a uniformed man. Now he hadn't the courage to knock on it, nor did he have the curiosity to discover to what secret world the gate would have given him access. He sat on a boulder by the side of the road. To his left, there was a stream whose banks were green with weeds. It appeared as though a fountain had, just at that instant, right in front of him, right in his presence, given birth to an aqueous marvel of a stream in which fishes of all sizes and descriptions chased one another without any sense of inhibition or forbearance.

And he discovered, looking up, that the sky above him was wearing the seven heavenly garments, whose colours matched that of a rainbow he had never seen before – one was of ruby; one of silvery pearls; one gold; another white silver; one of orange hyacinth; and, lastly, one of shining brightness, the likes of which no human, other than a mystic or a prophet, had ever perceived. To his right, when he turned, there was a tree on one of whose branches perched 'talking dolls'. He couldn't understand what the dolls were saying. However, he later wondered if these might possibly have been the product of an exhausted mind's aberrant way of expressing itself.

Then a voice (was it coming from within himself or without – he couldn't tell), a voice, alive with urgency, called to him. First, he was frightened and wouldn't stir at all. Then he heard a silky sound, that is, he heard the hissing sound of a snake approaching from his right, and, not in the least frightened, he moved towards the snake. Meanwhile, his hands, as he went to encounter the snake, gently touched a spot on his thigh where a snake had bitten him when small. He stared at the snake, expecting it would wear an expression of recognition; and yes; he saw the snake's forked tongue cut the air surgically, its head nodding, its throat throbbing with coded speech. Then all movements, within himself and without, ceased; and he didn't know where he was or who he was; and he no longer had any identity or name; nor was the snake there either. For a second or so, he was frightened, as if he were a traveller who had misplaced his travelling documents. Was it conceivable, he asked himself, that he had lost whatever knowledge he had gained about himself through the years?

Alone, melancholic, he sat on a boulder, his head between his hands, his expression mournful. He was saddest that there was no one else to whom he could put questions about his own identity; there was no one to answer his nagging, 'Who am I?' or 'Where am I?' Luckily, however, Askar soon found he had a premonition – that the snake would return wearing a mask. And lo and behold the snake did return, its face cast in the image of a man whose photograph Askar had seen before, a photograph identified as 'Father'. He couldn't, then, help remembering a relation telling him not to harm snakes that had called on the family compound years ago because some snakes were the family's blood relations. He had given this serious thought and requested that someone, preferably an adult, answer his query: 'He may be a snake in body and appearance although he is a human

relation in all other aspects that are not easily revealed to you or I —
is this possible?' Misra had answered, yes.

Suddenly, an overwhelming silence had overcome Askar. And a
voice nobody claimed, one which certainly did not emanate from his
sub- or unconscious, called him away. In other words, a voice lured
him on to a a field — a field greener with the imaginations's pasture
— and he spotted two horses neighing nervously as he approached
them. One of the horses was frighteningly ugly, the other handsome
like an Arabian horse of noble breed. The colour of the handsome
horse, saddled with the finest material man could make, was jet black,
sporting a white forehead, white forelegs and dark eyes, although its
upper lips were not as white as its forehead. The other was ugly, but
it appeared uglier standing by the handsome horse. It was sweaty and
smelly and its teeth were as sharp as a sword. Askar suspected the
handsome horse knew who he was, for it came up to him (the ugly
one stayed behind, greedily eating its grass), and, head down in
reverence, stood by him ready to be ridden. The speed, once he was
on its back, was great; the grace, enormous; and the comfort of the
ride indescribably refreshing. It galloped across rivers, it jumped any
mountainous hurdle and flew in the air, as if winged! A horse, was
this really a horse? It wasn't as big-boned as the horses he had seen
before, but was definitely a great deal taller, and of course heftier,
than an Arabian horse. It had legs which adjusted themselves to the
conditions of the terrain. When going down a hill, for instance, the
horse's front legs would stretch, they would become longer so that
he, who had never ridden a horse before and who didn't know how
to, wouldn't find it embarrassingly difficult to hold on to the saddle.

Without being told to, the horse stopped.

And a man, clothed in coarse garments of wool, appeared before
them. The man was so quiet, so still, it seemed Askar and the horse's
breathing disturbed him. The horse went nearer the man, and it
bowed its head low, as though in apology for some wrong done. The
man patted the horse on the head. And Askar dismounted. The horse,
as if dismissed, went away to the bushes behind Askar and the man,
out of hearing and hidden from them. Askar saw that the horse did
not condescend to eat the grass at all, but waited, its ears pricked,
blessed with the foreknowledge that it would be fed on nobler food,
on something ambrosial perhaps.

'Greetings,' said the man, his voice golden and sweet and deep.
'Greetings, young man, from our land of mysteries, snakes, spiders,

and horses and men in coarse garments of wool. Welcome amongst us, traveller. Greetings,' he repeated.

There was a brief silence which appeared endless to Askar, for it was during this period that he was to cross from the darkened area of a dreamscape to that of light. Uninitiated, it took him longer and the man repeated the greetings formula a couple of times until Askar was ready to hear and understand. The man continued: 'We met but briefly, you and I, my son. My vision had just begun to grow mistier and the fog had descended on my soul, and thus I could not see nor comprehend. Greetings.'

Askar stared at him in silence.

The man went on, 'And I have a message. Would you like to receive it? And will you promise to deliver it to its rightful recipient, my son?'

Askar nodded his head, but didn't ask who the rightful recipient of the message was.

'The Prophet has said, may God bless his soul, that men are asleep. It is only at their death that they are awoken. Can you repeat that to me, word for word, my son?'

Askar nodded his head.

'Please repeat it to me, word for word.'

Askar repeated it.

'And there is another message.'

Askar indicated that he was waiting to receive it, even if it were on behalf of someone else.

'Please listen very carefully.'

Askar waited.

The man said, 'An eagle builds a nest with its own claws.'

There followed a slight pause. And the man waited.

Askar repeated, 'An eagle builds a nest with its own claws.'

Then the man in the coarse garments of wool took Askar by the hand and the horse, without being called, joined them, but kept a distance, awaiting instructions. The man walked to where the horse was and he whispered something into its ear. And the horse nodded. The horse then indicated to Askar that it was ready to be ridden. Askar, as he mounted the horse, wondered to himself if it would grow wings as bright as dawn and fly in the direction of the morning sun. Whereupon, as they bid each other farewell, the man said to Askar, 'May you be awoken in peace.'

And Askar awoke.

Awake and washed, handsome, shaven and seventeen years old, he now stood behind a window in a house in Mogadiscio – Uncle Hilaal's house. To his right, a writing desk on which lay, not as yet filled out, a form from the Somali National University Admissions Committee, a form he hadn't had the peace of mind to look at, because he didn't know whether he would, after all, choose to go to university although he had passed his school certificate examination with distinction and was within his rights to say which course or faculty he wanted. There were, besides the unfilled-out form, two other notes – one from Uncle Hilaal, in whose charge he lived, telling him that Misra had been seen in town and that she had been looking for the whereabouts of Askar and was likely to turn up any day at this doorstep; the other from the Western Liberation Front Headquarters, in Mogadiscio, requesting that he appear before the recruitment board for an interview. He stood behind the window, contemplative and very still – resembling a man who has come to a new, alien land. Presently, he left the window and picked up the forms and the notes in turn. He realized that he couldn't depersonalize his worries as he had believed he might. It occurred to him, as an afterthought, that on reading the note from Uncle Hilaal last night when he got back (he had spent a most pleasant evening out in the company of Riyo, his girlfriend), his soul, out of despair, had shrunk in size while his body became massive and over-blown. He wondered why.

Misra was here, in Mogadiscio!

Askar was now big, tall, clean as grown-ups generally are, and healthy. What would she make of him? he asked himself. He remembered how she used to lavish limitless love on him when sick; how she took care of him with the attentiveness of a child mending a broken toy. She would wash him, she would oil his body twice daily and her fingers would run over his smooth skin, stopping, probing, asking questions when they encountered a small scratch, a badly attended to sore or a black spot. Boils were altogether something else. They never worried her. 'Boys have them when and as they grow up,' she said, repeating the old wives' notion about boils. 'They are a result of undischarged sperm.'

But how would she react to him and to his being a grown man, maybe taller than she, who knows; maybe stronger and more muscular than she? Would absurd ideas cross her mind: that she would like to give him a bath? Or would she offer to give him a wash or help him soap his back, or–why not?–sponge those parts of his body his hands can't reach, would she? Whose look would be earth-bound, his or hers? Would he be able, in other words, to outstare her?

Standing between them, now that he had turned seventeen and she forty-something, were ten years, each year as prominent as a referee stopping a fight – ten years in which he shed his childish skin and grew that of an adult, under the supervision of Uncle Hilaal. He was virtually a different person. Perhaps he wasn't even a person when she last saw him. He was only a seven-year-old boy and her ward and, sometimes he thought to himself, her toy too. Anyway, the ten years which separated them were crucial in a number of ways.

The world Uncle Hilaal and Salaado had introduced him to, his living in Mogadiscio with them, his schooling there and the world which these had opened up for him, was a universe apart from the one the war in the Ogaden imposed on Misra's thinking. But how did she fare in war? Why did she become a traitor? For there was a certain consistency in one story – that she had sold her soul in order to save her body – but was this true? Was it true that she had betrayed a trust and set a trap in which a hundred Kallafo warriors lost their lives? Or did she surrender her body in order to save her soul? He then remembered that living with Misra wasn't always full of exhilaration and happiness, that there were moments of sadness, that it wasn't always fun. It had its pains, its agonies, its ups and downs, especially when the cavity of her womb overflowed with a tautology flow of blood once every month. When this occurred, she was fierce to look at, she was ugly, her hair uncombed, her spirit low, and she was short-tempered, beating him often, losing her temper with him. She was depressive, suicidal, no, homicidal.

That was how Karin entered his life.

[3]

Once a month, for five, six, and at times even seven days, Misra looked pale, appeared to be of poor health and depressive, and was of bad temper. And she beat him as regularly as the flow of her cycle. He used to think of her as a Chinese doll which you wound – if you waited long enough, its forehead would fall lifelessly on its chin, when unwound. A makeshift 'mother' substituted her. Not one of Uncle Qorrax's wives, no. The woman's name was Karin and she was a neighbour, with grown-up children who had gone their different ways, and a husband who lay on the floor, on his back, almost all the time, perhaps ailing, perhaps not, Askar couldn't tell. Karin carried or took Askar wherever she went, as though he were running the same errands as herself. For a long time, he called this woman 'Auntie' and never bothered to find out what her name was, wondering if she had any. For all the children in the area, including Uncle Qorrax's, referred to her as 'Auntie', too. One of Uncle Qorrax's sons said she was the wife of 'the sleeping husband'.

Karin didn't tell him what the matter with Misra was for a very long time. And when she did, she simply said, 'Oh, Misra is bleeding'. This made no sense to Askar. He had not seen any blood (he had once had a nosebleed himself and of course knew what blood looked like) and therefore said he didn't understand. He reasoned that this must be an adult's way of hiding something, or Karin's liking for speaking in parables. He couldn't forget that it was she he had asked what was wrong with her husband and she replied that he had a backache. On inquiring further, he learnt from Misra that he had a more serious problem than a backache. On making inquiries still further, this time from Uncle Hilaal, he was given the scientific name of the ailment. Now he asked, 'Do you "bleed" too?'

Karin said, 'I'm too old for that, thank God.'

This puzzled Askar. And Karin, with grandmotherly patience, explained: 'What Misra has is called *Xayl*. We women have other ugly names for it. Only women, above or below a certain age, have it – or suffer it. Men don't. When women are in their fifties or older, they stop having it. I haven't suffered from it since I was fifty-three. Do you understand?' she said, her bloodshot eyes fixed on him.

Askar needn't have spoken – she could see from the expression on his face that he didn't follow her explanations. She wished she could make him grasp her meaning – she, who took delight in talking to him about things she hadn't dared talk about with her own children. She said, 'When you are a little older, you will understand', in the manner in which a doctor assures an ailing person that all will be well if they take the tablets as prescribed.

'But I won't bleed?' he asked.

She forgot to repeat that only women suffered it – a fact he either hadn't registered, or which had escaped him, when she said, 'It brings with it lots of pain and suffering.'

'If I had some of it, then Misra will have less of it, yes?'

She wore the pained expression of somebody who felt misunderstood. Her head, as though it weren't on its neck any more, began to shake, 'No, no, no. Misra is a woman,' she said to Askar.

He shrugged his shoulders, 'So what?'

Without her speaking, he realized he had misunderstood her. Then he heard her say: 'Only women of a certain age have their periods, women between the ages of twelve and let's say fifty. Not men. And definitely not boys.'

He stared at her in wonderment, in silence. She went on, speaking slowly, articulately, 'My husband and my sons do not suffer the monthly pains of menstruation. My daughters, yes. I, yes – when I was younger.'

'Suppose a woman doesn't have it? Suppose she misses it?'

She wanted something clarified before she answered that: 'You mean, when these women are still young enough to be afflicted by them and they're not as old as I?'

Askar nodded.

Karin was sure. 'It means that they are with child.'

He appeared puzzled. Nor did the following explanation which she offered enlighten him, any more than a nomad listening to a news broadcast about the devaluation of the Somali shilling finds the subject comprehensible. She said, 'Women who miss their periods are pregnant, unless they are unwell.' Rather, this complicated matters.

Was Misra with child once monthly since she was unwell? Misra's periods used to be accompanied by depressive days and nights, and her breasts ached. She was unwell and she bled a great deal. Her monthly agony flowed for almost a week. Her pain was most acute in the lower abdomen to which she held constantly, and which she pressed as though she were squeezing pus out of an infected wound – so severe was this pain, at times she fainted. When the tension in her body was greater, she doubled up with it – as though she were in labour.

Karin, mixing kneaded dough with ground millet and water to make *canjeera* for Askar and, if she could eat it, for Misra as well, was saying, 'Remember when you're a grown man – remember the suffering and the pain on her face. Remember how women suffer. And do not, please, do not cause her further pain and suffering.'

He wished he had the will to make the required promise. Also, he wished he could remind Karin that Misra was not always in pain during this period. At times, he could see her sit in a palatial silence, daydreaming. He didn't know if Misra had ever told Karin of the two men, namely Uncle Qorrax and Aw-Adan, who called after nightfall.

With no after-dark visitors, these nights were quieter when Misra stopped moaning with excruciating pain. At any rate, neither of the men visited her when she was in season. He wished she was never in seasonal agonies. He wished the two men did not come after nightfall.

But there was one occasion when Misra didn't have the monthly, excruciating pain. Karin came and inquired after their health, all right. In fact, she called oftener, arousing suspicions in Askar's mind – and something told him something was amiss. Came a woman whom he had never seen before and the three of them were closeted in the room, speaking in whispers. What were they hiding from him?

Although there was no visible pain – the kind that he had associated with her periods – there was the same kind of pronounced tension in her body and she daydreamed a lot and for long periods of time. She didn't beat him, however, and had no temper to lose, it seemed. But she was most firm with the two after-dark callers – she wanted to see neither of them. Aw-Adan was very persistent. She didn't hesitate. She said to him, 'Go.' And he went.

There were changes in Misra's diet. She began chewing clayey lumps which were brought for her from the river bed; she ate a great many sour things; she also brushed her teeth with coal.

One evening, Aw-Adan came and the two of them entered the room and Askar could hear the key turning in the door as they locked it from inside. And Askar went to his favourite spot below the window. Undisturbed, he eavesdropped on their conversation. It was very brief. She wasn't willing to enter into a long dialogue with him. 'No marriage', he caught the phrase and held it in his mind long enough for him to hear her snappy, 'In any case who says the child is yours? He isn't.' And she came out.

There was a great deal of movement that night, with Karin and another woman coming and going. Something was being prepared but he didn't know what. Then, the following morning, the women made Misra lie on her back and they trampled all over her body. As if that wasn't enough, they made her sit up and be fumigated with cardamom and then improvised for her a suppository of cinnamon with myrrh. After which, they made her take concoctions which, among other things, included the broth of roots and shrubs which were known to have abortifacient powers. And as if this wasn't sufficient, one of the women inserted a metallic rod into her insides and Misra made a most frightening noise.

Misra convalesced for about a week. She was weak. What a kind woman Karin was, he used to think, ploughing the space between a husband who lay on his back from before Askar was born, and Misra whose wounds were fresh and whose memory of the pain therefore most acute. Playful, although he was now old enough to run faster than her, Askar rode on her back as she went back and forth, ecstatic at having found a person as patient, kind and generous as she.

Now. Years later. In Mogadiscio. At Hilaal and Salaado's.

And he saw a child crawling – and he could see this from a slight distance. Then the child clambered to its feet and walked for a bit, its gait shaky, its legs infirm and wobbly; he walked for half a metre and fell on his bottom but got up instantly and fell again, this time forward; his mouth, when he turned to Askar, was marked with the earth it had struck. But he did not cry. He continued falling and rising, without ever getting tired, without hurting a muscle or breaking a bone. And someone's voice (he couldn't see the person – but the voice was a woman's) said: 'Children fall without ever coming to harm because some protecting angels lay themselves between the falling child and the concrete floor, serving as the mattress on to which athletes drop from great heights of record-breaking dreams.' And he remembered his physical instructor at school say to him recently: 'Take care when you jump high, Askar. Yours is the age when you must account for every fall, lest you break a bone.'

His mind wandered – he watched with fascination a woman on 'fours', a woman crawling playfully towards the child, and, following lustily in the woman's wake, there was a man. It didn't matter to Askar if the child was theirs. This was not his concern. He asked himself a question: was this how Uncle Qorrax and then Aw-Adan first seduced Misra?

Imagine: a maid, wet to her elbows in the master's muck, a maid who is on her fours, whose bottom is high and is spread out in a protruding manner. And the master comes from behind and he takes her. How many films in which maids were raped by their employers had he seen? Or a secretary by her boss? How many stories in which a slave is raped by her south-of-the-Dixon-line master had he watched? Did Aw-Adan make her read the Koran and, while she was busy deciphering the mysteries of the Word, did he insert *his* in? Many stories of Ethiopian atrocities invaded his thoughts. And not in all of them were the raped women maids, mistresses or whores. In all of them, man was 'taker', the woman the victim. 'Why, if she isn't your mother, your sister or your wife, a woman is a whore,' said a classmate of his. How terribly chauvinistic, thought Askar. Women were victims in all the stories he could think of. Misra. Shahrawello. And even Karin. The soul is a woman – victimized, sinned against, abused.

Karin was such a dedicated soul and he trusted the truth of all that she had told him about Misra, trusted the truth of Misra's surrendering her body in order to save her soul – giving in ransom the warrior's faith in her integrity.

[4]

Why did she incestuously surrender the body he knew better than he knew his own? For weeks, his mind felt numbed at the idea that he had been part of the body which had been given away incestuously. 'How much of a child's body, or a woman's for that matter, can be said to be his or her own?' he asked Uncle Hilaal. 'Precious little,' had responded Hilaal. But even this did not damp down the fire of disgust burning inside of him. Uncle Hilaal wondered if, in Askar's opinion, Misra's betrayal was comparable to a woman who was unfaithful to a husband? No, no. It was more like a mother who brought dishonour upon the head of her child – right in the child's presence. What is in surrendering a body that is not one's own? But what soul is there that's worth saving? The noon was high and the sun climbed the steps of time.

'Possibly, Karin is not telling the truth,' said Salaado.

Askar retorted, 'Possibly she is.'

'And maybe you didn't know Misra that well,' suggested Salaado.

Askar nodded.

'And wars kill friendships in the same way as they bring into being other forms of trust and interdependence, don't you agree, Hilaal? Don't you agree, Askar?' said Salaado.

Hilaal, not reacting to what Salaado had said, nodded his head in silence.

'True, they were once the world's best friends. To each other. And to me, too,' said Askar.

'Well, there you are,' said Salaado.

A question imposed itself on Askar's mind: how much of a man's body can be said to be his own? A man is a master, a part of him said, he is a master of his own body.

Hilaal then said, 'Hadn't he better ask her to account for her life before he totally condemns her? Hadn't he? She, who was once his only world?'

In silence, Askar's mind continued along the same lines as Hilaal's thoughts – Misra, who was his only world, the content and source of his secrets, the only one whom he trusted and in whom he confided; she whose arm, large as anything he had touched or seen, would extend upwards and with short fingers point at the heavens, naming it; the same fingers which cleaned his face or dried his nostrils and had the agility to point subsequently at the earth on which she sat, her thoughts, like a pendulum, going from the sky (God's abode?) and the earth (feeder of man?) and then himself or herself. It was she from whom he learnt how to locate and name things and people, she who helped him place himself at the centre of a world – her own!

'Where is the sky?' she would ask him.

He would point at it.

'And the earth, where is the earth?'

And he would point at *her.*

'The earth, I said, where is the earth?'

Only after a number of attempts would he get it right. Then Mother, where is Mother Misra? And she would point herself out, her short finger placed between her breasts, saying 'This is I'. For years, he had had enormous difficulties pronouncing his Somali gutturals correctly, since he learnt these wrongly from her; for years, he mispronounced the first letters of the words in Somali for 'sky' and 'earth' – just like she did; for years, too, he remembered her favourite phrase: 'You are on your own!' She used this when she was fed up with him because he wouldn't stop crying or wouldn't sleep and she used this very shibboleth as an avant-courier of unhappy tidings. And the world, because she decided to walk out of it, would disintegrate right in front of him and he would, faithful to the formula, burst into a cry the instant she walked out of his sight, out of his world, and into one he couldn't get to, a world whose code of conduct he was not familiar with. At times, she would step out and hide behind the first available wall and listen to him express himself via a fit of weeping, his cheeks sooty with tear-stains, his heels painful from pounding them on the paved floor; on occasion, she would return after a long absence when he had tired and fallen asleep; on other occasions, she would come back to him playfully and teasingly, and she would tickle him and kiss him and hold him tightly to herself, speaking to him endearingly, calling him 'my man', addressing him as 'my love'.

Misra is here, in Mogadiscio, he read the note again.

Does that mean that I will have to touch her, kiss her, hug her to myself and hold her in my embrace? he asked himself. He wondered to himself how loathsome any physical contact with someone one doesn't love any more turns into; when the person to be touched, to be kissed, to be hugged, is now hated. Why is it that we love touching, animal-like, the one we adore? Why do we shun contact when this very person becomes the one we hate most? The body speaks, the soul obeys – is that not so? The body refuses to make contact with a love gone senselessly numb – is that not so? But to touch Misra, to kiss her, to hug a woman who has betrayed one's trust – here in Mogadiscio – when one is to make a decisive decision such as whether or not one should join the Liberation Front or choose a career in the world of academia? Had he not better write to the Front intimating his immense wish to join its ranks? That way, he would wash clean his conscience – and live at peace with it. Neither the members of the panel nor Uncle Hilaal would know of the connection, and his going before them would undo the fetters tightening on his conscience. If killed when defending his country, he would die a young man at peace with his soul – and therefore a martyr.

And if he joined the university? It worried him that, at a university, he was likely to indulge his thoughts in higher intellectual pursuits and that he might not think it worth his while to fight until death in order to liberate the semi-arid desert that was the Ogaden. He was sure, in the camaraderie characteristic of the times in which he lived, that there would be a great many people who would dissuade him from dying for a nationalistic cause, such as the Ogaden people's. Many Somalis, he knew, were inarticulate with rage whenever the argument they put forward was challenged. Wouldn't a university education equip him with better and more convincing reasons, wouldn't it provide him with the economic, political and cultural rationalizations, wouldn't he be in a better position to argue more sophisticatedly? He would, perhaps, write a book on the history of the Ogaden and document his findings with background materials got from the oral traditions of the inhabitants. So would he take the gun? Or would he resort to, and invest his powers in, the pen?

Once in Mogadiscio, Misra was not likely to return to the scene of her treason. Her past, now that it was dishonoured, as was her name, would come before her, naked like a child. But instead of touching and fondling her newly found child, Misra would shun contact with it. She would double up with guilt, he hoped, and would suffer from the cramps of disgrace. The marrow in the cavities of her bones, he hoped, would congeal, due to the chill of exposure. Cursed she would remain, he prayed, and unforgivable too. May the tendons of her neck snap, he prayed to God, as should every traitor's neck and may her blood, startled, rush to her eyes and blind her. May her mucus dry and may the pain this caused, in the end, bring about her death. May the earth reject her, may the heavens refuse to grant her an audience. If and only if she had betrayed!

It pained him to remember that he had once shared his life with her, it made him feel embarrassed to recall that he had been so close to her once, that he had been proud of her. Once she upheld him, like water – she lifted him up and threw him, as though she were a wave followed by another and another and another. He tasted the salt in her tears, he smelt of her menstruation. He called her 'Mother' years ago. Could he undo all the ties which held them together? Could he, like time, sever all their links? Oh, how he wished he could hang 'time' on a peg like a wet cloth, and how he wished it wouldn't stop raining so the cloth would not dry; yes, how he wished he could suspend 'time' so he would not grow up to be a man – a man on his own, and to whom Misra would say, 'You are on your own!' No. As a child, he never wanted to be on his own, never wanted to be alone, for he couldn't find himself inside of himself, only in others, preferably adults like Misra and Aw-Adan, who would analyse situations and tell him things he might never have known about himself if not informed by their experience. Misra's 'Your are on your own!' reeked of the same vindictiveness as a man's throwing out of the house a pet he kept and fed for years, a pet expected to fend for itself. One morning, when he had wet the bed the previous night, she spoke the formula shibboleth 'You are on your own' (this was he when he was a little under five-and-a-half years old) and made as if to go out.

'Wait, wait, Misra,' he said.

The voice sounded grown-up to her and she did as told. Also, she saw that he had wrapped her *shamma*-shawl round his shoulders, looking very much like a woman; and he started saying: 'When I grow up and I become a man ... ', purporting, as it were, to speak for a long time, although he suddenly stopped, since he suspected she might not have noticed what he had wrapped round his shoulders.

Her voice, teasing and friendly, 'And I an old woman ... , yes, when I grow older and I have no teeth left and no help forthcoming and you a grown-up man and I a helpless old woman ... ! One day, when you are a youth . . . and I an old emaciated woman, friendless . . . ,' and she was standing a few inches away from him . . .

Firmly, 'No,' he said, indicating that she had messed up his plans. 'No,' he repeated, shaking his head as if saying, 'This is not what I meant.'

'What no? Why not?'

He was silent. She thought that perhaps she had upset him greatly and so she extended her hand out to him and he took it in silence. They hugged slightly, neither speaking. Then his hands, when he tried to clasp them round her, wouldn't make a circle, the fingers wouldn't touch, they wouldn't reach one another, and he was now saying, half-playful and half-serious, 'No, no, no.' She looked at him and saw that the *shamma*-shawl had slipped away to the ground, trapping his feet, and the face that emerged was that of a half-man, half-child.

'What no? Why no? What are you telling me, my man?'

Again his voice sounding grown-up, 'When I grow up and I am a man . . . I am trying to tell you if you care to hear it . . . Misra dearest . . . ,' and he took a distance and stood out of her arms' reach.

'Yes?'

'I will kill you.'

She stared at him in silence for a long time. 'But why?'

'To live, I will have to kill you.'

'Just like you say you killed your mother?'

'Just like I killed my mother – to live.'

[5]

He asked himself the question whether, to live, he would have to kill her if he saw her in Mogadiscio – now that there were good reasons for him to do so.

CHAPTER FOUR

[1]

You began debating with the egos of which you were compounded, and, detaching itself from the other selves, there stood before you, substantial as a shadow, the self (in you) which did not at all approve of your talking with or touching Misra, lest you were lost in the intensity of her embrace. For a long time, your selves argued with one another, each offering counter arguments to the suggestions already submitted by the others. Undecided, and undeciding, you stood in front of a mirror and you studied those aspects of yourself which could be seen with the naked eye and you concluded that Misra wouldn't recognize you, even if she saw you in the street that day. You wore your age on your face, for instance. And your hand felt a day's growth on your chin as you wondered if you should shave. An instant later, you were on the mat of your younger stubble, watching Aw-Adan help Misra study her future in the flames of a fire she had made. Oh, if only . . . !

If only you and Misra could meet in a room darkened for that very purpose, you told yourself. If only there were no mirror to divulge the secrets of your inner torments; if the two of you could touch each other in the dark; if you could get used to each other while still in the unlit room; if each could claim to be someone else, until you were together long enough to want to know the other; if each could fabricate a story which would go well with the identity you wished to assume (you hadn't, by then, been told that she had entered the country in disguise!); if only you could speak to each other without recognizing each other, remembering hardly anything which might generate suspicions, anything which might activate emotions within, anything which might stir dormant memories of your life together.

And if the two of you met in broad daylight, in the presence of other people, when, say, Hilaal was here, or one of your friends, one of your acquaintances or one of your neighbours? You were certain your confidence would be so shattered you would break into pieces; at best, your dignity would drop at your feet as though it were a shawl flung by its wearer; possibly your tongue, short as the midday shadow, would curl up and lie exhausted in the sweaty siesta of the moment's lethargy and you wouldn't be able to speak.

What you needed to confront her with was an innocence with which to protect yourself, you thought. Alternatively, you could do with the kind of powered stare you were born with – that unmitigatable, impenetrable, 'whole' stare, one which might have caught sight of her guilt and focused on it. Could this be why you felt comfortable standing in the curtained silence of the darkened hour, standing, to be precise, in the confluences of your past and your present; standing your ground, withstanding the wholesome flood of your future! 'You behave as though you were a husband to whom a woman has been unfaithful,' commented Uncle Hilaal, 'as though you couldn't bring yourself to touch the body which had betrayed your trust. It is unbelievable that you would avoid any physical contact with the woman who could justifiably say that "by touching me, it seems as though he were touching himself"!' You lifted your eyebrows as if in wonder, and no wonder! For there stood before you, upright and as though waiting, *another* you, younger surely and more confident. You couldn't think of anything to say – you didn't speak to your younger self. Instead, you moved away from the mirror and stared ahead of yourself.

The world was open as the field you could see from the window and. . .

[2]

You were very old and your skin had started to sag and so you had it altered – that is, you exchanged your old body for another, one which belonged to a young woman. How this had taken place, or why, was something beyond your conjecture. Why, for instance, first wear the mask and features of an old man, only to discard them the following moment in order to don the visage and look of a young woman? Or why, for that matter, resort to a metamorphosis, changing face, visage, age, sex and features too?

Anyway, the signs of your body's sagging began to appear first in the hands and fingers which shrank to the size of a small child's little fingers. The logic behind all this metamorphosis was so dim to your unilluminated perception of things that you couldn't see anything clearly. Your legs had stiffened so you couldn't get up, walk or rise to your feet – the legs themselves having been reduced to the size of a monkey's paw. And you were seventy years old.

A second later, you were watching a young woman's body being dismantled, right in front of you – each limb, part and organ was first shown to you so you could examine its fitness. Every now and then, you offered your approval or disapproval by nodding or shaking your head. You wondered why the young woman accepted the exchange. You were told that she was disgusted by her young body – a body which was beautiful, smooth and seductive. You were told that her father had raped her, that her elder brother had desired her and that her mother and sisters were envious of her. You were told that she couldn't walk up or down a street without someone proposing to her, without feeling eyes of lust piercing through her body to the core of her soul. You were told that she felt she was a dartboard and an intrusion of eyes were penetrating through her. And why was she interested in yours? 'Yours is a maturer kind of anima,' she said, standing in front of you, half old and half young, half you and the other half herself. Parts of your body mingled well with hers.

You noticed that her head, hairless and smooth like a peeled onion, lay within your reach. You wished you could stretch out your hand and touch her but apparently your arms hadn't been screwed on. Also, you didn't like the ugly sights in front of you now that you could see better, nor did you like eating the food that was on offer, now that your appetite was that of a young person. So why did you accept the exchange? someone asked you. 'You must know,' you said. 'Only in dreams do such impossible things happen.' And you were silent, thoughtful – and concentrating.

So far, you and the young woman coped grandly with the exchanges and you were civil to each other. Now, however, there was tension. You both remained hesitant and contemplative, and neither was willing to offer the final approval once it came to the exchange of the mouth and lips. You didn't know what language she spoke; she didn't know what syllabic, consonantal or guttural formations would come with your mouth and lips. You were worried what her political views were; she, whether you were conservative or no. You asked yourself what continent she was born in, whether her family was rich, if she had many friends – and what kind. She wondered to herself if you had a good or a bad conscience, if you were guilt-ridden and whether you had a happy life. These questions, these ideas, so far unhoused, unclaimed and unspoken, roamed about in the air, ideas without flesh, without soul and this made you wish you were whole again, this made you wish you were yourself again, a young man, barely seventeen. How very weird: to dream that you were dreaming? Or were you simply confronting your various selves, which consisted of a septuagenarian and of a young woman, not to forget the self whose identity you assumed when awake?

You felt there was something unfinished about *you*, as though you had made yourself in such haste you roughened your features unnecessarily. You had the feeling, however, that your face fitted you extraordinarily. And the identity of *your* newer self? It was like a dot in the distance which assumed features you could identify, becoming now a man, now a woman – or even an animal, your perceptions of the new self altering with the distance or nearness of the spot of consciousness. Then the mirror vanished from right in front of you and the wall which had been there replaced it. And there on the wall appeared shadows and the shadows were speaking with one another, some laughing, some listening and some holding hands or touching one another.

'And you – who are you?' one of the shadows asked you.

You answered, 'I am in a foreign body.'

'Now what does that mean?'

You paused. Then, 'It means that I am in a foreign country.'

'Yes? Go on.'

'I was once a young man – but I lost my identity. I metamorphosed into an old man in his seventies, then a young woman. I am a septuagenarian wearing the face, and thinking with the brain, of a young woman, although the rest of my body, my misplaced memory if you like, partly belongs to yet a third person, namely a seventeen-year-old youth.'

The wall in front of you shook with laughter and all the shadows joined in making fun of you, some mimicking your voice, others mocking the rationale of your complaint. You didn't know what to do; you felt uneasy and looked from one shadow to another. Finally, your eyes singled out a smiling face and it belonged to an old man. He was saying, 'And what do you think is the cause of this torment? What have you done?'

'My mother placed a curse on my head,' you said.

The old man's look took on a most venomous appearance. 'What did you do to earn her curse?'

'I ... er ... I ... ,' you started to say, but stopped.

He commented, 'Mothers are the beginning of one, they beget one, they give one a beginning. You must have done something unpardonable. You must have. Otherwise, why on earth would she place a curse on your head? Why, why, why? I imagine she must have suffered gravely: first under your father and then you, her own son. Poor woman, your mother. To have carried you, as a blessing, for months, inside of herself, to have loved you as her child for years and then to have had to curse you. It must have been agonizing to her.'

You were clearly misunderstood by this old man, you said to yourself. Perhaps, you should tell him that the woman wasn't actually *your* mother in the sense in which he took it, that the woman didn't give birth to you in the way mothers as we know them give birth to their children. In other words, this woman wasn't where you began in the clotted form of a tiny germ which grew, lived and developed on its own inside the body of another. But you loved her as you might have loved your mother – if she had survived your birth.

The old man was saying, 'I knew of a young man who was cursed by his mother because he refused to carry her on his back when they were crossing a stream lest she drown and because she didn't know how to swim and he did. The arrogance of youth had gone to the young man's head, the desire of a woman had lodged itself in his loins and the beating of love's wings compelled him to run to where the woman of his lust was. He left his mother, an old woman who was lame and aged and decrepit, he left her to her own devices, impervious to her plea, "Just help me cross this stream in which I might drown." He flew off in a mad rush. No one ever heard of his mother ever again. The beasts made a meal of her. Or perhaps the angels of mercy saved her. But we heard of the youth, and saw him again and again.'

'What became of the youth?' you asked.

'He complained again and again of hearing the noise of a chain-saw inside his head. He heard that noise at night, he heard it by day, he heard it in his sleep and heard it when awake. In the end, he went insane. And the woman he loved? you ask. Whatever became of the woman he loved? They were separated by the noise of the chain-saw: she couldn't bear sharing a bed and her life with a man who always heard something she couldn't. Besides, she took her distance because she believed that a young man who was so insensitive as to remain indifferent to his mother's pleas couldn't or wouldn't be bothered about her the fortnight following their own honeymoon. And she paid heed to society's advice and rejected his advances. He was reduced to an ugly sight, this young man. And you could see him roaming the streets of our town, garbed in tatters, looking into the town's refuse bins as hungry dogs and parentless urchins do. One day, right in the middle of the largest market, he set his tatters on fire. Ablaze, he died, unhelped, and his body lay unburied for days. A mother's curse is to be taken far more seriously than a father's. Give heed. A mother's blessing is far more worthy of God than a father's. What I do not know and what no one but God knows is whether it was the curse placed on his head by his mother that did it, or the woman's rejection of his marriage proposal, the woman's refusal to reciprocate his love. My feeling is it was the curse. Someone else might argue that it was society's turning its back on him that persuaded the young woman and so on and so forth. Yes, young man. A mother's curse is by far the heaviest burden a human has carried on his head. Don't earn it. That is my advice.'

Silence. Then the wall became just another speck in the huge space surrounding yourself. And in the miraged distance, prominent as an oasis, there was a colt, riderless – but saddled. You sighed – relieved. You knew Misra was back, you knew she hadn't, as yet, placed a curse on your head.

[3]

Your childhood, excepting activities involving either Misra or your dreams, you once said, is one great oblivion. You couldn't remember much, you confessed; couldn't remember what people looked like, although you could recall some names to which, at any rate, you couldn't put faces; couldn't remember whether your feet ached as you pushed them into shoes a size too small; whether the papulae on your measle-affected body broke on their own or whether you pressed them playfully yourself. In one sense, you considered yourself a solitary child and spent a great deal of your time alone. Unless you were with Misra, you found all other company 'demanding, boring, in short, lifeless'. You would stand by the tree, born a day or two after you, and look up at its branches swinging in the wind, a tree much taller than you, and you would water it. Then you would take a handful of the earth sorrounding it and you would take a mouthful of its nourishment, making sure Misra wasn't watching you, believing, of course, that eating earth would do you a world of good, and that you would grow taller and heftier, just like the tree. Alone, again, once you knew how to write your name, you would secretly graft your name, born the same day as the tree, on its bark.

Dreams separated you. You shared everything else – but not your dreams. She knew every one of your secrets, touched every inch of your body and felt your heartbeat too. You slept on the same bed, under the same cover and partook of the same atmospheric pressures, air and oxygen. But not your dreams. Even at night, asleep, in the dark, it was your respective dreams which separated you; dreams which lay between the two of you; dreams which were (in your case) dressed up in 'mantles of water, in jackets of fire, in suits of green wear, in fatigue-uniforms, one day as a woman, another as a man'. The rivers in your dreams flowed away from the streams in hers. Whereas you saw a companion very like yourself walk beside you in an empty street, Misra saw a man holding her right hand, she saw you hold her left and the three of you walked together towards sunset. Your dreams overflowed like buckets of water; at times, you saw rivers burning; at times, the water in your dreams was on fire; at other times, your volcanic eruptions made you speak in your sleep, and Misra could hear and understand the odd word that she had heard. She asked you to tell her what you saw in your nightmare the following morning. You didn't. It was as if you were claiming your dreams as your own.

Nor would you share with her the dream in which you saw a woman drown in a muddy river, a woman who appealed for help, calling out your name. Do you remember what you did? You waded to where the woman was drowning. You extended out your hands as though you were offering help. Your fingers, immediately they came into contact with her body, rolled into a fist and you pushed the head of the woman down and down and down – until she died.

In its wake, the dream made you shout in your sleep. Uncle Hilaal rushed in and woke you up. You were wet with perspiration. In an effort to persuade him that it wasn't anything serious, you told him a story you made up on the spot. He said he didn't believe you had given him the true story. And only then did you speak the truth. He inquired if you recognized the woman's face. You insisted you didn't.

'What did the woman's voice sound like?' he said.

You answered, 'She spoke as though there was water in her mouth.'

'This doesn't say much, does it? After all, the woman was drowning.' He explained himself, unnecessarily. 'You said the river was choked with mud, didn't you? Or was it simply stagnant?'

'It was salty and stagnant,' you said.

'Do you remember anything else?' he asked.

Here again the dream stood between you and Uncle Hilaal and you chose to wrap yourself with it and not share it with anyone else – not even him. He waited, expecting you would answer his question. Indeed, he was surprised when you said that you were thirsty.

He got you a cold glass of water. As you drank, you apologized saying: 'I'm thirsty as the earth. I could drink an oceanful of water.' He returned with a jugful of cold water. Your thirst was insatiable. Anyway, you were justifiably relieved when, of necessity, the subject had to be changed – from your dream to your thirst.

[4]

Uncle Hilaal's saying that your life was 'an answer to a fictive riddle asking a factual puzzle' when you refused to talk to him, take walks with him and Salaado, his wife, or eat anything save bread and water and occasionally a glass of something whilst they weren't looking – your uncle's statement set into motion a cavalcade of memories, each of which rode, as if it were a wave, on the bigger crest ahead of it. And, in no time, you managed to discrete the dreamed anecdote from the one really lived and personally experienced, you managed to separate them so they didn't overlap, so they didn't go over the same ground, telling the same story with a repetitiveness which bored one. You ran the whole course, without once looking back to see who had dropped and who hadn't. Misra, too, stayed the course, always within view, always there – motherly, lovely and good. Others were wicked. Not she. She was your 'mother'. Hence, she was very good.

And *now*! A he-dog was copulating with a bitch. Then you saw a little boy come out of a house and, immediately behind him, a woman – most probably his mother – calling him back. The boy was apparently very angry and was desperately throwing pebbles at the copulating dogs. He didn't stop pelting pebbles at the mating dogs, although none hit his target. The woman finally managed to hold the little boy's arm suggesting that he restrained himself, asking, 'But what's got into your head?'

'But they shouldn't copulate,' said the little boy, barely eight. 'They shouldn't copulate, they shouldn't copulate, they shouldn't copulate. These two dogs shouldn't copulate,' he half-shouted.

The woman bent down and wiped away his tears with the edge of her *guntiino*-robe. Then she noticed the sticky, white after-sleep fluid in his left eye. She wet the cleaner edge of her robe by licking it and she applied her saliva caringly. The boy was calm. She asked, 'But why not?' seeing the dogs unlocked and playful.

'Why not? Because the bitch is his own mother,' he answered.

The woman, taking his hand with a view to persuading him to go with her back into the house, said, 'I know!'

'You know the bitch is his mother?' he said, in disbelief.

She said, 'Yes, I do.'

'And that they shouldn't copulate?'

He wouldn't go with her until she answered his challenge. He hid both his hands behind his back, his look defiant, his reason enraged, his body intent on fighting, if need be, for what he understood to be morally wrong.

'It is different with animals,' said the woman.

(Perhaps the woman didn't know, and neither could you have known then, that the young man had been taught at school that human beings were animals, too – rational beings, endowed with the power of speech – a higher animal, if you like, the teacher had said.)

'Look,' he was saying, pointing his finger at the dogs which were locked in incestuous fornication. 'Look at them doing it again, right in front of us, lower animals that they are,' and he went and kicked at them, but they wouldn't unlock. He turned after a while, half in tears, to his mother and appealed, 'Mother, do something. Please, Mother, do something. Don't let them do it.'

The woman received her son's appeal in a mixture of good humour and serious intent. First, she chased away the dogs, who limped away, still locked in love, then she picked up her son and kissed him, saying: 'You are impossible, my dear. You're impossible.'

And he was saying, 'Lower animals, dogs and bitches.'

[5]

You were young again, you were in Kallafo again, remembering an anecdote involving a man originally from Aden, the Democratic Republic of Southern Yemen, a man on whose lap had been found, when surprised by unannounced visitors, a hen. You didn't quite comprehend the implications of the scandal. The old Adenese had been one of your favourite old men and he was a neighbour and you were fond of the chocolates he presented you with whenever you happened to have called on him. But you were often told not to go to his house, alone. You were often told not to accept his gifts – ever. You were warned against keeping his company ('A most evil company!' had said Aw-Adan). You were warned against the man's wicked ways. And yet you went, like many other young boys of your age, and you played in his spacious yard, you plucked lemon and other fruits and ate of his garden what pleased you most. You slept, exhausted, in the shade of his trees. You swam in the pond of his irrigation scheme. You watched him, strong and muscular for a man of his age, start his engine or switch it off; you watched him with great admiration, lean and tense, loving and lovable.

'But what was he up to,' you asked, 'with a hen on his lap, with plucked feathers on his naked thigh? What was he up to? Will somebody kindly tell me?' you appealed.

Misra said, 'He was up to no good, that wicked Adenese.'

'What foul things was this Adenese up to?' you asked.

Misra was insistent that you were spared this old bachelor's wicked involvements with young boys: how he used to lure them with chocolate and other gifts; how he used to run an open house to which the urchins of Kallafo as well as other boys from the well-to-do would find their way; and how he would entice one of the small boys into his bedroom every now and then. You were very upset at learning what the Adenese had done, so upset you took ill. You had a temperature. And when Aw-Adan came with a suppository, you suspected him of vicious intentions. You cried and cried and cried and you wished you had never known the Adenese, had never been so sick you would need a suppository. Indeed, you were too shocked to allow one of your selves to stand out from the others, with a view to studying the activities, thoughts of your primary self. You would have nothing whatsoever to do with an Adenese, you said to yourself, never would you befriend any Adenese, you thought to yourself, never would you trust them – ever. And it was only then that remarks made by Misra or Aw-Adan began to make sense, remarks which were to do with 'respect for human dignity'. You forgot who it was, precisely, that had made the remark following the scandalous Adenese's copulating with a hen – and therefore didn't know how to interpret it. You then asked Misra: 'Am I to understand that any person who has respect for human dignity does not copulate with a beast? Or am I to understand that any elderly bachelor with respect for human dignity doesn't rape boys?'

She was on her knees, scrubbing the floor. Her clothes were filthy, her hands soaped, her headscarf unknotted, her knees squarely on the wet floor and her elbows covered with the brown mixture of dirt and sweat. And she looked at you, not yet seven, you, who stood as men do, clean and washed and yet unperturbed by the unclean job which must be done by women; you who stood in the doorway, with your back to the sun which was in her eyes, speaking of 'human dignity' as though the phrase meant nothing to you personally. She rose to her feet. Her look went past you, dwelling, for a moment, on the upturned chairs, the dismantled bed and the mattress standing against a wall in the courtyard; then her quizzical look rested, for a while, on you and her lips moved, mumbling something inaudible to you. Maybe she was repeating to herself the phrase 'respect for human dignity', you thought, or maybe the many-stranded views of Misra were taking shape, and, you thought when at last she spoke, you would have a response to your question. But the silence was too painful to bear and the world you and Misra inhabited was not one in which you could merely pay lip service to lofty, meaningless phrases like 'respect for human dignity'. It was as though her silence was saying that you should take an objective, honourable look at yourself as a man and then at the position of women in your society before using phrases that were loaded with male hypocrisy.

She was back on her knees, scrubbing, using as a brush her open hand, and at times her nails, to rub away the sticky filth which wouldn't be removed easily. She didn't look up at you at all, pretending that you weren't there, that you hadn't asked her anything. She was defiantly quiet. Until you were about to move away. Then you heard her sobbing between the noises her scrubbing had made.

'Am I to understand,' you started, but lost interest in what you were going to say when you heard Misra's chest explode in a convulsive cry, like a child's. And you fell silent.

[6]

That night, cuddled up in each other's embrace, and in bed, she spoke to you of a raid, so far undocumented in history books. Out of the raid, out of the dust of triumph, emerged a warrior, she told you, a warrior riding a horse, and as he hit his heels against the beast's ribs, the warrior held tightly to a little girl, barely seven. The girl was his loot now that the enemy had retreated in haste, defeated. Other men returned with gold and similar booties – but not he. The little girl, now a young woman, would remember forever her dog howling with fear and anxiety and hunger, her cheeks shiny with mucus and with streaks of tears running down them; and she cried and cried and cried, seated, as though tied hand and foot to a bedpost, on the horse's back, a horse whose speed frightened her, as did the fact that he was taking her away from the world she had been familiar with so far. She was very pretty. Her hair had been shaven in the style your people shave children's skulls when suffering from whooping-cough, although the little girl's tuft on the skull was longer and slightly curlier. When the warrior arrived back in his hamlet, Misra went on telling you her story, his people intimated to him that they were afraid the girl might be traced to them – the soldiers of the Empire would follow the civilian invaders and the punitive expeditions would find many unburied dead. So he rode away, travelling as far south as he could, and the two of them, on a horse's back, ended up in the vicinity of Jigjiga.

In Jigjiga, the warrior, weary and fatigued from travel and worry, took ill. He stopped at the first house and knocked on the first door and spoke with the first man he met – luckily for him, the owner of the house, a very wealthy man. The warrior and the little girl were both given generous hospitality. A day later, the warrior died. And the little girl, who had been taken for his daughter, fell into the caring hands of the wealthy man. He raised her with his own children, making her embrace the Islamic faith, making her undergo the infibulatory rites, just like the other girls of the community. But he raised her with an eye to taking her as his wife when she grew up. And this he did, when she was seventeen. So, the man the little girl thought of and addressed as 'Father' for ten years of her life, overnight became a man to her, a man who insisted he make love to her and that she call him 'husband'. In the end, the conflicting loyalties alienated her, primarily from her self. And she murdered him during an excessive orgy of copulation.

To escape certain persecution, she joined a caravan going south to Kallafo, a caravan in search of grain to buy. She introduced herself as Misra Haji Abdullahi – taking anew the name of the man who became her father and whom she murdered as her 'man'.

And you asked, 'The girl's father and mother? Does anybody know whatever became of them? And whether or not they are still alive? Or if one of her parents has remarried or has had another child?'

You were surprised to learn that the girl was the offspring of a *damoz* union between an Oromo woman and an Amhara nobleman. She was the female child of the union, one in which her mother agreed, as is the custom, to live with an Amhara nobleman, none of whose other wives gave him a male child. The contract was for a period between a fortnight and six months. The girl was conceived by the 'salaried' concubine. Because the issue was a girl, the man lost interest in her, abandoning mother and child to their separate destinies and uncertain fortune. 'Yes, yes, but did the girl have a half-brother or a half-sister?'

'No one knew.' That was her answer.

'And then what happened?'

Again, she entered the household of yet another wealthy man. This time, she entered the household as a servant but was, in less than a year, 'promoted' to the rank of a mistress and eventually as a wife. By the time she found Askar, the woman had been divorced. She had had two miscarriages and was discovered to be carrying, in secret, a dead child in her.

'A dead child in her, carrying a dead child in her living body?'

'That's right.'

'And then? Or rather, but why carry a dead child?'

'Then the living miracle in the form of Askar took the place of the dead child inside of her,' she said, holding you closer to herself, you, who were, at that very instant, dreaming of a horse dropping its rider. But you weren't alert enough to note a discrepancy in this and Misra's true story. For she had her own child who died at the age of eighteen months. Nor did you ever ask her why she told you this fictitious version. Or is your own memory untrustworthy?

[7]

A week later, the following:

Late one afternoon, the Archangel of Death called at Karin's place as though he had been invited to tea, just as you were invited to partake of the festive atmosphere, have a cake or two and biscuits too – and his share of the flowing conversation. When the opportunity presented itself, the Archangel whispered something discreetly in Karin's old man's ear, saying (you were told afterwards) that he, the Archangel, would return in precisely seven hours. So, would the old man finish, in elegance, all he had planned to do – wash, pray, say a few devotions, make a number of wishes, give his *dardaaran* to his Karin and, if it pleased him, tell her that time was up? In retrospect, you recall that the old man kept giving furtive glances to a timepiece by his mattress on the floor, rather like somebody who didn't want to miss an important appointment. Together with Misra and Karin, you were making joyful noises and nothing seemed to be amiss. It was the placid look in the old man's eyes that said to you that something was taking place, but you didn't know what. First, Karin looked at you and then Misra and there fell the kind of silence which precedes an event of great significance. Somehow, Misra and you sensed your presence was standing in the way of Karin and her husband's communicating a secret to each other. And so you left, leaving in your wake, you thought, a silence so profound you were sure a change of inestimable importance would occur in your lives.

Before midnight, the old man's leaf fell gently from the tree on the moon. It was a most gentle death. Hush. And the soft falling of the withered leaf didn't even tease the well of Karin's emotions, nor did it puncture the lacrymatory pockets. She didn't cry, didn't announce the departure of the old man's soul to anyone until the following morning. She stayed by him, keeping his death all to herself. She lay by him in reverent silence, he dead, she alive – but you couldn't have told the difference, so quiet was she beside him.

She washed him as she washed him every day of all the years that he had lain on his back. Alone, but not lonely, her hands white with soapy foam, her eyes tearlessly dry, her throat not at all teased with the convulsive wishes of mournfulness, she moved back and forth and her hands washed and touched and felt a body she had known for years, the body of a man who had 'possessed' her, a man who had given her love and children – and who, at times, made her hate herself. She married him when very young. She wasn't even fifteen. You might say she could've been his daughter. She was small and a woman, and he was muscular and shapely as a man, and was popularly nicknamed 'Armadio'. He came one morning and made a downpayment for her. He went 'somewhere' (he had a job to do, that was all he was willing to tell anyone) and returned, his going as mysterious as his returning. He wasn't a man for formalities, weddings and parental blessings. He shouldered her in the manner porters lift any weight. He spoke little, said little, the night he deflowered her. 'I have a job to do,' he said, and she carried his child.

He gave her children. He gave her lots of space and silence and love, when there. But he disappeared every now and then, saying, 'I have a job to perform'. One day, he came home to a woman who suspected him of being with other women. He didn't explain himself, didn't scold her when jealousy threw her into tantrums, even when she maliciously described him as 'the man with a job to do'.

A month later, he called her into the bedroom before he parted on one of his mysterious missions and he did something he had never done before. He told her he might be away for a long period. He suggested she sell the house in which they were living and that she buy a smaller one, if, yes if, he didn't come home before the rains. He was most tender and he gave her money which he was sure she and the children would need. 'But what job is taking you away from us?'

'Death might,' he said.

'Now what do I say to people when they ask me where you are? You are my husband, the father of my children, the man I've lived with and loved all these years. What am I to say?'

'Tell them I had a job to do.'

'I want to know more.'

He said, 'Don't worry. I'll not allow death to take me away,' half-smiling, as though Death was the name of a woman with whom he was madly in love. 'I'll come back, sooner or later.'

He didn't come home before the rains and not even after them. She received news of him over the wireless. Armadio was apparently a member of a cell of the Somali Youth League which was agitating for the reunification of all the Somali-speaking territories. He was the chairman of the cell under which fell the activities of the movement within the Ethiopia-administered Ogaden. He was caught when doing a job and ended up in one of Haile Selassie's many prisons. When she didn't hear from him, she sold the house and moved into a smaller one and, as told, did her job. It consisted of taking care of the children, sending them to school and making sure they all left for Mogadiscio, where it was safe to be a Somali and be proud of it, and where they would join cells from which to launch spearheads to open the way for a united Somalia. She stayed – and waited. She was sure he would come home. One day, he did. He was seen standing at her door. He looked tired, 'like a man who had done a heavy load of a job', she said. He didn't speak of his ordeals and his years in prison. He was carrying a holdall which was empty save for a portrait of Ernest Bevin.

She said, 'Who is this man, Armadio?'

He answered, departing, for once, from his job-to-do formula, 'He is the one British friend Somalis have.'

'How so?' she asked.

'He is the one powerful figure in British politics who has advocated the reunification of all the Somali-speaking territories.'

He stuck Bevin's portrait on the dung-plastered wall with the help of a couple of thumbtacks someone gave to him. And he spoke no more of jobs to do or places to go to. He fell unwell. He complained of acute pains in the spine, but whether he had been tortured in the Ethiopian prison, he wouldn't say; nor would he talk of what it was like to be in a dark room year after year, isolated from the rest of humankind, from his Karin and from his children.

One morning, he didn't get up to say his *subx*-prayers. 'My back,' he said. And from that moment on, he lay on his back, on a mattress on the floor. His wife washed him once daily – no, washed is not the right word. What she did was to wet a cloth a little bigger than a face towel in soapy water and run it all over his body, rubbing harder where it was hairier. For ablutionary purposes, it was he who performed it, whispering the right traditions and verses as she dipped the cloth in cleaner water, massaging the proper places himself. He prayed, lying on his back. He didn't go through the body-motions of *sujuuds* and *rukuucs*. To the suggestion that they consult a doctor, cost what it might, his response had been, 'I have no more jobs to do.'

Bevin's portrait was transferred from the dung-plastered wall to a spot in the ceiling directly above his bed. Karin spoon-fed him, holding him by his nape with her left hand and wiping away whatever mess his mouth made with her right. She treated him as she might have treated a child – if she were blessed with a sickly one at her age – with knowing kindness. And when someone asked Armadio why he was still holding on to life, he said, 'Unless I know there is a job for me to do, is there any point my going *there*? In the meantime, I'll wait for a word from Him.'

The word came. His last words, 'No mourning for one who has done little for his country, his wife and his children. Promise, Karin. No mourning.'

She noticed there was a stain of blood on his mouth. She was trying to discover the cause, when he breathed his last. She promised, she, the living, promised to the dead, 'No mourning'. But she couldn't find out the cause of the bloodstain on his mouth, and in the end gave it up.

And there was no mourning.

The old man lay, just as he had always lain in the room, on his back, on the floor. The only difference (and you noticed this) was that now he lay in state and would be buried. Also (since you and Misra were allowed to take a look at him before others came), you saw that there were bloodstains on his lips. You were assured that he had died a gentle death and that his soul parted with its user for so many decades – peacefully. As the mourners came from far and near, as the kettles sang a rosary of teas and blessings of the appropriate suras, you asked Misra, why the bloodstain on his mouth? She did not know.

The subject of death enabled you to return to your own beginnings, to the day when Misra found you with a mask of blood for a head – and a stare. You stole in on Armadio's corpse. Is this what Mother looked like when dead? Perhaps not. Death here was clean, you thought. An angel had prepared him for the moment. You had this thought, not in Karin's but in your compound, with your shadow falling across the one cast by the tree planted the same day as you were born.

'It wasn't clean, was it?' you wondered, springing upon Misra a question she wasn't in the least ready for. 'It was blood and pain and struggle all the way to the end for the old man, wasn't it?'

'On the contrary,' she said.

'And my mother's death?'

'Come, come with me,' she said, and you obeyed.

And she walked the ground of her memory over again, with you beside her, repeating all she had told you before, word for word, telling you all she knew about your mother's death.

'My father, what do you know about him?'

'He died for a struggle, he died for a national cause.'

'My father had a job to do, did he?'

'That's correct.'

'And he died doing it?'

'That's correct.'

And when night fell and most of the mourners had gone, the two of you were joined by Karin. 'Here is a gift from the old man,' said she, giving you the portrait of Ernest Bevin.

You accepted it with a great reverence that befits the memory of the old man you loved, and the British political figure for whom the old man held high admiration. 'Do you know who this man is?' said Misra, pointing a finger at the portrait.

You said, 'Ernest Bevin was a dream of a man for well-informed Somalis.'

CHAPTER FIVE

[1]

There was nothing like sharing the robe the woman carrying you was wrapped in, nothing as warm, with the bodies, yours and hers, touching, oozing and sweating together – I naked and she not – and the rubbing together of the bodies producing itchy irritations, scratchy rashes and crotchy eruptions of skin. Then the quiet of the night would crawl in like an insect up one's back – ticklish and laughter-producing. The darkness of dusk would take over one's imagined sense of being: this time, like an insect bite so scratchy that you cannot think of anything else. And so, for years, I contemplated the world from the safe throne carved out of Misra's back, sleeping when I pleased, swinging from her back as a fruit the thorn which is its twin, making water when I had to and getting scolded for it; for years I viewed the world from a height slightly above that of a pigmy's head.

I seem to have remained a mere extension of Misra's body for years – you saw me when you set your eyes on her. I was part of the shadow she cast – in a sense, I was her extended self. I was, you might even say, the space surrounding the geography of her body. And she took me wherever she went. As a result of which, I became the invited guest to every meal she was offered, partaking of every generosity she was given. I was the overhearer and eavesdropper of every conversation she had – the first to know if she was in pain or no; the first to notice if she had her period. Which I could tell from the odour her body emitted, from the way she shuffled about, from the constant washing she undertook and from the fact that I would get spanked for the slightest noise and she would shout at me more often. Yes, I was the time Misra kept – she woke when I awoke, clocking the same number of sleeping hours as I had done, feeling unwell when I was taken ill. Now, if I were circumcised, I thought to myself, and I became a man, yes, if . . . ! What would become of our bodies' relationship? Surely, I wouldn't remain an obvious extension of Misra's physicality? Surely, I could no longer be her third breast or her third leg? Perhaps she would put me down on the dusty ground to fend for myself, play by myself, and the relationship which the years had forged between our bodies would cease to exist. If seen alone by a neighbour, she wouldn't be asked to explain where I was. I wouldn't be the clothes she wore to a wedding party; I wouldn't be the bringer-about of conversations, of friendships, and because I wasn't with her, wouldn't be seen with her, no man would make advances to her using my presence as a safe ploy, saying something like, 'Oh, what a good-looking boy', pinching my cheeks, asking me my name, how old I was and so on and so forth, until he and Misra spoke to each other and exchanged addresses and agreed to meet again – but without me. In other words, I wouldn't remain the subject of conversations, when she was really the object of someone else's real interest.

Her body (or should I speak of her bodies: one of knowledge, another of immortality; one I knew and touched and felt, the other for others such as Aw-Adan and Uncle Qorrax) anticipated my body's needs (because I was a child, I had only one body, with hardly a shadow to speak of, this shadow being the size of a bird's dropping whenever I looked for and found it) only to satisfy them. If I couldn't pluck a fruit off a tree, Misra's hand reached out and got it for me, and when I couldn't soap the small of my back, her palm was there to scrub it. Likewise, when I couldn't move my obstinate bowels, it was her applying massaging or kneading techniques which helped me do so.

Then I remembered the first painful separation: when I was sent to the Koranic School run by Aw-Adan. I was very, very unhappy. For some inexplicable reason, it felt as if, between my feet and the rest of my body, there existed an unfillable space. It was only much, much later that I rationalized that perhaps this was the unused space (previously Misra's) which had surrounded me for years but wasn't there any more. My body had gone numb, my hands disobedient and unable to hold the reed with which I was supposed to trace the *alif*, *ba* and *ta* of God's words in the flesh of His wisdom. And I was beaten by Aw-Adan, the teacher who ran the Koranic School, beaten until I made a pool of pee in which I sat, something which allowed the other children to make fun of me. Wet and miserable, I returned home to a Misra who didn't show as much sympathy as I had looked forward to. Nevertheless, she scrubbed me clean, fed me and insisted that I learn to copy the emaciated Aleph which she wrote on my slate; that I learn to do properly the under-weighed Ba and the Ta as well. But I couldn't make the letters take shape – my Ba appeared sagged, my Aleph short and squat and very much unlike what either Aw-Adan or Misra had written; whereas my Ta was inundated with the messiness of the two dots above it, each big as the tears I shed. However, the sounds I made as I chanted were so beautiful, Misra admitted she sensed their charm pierce through her flesh. Each sound came out marvellously pronounced, shapely, smooth, with all the outer roughnesses removed, all the redundancies discarded. And together we moved forward. I repeated the letters after her, trembling with joy, shaking with delight, as I said what had been, to me, the joyful names of God. Deliberately, I would mispronounce a letter so she would correct me. With Misra, God became fun. To me, He was the letters I couldn't draw, He was Misra's thigh which I hit playfully as I chanted the alphabets of rejoice. In a week, I knew how to write my name, Misra's as well as God's. And when, three months later, I could recite the *Faatixa*, my uncle was invited to hear me perform. As I recited, each word was hot as a brand impressing upon my listeners the intensity of my feelings.

But I hated Aw-Adan, my Koranic teacher. I hated him more when he caned me, because I thought that each stroke struck a blow, rending a hole in the wall of my being. When with him, when at his school that is, I uttered every sound so it was inlaid with the contemptuous flames meant for him. Which was why I shouted loudest, hoping he would burn in the noises – ablaze with hate. In any case, once I got home, Misra studied my body as I did the slate upon which I had scrawled verses of the Koran, she studied it for sores and cuts as I re-read the suras to her.

One day, when taking the *Juzz Camma* examination, Aw-Adan interrupted me, and he beat me too. I didn't see the reason why. I hadn't done anything wrong and so I said what I always thought of him, speaking in the full presence of a crowd of youngsters who hadn't known or heard what I had to say. And he caned me again and again. The haemorrhage of hate had run profusely to my head first, and then to the rest of my body: this meant that by the time I regained consciousness, I came to, shouting: 'I am going to kill Aw-Adan; I am going to kill Aw-Adan; I am going to kill Aw-Adan.' I had a temperature the following day. Misra and I stayed in bed. Together, we recited Koranic verses; together, we re-created our bond of bodies, hers and mine. Then I repeated with the premeditated sanity of a murderer determined to kill an opponent, 'Do you know I am going to kill Aw-Adan?'

After a long pause. 'Tell me. Why are you so vindictive?'

'I vindictive?' I asked.

'To avenge, you're the kind that would drink his enemy's blood.'

I remembered the pain on her face when the metallic rod was

inserted, along with abortifacient herbs and root concoctions, into her vagina; I remembered the agonies he had caused her; I remembered her inability to avenge herself – was I really vindictive? I thought she was unfair to me. I could enumerate for her the terrible things he had done to me and to her.

'To begin with,' I said. 'This calendar ... !'

She was shaking her head, recalling a previous argument we had had the night before.

'What's in a calendar?' she said. 'Yes, my Askar, my man, what's in a calendar?'

[2]

What is in a calendar? What is in a table giving you the days of the week, the months and the year, be it a Year-of-a-Monday, a Year-of-a-Tuesday or one beginning with another day of the week, a year belonging to signs of the zodiac which are based neither on the Gregorian system nor on the Julian but whose calendary makes overt reference to the cyclical and menstrual ordeals of a woman – Misra! She had apparently aborted a child. That was what the metallic rod with the bandaged head appeared to have done – it killed a foetus. And Misra bled a lot. Had she become pregnant because she had miscounted? Here was a calendar that would help her count properly, 'provided', I overheard him say, she put a red circle round the unsafe days with green circles for the good ones.

On the 'green' days, the room smelt of musk and other *cuuds* of such sweetness I recall commenting on how much I hated these perfumes and any who wore them. Whenever I was in a bad mood, she went out herself, out, I think, to meet Aw-Adan or Uncle Qorrax, I couldn't tell. She tiptoed out of the room once I was deep in sleep. Sometimes, she returned before daybreak.

She woke me on one such day, before dawn. The *baaf* was ready, the water lukewarm and I was to shower, she said. From her voice I sensed that a decision had been taken about me when I was asleep. Neither did the fact that she was in the same dress as the night before escape my vigilant eyes. She didn't smell of sweet perfumes and freshly prepared *cuuds*. She smelt, if anything, of dried sweat, and her skin, when I touched it, was ugly, I thought.

'Where are we going?' I asked, when bathed.

She said, 'You just wait.'

And so we did – together. She unburied the live coals she had preserved in the brazier, by pushing to the sides the top layer of the ashes, using the handle of a fan. Then she drove gentle air upon the exposed coals with the strawed end of the same implement. Although I was dying to comment on the suspicions circulating like the fan's agitated air inside my head, I am afraid I didn't dare question if Misra didn't think she had lapsed from virtue – the virtue of being 'my mother'; the virtue of my knowing what was to happen to me. But the idea of discussing questions of moral virtues disgusted me.

We had our breakfast in silence. We had difficulty choosing a pair of shorts which wasn't either too tight for my waist or too short. This gave me the opportunity to make sarcastic remarks about adults who never stopped keeping under lock and key clothes for a growing boy. I said, 'Blessed is the intelligence of adults.'

She didn't open her mouth to say anything. But I was dressed now and it took me quite a while before I was sufficiently aware of anything or anyone outside of me. And she was rummaging among her clothes for something for herself, something decent for her to get out in. 'Where are we going?' I said.

'You'll know in a moment,' she promised.

'But why won't you tell me?' I demanded.

She was dressed to kill, I thought. I wondered if it was Aw-Adan she had spent the night with, or was she with Uncle Qorrax? But did this matter to me? I heard Misra say, 'Let's go.'

Before long, I knew where we were going: to Uncle Qorrax's compound. As always, the compound was feverish with activity. Today, it appeared more so than ever. There were at least a dozen camels, many heads of cattle, twenty or so goats and naturally the nomads that owned these. As was expected, there were some of Uncle Qorrax's children and their chatter, which I thought of as their other selves. Misra and I walked into the compound looking a little frightened by all the noise. She gave me her hand the very moment I offered mine for her to take. Having made contact, we sat in what served as Uncle Qorrax's ante-room – waiting. Half-shouting, perhaps because I was nervous, I said, 'Do you know if Uncle is in?'

As though to answer my question, I saw the body of a woman push through a curtain to Uncle's door. And there she was – a woman I hadn't known he married. I thought of him as a magician, making one of his wives disappear between dusk and dawn, only for another to replace the vanished concubine. I cannot tell how many he married and divorced in the short period I began to take note of these cruel happenings. In fact, many of his children, for purposes of identification, carried not only his name but that of the maternal-*bah* line to which they belonged. 'He's coming,' the woman said to us and walked past us, out of the ante-room in which we had been.

Tall, handsomely dressed, his shoes elegant and shiningly polished and towering above Misra and myself – Uncle Qorrax. I was frightened of him, afraid I might earn his rage, worried that he might knock my ears deaf and my head insane. Especially now that he was staring angrily at me, I thought. Poor me, what have I done? I must say I was relieved to learn he was mortally offended with Misra. He said, 'Where on earth were you returning from early this morning, Misra?'

Unperturbed, she mumbled something, as wives do when their husbands put indiscreet questions to them in public. Perhaps she suggested they postpone their argument until later. Anyway, he didn't pursue the matter. Addressing me, because he wanted to change the subject to something less personal, he asked me how I was. The lump of fear in my throat allowed little beyond a grumble. It was just as well, I thought, for I might have spoken long-windedly and mentioned that Misra had been with Aw-Adan until daybreak. He said, 'Let's go.'

In awe, I looked from one to the other. Misra unclasped my hand from hers and, so to speak, pushed me towards Uncle Qorrax. I didn't know where I was being taken to and was worried I was to go alone with Uncle. He said, 'You and I will go together.'

I said Misra's name and hung it on a peg for both of them to see. 'No. Alone. You and I,' he said, and took my hand.

Like a bewildered African nation posing questions to its inefficient leadership, I kept asking, 'Where are we going? Where are you taking me to?' My thoughts crossed my mind. The most pressing one was addressed to myself: will I be able to cope with this separation from Misra?

I cannot vouch for the accuracy of my memory here. Possibly I've invented one or two things, perhaps I have intentionally deviated from the true course of events. Although I tend to think that I am remembering in precise detail how things happened and what was said. I admit the abrupt removal from Misra's reassuring presence was similar to being weaned – despite the fact that I don't know what 'weaning' means (I was bottle-fed or 'cup-fed'). However, there was something formal, something ritualistic about the encounter which took place between Uncle Qorrax and Aw-Adan, an encounter which occurred on the periphery of the latter's kingdom.

I was tense. I stood away from them, timid-looking, avoiding any eye-contact with Uncle Qorrax's children, one of whom was putting out his tongue (at me) in a gesture of derision. The pupils fell silent directly they saw us. The two assistant teachers held their canes in their tight grips but grinned noddingly at Uncle Qorrax. Aw-Adan came forward. He and Uncle exchanged greetings. They both then looked at me and then at themselves. Then I was no longer afraid, because I knew that I knew something about both of them – things that neither knew about the other. This fresh sense of elation gripped me unawares and my imagination flew away with me, which is why I cannot remember if Uncle Qorrax said the following to Aw-Adan as he formally handed me over as the latter's newest pupil at the Koranic School of which he, Aw-Adan, was head:

'I bring to you, this blessed morning, this here my brother's only son, whose name is Askar. The young man is ready to be introduced, by no less than yourself, to the Word of God as dictated by Him to Archangel Jibriil, and finally as heard by Prophet Mohammed in the trueness of the version; the Archangel was authorized by His Almighty. Young Askar is nearly five years and, although he is younger than most of your other pupils, I bring him to you nevertheless. For there is no man in the compound in which he lives and one must take boys away from the bad influence of women. Will you accept him as a pupil of yours – in this and in any other life?' he said, giving him my wrist in the way a seller at an abattoir offers to a buyer the front leg of a goat that's been paid for.

Aw-Adan said, 'I accept.'

'Like all human beings given life by the Almighty,' continued Uncle Qorrax, 'Askar is part bone and part flesh. The flesh is yours and you may punish it to the extent of it letting or losing a bit of blood. Teach him the Word, punish him if he is disobedient, show him the light which you've seen when he is still young. The bones are, however, ours, by which I mean the family's – and you may not harm them unnecessarily, or hurt them or break them. The flesh on the head and the hair thereon is yours, but the fluid in the brain may become yours only in so far as you've put in it the right amount of illumined knowledge. But you may not split his head with an axe.'

Aw-Adan nodded in silence.

'Do you accept Askar as your pupil as you accepted before him my own sons of my own body and blood?' he said to Aw-Adan.

'I do.'

'The same conditions, the same monthly pay?' he asked.

Aw-Adan said, 'I do.'

My uncle then formalized the deal by shaking Aw-Adan's hand. This done, it seemed to me, at first, that he was ready to depart. No. Instead, he went over to and looked at the slates his children had scribbled on. Satisfied and appearing impressed, Uncle Qorrax left without so much as saying anything to me.

Scarcely had I taken my bearings than I was caned by Aw-Adan. You might want to know what I did to deserve such a sound beating. 'That satanic stare of yours,' he said, when I asked why he was caning me, 'dim it.' Could I? Even if I wanted to?

And you say that I am vindictive?

The letter *alif*, because I was hit by Aw-Adan and I bit my tongue, became *balif*; and *ba* when struck again sounded like *fa*; whereas the letter *ta*, now that my mouth was a pool of blood, was turned by my tongue into *sha*. (I can't explain why, but for a brief period that nobody except me remembers, I had difficulty pronouncing the letter *ta*, which is the third letter of the Arabic and Somali alphabets. I guessed this was rather odd, given the fact that I could accurately pronounce the letter *tha*, as in the English word 'thorough', and also *fa*. Mind you, it wasn't because my upper, front teeth were missing or anything, no. It was as if the sound *t* was altogether absent from the repertoire of sounds I could make. Years later, Karin came to Mogadiscio, Karin who had fallen out with Misra. And Karin gave me a startling bit of gossipy news: that Misra's given non-Somali name had a *t* in it, a *t* with which it ended but which she got rid of so that her name wouldn't raise eyebrows or provoke monstrous suspicions in the heads of the Somalis amongst whom she lived. But she restored the *t* when she fell in love with the Ethiopian security officer. Now how about that, I had thought. A *t* ending Misra's name would make it Misrat, no?) Anyway, when beaten by Aw-Adan, I could only produce an ABC of confusion. Now I had enough evidence that he hated me. I was convinced he hit me whenever he had the opportunity to, caning me ruthlessly, hitting me as one vindictive adult hits another. He was far from being a responsible teacher disciplining an errant pupil. I could see hate in his eyes, I could hear contempt in his shallow breathing as he lifted his arm as high as he could in order to strike me. I could sense that he invested all his power and muscle into the hit. I don't know how long it was before I made the resolution that I had reached the point of human evolution where I could seriously plan to murder. Then something became obvious to me – or rather something was revealed to me – that I could kill, at least in thought. That was how I willed Uncle Qorrax and Aw-Adan out of my way and, for whatever this is worth, declared them dead. And it was the first, but definitely not the last, time that I tasted hate in my saliva – which is to say that I tasted blood in my mouth, which is another manner of saying that I tasted someone else's death inside of me.

There were bloodstains on my back; and lots of sores which have left memories of scars, a dozen or so of them, some as straight-backed as the letter *alif* in Arabic calligraphy, others with a curve as that of the letter *ba*, and yet others with three dots above the letter of *tha*. Misra applied the proper medicaments. Her position was that no child could deal with the intricacies of the sacred Word until his body was subjected to, and made to undergo, physical punishments beyond his own imagination. No sooner had I begun cursing Aw-Adan than she put her hand on my mouth, beseeching that I unsay all the wicked things I had spoken. 'Please unsay these things,' she pleaded. Of course, I did not.

How the sores ached! And I had a temperature too. My hot blood had poured into my head. I became dizzy and was certain I would fall were I to get up and walk. My eyes fell on the calendar on the wall. I counted in my head, counted over three-hundred-and-sixty-five reasons why I hated and wanted to murder Aw-Adan. I worked out in my thoughts some three-hundred-and-sixty-five ways of killing Uncle Qorrax; I named the three-hundred-and-sixty-five days in a future in which I would make this possible. I, who had murdered my mother, I said to myself. Why should it not be possible to murder a hated Aw-Adan? And why should killing Uncle Qorrax pose any difficulties?

'Now, Askar. Why can't you collaborate?' she said, in my opinion putting the blame squarely on me. 'Why don't you simply acknowledge the fact that I taught you to read and write? Why don't you admit that you know the alphabet backwards and forwards?'

I cried, 'Ouch,' when she touched a sore. 'It hurts,' I said.

She dabbed another sore and I shouted louder. She said: 'This is no lay education. This is sacred education. And children are beaten if they don't pay their full attention to the Sacred Word. No sympathies. Learn to read the Koran, learn to copy the verses well – and you may go far. One day, who knows, you may be in a position to pray for my displaced soul.'

My saliva was tasteless and I was tongue-tied, and it was a relief because I didn't want to say something I couldn't unsay. But the pain, what pain! I thought, God, why did you have to create such pain? To test the man in me?

When the sores began to heal, I was escorted back to the Koranic School. I might not have gone back if Uncle Qorrax hadn't taken me there himself. 'Discipline,' he said to Aw-Adan, 'is the mother of learning. Here,' he handed me over to him again, 'teach him to read and write.'

And someone says: why are you so vindictive?

In a 1956 speech to the Somalis of the Ogaden, Emperor Haile Selassie said: 'Go to schools, my people. For there, you will have a good chance to learn to read and write Amharic. Only then will you be able to take over the various positions in the central government administration. And remember this: lack of knowledge of Amharic, which is the national language of Ethiopia, will prove a great barrier to economic improvement and individual and communal betterment. Learn to read and write Amharic. It'll do you a lot of good.'

Nomadic camps were rounded up and their children taken away to schools in Upper Ethiopia – boys and girls who were barely six years old. They were sent to different schools in the non-Somali-speaking regions of the country, so they would lose contact with other Somalis and with one another. Amharic – the language of a minority imposed upon a majority. Arabic – an alien language with its alien concepts and thoughts imposed forcefully upon the mind of a child. One is not beaten as harshly when one is learning in one's mother-tongue, surely? Does learning come naturally? Do things flow smoothly, then? The brutal force of the written tradition imposed upon the thinking of one belonging to a non-written tradition? The brutal force of adults imposed upon a child? I am not sure why I kept the cutting giving the full text of the famous 1956 speech which Emperor Haile Selassie delivered to the people of the Ogaden. On its margin, I can read Uncle Hilaal's scrawling hand: 'It is revolutionary, isn't it, that we vindicate our people's language, culture and justice?'

To vindicate. To be vindictive?

Following the confrontations between Aw-Adan and myself, one day, Misra said: 'It worries me to think what you will do when you grow up. You're not yet six years old but the hate in your eyes frightens me. As though you really mean it when you say you will kill Aw-Adan, or kill Uncle Qorrax or, for that matter, me.'

'True,' I admitted. 'I am vindictive.'

'But why?' she said.

I wouldn't tell her. She looked miserably worried and frightened. I began to recite a Koranic verse which she repeated after me. My hand rested under her ribs and I could feel her heartbeat, I could sense the tremor of her caged emotions.

'I'm sorry I cannot help myself being who I really am.'

'Of course, you can,' she said. 'You're very young, almost a baby.'

We made peace.

I behaved as though I were convinced that being caned by Aw-Adan was part of the ritual of growing up, that in a way, it was for my own good – didn't learning the Koran form a part of the ritual of growing up spiritually? It was also a trade. After all, I could teach it if I landed with no other profession. Also, she reminded me of something Uncle Qorrax had said: that the flesh was the teacher's and he could treat it as he wished. And if, for purposes of teaching this young boy the Word of God, you were to discolour his body with bruises or injure it slightly, so be it. Uncle had said it was to train my spirit so it would dispel Satan.

Yes, Misra and I made peace. We forged a union of our bodies. After all, she was a woman and she could be beaten or taken at will. I was a child and the same tyrannical persons could beat me or maltreat me.

'You promise that you will not see either of them?' I said.

She promised. Then she said: 'You promise that you'll learn the Koran and will behave well.'

I promised.

There was a very long pause. Then she said: 'What we must do one of these days, so you can be a man, is to have you circumcised, have you purified.' And she looked at me.

My head moved, as though of its own accord, away from the body to which it didn't feel at all connected. I shunned contact with her, I wouldn't permit her to touch me. I scrambled over to the other side of the bed and sat on the edge, my feet danglingly touching the floor. It was such a plague to think that I would finally be separated from Misra and the thought gripped my heart and played tricks with its beating rhythm. I would live in a territory of pain for a fortnight or a month following the circumcision and then in a land of loneliness –

forever separated from Misra. Maybe I would be given a bed of my own and I would have to sleep by myself after that.

[3]

I would sleep with the *loox*-slate between my legs. This not only enabled me to keep her from coming anywhere near me but it also gave me the warmth, the security and continuity I most deservedly needed: that of reading the slate night and day; and that of seeking nobody's company save that of the Holy Word. I slept with the Sacred Word sweet on my tongue and awoke chewing it in place of Misra's profane name. In secret, I would drink the writings which I had washed off the slate, believing it would help retain the Word's wisdom, a day, a week or a month longer. During the long silences between myself and Misra, my thumb would busily trace and retrace, with the help of the index finger, a Koranic verse or a tradition of the Prophet's; at times, I would copy, using my body instead of the slate, a short verse which I had committed to memory; I would copy the verse again and again and again until my veins flowed, like ink, with the blood of the Word. The Word became my companion, the slate the needed extension of my body and I chanted selected verses of the Koran whenever Aw-Adan called on Misra, as he was accustomed to doing after dusk, verses which promised heaven for the pious and a hellish reward for the adulterous and the wicked.

'Do you know that Askar will be circumcised the day after tomorrow?' she said to him one evening, speaking loud enough for me to hear it. 'He'll become a man from then on, you'll see,' she predicted.

A stray dog howled in the distance and, right there and then, I choked on the Word and my speech flew in fright, like a bird at the approaching of boots crushing under their heels a mound of gravel. Above all, my ears were filled with a din associated with that of fear. I held the slate tightly in my grip until the blood that had rushed to my heart began to circulate normally again. When I resurfaced, I was back where I had begun – I was motherless, I was fatherless, I was an orphan and had to give birth to myself. Yes, I was to re-create myself in a worldly image, I thought to myself, now that the Word had deserted me, now that I couldn't depend on its keeping me company. The Word, I said to myself, was not a womb; the Word, I convinced myself, wouldn't receive me as might a mother, a woman, a Misra. And so I waited for Aw-Adan to leave and, just as Misra returned, she saw me standing in the doorway, suggesting that we embraced – opening my arms like a bird opens its wings when about to fly off. We embraced warmly, we embraced tightly, then she laughed, laughed in such a way that I could sense mockery in it. Offended, I let go. Once apart, I saw why. Apparently, the slate had become an impediment disallowing her to hug me comfortably, since its sharpened edge embarrassingly pressed itself against her pelvis.

'You naughty little boy,' she said, teasing me.

I said, 'I'm sorry.'

Again teasing me, she said, 'I'm not sure if you are sorry.' And while laughing, she bent double, half-leaning against me, while supporting her great weight on her knees which were on the floor. A spatter of her saliva had begun to descend on the slate which was lying flat on the floor, nearer me. And I noticed the letters of a verse I had written on my bare thigh run into one another, with the letter 'o' closing its eyes in misted tears as of remorse. The other letters were reduced to tawdry shapes and a straggle of formless figurines.

'You naughty thing,' I said, teasing her.

She stopped laughing to say, 'I am sorry,' only to continue laughing away.

'I am not sure if you are sorry,' I said, teasing her as before.

In silence, we listened to the crickets call to one another. A little later, Misra was moving about, preparing a bath for me. I knew what she would do – she would dip her finger in the water to feel how warm it was, for she knew, more than anyone else, what my body could or couldn't take. Now she mixed hot and cold water and took a long time deciding whether the temperature was right. I asked myself if it was possible that she might have forgotten what she had known about my body in the few days she and I were separated by the slate or what had been written on it. Before I could answer the question myself, Misra was dragging me to the open courtyard: and under the starry night, we stood in the *baaf*. She was fully dressed and I, naked. And with a tin which had originally contained tomato-purée, or some such manufactured item, she scooped the lukewarm water and washed me. I felt her calloused palms on my young, smooth skin, and felt ticklish and laughed and laughed and laughed and was very, very happy as only children can be. She was playfully rough and rubbed the soap in my hair but said 'I am sorry' when she realized that soaped water had entered my eyes. Then she kissed my soaped forehead and looked into my eyes, which I opened as she splashed water on my face. The moon was up and bright, the stars too, but I couldn't see the colour of the water which I imagined to be as blue as a bruise. I jumped up and down in glee, oblivious of the fact that the Koranic writings had ended up in the same *baaf* as the dirt between my toes. I decided I wouldn't hold the slate between my legs that night, and the following night too. Misra and I slept in each other's embrace and the slate was left in a corner until after I was made a man.

[4]

The man who was brought to circumcise me, when my turn came, made me sit alone, insisting that I read a few Koranic verses of my choice – and that I wait for him as he honed the knife he was going to use against a sharp stone he had come along with. I was overcome by fear – fear of pain, fear of being lonely, fear of being separated forever from Misra. (She wasn't there anyway; she wasn't allowed to come. In her place, there came a man, one of my many uncles.) The sticky saliva in my mouth, the drumming of fright beating in my ears, the numbness of my body wherever I touched, felt: my legs, my hands, my thighs, my penis, what pain!

Then the man asked me to look up at the heavens and to concentrate on anything my eyes fell on. There was an aperture in the clouds and there was a bird which I spotted, a bird flying high and in haste towards the opening in the heavens. I concentrated on the bird's movements, concentrated on it until it became a dot in the heavenly distance. To mask my fear, I invested all my energy in the look and the bird's flight reminded me of similar flights of my own fantasies. When I looked again, I couldn't see the bird. I could only see a tapestry of clouds which was woven in order to provide the bird with a hiding-place. The world, I told myself, was in my eyes and the bird had flown away with it, carrying it in its beak, light as a straw, small as an atom. Now that I had lost sight of the bird (I wasn't sure if it was an eagle or if it wasn't!), there was nothing but sunlight for a long while, and the sun was in my eye and it blinded me to the rest of the cosmos. Until the bird re-emerged out of the sun's brightness, beautiful, feminine, playful, and it became again the centre of my world and I was inside of it, in flight, light as are children's fantasies, impervious to the realities surrounding me – and then, sudden as bushfire, ZAK!

It is such a horrid territory, the territory of pain. And I crossed it alone – no thought of Misra, no amount of consolatory remarks made by the uncle who had come with me and no verse of the Koran could've reduced the pain or even eliminated it altogether. Do I remember when the pain lodged in my body which it lived in for almost a month thereafter? It entered my groin first. Or rather, that is what I seem to remember. I recall thinking that I had seen the bird's apparition and that the rest of the world had been small as a speck in the sky – then the man pulled at the foreskin of my manhood, producing, first in my groin, then in the remaining parts of my body, a pain so acute my ears were set ablaze with dolorous flames. These flames spread gradually – then my feet felt frozen, my eyes warm with tears, my cheeks moist with crying and my throat dry as the desert. It was only then that I looked and I saw blood – a pool of blood in whose waters I swam and which helped me cross to the other side so I would be a man – once and for all.

I saw the man break an egg. I couldn't tell why he did so. Perhaps the idea was to reduce the pain or help stop my losing any more blood. I thought that the white and yellow of the egg mixed well with my own blood and the colours which I saw, the beauty of what I saw, took the pain away, for at least a few decisive seconds. My bare thighs were spotted with cold sprouts of pained hair and I rubbed them, smoothing the hair-erections so the blood would return. I was helped to stand, I don't remember by whom, and was led away from the spot I had been sitting on. Possibly, the eggshell was the hat my manhood wore, possibly not; possibly, once the skin was pushed back, I was bandaged with cotton or other similar material, although I cannot remember anything save the pain, which made me faint. I awoke – alone, on a bed.

Pain, *per se*, I discovered, was no problem. I could cope with it, I could dwell in its territory. But there was the problem of space. For pain not only defined my state of mind but my movements as well. I couldn't come into bodily contact with anybody, not even Misra. I became the bed's sole occupant. People kept their distance. I was like a man with an arm in plaster. And people were careful not to come unnecessarily near me, surrendering up the space surrounding them to me – how generous of them, I thought, how kind! Misra slept on a mat on the floor. Because I was sore, I was given the bed to myself. Traditionally, it is taboo for women to stay near newly circumcised boys, and so Misra was sent away. But I created such an uproar Uncle Qorrax allowed me to have my own way, yet again. I didn't care much for traditional taboos, especially when they severed me from somebody who wasn't herself Somali and whose psyche they wouldn't affect. When she was allowed to return to me, I didn't think 'How kind of Uncle to allow her to come and stay by me in this hour of need'. No, I thought of how clever I had been in making her return possible. I had my own sheet to cover myself with, one that I had had to hold at a certain distance from the wound – again, a question of space, a question of the geographic dictates of pain. And once Misra was offered a bed of her own which was brought into our room, I began to claim *our* bed as mine – and I was delighted. One other item had had to go too – the slate which I had kept between my legs. I discovered I needed space for myself, that I couldn't tolerate anyone or anything standing in the space between myself and *where* I had intended to move. In short, the dimensions of my body occupied the centre of my world of pain, my preoccupations, and I took in the body's measurements, as it were, and followed the guidelines suggested by its dolorous perimeters. I moved or lay on the bed accordingly.

When asked how I was, I lied. I said I was well and that the pain had more or less confined itself to the *de facto* boundaries of the wound. The truth I didn't tell anyone was that I had, in effect, become two persons – one belonging to a vague past of which Misra was part, of which painlessness was a part, a vague past in which I shared wrappers with Misra, shared a bed with her. Yes, a vague past in which I felt so attached to Misra I couldn't imagine life without her. The other person, or if you prefer, the other half, was represented by the pain which inhabited the groin. I held the citizenship of the land of pain, I was issued with its passport and I couldn't envisage when it would expire or what would replace it or where the urge of travel away from it would eventually take me to, nor at what shores this would abandon me. In the territory of pain, there is a certain uncertainty, I thought, of a future outside of it.

On the fourth day, Uncle called on me. Misra placed herself between him and the bed which I lay on. And she explained what I had done, she talked about me in a way I thought recalled to me a history of her concern and worries; one in which she was the guide. She told Uncle how many times I got up to make water, how many spoonfuls of soup I had eaten, what I did and what I didn't do. She spoke about my condition as if I were a monument with a background worthy of delving into. Uncle, because he wanted to see the wound for himself, told Misra to leave us alone. It was only then that the thought that she hadn't seen it crossed my mind and I remembered her saying that society believed it to be bad for a woman to see a boy's wound of circumcision lest it fester and never heal. Anyway, she left us alone. Uncle, gentle and playful, took a peek at it and was visibly satisfied all was well. He called Misra to return, which she did. He asked her what gifts I might like.

She looked at me considerately, silently. Uncle looked from her to me and then back at her. Was she saying that I was now a man and I could decide for myself? Maybe. Uncle asked: 'Is there anything you'd like brought to you as you lie in bed?'

I had already worked it all out in my head. I said, 'A pen.'

'A pen?' he asked in disbelief.

I said, 'A pen and a sheet of paper.'

Again, he looked at Misra, whose head nodded approvingly, and then at me. He was obviously pleased with the choice I made, especially when I added, 'I would like to practise copying and recopying the verses of the Koran which I've already committed to memory. Otherwise, I might forget them.'

He was thoughtful for a second or so. Then, 'Anything else?'

I was silent for a long time. To Misra, 'Can you think of anything?'

I watched them exchange smiles. I knew they used to meet occasionally in the dark. I wondered if I was in their way; I wondered, did they need the bed on which I lay?

And again back to me: 'Askar?'

If I could I would've said that I wanted Misra taken away from me, sent away somewhere else, away from me anyway for a week, a month or two. If she were away, I said to myself, perhaps the act of weaning would occur less painfully and I would be able to bear the loss well. I would, in time, be able to replace the loss with a gain, I thought, looking up at Uncle who was still awaiting a request from me.

'I can't think of anything else,' I said.

But Misra spoke and we both turned to her. (In the meantime, I realized that, while thinking thoughts and listening with attention to Uncle and Misra, I had taken temporary residence in a land-of-no-pain.) She said, 'I can think of something he's always wanted.'

'Yes?'

'A globe,' she said. 'Or an atlas. He loves the blue of the sea. And a picture-book of horses and birds. Please get him a globe and a map of the seas and the oceans,' she appealed.

I was as surprised as my uncle. I didn't know I loved the blue of the sea – not then anyway – nor the world of the oceans, or picture-book horses and birds. But I was grateful to Misra – grateful that she chose to introduce me to a world in which I have felt happiest since then.

[5]

During my brief sojourn in the land of pain, two things occurred: one, I lost myself in it (I wondered, was this why Misra suggested I was given a map of the globe and of the oceans?); two, I took hold of a different 'self', one that had no room and no space for Misra and no longer cared for her. I let go of Misra and, with self-abandon, roamed about in the newly discovered land, thinking not of her, but of pain. It rained a lot and the rain levelled the terrain which wiped out the readable maps, the recognizable landmarks and milestones. And there I met the children of sooterkin and I shook hands with them. I was introduced to my future, my destiny – indeed, somebody pointed it out to me, and there was no Misra. Or was I in the land of dreams?

The waters of the rain washed the slate on which I had written my prayers and the thunder drowned my chanting of the verses which praised the traditions of Islam. The world, crowded like Noah's ark, lay under my feet. Lying on my back, contemplating the ceiling, I roamed in a state of stupor; I roamed in the darkness of a rainy night, my body soaked in pain; I roamed – spreading myself as though I were water; I roamed inside of my body, which was ablaze with the flames of an untold future. Then I heard a voice, I heard, loud and clear, a voice, peculiarly like my own. I heard, not the blabber of a child whose tongue stumbled on Misra's name, but that of a man, saying what, in essence, could be translated as 'I am I!' And I was calmed by what Uncle Hilaal was later to call my 'existential certainty'.

And I was asleep and alone.

And I was *suddenly* a bird in ascent, a bird, holding, in the clutch of its beak, the foreskin of a boy's circumcision; a bird, inside of which was folded up, like a map, the entire experience of the cosmos; a bird that had walked out of my human body and been metamorphosed into a dream-animal, free to fly as it pleased. I surveyed the world of which Misra had been an integral part from a reasonable height, after a dreamy flight that nearly took the breath out of me. And I noticed that her hand had been severed from the rest of her body and her

92

head, not in the least plaintive, shouted, 'Askar, what's the meaning of all this?'

It rained non-stop for hours and the darkness of the night was thick-bodied. I made sure I held a tighter grip on myself. Then I saw a figure in the distance, a figure standing tall as an obelisk. I walked in the direction of the figure, above whose head, clear as a halo, there now was a lantern. The nearer I moved to the figure, the further we got from each other. Wet, exhausted, my body ached and I walked and walked and walked, and it rained and rained and rained. I walked, holding my sarong at the edges, my body alert, my every step careful. Finally, I reached where the figure and the lantern had been: there was no figure, no statue, no lantern – only the remnants of a corpse, blown up in an explosion of some kind. I went here and there, collecting the unnamable parts of the blown-up person's body, until I got to where the head had dropped – and I screamed with fright.

I don't know what curses I shouted or uttered. All I can tell you is that I woke up, my body wet with sweat, my throat aching from crying and saying again and again and again, 'Who am I? Who am I? Where am I? Where am I? Who am I?'

Misra was not there. I was alone.

And no one told me where I was, no one told me who I was.

[6]

By the time I started to limp my way to places (although there was a slight pain between my legs) I noticed there was a halo of silence above many a person's head – an ominous silence, a silence punctuated by prayers and sacrificial offerings. I had never seen as many beasts sacrificed as I saw in the following few days, beasts whose meat was offered, with blessings, to the sheikhs who were invited to pray for the safe conduct of those whom Kallafo, our town, sent to the war front.

I asked Misra, 'A war? And whom are we fighting?'

In those days, everything and everybody was throbbing with inexplicable activity in so far as I was concerned and a number of people were said to be getting ready to marry. Once married, the men went off, leaving behind them the dust of victory, the women whom they had just wed, their old parents and the very young. Not until weeks later did we see the full-blooded men in our midst and no strong men returned for long periods unless they were wounded and in need of medical attention. That was how I learnt where Aw-Adan had gone – to the war front. People sat next to the radio and names like Jigjiga, Harar, Iimey and Dire Dawa occurred frequently in their exchanges – which was when the atlases Uncle had given me became very useful to own. Most of the women were illiterate and had never seen or owned a map. And our room was turned into something like a war-room. We spread the maps on the tables and calculated how long it would take the Somali army to capture a given town and how far this was from us or from Mogadiscio or, for that matter, Addis Abeba.

It was only gradually, however, that it dawned on me that Misra's heart wasn't in it as much as mine or the other people's were. She was excited, of course, whenever any town or village fell to the Somalis, but she was exaggeratedly cautious, saying something like 'How long will this victory last?', or 'Where will it take us to?', or 'What will the Russians do?' Somebody called her a 'spoil-sport' once or twice and I heard many more wicked things said behind her back. Then, a few days later, I felt that the mood which prevailed was one of hostility towards her. I could sense that more and more people were coming less and less to our war-room. I remembered that she was different from us – that she wasn't a Somali like me and the others; I remembered how often people teased her about her pronunciation of Somali gutturals; I remembered about the warrior of whom she had spoken and of the saddled horse which had dropped its rider. And I, too, saw her in a different light. She wore a grim appearance and was ugly. I recalled a dream I had seen previously, a dream in which the finger of collective guilt was pointed at the Somaliness in me and the others. I asked: hasn't Misra chosen to be one of us? Hasn't she chosen to share with us our pain and pleasure? Now she was undecided whether to leave us or share our bitter destiny with us. She spoke of this too, although I do not think I understood it at the time. '*I* am an Ethiopian,' she said. But how was I to know what species an 'Ethiopian' is? I asked the appropriate questions and got the appropriate answers. The image which has remained with me, is that of a country made up of patchworks – like a poor man's mantle. She wasn't decided whether to go back to the Highlands or stay, she repeated. Although she no longer spoke or understood the language of the area of Ethiopia in which she was born.

I said, 'I'll come with you.'

She greatly belied her pleasure by saying, after a long, long silence, during which she wiped away the tears which had stained her cheeks, 'I will not want you to come with me.'

'Why not?' I asked.

She turned towards me, her eyes aflame with hot tears. 'Because it's not safe for you. They will kill you, my people will, without asking questions, without wanting to know your name or what our relationship is.'

I asked, 'Your people, my people – what or who are these?'

'One day,' she said, speaking of a future in which we would meet, 'one day, you will understand the distinction, you'll know who your people are and who mine are. One day,' she prophesied, speaking into that void of a future in which she hoped we would meet again, 'you will identify yourself with your people and identify me out of your community. Who knows, you might even kill me to make your people's dream become a tangible reality.'

'Kill?' I asked.

'Yes. Kill. Murder. Loot. Rape. In the name of your people. Kill.'

I said, 'One day, I might kill you?'

'Maybe,' she said, and walked out of the room.

CHAPTER SIX

[1]

In a month or so, especially now that his manhood was ringed with a healed circle, the orgies of self-questioning, which were his wont, gave way to a state in which he identified himself with the community at large. And he partook of the ecstasy of madness that struck the town of Kallafo, an ecstasy that expressed itself in a total self-abandon never known, never experienced in the history of the Somalis of the area. The war was on. At first, the war was mentioned in whispers and was spoken about as one talks of a certain calamity. But what mattered to Askar was that it presaged, for him, a future maturer than he had awaited, that it predicted a future in which he would be provided with ample opportunities to prove that he was a man. In his mind, he didn't exclude that some day he might even be recruited as a member of the Western Somali Liberation Front, the front fighting for the liberation of the Ogaden from Ethiopian domination. Who knows, he thought, he could become, at such a tender age, the movement's flag-bearer; who knows, the Ethiopians might forcefully conscript him if the Somalis lost the war; who knows!

What mattered, he told himself, was that now he was at last a man, that he was totally detached from his mother-figure Misra, and weaned. In the process of looking for a substitute, he had found another – Somalia, his mother country. It was as though something which began with the pain of a rite had ended in the joy of a greater self-discovery, one in which he held on to the milky breast of a common mother that belonged to him as much as anyone else. A generous mother, a many-breasted mother, a many-nippled mother, a mother who gave plenty of herself and demanded loyalty of one, loyalty to an ideal, allegiance to an idea, the notion of a nationhood – no more, and no less. And his tormented spirit was calmed the instant he walked down the same steps as everyone else, to encounter this common mother, to be embraced by her in joyful reunion, to be breast-fed and helped to rediscover in himself the need for a mother of a general kind.

In those days, Misra sat alone, immured and inert, right in the quiet anxiety of one who had just been transferred to a country alien

96

to herself, a territory of whose earth one didn't eat mouthfuls when one was an infant, when one was but a mouth perpetually open, a mouth famished to the point that it would cry unless it was stuffed with anything – a handful of dirt, a piece of metal one's groping hand got hold of, anything and everything. Anyway, she sat, waiting (Askar didn't know for what or whom!); she sat mantled in her mourning garments; she sat friendless, now that Aw-Adan had gone, now that the men who used to lavish their lusty interest on her were away at the war front, fighting the Somali people's common enemy (she was not herself Somali and Askar by then knew what that meant); men who came home, who touched base every now and then, maybe for a day or two, and who, in haste, contracted matrimonies so they would leave behind themselves widows whose memories they hoped to inhabit, and children onto the end of whose given names theirs would be attached. In such an agitated air, the schools had to be closed and many families changed houses and a great many left for Mogadiscio, the capital of Somalia. And yes, there was much talk about 'Somalia', a country that was referred to as 'Mother' in a tone suggesting a getting together of her and the Ogaden/child separated from her. To mark the progress each had made, Askar noted the mother and the child's efforts on the map Uncle had presented him with, just as he traced, on another mental chart, the uncoverable distance between Misra and himself. She began to lose weight; he, to grow it. She sat in a corner, sulking; he, as prominent as the map he read to the illiterates surrounding him, spoke knowledgeably, enthusiastically about the liberation war which his people were waging against Misra's people.

He was adrift (and so was the Somali nation everywhere) on a tide of total abandon. At least, he kept thinking to himself, staring at the map on the wall, there would be changes in the cartographer's view of the Horn of Africa. And so, with his felt pen, using his own body, he re-drew the map of the Somali-speaking territories, copied it curve by curve, depression by depression. Which reminded him of his father's nickname: Xamari. At last, he would be reunited with the city of Xamar from whence came his father's nickname.

'Why are some countries referred to as "Motherland" and others as "Fatherland"?' Askar asked Misra one day when both were in a mood to talk. 'What is the logic behind it?'

She didn't know, she said.

'I wonder if it indicates a people's mind, I mean if their choice indicates what kind of people they are. People of the heart, people of the head, if you know what I mean.'

She was silent for a long time.

'You know, of course, that Somalia is seen by her poets as a woman – one who has made it her habit to betray her man, the Somali, don't you?' she said.

He nodded, 'Yes.'

'You know the poem in which the poet sees Somalia as a beautiful woman dressed in silk, perfumed with the most exotic scents, and this woman accepts all the advances made by the other men – to be precise, the five men who propose to her. She goes, sleeps with them, bears each a child named after its progenitor and has a number of miscarriages,' she said, stopped – and wouldn't look at him, as though she were apologetic.

He asked, 'How do Ethiopian poets see the country?'

'I don't know,' she said and was very sad.

What could he say that would make her interested in the flow of their conversation? First, he pulled a sheet over his bared thighs on which he had redrawn the map of the land so far reconquered by the Somalis, then he gave himself time to study her expressions, her movements – deciding that she was, in all probability, having her period. It was something he envied her: the fact that she had periods whose monthly occurrences, he thought, had cleansing aspects about them. 'You get rid of the bad blood,' she told him once, jokingly, 'and you do the same a month later and so on and so forth until you reach old age. Men don't have it,' Karin had explained. 'Why not?' he had inquired. He couldn't now remember for the life of him what explanation Misra had given, but could remember thinking about her periods whenever he stood by the tree in their compound and saw its life flow into waste and he tasted the sap and was coincidentally sick the following day, believing that the tree, born the same day as he, although taller and shadier than he, was poisonous. Was life a poisonous potion which, if taken in the right doses, offers sustenance, but if not kills?

She was saying, 'Do you know that Somalis are fond of talking about their country, in their poetry at any rate, as though she were a camel – the basis of this being that a camel is, after all, "the Mother of Men", do you?'

'Camel, the Mother of Men?' he repeated.

Silence. Then, suddenly, there was an explosion, and after a small pause, another, then a third and after that a fourth. Had the war come to Kallafo? Almost. For there was an ochlocratic roar every now and again. Curious, Askar came out, wanting to know what might have caused it. Whereupon he saw a group of young boys running in the direction of the 'Hill of Government', and at the head of the group was a boy a year or two older than Askar and this boy was the group's flag-bearer. The five-starred flag of Somalia fluttered in the vainglory of victory.

And Askar became the child he was – he abandoned thinking philosophically, he gave up the thought whether or no Misra too needed a mother in the same way he did and ran and joined the boys and girls of his age. For them, it was fun to be on the winning side, it was fun to disarm the disheartened, already defeated Ethiopian soldiery – for them, war was fun. It was fun to be strong, fun to be the toughest, fun to lead.

Askar proved to be the toughest when it came to receiving Aw-Adan's humiliating lashes. He didn't flinch if caned. He found his first fans among the other pupils. He was also the most brilliant, needing no time at all in order to commit any verse to memory: he heard a verse once and he gave it back in the form he was given it. Aw-Adan nicknamed him 'little devil', his peers 'little hero'.

He was naughty, pulling loose the girls' plaits or skirts, calling them names or challenging older boys to wrestling duels. He was very active, he was a busybody, arranging football matches to happen, organizing running and other physical challenges to take place. Boys liked to gather round him. Before he was six, Askar became the undisputed leader. Besides, he had one advantage over all the other boys. Misra appeared to be more tolerant than most other parents. She didn't mind how many of them he brought home with him to share his lunch, didn't mind his going away as long as he showed up for his meals, didn't mind if he omitted his siesta in the afternoon. At times, however, he would invite her to go and watch him – she being the only adult member in the audience.

Misra discovered, to her pleasure, that the children's inventiveness never ceased to surprise her. And she watched them, with admiration, as they built an effigy resembling one day this historical figure, the following day another, whose portrait they had seen – and they took shots at Aw-Adan's effigy one morning and in the evening, they burnt Haile Selassie's. They sculptured the Emperor's image out of tins, bits of wood and metal scraps, but you could see the likeness of the constructed effigy to the small-bodied man who ruled the Ethiopian Empire for nearly five decades. But did they know that Haile Selassie had died? Of course, Askar did. And so why were they burning the image of a man who had fallen out of popular favour? 'Do you think,' Askar said, 'that contemporary Ethiopia can be seen in an image other than the one created by Haile Selassie or Menelik?'

She agreed with him. She became a member of his fan club. Why, he was capable of drawing a dividing line between personalities that were in the public memory and those that were not. Why, Askar never contributed a scrap towards the construction of an effigy in the likeness of Uncle Qorrax. It was not that Qorrax's children would have minded. They would've been the first to rally round their leader, their cousin. His awareness of the thin line separating the personal from the political was such that he brought the play to an abrupt halt the moment he suspected it had crossed into the forbidden territory.

Askar and his friends had, themselves, a large repertoire of pieces which they often enacted. His was the largest stock. His body, it appeared, was an instrument where different parts produced different sounds and different bird noises. He made the weird twang of a boy born with a cleft palate, for instance. Then, immediately thereafter, turned outwards his upper eyelid as though he were showing it to an eye doctor. But he didn't stop there. Now, he acted as if struck with paralysis and foamed at the mouth; now, he was a child born with a weak mind. And before the enthralled crowd recovered its breath, Askar would move away slightly, then turn round and look at everybody with crossed eyes. Then he became a hunchback or a child with rickety legs.

One day, he and his group of playmates sneaked into the orchard belonging to the Adenese and they let the camel loose. Before they untied the beast, Askar took off the blindfold. You can imagine – a beast that for decades, day in and day out, turned round and round, now hauling a cart, now helping in the mill, now pulling bucketfuls of water from a well – a beast that had remained blindfolded day and night for years, never seeing natural or artificial light – and not only did they let it loose, but they removed its blindfold. The beast cried a most hideous cry: and died. When questioned, each denied he was not present when this occurred. But they all mentioned Askar's name. Not that he had done it, no. It was possible, they insinuated, that he might know who had been responsible.

They could not go unpunished. Uncle Qorrax suggested that he should be made very busy. And a school in which to discipline these unruly boys was started with Aw-Adan appointed as its headmaster. Arithmetic. Geography. History. Arabic. The school's name was Kallafo Public School, since it was funded and founded by the community, and since the Ethiopian government didn't provide any schooling facilities for the Somalis in the Ogaden. So, for the first week or so, Askar returned home exhausted. Naturally, the morning's Koranic School plus the afternoon's arithmetic, etc., took their toll and by the time he staggered home, he wasn't willing to spend his energy on inventing a new set of rules for games to be thoroughly enjoyed by an improvised audience.

A fortnight later, he thought of new games, which attracted larger audiences. Misra heard that the young man in her charge had been up to no good. And there was no way she could've held him in the house. What was the point of beating him? At times, he removed his shirt from his back, brought a cane himself and asked her to 'go on, punish me, go on'.

She only pleaded, 'Please, do not attract *eyes* to yourself. People can be bad, envious, wicked. People's *eyes* can make you fall ill. They are terrible when they are bad, people's *eyes*.'

He paid her pleas no heed.

He was taken ill.

He looked bloodless – too weak. 'How do you feel?' she asked.

He shook his head. He had no temperature, thank God. Neither did he vomit. He ate as normally as he used to. And yet he was 'sick'. The 'sickness' showed in his look, which appeared startled. What could be the matter? His head between his hands, he said, 'I don't know.' It was a weird kind of illness. 'Bad eyes are wicked!' Karin had commented.

'Is there any part of you that is in pain? Your head, your stomach, your heart? Tell me.' Misra touched him all over. 'Which part of your body does pain reside in?'

'*I cannot think,*' he said. 'It's that kind of sickness!'

'What do you mean, you cannot *think*?'

He said, 'It's odd, but it feels as if my brain has ceased thinking, as if I will never have new thoughts. It's a strange sensation but that's what I feel. No fresh ideas. And my eyes – look at them. Pale as white meat.'

Misra thought, it is the bad eye. All that night, she prayed and prayed and prayed. Oh Lord, protect my little man from the rash of measles; from diarrheal diseases and complications; from conjunctival sightlessness; from tubercular and whooping coughs. Protect him, oh Lord, from droplet-bone infections and from migratory parasites – and such diseases for which we have no names. Oh Lord, restore to him his thinking faculties. Amen!

*

A day later, she consulted Qorrax and Aw-Adan. Interestingly enough, each suggested two remedies. Aw-Adan offered to read selected verses of the Koran over Askar's body 'astraddle the bed in satanic pain'; alternatively, he said, someone ought to belt the jinn out of the little devil. Uncle Qorrax suggested he sent his wife, 'Shahrawello', over – she was an expert at blood-letting. Otherwise, he went on, he would pay for the *cuudis*: 'Blood-letting works when the blood of the patient is bad; fumigating if there is suspicion that somebody's covetous, evil eye needs to be appeased,' said Uncle Qorrax.

Askar retorted, 'Blood-letting? For whom? For me? No, thank you.'

Half-serious, Misra said: 'Maybe that's what you need.'

'I've seen it done, no, thank you.'

He remembered someone saying that Shahrawello prescribed blood-letting for Uncle Qorrax if he wasn't happy with his perform-ance in bed, if he wasn't content with his respiratory system or if he was believed to be suffering from bronchitis. Hours later, she would show him the blood that had rushed to the surface and which she managed to capture in the cup, a cup full of darkened blood which she held before him as evidence. Uncle Qorrax would stare at the dark blood and, nodding with approval, would say, 'You see, I told you. I am not well.' Some people were of the opinion that Qorrax was healthly until Shahrawello decided it was time his pride was punc-tured. To humiliate him, people said, she made him lie on a mat on the floor, helpless and submissive. Flames, tumblers, used razor-blades – she gave him the works. Lethargic, and drained of blood, he would remain on his back, at the same spot for hours. From then on, he beat his wives less often. From then on, he bullied his children less frequently. And this was the amazing thing – Qorrax acknowledged his unlimited gratitude to Shahrawello who, he said, kept him fit and on good form.

'No blood-letting for me. No, thank you,' said Askar now.

'What about *cuudis*?'

He said, 'No, thank you.'

He had watched it done. Karin was the patient. Poor woman, he thought. They forced her to tell lies, heaps of lies. Otherwise, how could she give as her name the name of a man? How could Karin say, looking straight at her 'confessor', 'My name is Abdullahi', giving as her own an identity which didn't match her real identity. Maybe, it was because they 'fumigated' her by placing a towel above her head, making her sweat, making her swelter under the suffocating smoke and she coughed and coughed. The woman who had been hired to dispel the bad eye out of Karin's system spoke to Karin in a language which definitely was not Somali. A couple of other women beat Karin on the chest as though she were a tin drum, they beat her on the back of the neck like one who's choked on a large piece of meat but won't vomit it out voluntarily. Askar wondered if Karin might have swallowed the 'bad eye'. No? Although it didn't make any sense, he wasn't averse to the idea.

'The Koran, then?'

No, no. He knew the Koran from back to front. He didn't want it read over his body astraddle a bed – not by Aw-Adan. Who knows, argued Askar, the man might have weird ideas. What if he read the wrong passages of the Koran, passages, say, which could make him turn into an epileptic? He had heard of such a story. As a matter of fact, he knew the brother of the boy to whom a similar experience had happened. A 'priest' had chosen the wrong passages of the Koran deliberately, mischievously, and read it over the little boy whom he didn't like. Did Misra know what became of the boy? 'He now has extra fluid flowing into his skull. They tell me his brain is over-flooded like a river with burst banks.'

Misra was worried. 'Who is this boy? Does he really exist?'

'His head is larger than the rest of his body; his sight has begun to fail, his hearing too. And all this because a wicked "priest" has read the wrong passages of the Sacred Book over the body of an innocent boy.'

'That's criminal,' said Misra.

'I agree with you,' he said.

They were silent for a few minutes. 'So what do we do?' she said.

His eyes lit with mischief. He pretended to be thinking. 'What?' she asked. 'What is it, Askar?'

'Go and call Aw-Adan,' he suggested.

'And I ask him to bring along a copy of the Koran?'

'No.'

'What then?'

And he became the great actor she had known, and his stare was illumined with the kind of satanic naughtiness his eyes brightened with when he was being mischievous. 'What then?' she repeated.

'Tell him to bring along his cane. I prefer his caning me with my eyes wide open to his reading the Koran over my body astraddle a sick bed when they are closed and trusting.'

In a moment, he was up and about. He was changing into a clean pair of shorts and looking for a T-shirt to match it. He was all right, she told herself. He was *thinking*. However, she saw him rummage in a cupboard. 'But what are you looking for?' she said.

'I am going to shave,' he said. 'Shave my chin, grow a beard, be a man like any other.'

'Shave? What . . . ?'

He was gone.

[2]

He cut himself when shaving. He cut his chin and his lower lip bled when he held the razor the wrong way, when he didn't adjust the disposable blade properly. There were shaving things lying about and he knew where to get them. His uncle was away at the war and so were many other men. Now he washed his face in the after-shave lotions, trying to see which one would stop his chin's blood running. The lotions made him smell good and so he sprayed them on his groin – determined that this would instantly remove the odour of his perspiration – and now, as there was still some of it left in the bottle, he hesitated whether to sprinkle it on his armpits, something he had seen older men do. But no. For this he chose the talcum powder, he decided that would do. He smiled. He breathed hot vapoury air and wrote his name on the mirror's mist and saw bits of himself, bits of his coagulated or running blood in the 'A' or the 'S' or the 'K' and the 'R' of his name.

He could not remember which came first – the thought that if he shaved, hair would automatically grow on his chin and his lips – or that he should take note of the hourly changes in his body. He was said to have developed the habit of getting up earlier than Misra so he would see for himself, placing his head against the dot he had marked on the wall the previous day, whether he had grown an inch or two taller in the past twenty-four hours. Very often, he was disappointed that he couldn't determine if he had, but he never felt as disheartened as when he stood against the tree planted by Misra the same day he was born.

'You must eat and eat and eat if you want to grow fast,' she said, one early morning when he woke her up because he moved about noisily. 'The tree lives off the earth and its water, it eats grandly, drinks huge quantities of water and breathes fresh air all the time. You must eat more so you'll become a man, a fully grown man, tall, broad-shouldered and perhaps bearded too.' And having said so, she went back to sleep.

And the anxiety to become a fully grown man, a man ready for a conscription into the liberation army, ready to die and kill for his mother country, ready to avenge his father, the anxiety made him over-indulge himself in matters related to food, it made him eat to excess until he felt so unwell that he vomited a couple of times. He had appropriated Misra's food since she couldn't eat anything anyway and stuffed himself full of anything he could lay his hands on. Hardly able to breathe, he would then lift rocks, flex his muscles so as to develop them, climb up the tree for further leg and arm exercises and then swing from it. Exhausted, he would fall asleep.

What distinguished this period's dreams from any other, what set these dreams apart from the others, was the presence of a huge garden, lush with an enormous variety of tropical fruits. He ate these fruits, he made himself a long list of salad fruits, and swam in the cool stream whose water was warm and whose bed was grown with weeds which were nice to touch and feel and pull and tickle one's face with – a face which grew sterner, and upon whose chin sprouted hair, silky, smooth, young and tender. Yes, what made the experience unique was that the garden was green with paradisiacal tropicality, it was calm with heavenly quietness. And in the Edenic certitude he found himself in, he discovered he was confident, happy to be where he was happy to be who he was. There was – almost within reach, wearing a smile, motherly – there was a woman. The woman grew on him. One night, dreaming, he 'picked' her up like a fruit and studied her; she, who was small as a fruit, lay under his intense stare. He had never seen that woman before. Of this, he was most certain. And yet he knew her. Where had he met her? He didn't know. She was calling him 'my son' and was talking of the pain of being separated from him – she who had borne him, she who had carried him for months inside of her, she who claimed she 'lived' in him who had survived her, she who claimed to be his guide when everyone else failed him. The following morning, he awoke and was confronted with an inexplicable mystery: there was blood on the sheet he had covered himself with, blood under him too. Most specifically, there was blood on his groin. He sought Misra's response.

'You've begun to menstruate,' she said, looking at him with intent seriousness. 'The question is: will you have the monthly curse as we women do or will yours be as rare as the male fowl's egg?'

He said, 'But I am a man. How can I menstruate?'

Enraged, he strode away from her in a manly way. He wouldn't give her the pleasure, he shouted, of her making fun of him any more or even of washing his 'womanhood' if it came to that. But what did this mean anyway? he asked himself, when he had washed. How come his own body misbehaved, how come he menstruated? Come what may, he said to himself, he wouldn't allow such thoughts to dissuade him from doing whatever it took to be a man who was ready to be conscripted into the army, a man ready to die and kill for his mother country, a man ready to avenge his father.

[3]

That day, he rejected the food she gave him. He tossed aside the plate she extended towards him and scolded her for what she had done when he was sleeping – smear his sheet and groin with blood. Why did she do it? She swore that she didn't go anywhere near him, that she didn't smear his body or sheet with blood.

'And so where did the blood come from?' he said.

She answered, 'I don't know.'

He reminded her of a conversation they had had a few days ago, one in which he admitted that he envied women their monthly periods. 'Could it be that in my dream, *I* menstruated?'

'There's a war on, there's a great deal of tension – and so everything is possible. I wouldn't know the answer, to be honest with you. I've never known of any man who menstruated. Could it be that the tension, the war . . . ?'

And he interrupted her. 'The war, the tension – what nonsense!'

'Do you have an answer then?'

He reflected; then: 'Men wet themselves occasionally?'

'When sleeping, yes.'

He sighed. 'And the colour of sperm is white?'

'White as silver.'

She heard a whine and waited.

'You know Uncle Hassan, don't you?'

She nodded her head, 'Yes.'

'You remember he urinated blood and was taken to see a doctor?'

She agreed that that was true.

'Perhaps that explains it all.'

She didn't like his explanation. 'It means you prefer being sick to being a woman.'

'Naturally,' he said. 'Who wouldn't?'

She said, '*I* wouldn't.'

'That is easily understandable. You are, after all, a woman.'

And he left the room.

[4]

'Tell me, why are there truckloads of women and infants leaving Kallafo?' Askar asked Misra when it became obvious that the Ethiopians were sending away their women and children from the war zone. 'Why?'

'Where there's a war,' she began to answer, but continued mixing hot and cold water so she could give Askar a bath, 'man sends ahead of himself his wife and children and stays behind to defend his people's honour, dignity and also property. Perhaps a bomb will cut the women's and children's lives short before they get home; perhaps the dozen or so armed soldiers with their primitive rifles will manage to deter a few equally primitively armed Somalis from killing them.'

There was a pause.

'And you won't go?' he said.

Her hand stopped stirring the water whose temperature she was testing. She was reduced to a stare – speechless. He said to himself, 'Maybe this is what death looks like – Misra sitting, speechless and staring, with her hand stuck in a bucket full of lukewarm water, the dust round her unstirred, the lips of her mouth forming and unforming a roguish smile – maybe this is what death looks like. And not what I saw last night – the back of a woman's head, a hand flung aside, a nail cut and then discarded.'

She was saying, 'Are you sending me away, Askar?'

'Not ahead of myself, no.'

Again she smiled rather mischievously, reminding herself that Askar was not yet eight and that here he was behaving as though he were a man and she a creature of his own invention. She declined to comment on what was going on between them, she declined to go into the same ring as he, she bowed out. However disreputable, she believed she was the one who made him who he was, she was the one who brought him up. She changed the mood of the exchange, changed the subject. Searching for his hand, she said, 'Come.'

He stood away, his hands hidden behind him. 'Where?'

'Come,' she said, half rising to take grip of his hand. 'Let me give your body a good scrubbing which is what it needs most. And then we'll go for a walk and, if you wish, watch the Ethiopian men send their women and children away to highland safety.'

He was rudely noisy, shouting, 'Don't you touch me.'

'I'm sorry,' she said, taken aback.

It was then that the thought that he was now a man and didn't want to be helped to wash impressed itself upon her mind. She would have to make an auspicious move, one which would make him relax until she poured the first canful of water on his head, and until the water calmed his nerves. His determined voice of defiance resounded through her body – and she had to wait for a long while before she was able to say anything. Then, 'Do you want to bathe yourself?' she asked, keeping her distance.

And saw (the thought took a long time to mature) how methodically 'dirtied' he had been – as if he played rough with boys of his age and wrestled and somersaulted into and out of challenging hurdles. He didn't look helplessly dirty – if anything, he was deliberately dirty. This thought descended on her like a revelation. She wondered where he had been – and with whom. She suspected he wouldn't tell her, but thinking she wouldn't lose anything anyway, she asked: 'Where have you been?'

He wouldn't tell her.

'Why won't you tell me where you've been?'

He behaved like one who had a secret to withhold.

'You'll not tell me?'

He shook his head, 'No.'

With harrowing clarity, she saw what he was after – to tell her he would go where he pleased, tell her that he would roam in the territory of his pleasure, alone, and at any rate without her help, wash when he decided he wanted. She reasoned: the world is reduced to chaos; there's a war on; boys, because of this chaotic situation, have suddenly become men and refuse to be mothered.

And then, with frightening suddenness, he said, 'Not only can I wash if I choose to, but I can kill; and not only can I kill but I can also defend myself against my enemy.'

The fierceness with which he spoke the words 'I can kill' alarmed her. She stiffened, her heart missed a beat, then drummed faster, beating noisily in the caged rib of her seemingly discreet reaction. She appeared uneasy and stood up taller, higher, supporting her weight on the tip of her toes, like one who is looking over the edge of a cliff. 'Kill? Kill whom?'

He wouldn't say, just as he wouldn't tell her that he was a member of a small body of young men who trained together as guerrillas and who rolled on the dirt as they felled one another with mock blows, issuing, as they dropped to the ground, a most heinous kung-fu cry, or some such like. What mattered, in the end, was you killed your enemy, said these young men to one another. The idea to train with these boys wasn't his, but the boy who had been raped by the Adenese – who proved to be the toughest, not least because he had something to fight against and he had in him a bitter contempt for everybody in this or any other world. It was he, and not Askar, who made a hole in a thinly mud-plastered wall which enabled the body of boys to take a quieter look at the men (believed to be away at the war front) who trained to kill and, through the hole in the wall, the boys imbibed an ideology embodied in the dream they saw as their own, the dream they envisioned as their common future: warriors of a people fighting to liberate their country from colonial oppression. Nor would he tell her of his friends' suspicious finger pointing in her direction. Was she not from the Highlands? they said. How could she be trusted? They most insistently repeated their suspicious worries that she might speak, might pass on the information. It bothered him greatly that he couldn't share with her the joy of his secrets; it pained him that he had to be distrustful of her motives when she probed into his affairs, asking him where he had been and with whom. 'It was as if you were born with a deformity that you had to carry with you everywhere you went,' he said to the boy whom the Adenese had raped. Indeed, who better could he say this to, than to another boy who carried on his head another shame of another kind? 'Yes, I understand,' said the 'disgraced' boy. Askar said to himself now, 'I will not allow her to wash the dirt my body has accumulated when training to kill my people's enemy.'

Whereas she was saying, 'There are a number of blind spots the body of a human has. We may not know of them until we are self-conscious; we may not sense how helpless we are until we submit ourselves to other hands. A child's body's blind spots are far too many to count – the small of the back, the back of the neck, the dirt in the groin, the filth on either the left or the right of the lower reaches of the bottom. A mother sees them all, she soaps them all and, in the end, washes them clean.' She was going nearer him and he was withdrawing and she was saying, 'They are difficult to live with, these blind spots, these blind curves in one's body, the curtained parts of one's body, the never-seen, never-visible-unless-with-the-assistance-of-a-mirror parts – and here I am thinking of the skull – or the difficult-to-see parts – and here I am thinking about . . . I am thinking about . . . ,' and speaking and moving in his direction and he was retreating and was about to stumble backwards into the tree planted the day he himself was born, his blind spot, that is his back, ahead of the rest of his body, when . . . a bomb fell – and it fell almost between them, although nearer where he was standing – and it separated them.

Panic gripped her throat: and she couldn't speak or shout but lay on the ground, inert, covered in dust – once the noise died down and the shower of dust began to settle. He? He was – he was there, more or less dusted, and his eyes were two spots of brightness which focused on their surroundings and it seemed as though he mobilized his alert mind to determine where the shelling had come from.

'Are you all right?' she managed to say after a long silence.

He looked at her – she appeared like one who had just risen from the dead.

Still defiant, he said, 'Who do you take me for?'

She had gone browner with dust and her headscarf had fallen off, exposing a most unruly head, as ugly as the knotted, uncombed curls. She walked away in a defiant way – defiant and indifferent as to what might happen, impervious to what he thought or did, or whether a shower of shells fell on her head, or anyone else's head.

'It's worthwhile your considering giving yourself a good scrubbing. Maybe the water is still lukewarm and you surely need a wash and something that will keep your soul active and alive and your body clean,' he said.

Then another shell fell – this time nearer where she was standing. And, at the wake of the explosion, when again she had managed to stand to her feet, both of them saw before them a crowd, brown as mud – a crowd of women and children armed with pangas, sticks and machetes, a crowd that was moving in the direction of the hill where the enemy had fired from. A spokeswoman of the crowd promised they would take 'Government Hill'. Askar felt he had to join, to give victory an indispensable hand.

And he ran after the crowd.

The following day. Noon.

'Misra, where precisely is Somalia?' he asked suddenly.

She was pulling at a chicken's guts, a chicken she had just beheaded. She stopped and stared at him, not knowing what to say. Her forehead wrinkled with concentration, like somebody who was trying to remember where he was. Then: 'Haven't you seen it on the map?' she said, holding her bloodstained hands away from her dress.

'A map? What map?'

'Go look it up. You seem happily engrossed in it.'

He surprised her; he admitted in a sad voice: 'No one has ever explained how to read maps, you see, and I have difficulty deciphering all the messages.'

She looked away from him and at the decapitated chicken. She wished she could get on with her plucking of the fowl's feathers (Askar thought of the chicken's blood as being exceptionally red – not dark red as he expected) and she said: 'If you go east, you'll end up in Somalia.'

Offended, he said, 'I know that.'

'What don't you know then? Why don't you let me get on with what I am doing? Don't you realize there is little time left for me to prepare a decent meal?'

He bent down and picked up a feather flying away into the cosmic infinitude. He looked at it, studying it as though under a microscope, one among a hundred other feathers joining the unbound universe. Then he looked at the white meat of the chicken – goose-pimpled, dead and headless, the fowl lay where Misra had dropped it, in a huge bowl. Did it have a soul? Did it have a brain? He remembered testing its motherly instinct when he threatened the lives of its chicks. It attacked, its wings open in combat readiness and its rage clucking in consonants of maternal protectiveness. Askar had run away for his own life. From a hen. He was glad none of the boys saw him run away.

From then on, whenever he entered Karin's compound, he suspected that the mother hen, or the others, now as tall as they were ever likely to grow, eyed him menacingly, goose-stepping sideways as if only their preparedness for a full-frontal attack, and together, might save them from his mischievous threats. Poor hen – dead. Dead because it was killed to celebrate a victory – and the fact (this was in the air) that Askar might be leaving for Mogadiscio. After all, Uncle Qorrax said he would come and speak with him.

Then, something attracted his attention. Misra had laid the plucked chicken on its side and was pulling at its guts, when he noticed an egg – whole, as yet unhatched, and, he thought, indifferent to the goings-on outside its own complete universe. An egg – oval-shaped as the universe – with a life of its own and an undiscovered future. 'Don't touch it, Misra,' he ordered.

She looked at him in wonderment. 'This?' she said, touching it.

'Don't hurt it,' he said.

She gave it to him – slowly but delicately. She handed the egg to him with the same care that she might have offered the world to him. And he received it with absolute reverence, with both hands joined together as if in prayer. Something warned him to be careful and not to drop it. It was warm. He believed life quivered within it as he closed his hands on it, not tightly, but gently. Reluctantly, he entered into a dialogue with himself. Was there no similarity between the egg and his own beginnings? In the corpse of a hen, there lay another potential life – just as he lay in his dead mother – but alive. He was glad the egg was salvaged out of the dead hen.

Misra was saying: 'I thought you wanted me to tell you where "Somalia" is?'

Askar nodded his head.

'There,' she said, pointing with her blood-soiled index finger.

He repeated the question, 'Where?' apparently because he had been staring at the index finger, which was dripping with blood, and hadn't taken note of the direction in which she pointed. 'Where?'

Her 'There', this second time, was so suddenly spoken, Askar could've sworn 'Somalia' was the name of a person, perhaps a friend of hers, somebody who might be invited to partake of the meal she was preparing. 'That's Somalia,' she added. 'Easterly.'

He thought he heard someone's footsteps coming from the easterly direction – he looked, and there was Karin. She had come with an empty bowl. Today, she was in near rags but charming-looking, and smiling too, and talking and friendly, and had the look of somebody who wanted something. She said, 'Give us some of God's charity and you'll be blessed forever.'

Askar said, 'The meat is yours, the egg is mine.'

Karin, puzzled, looked at Misra. 'What's he talking about?'

'Ask him,' she said.

By the time Karin was ready to ask him a question, he was gone.

*

Three days later. Another festive occasion. The three of them: Karin, Misra and Askar. Somebody had delivered a large consignment of raw meat, a gift from Uncle Qorrax. Karin was sitting apart and seemed to be having difficulty determining in which direction the wind was blowing. She appeared littler, barely a girl in her teens. This was how she looked to Askar, who saw her go closer to the earth as if she were listening for a secret. He thought of a beetle, which, sensing that an unidentified shadow might strike it dead, waits, and while doing so, curls up, making itself smaller, leaving no part of it exposed other than its wing-cases hard as a turtle's back – and like a turtle, it is able to remove its head and neck out of danger: that's it! 'What are you doing, Karin?' said Misra.

'Thinking. Thinking of asking you to divine,' she said.

'What with?'

'Meat.'

She thought for a minute. 'I've used meat only once. Water, yes, and blood. It's difficult to divine with meat. Meat is short-lived, there is something temporary about meat in hot climates.'

Misra gently stroked the entrails and he could hear the groan of an intestine, the moan of a bladder. She washed the meat. Then she held a handful of it and stared it it for a long time. She fell into, and dwelled in, a state of suspense. Her posture was that of someone praying, her silence concentrated like a treasure. Then she began speaking words belonging to a language group neither Karin nor Askar had ever heard of before and she repeated and repeated the mantras of her invocation. She uttered a shibboleth, or what must have been a test word, and looked happy like somebody who has found a lost friend. She spoke slowly this time. Her voice – ripples (as of water) in the wake of other ripples, each following waves of more ripples falling upon further ripples. And each of her incantatory phrases was shapely like predictions that would come true. Finally, she put the meat back in the bowl.

And the meat quivered.

And Askar watched her stare at the fatty portion of the meat, as though she were reading the future in a palm – which she probably was. And the future trembled, red like the season's flower in bloom, living and yet dead: the meat. And the future-in-the-meat, whatever its colour, whatever its own future, beckoned to Misra's questioning mind – and her palms, from which she was reading the future, were bloody. What did that mean? Karin asked: 'Tell us what you've seen, Misra. Please.'

Misra's breathing was deep, Askar's shallow, Karin's, choked.

'To the traveller,' began Misra, speaking with a voice that was not her own (this reminded Askar of when Karin had assumed an identity different from her own, claiming she was called Abdullahi), and then paused for a while. Then she continued, this time with her eyes closed, 'To the traveller, the heat dwells in the distance in the dilute forms of mirages and such-like hopes as may make the fatigued voyager believe in the eternal nature of the state of things.'

She paused. She breathed in and breathed out. Her brassiere came undone, there was a great deal of motion in her heavy chest. Involuntarily, the thought that each of her breasts was ovally shaped – almost like immense eggs – shocked Askar, bringing him back to a reality of sorts – to the present.

Karin said, 'Now what, in plain language, does that mean?'

Askar was thinking how, the other day, the air had been thick with falling feathers and how, today, meat was employed to foretell a future full of death and blood and journeys.

Misra said, 'He will travel,' this time speaking with her own voice. 'Who will?'

'I saw a pearl, as clear as the water of the ocean is blue. Did you ask, who will travel? Askar will travel and will put his feet in the Indian Ocean. And he'll be happy as one who's discovered his beginnings.'

Karin asked: 'And you? Will you, too, travel?'

'I will join him eventually, but not immediately. He will first be reunited with his maternal uncle. Arrangements are being made. But I see death and distress and disaster in the offing.'

He asked, 'He will travel soon, will he, this rascal, this Askar?' very excited. 'Tell us how soon.'

'Shortly.'

Then, almost simultaneously as he jumped up in glee, he sensed something weird had taken place – he tasted blood in his mouth. He took hold of himself and noted that, for one thing, he hadn't bitten his tongue; for another, when he examined the floor or palate of his mouth, he didn't discover any sores or cuts. Now what in heavens did that mean? He remembered it was happening for the second time in his life, the first, when Aw-Adan caned him unfairly, and with unjustified contempt, on his first day at the Koranic School. He might not have admitted it, but he was frightened. In any case, he decided not to tell them about it.

As more steam rose from the huge pots which were on the fire, and more smoke from the one just built, Askar's worried look settled on Karin's chin – the old woman had a faint beard. Some women are known to grow thin hairs on their chins when their bodies enter the age of menopause. Now, who could've told him that? he asked himself. From Karin's chin, his eyes travelled to Misra's hands, still stained with blood. A future of blood, of death and disasters – and a journey to Mogadiscio for him.

Well!

[6]

That night, when sleep came, he moved his bed to the centre of the room he and Misra shared, placing it right under the opening a bomb had made in the roof, so he could keep his eye on the sky; and slept cradled in the warmth of a stick carved in the shape of a rifle – this being a gift from the boy whom the Adenese had raped. And his dream garden was emptied of its greenness – the trees had been disrobed, the branches had gone dry, the leaves had begun to become wiltingly lifeless and what fruits there might have been had dropped to the ground to rot – unpicked, uneaten. From one end of the garden, a fire ate its way, ruthless, tongued, and Askar could hear its crackling noise as each tree, limb, stump, twig or dry leaf was licked dead by its famished rage. The fire was helped by the fast-travelling, angry wind. At times, the wind levelled the ground so the fire would find the job – already half-done, or almost – easier. The earth was thus pillaged of its water. Dry, it wore a dark coating of charcoal.

And he?

He was fixed to the ground – waiting. And he was sure that the fire – which had devoured the wind, emptied the earth of its water, the garden of its greenness – he was certain the tongued flames would finish him. Frightened, he froze. He believed that was the end of him: with a heart already frozen and a body dipped in the red fluidity of fire. The tongued flames stopped at his feet, then, in a moment, like a cobra, it was gathered into and moved up spirally, climbing his body until the chill disappeared. He felt his body being tickled back into life.

He looked about – no fire, no wind. Did that mean that the fire which had devoured the earth and the sky had found a home inside him? That he would burn, sooner or later, and nothing would extinguish him?

And then it rained.

And the rain cut short his dream.

For the water poured down from the heavens and a few drops fell into his open mouth. From the way he gulped, from the frightened way he gasped, seeking his breath, etc., one would've thought he was drowning. He sat up, preoccupied. His face was wet, his body was soaked in the ablutionary waters of a heavenly downpour and there seeped into his soul a sense of irrelevance. 'What am I doing here sleeping dreamily when my mother country needs my help?' He crawled out of bed, his 'rifle' in his tight clutch, and he heard bombs fall. The horizon in the distance was lit by tiny fragments of brightnesses, small and fretful, like fireflies in the thickness of a tropical night's unmitigated darkness. Placing his 'rifle' in his bed, he stood motionless, thinking.

A little later, he began moving about, quiet as the smoke of gunpowder, and he lit a paraffin lamp. He strode towards Misra's bed to wake her up. But he stopped. He then saw that his 'rifle', which lay astraddle his own bed, was pointed at Misra's head – Misra, who lay on her back, asleep in paradisiacal disorder. (Her knees were up, her legs open and her private parts exposed.) He chose to leave her *be*. And he went out of the room.

Outside, the night was infernally dark. Not a single star was in the sky. The wind was still and nothing stirred. Then he noticed a few women, who emerged out of the now opened doors of sleep. A bomb fell, not very far from where they were standing. This helped unbolt the locked gates of conversation and floods of information came forth. He could gather from the conversation that the 'enemy hill' was aflame. Somebody was saying that the Ethiopians had set fire to their houses in an apparent attempt to prevent the Somalis taking their houses, and other belongings, intact. Which was why everybody who was there, save Askar, went towards the fire on the hill with a view to snatching a slice of the fire before it died! He had had his share of fire, he thought, and wished Misra was awake to celebrate the birth of 'Somalia' in Kallafo.

He was very sad. For her.

INTERLUDE

Life can only be lived forward
and understood backward.

Kierkegaard

The joy of travel, you said to yourself, there is nothing like it. The joy of open spaces, that's divinity itself. And for a few minutes, your mind dwelled on guilt and on loss, yes, your mind spoke to itself of the fact that Misra wasn't going with you to Mogadiscio. You were in distress and insisted she go with you. You didn't hear her say it yourself but Uncle Qorrax had told you that Misra had indicated her desire to remain behind. But why? you asked, and you were hysterical, why? 'Misra says, and I am quoting her own words,' said Uncle, 'that she prefers being here until the white bones of the unburied corpses assume a browner tinge, resembling the earth's. This is what Misra says, but she promises to come to where the lorry is leaving from.' And you travelled as arranged. Together with a number of men, women and children, you left Kallafo in a lorry travelling to Mogadiscio, one of the first to do so. And Uncle Qorrax asked a man to look after you, a man whom he knew and who happened to be going to Mogadiscio. Not only did he request that the man help you if the need arose, but he entrusted to him a letter in a sealed envelope, addressed to Uncle Hillaal, your maternal uncle. Strange how certain names never come up and when they do, they mean a lot to you. It is true that you had never 'heard' of Hillaal's name nor of Salaado, his wife. But then there you are. Life is full of surprises.

Uncle Qorrax explained to the man to whom he entrusted you, 'His maternal uncle's name is Hilaal Cabdullahi and his wife's name is Salaado. The address is on the envelope you're carrying with you. If you encounter problems finding him, please go to the National University and someone will know where he lives, for he teaches there. We've never met, he and I, and have never corresponded.' Then Uncle Qorrax did something which made you cast your memory back to the morning when he handed you over formally to Aw-Adan as the latter's pupil. Now he gave your hand to the man who took you by the wrist, saying, 'Come', as though you were a goat he had paid for. You would have preferred it if he had formally shaken your hand.

And so, for the first time in your life, you travelled away from where you were conceived and born and where your parents and your umbilical cord and your first teeth were buried. For the first time in your life, you would cross a border that has never been well spoken of among Somalis, for such borders deny the Somali people who live on either side of it, yes, such borders deny these people their very existence as a nation. Uncle Hilaal would say of this that 'Somalis went to war in order that the ethnic origin of the people of the Ogaden would match their national identity. That's what gives the Somalis their psychical energy, a type no other African people have, only Somalis. Imagine, Askar. A nation with a split personality, Askar. How tragic! Of course, the economic and political considerations are to be given their due weight and they are important. But it is the psyche of the Somali – his peace of mind and that of the community – these matter a great deal more.' But will you hold a second, please? You don't have to rush the story and its audience, do you? Why not introduce Uncle Hilaal and Salaado when their appropriate time comes? Now go back to the lorry before it left Kallafo. And where is Misra?

You could now see Misra lost in a limbo of despair. She was a woman sunk to the bottom of distress, and she wasn't saying, or capable of saying, anything save your name again and again. You had already begun thinking about Uncle Hilaal and of the future linking you with him, a future as long as the distance on the map between Kallafo and Mogadiscio. You averted your look from Misra because it pained you to see her so unhappy and, in any case, you knew Uncle Qorrax wouldn't approve of your request that she come with you. So you looked at other people and they were hugging lovingly and exchanging farewell kisses. The young were taking their parents' or guardians' hands and were kissing them and some were shaking hands as adults do, while others embraced as friends and equals do, you thought. You heard the promises they made to one another. You could feel a touch of fear in their voices, for the war in the Ogaden was still raging and nobody could know where victory would fall, on whose side victory would fight. They promised to one another that they would write, give one another news frequently. And there were prayers and beggars were given their *xaqqas-salaama*, a farewell fee given by every traveller to a man or a woman who would pray for his or her safe journey. You watched your uncle pay, on your behalf, your *xaqqas-salaama* to a man looking not at all like a beggar. Well, you thought, he doesn't wish me luck. And then you looked in Misra's direction and were pleased to see Karin was there too. And Karin came to you.

'How do you feel,' she asked, 'leaving us all?'

You had already been helped up and into the lorry and so, because of this and because there was a great deal of commotion and a lot of overflowing emotion, the place was hellishly noisy. You shouted to Karin: 'I've already begun to feel the loss, and it takes a most weird form.'

She stood aside, letting an anxious man pass who was bidding another farewell. Then she said: 'How do you mean?'

'It is as if I have no inside,' you said to Karin. 'I can feel my rib-cage with my fingers, or knock my knuckles against it, and it drums emptily, as if there is nothing inside, nothing whatsoever; it feels as though I have no heart which beats, no lungs which breathe and no head which can think lucidly.'

She was a dear! She said: 'Nonsense.'

You noticed that Misra was keeping a deliberate distance from you, as though she didn't want to make any bodily contact with you. Perhaps she thought that once you had touched, it would be difficult to part again. But now that you were returning to Xamar from where your father took his nickname, was she, too, likely to return to hers? Since everybody comes from somewhere, you decided she, too, would go back to where she had hailed from. Who knows, she might ride the horse which had dropped its rider; or meet her father who was of a noble Amhara family; or her mother or one of her half-brothers or half-sisters or cousins. Wars have a way of springing surprises on one, some of which are pleasant and some deadly unpleasant.

Oh, and the mystery of things! Karin now stepped aside and Misra was giving you something. Taking it, you felt something move and the tin-foil in which Misra had wrapped it glittered in your eyes. But what was it? It was food which was still warm. How did she know you felt empty? You began eating voraciously and you guzzled and guzzled. Uncle Qorrax, who was talking to some friends, was joined by Shahrawello and some of your cousins. They inquired as to who had given you the food that had 'bewitched' you? 'Why, look at him. You would think there was famine in Mogadiscio.' It was then that Shahrawello mentioned that a rumour had been spread that Misra had hung above your head, one early dawn, a slaughtered fowl, dripping with blood. You thought, let them say what they like. I hope that when I've filled my empty viscera with food prepared by Misra, I'll be able to express my emotions better.

You were busy eating and could hear the engine of the lorry revving, you could see the exhaust-pipe's white smoke – and before you knew what was happening, you realized that the lorry was in motion. When you looked back, you saw hands wave and heard shouts of farewell but couldn't determine which hand was Misra's, Karin's or anyone else's; nor could you distinguish one person's cry from anybody else's. You rose to your full height. By then, distance was making Misra smaller, distance was making her shorter than half her size. However, when she finally vanished, together with her the township of Kallafo, Uncle Qorrax, his wife Shahrawello and your cousins – yes, when Kallafo was but a dot in the dusty distance, smaller than the speck of dust it is represented as on the map, it was then that you sensed that your heart had begun beating again and that you had lungs with which to breathe, and you were whole again. And the man to whom you had been entrusted was saying: 'It is like sea starting where the earth ends. Because Mogadiscio, or any other town in the Republic, is a road leading to other roads, a road with a purpose that takes one to other possibilities.'

You thought that the conversation must have reached an advanced stage, since you couldn't recall what had gone on before. You listened intently, and somebody put a question to the man sitting next to you. 'Could you tell us, in the simplest language possible, why you are crossing a border which exists no more, to a Mogadiscio to which you've never been?'

The man took his time. Years later, you would remember his posture as one resembling that of a person from other war-torn areas of conflict, a man residing in the spacious pause of a peace truce in Lebanon or a Ugandan enjoying the quiet following army looting. The man responded: 'I am journeying away from graves.'

A number of heads nodded approvingly.

The man continued: 'I am travelling, leaving behind me unburied corpses. The tombs are, you might say, those of history. That is to say, these are corpses that should be buried in the tomb of history but that are not; corpses that, at any rate, will be undug every century or so. Somalis come, "Ethiopians" go, every twenty, fifty or a hundred years or so. Waves of atmospheric spirits fill the air of any place where the dead are not buried, ghosts, ferocious as hounds, hunt together, in groups, in the dark and they frighten the inhabitants – it ill-behoves a displaced soul to search for a body in which to take residence.'

Somebody commented: 'I dare say!'

Another asked: 'Whose are the unburied corpses?'

Then the man smiled. He said: 'Our memories, our collective or if you like, our individual pasts. We leave our bodies in order that we may travel light – we are hope personified. After all, we are the dream of a nation.'

You wondered if the man had made sense to the others since you didn't understand him. You were looking at the other faces for clues when Misra's image came right before you, placing itself between you and the men you were staring at. You would remember the same image when, years later, at school and in Mogadiscio, you were shown the pictures of Egyptian mummies by one of Salaado's relations, namely Cusmaan. The image which insisted on imposing itself on your brain was that of a Misra, already dead, but preserved; a Misra whose body, when you touched it, was cold as ice, as though it had spent a night or two in a mortuary. But there was an incredible calmness about her corpse, as if she herself had abandoned her life much with the same preparedness as Armadio, Karin's late husband, had surrendered his to the Archangel of Death. There was no struggle, no pain, death came as a welcome guest – and stayed, that was all. Somehow you consoled yourself, remembering that she looked like a corpse when asleep, with her hands neatly clasped together across her mountain of a chest and barely a snort or noise issuing from her nostrils. Did she not playfully act as though she were dead a couple of times? You rationalized that your mind conjured up these ugly images because you felt guilty at parting with her, guilty at leaving without her. Then you told the image to vanish – and it did. And you were staring at the men's faces, in silence, in the kind of thank-you-God hush which comes after a Muslim has sneezed.

Then one of the men burst into a nationalist song, but his voice failed him. Another man, this time the one to whom you had been entrusted, picked it up, lifting it to that undefined zone between the earth and the sky, which is said to be the angels' abode. The man had a wonderful voice and, what is more, he knew it. He sang one of the fifties songs, of the Qershe and Jawaahira-Luul era and fame. This, together with the speed of the lorry, transported your imagination to the high seas and you thought you were floating, one and all, in the pure silver water of total abandon. Nothing mattered any more. You could've all died in a single somersault of the vehicle and your bodies would probably not have felt the slightest pain in parting with life. Beautiful voices that sing beautiful, nationalist songs beautifully are seldom found and you appreciated the man's exquisite voice for another reason: that it made you re-play in your ears Uncle Qorrax's voice, which was ugly and short of breath, like an angry half-wit only good to give commands. You would later, of course, reconsider your judgement, once you got to Mogadiscio and heard Uncle Hilaal's. In any case, it seemed you had bodily gained access to the buffer between reality and dream as you listened to the song and thought if you died, you wouldn't, in all probability, be woken up from the dead and therefore you might not have known you were alive. One song was followed by another. Others contributed or requested which song the man should sing next and when he didn't know the words, or couldn't remember how its rhythm went, they helped him out. But you didn't contribute any songs, nor did you suggest he sing any for you. Because in you, your soul was rising up, climbing higher and higher up your body, the way breathlessness rises in one, only to be replaced by the delirium one feels when going up a very, very high mountain.

Then the lorry slowed down. For you, the speed meant a lot – it had enabled you to leave below you, as though on the earth, the worldliness that had been your past; it had helped you gain an unreachable height, a territory formed only by the most fertile of imaginations. You paid more attention now that you read signs of worry on the other passengers' faces. 'What's happening? Why are we slowing down?' someone asked.

Only the passengers in the cabin sitting by the driver knew why. And when one man half-climbed over the side of the lorry to ask why, you learnt that you were nearing the town of Feer-Feer, formerly a border town. And someone was asking: 'Does anyone know what flag Feer-Feer is flying today?'

In chorus, the men said: 'Of course. The Somali flag.'

And the idea produced poetry in another man who said, 'The sky is blue and heavenly and so is the Somali flag; a flag whose colour matches that of God's abode. It has, right in its middle, a five-pointed star and, for each point, a Somali-speaking territory. The former British Somaliland and the former Italian Somalia have been recently joined by the Ogaden.'

Heads nodded. Silence. The question how long the victory would last was in everybody's mind. But because you were being welcomed by the townspeople and Feer-Feer was in such a festive mood, it seemed inappropriate to worry. The lorry came to a halt. Before you could alight, many of the townspeople joined you in the lorry and together you sang nationalist songs which were composed in the 1940s by the founders of the Somali Youth Club. You sang songs until you reached what could be considered the centre of town. You finally alighted. While food was being prepared for you, some of the men prayed and you and a couple of others went to have a look at the Somali flag, flying in the heavens of your nationalist dreams.

A little later, someone set fire to the Ethiopian colours; after him waved flames of joy as he ran in circles in the clearing made for the purpose. In stunned silence, you watched the red, the yellow and the green of the Ethiopian flag being reduced to charcoal.

[2]

You stood aside. You didn't take part in the flag-burning exercise. Not because you thought it was the wrong thing to do. You had other thoughts to attend to. You remembered, earlier on, you had taken possession of the thick envelope Uncle Qorrax had entrusted to the escort who was to lead you to Uncle Hilaal's door. The man was far too excited to stay away from the flag-burning exorcism. He threw himself in headlong, like a *mayooka*, dancing frenziedly round the flames of the burning colours. He hurled himself, now forwards, now backwards and then to the sides – now he grew wings and flew like a firefly; now he was no longer impeded by legs and could jump as high as a leopard; now he roared with joy, surrounding himself with a myth, like a lion. When the man was too busy to look, you opened the envelope.

Briefly, you studied her handwriting, which, in any case, you couldn't read because it was in Italian, and imagined her to be under a great deal of stress when jotting her notes. Maybe the rush of thoughts had come to her the same moment that she felt your kick in her ribs. Or maybe she was in a hurry to get somewhere. But you saw dates – days of the weeks, months as captions. You could read these. You could also read one name – that of Uncle Qorrax, spelt as *Korrah*. Something brought back a sad memory – of a calendar on a wall, Misra aborting a foetus, of dates in red and green in accordance with a code of safety. Why was Uncle Qorrax's name often in your mother's journal? you asked yourself. You tasted your hate for Qorrax in your saliva, you tasted blood. I could kill him, you thought.

Your escort came and fetched you. He saw that you had opened the envelope and said he didn't mind your keeping it yourself. When you were putting it into your bag, he noticed two other items – the portrait of Ernest Bevin (you explained who he was to him) and an egg. 'What's that?'

125

You stammered something.

'I like eggs. Is this one boiled, ready to be eaten?' he asked.

'I am sorry. But I have a question,' you said after a pause. 'When an egg goes bad and there isn't a hen to sit on it, what happens?'

The man at first appeared puzzled. Then, 'How do you mean?' he said, but didn't wait for your answer. He asked you to tell him the 'history' of the egg, instead. He found your story amusing, at first, but when he thought about it, he found it enlightening. He said so to you as you joined the circle which had formed round the bus about to depart. Someone was speaking nationalist rhetorics, in which plenty of Somali as well as enemy blood was shed.

Then someone else insisted that passengers be told where the 'inexistent' border used to be – inexistent, because Somalis never admitted it, neither did they allow it to enter into their logic. Non-Somalis, because they were total strangers or knew no better, looked at maps, where they found a curvy line, drawn to cut one Somali people from another. Presently, somebody pointed a finger at a row of huts where the Ethiopian sentries used to live, their guns in their tight embrace.

Of the rest of the journey to Belet Weyne, and then eventually Mogadiscio, Askar would remember when the bus was stopped and the men and the women passengers parted, the men going one way, the women and children the other. Of course, he didn't doubt with whom he would go – the men. He was the only one who did not strip naked to take a dip in the Somali end of the Shebelle River. Because Aw-Adan was the first man he had seen wholly naked, he now wondered where he was and whether alive or dead.

He betook himself to a spot hidden from the men and the women, who were busy performing their cleansing rituals – a spot under the trees from where he could watch both groups. He was thrilled to be the sole inhabitant of a garden. This garden was green, as was his recent memory of another he had seen in a dream. He saw a footpath and something told him that the footpath might take him to his own beginning – had he the courage to follow it. But the thought of encountering his own starting-point frightened him, it threw him into some distress. He felt so uncomfortable he decided to join the other men. He stripped naked in order that he might indulge in the washing rite, just as the others. Acrimonious in expression, he went into the river. Directly his body came into contact with water, he regained his calm. The water was calf-deep for quite a distance and his body sipped through its pores the right amount, which eventually induced in him a peaceful harmony reminiscent of the day he was born. One of the men backstroked to the deeper end and dived, disappearing for quite a while in the water. And Askar was full of envy.

Still naked, he got out of the water and sat by himself. Should he return to the dark garden behind all this sunlit wateriness, he asked himself, and follow the footpath? Why on earth did he feel such an imbalance in his psyche, why was he frightened? Where did he think the road might have led him? To his own beginning or to someone else's?

Misra was before him again. She was there and he was small and she was washing him, fussing over him, playing with him, addressing him in a language of endearment, calling him 'my man'; there she was, real as the border; there she was, talking about how self-conscious he was on the day he was born, how he wore a mask of dried blood, how he appeared, or rather behaved, as though he had made himself. And she was there, teaching him the rudiments of things, calling each item by its name, 'That is the sky', and 'This is the earth'; and there he was, pointing at her repeatedly in reply to the question, 'Where is the earth?', although he would point correctly at the sky whenever the question was 'Where is the sky?' She would burst out laughing, saying she was 'Mother' and not 'earth' while his finger that had pointed, and maybe even the hand, was busily taking a bit of the earth to eat. Indubitably, she had done a most commendable job, training him in the nomadic lore of climatic and geographic importance – that it was the earth which received the rains, the sky from whose loins sprang water and therefore life; that the earth was the womb upon whose open fields men and women grew food for themselves and for their animals. And man raised huts and women bore children and the cows grazed on the nearby pastures, the goats likewise; and the boy became a man, the girl a woman and each married to raise a family of his or why not her own and the married couple drew joy out of being together with their offspring – thanks be Allah! (And all this time, Askar was thinking of the inherent contradictions – that she wasn't his mother, and the country wasn't hers; that she was teaching him *his* people's lore and wisdom, and occasionally some Amharic when night fell; that she wasn't married and hadn't a child of her own or a man she called 'husband' but was happy for whatever that was worth; that he had no one to bestow the title of 'Father' on, but a great many uncles, one of whom was once married to Misra.)

And Aw-Adan was there too. And he was teaching him things about astrology and how to locate the Milky Way; how to answer when the

Ciisaanka-yeer calls, or what to do; how to spot the afa-gaallo constellation of stars; plus one scientific truism – that in Islam, Nature – capital N, he insisted – is conceived of as a book, comparable, in a lot of ways, to the Holy Koran: a genus for a sura, a species for a verse and every subspecies shares a twinship with the *alif, ba* and *ta* of mother nature – *maa shaa Allaahu kaana!*

'The bus is ready to leave for Mogadiscio,' somebody shouted.

Askar saw men look for their clothes, men who were holding their members covered with both their hands; he did the same. He shook his shorts so they would be free of the sand which might have lodged itself in the pockets, etc., and stumbled into them in great haste. He put on his T-shirt as well, and the shoes. But his body was sandy as he had no time to wash off this earth's light coating. The driver waited until all the women and the children were accounted for. He asked if everyone was there. When he received the affirmative, he said, 'We shall be in Belet Weyne in less than an hour.'

[3]

Standing against the morning wall of sunshine, two oblong lines of light, each solid as a hem and clearly visible as the border of a dress. And there were two horses – one of them black, the other white; the black horse led the way, the other followed him immediately after, like white smoke after black before the red flames pursue each other into invisibility.

The horses were in a garden rampant with tropicality, a garden wild and virginal as the first day of creation must have been. It had rained heavily and the horses dripped, moistening everyone and everything near them. I admired them from a distance. I picked what fruits I could reach without any effort on my part and bit into them until I sucked out the juice. I discarded the pulp, leaving behind me a trail of formless mass.

A young girl, innocent as her smile, emerged from behind the horses. She looked intimidated – I don't know if my presence frightened her, or even if she saw me. I could detect a streak of fear in her eyes. But the girl fascinated me – especially her eyes. So I gave up looking at the horses altogether and I concentrated on the girl. I couldn't explain what was the cause of this bemused attraction to the girl, why this fascination. I couldn't look anywhere else for a long time.

I asked her what her name was. She said she had no name, that I could give her one if I wanted. I asked her where she came from. She said she had no country she could call her own, that she was a refugee although she didn't know from where, and from whom she was fleeing and to what safe shelter. I asked her if she had any parents. She said she had no parents. In short, she was a young girl, more or less the same age as myself, a girl without a name, without a country, without parents – but a girl and not a boy.

I held my hand out to her.

She said, 'Do not touch me.'

I asked why.

'Because I am standing in a skin I've borrowed,' she said.

I asked what else had she borrowed?

'The tongue I'm speaking with isn't mine either,' she said.

I inquired if there was anything she could claim as her own?

'At times,' she said, 'all I own, the only thing that I can hold on to for as long as I want, the one and only thing no one has come for so far, is, would you believe it, a shadow?' and she smiled.

'A shadow?' I repeated, in disbelief.

She nodded.

Then she walked away, in silence, from the horses. She stood by the bank of a river, a bank cowslipped with fresh excrement. From this I gathered that we were in spring – a season of rebirth, a period of renewal. The flowers were in bloom, the grass moist with tropical rain and the sky was overcast, threatening to pour with rainy vengeance. On the other side of the bank, I could see all sorts of animals and even a child or two and these were living together in total harmony. I couldn't, for the life of me, see how a lion could rub manes with horses without being tempted to tear them savagely apart with his teeth; could not imagine how a group of elderly men were in attentive reverence, listening to a speech being delivered by a young boy of eight; couldn't remember ever seeing (either before or after) how the men of the community paid respectful gallantry to the women upon whose demands and orders they waited. I was visibly delighted.

The girl asked, 'Have you ever seen leaves turn?'

I did not know what answer to give.

'You know,' she said, 'you remind me of another boy I once knew, a boy from Kallafo. You look very much alike, you and he. Or rather, you look like him in a number of ways.'

'For example?'

She said, 'It appears you never bother yourself about looking into the inside of things – and neither did he ever; and you never bother about studying, in detail, the inside of the statements others make – and neither did he ever; you're almost always satisfied with the surface of things – a smooth surface being, to you, a mirror in which your features, your looks, may be reflected, and so you see nothing in mirrors save surfaces.'

The girl reminded me of an old man I once saw sporting a young girl's head. But my tongue, tucked in like a dog's tail between its frightened legs, failed me, and I couldn't tell her of whom she reminded me. A girl with nothing but a shadow to claim as her own, a girl standing in a borrowed skin, and I, who am of flesh and blood, with a heart of my own, a lung, legs, head, eyes and shadow of my own, I who am a child of the age's spirit, I who am, in a sense, a maker of myself, I couldn't tell the girl anything.

'Anyway, come. Follow me,' she ordered.

I said I was thirsty.

'Follow me then,' she repeated; and I did.

She wore the distant look of a magician, trying to conjure up the images he impresses his audience with – and there was a human skull, old as the years of its previous owner. She shook the skull, emptying it of the sand. She then washed it in the stream, washed it until it was white as a priest's robes. We used the skull as a cup. The water was sweet as the season's sweet odour, its taste lingering on the tongue like delightful memories.

'What's your name?' she asked.

'Askar Cali-Xamari,' I said.

She was thrilled at hearing my name. 'So you are originally from Xamar, which, as you will probably know, is the local name for Somalia's capital, Mogadiscio?'

'My father lived there in the forties when all of the Somali-speaking territories were united under one colonial flag, all but one, Djebouti,' I said, hesitating whether to show off my knowledge about the background history to the period, mentioning Ernest Bevin's name and dropping a few others including my source, Armadio. But no. I continued, 'When he returned to the Ogaden, married to a woman from thereabouts, they added the Xamar bit to his name in order to distinguish him from all other Calis.'

She took a sip of water.

'Anyway, all will be well with you,' she prophesied.

I had a sip of the water. I asked, 'How do you know?'

'You're going back to *yourself*,' she opined.

I said, 'And so?'

I could see that she was unhappy at the question. I didn't know how to apologize, although I didn't see why I should. After all, I didn't do anything to offend her. I spoke my mind, adding, 'I ... er ... ,' but couldn't go any further.

'Surface again,' she interrupted. 'No depth, just surface.'

[4]

I resurfaced from the depths of my sleep and woke to shouts of joy announcing we were in Xamar, 'the pearl of the Indian Ocean'. I rubbed the sleep from my eyes and saw, down in the valley, the froth of the sea hug the blue of the sky: magnificent colours, I thought, watching the blue of the heavens and the white of the clouds embrace the blue of the ocean and the white of its foam. I was immensely happy. The man to whom I had been entrusted as his charge until we got to Uncle Hilaal's assured me that he wouldn't leave me before he made certain I was in the right hands. I thanked him profusely.

PART TWO

All is illusion – the words written, the mind at which they are aimed, the truth they are intended to express, the hands that will hold the paper, the eyes that will glance at the lines. Every image floats vaguely in a sea of doubt – and the doubt itself is lost in an unexplored universe of uncertitude.

Joseph Conrad

PART TWO

CHAPTER SEVEN

[1]

Physically, you thought Hilaal was the exact replica of Misra, only he was a man – which, at that point in time, didn't make much difference to you anyway – and older than she. He was better dressed and, you imagined, a great deal more knowledgeable. He was as large as she; he was as fat as she, although the echo of his voice, when he opened his mouth, resounded in your ears long after he had ceased speaking. You had been shown in by the maid who had answered the door. It was she who had led you down a small corridor to meet him. You didn't know why she had hesitated – could it be that she didn't want to disturb him? Or that she suspected he would've shouted at her for allowing you to enter in the first place? She knocked mildly on the door to his study – and you both waited. A minute or so later, he stood in the half-open doorway, as prominent in the landscape of your vision as Misra had been in that of your memory. For a moment, you failed to breathe; for a moment, you didn't know where you were and why; for a moment your tongue lay inert in your mouth and you stared at him in the half-dark, speechless. Half-dark? Yes, because the curtains in his room were drawn; yes, because he had shut out the daylight glare, and the small light which the table-lamp provided had made a soft space in the darkness and had pushed aside the opaqueness all around. Then he struck a matchstick and lit a cigarette; then he took a sip of the drink he had in his hand; and you could hear the ice shake against his glass, you could hear the dripping of a broken tap somewhere else in the house. Could it be that the alternating elemental presence in the form of water and fire decided you would feel at home in Mogadiscio?

Hilaal said, 'Yes?', looking from you to the maid.

She mumbled something you couldn't understand. As if to allow you into the room, he stood aside. His head, when moving, blocked, like a smothering hand, more than half the brightness the table-lamp light had given.

'Come,' he said to you, and you followed him.

He pushed open a door. He said, 'This is your room. That is the bed, and on it are the sheets, the bedspreads, the pillows – and all you need. The room has a wc too. The maid will make the bed, fix you a meal. You can wash, you can sleep, you can do what you please,' and, having said that, he walked away and vanished through the corridor, back into his study. Half a second later, his head emerged and he was saying, 'Welcome, Askar. I will see you later.'

You didn't know what to make of all this. The maid did – and suggested you didn't worry about what had happened, adding, 'He's a very warm person really. Today, he is exceptionally busy because he is giving a talk at the university this evening and is understandably tense.'

The room in which the two of you were standing made a claim on your attention. It was spacious, its floor-tiles Italian and therefore attractive, its walls decorated with lifesize pictures of horses and birds and maps of Africa, of the Horn of Africa – and of Somalia. The room was bright with sunshine, and because the windows had been left unclosed, the furniture was dusty. The bed was larger than the one you used to share with Misra. No wonder you asked yourself whether you had crossed the threshold of the great divide – and when? For not only did you find a frightening physical similarity between Misra and Hilaal, but you imagined your destiny in the hands of another maid, this time one whose name you didn't know and who was herself young and emaciated-looking. Did they have children? And how many? If so where were they? You suspected it was improper, putting questions about these and other matters related to Hilaal's family and life to the maid; the maid who was on her knees, scrubbing the floor clean, dusting the table and chair, making the bed and beating the dust out of the pillowcases before she used them again. Your aimless pacing up and down the room took you to the bathroom, whose tap was dripping. You went to the sink. You placed your open palm under the tap, collecting the water, a little later, in your cupped hand. The water tasted salty.

The maid was saying, 'Do you want to eat or shower first?'

You didn't want to admit to her that you had no clean clothes to change into if you showered, nor did you want her to know that it was the first time you were in a bathroom with showers and sinks and running water and electricity.

'How old are you?' she said.

You lied; you said, 'I am nine.'

'And where are your parents – your mother and father, I mean?' she asked.

You didn't answer her. She understood your silence to mean that they had died in the war and so she didn't push you any further. She changed subjects twice. She was nervous because she was afraid she might have touched a raw nerve, and she offered to do anything: help you shower, prepare for you something to eat, or even wash the shorts and shirt you were in so they would dry by the time you had had your afternoon siesta. Clearly, this was a world you hadn't imagined – a world of grown-ups, of siestas, of bathrooms with showers, sinks and running water; a world within which Hilaal created another world, out of which he refused to surface; a world in which you had lost your sense of direction, for you didn't know your north from your south and couldn't tell where you were in relation to the sea or in relation to where you came from.

She was very active – the maid. 'What do you want me to do?' she asked.

You appeared puzzled, and she said, 'I come thrice a week. It is not that I have the whole day and night. Do you wish that I make something for you to eat or that I make the bed or that I wash your clothes? Come on. Tell me. I have another hour before I go to the afternoon school. I am a student.'

You stood there, not speaking. Apparently, you didn't follow half of what she had just said. Was she a student? And at her age? You remembered one of your paternal uncles, as you left Kallafo, saying that the main purpose of your being sent off to Mogadiscio to your maternal uncle was that you would become a student. You prepared to ask her the age at which people stop studying at school. But she didn't give you time to put the question to her. Then suddenly, she pulled you by the wrist and was unbuttoning your shirt and shorts and saying that she was going to help you shower, get you into bed, wash your clothes which had been dusty from your long travel and put them out in the sun to dry, etc.

You felt abashed; you felt disconcerted; and you started to stammer something – but she didn't give heed to what you were stuttering; didn't bother listening to you. By then your unbuttoned shorts had fallen to your feet; by then you had your arms out of the T-shirt, but you were nearly choked because your head was clumsily caught in the narrowness of its neck. You felt outrageously insulted and you shouted a half-smothered cry of 'Don't do that', a cry which you repeated, and repeated as loudly as you could, until Hilaal was in the room with you asking, 'What's happening here?'

The maid stammered something.

137

You covered your nakedness with your cupped hands, as you saw adults do.

Then the three of you looked up and saw, standing in the door, a woman: Salaado.

[2]

Since we've been going backwards and forwards in time, let's continue doing so. But let us, for a while at any rate, spend some time with you, know how you were when you first came into their lives, arriving – diffident and shy – from a war zone. Your eyes said one thing to them, your silence another. And Hilaal and Salaado decided to wait, placing themselves somewhere between these aspects of yourself (as Hilaal put it), knowing full well that there was another you, which, if appropriately explored and defined, might give them a boy, as intelligent as he was bright, one who was acting, one who was hiding in the safe recesses of silence. They would love him when this emerged, love him as though he were of their own flesh and blood.

Uncle Hilaal pulled at your cheek and teasing you, said, 'Askar, where is *the third*? Where's *the other*?'

You looked about yourself, looked here, looked there and then at the two of them, but remained silent. In the quiet of your daydreams, you asked yourself, '*The third* – who's that?' One, Hilaal. Two, Salaado. Three? What does *the third* mean?

You withdrew from company, you preferred sulking in a quiet corner the first few days. You didn't speak much about Uncle Qorrax, his wives, his children – or how often he beat them; you didn't talk about the compound, of which he was the undisputed headman; nor of the nomads, many of whom were relations of his, and who came to Kallafo on a shopping spree, nomads whom you didn't like much (here are Misra's prejudices) because they tended to bring and leave behind them, as souvenirs, a colony of lice, and your head itched, your body too, if you got anywhere near them. (Is this true, Askar?) Nor did you say much about Misra in those early days following your arrival. You drew a skeletal picture of her. In fact, you offered so thin and so vague a sketch of her that Uncle Hilaal showed little interest in your relationship with her. What was more, you kept your mother's journal as your unshared secret, 'the only one I am left with, the only secret all my own', you said to yourself.

Do you know to what they attributed your silent withdrawals? Or rather how they explained them to each other at night, as you lay asleep, or perhaps dreaming, in a room all your own, all by yourself? 'Such horrors,' had said Hilaal, 'such blood-shedding and such terror in the frightened eyes of hunger and famine – part of young Askar is terribly suffering the loss of the world he has known.' Salaado argued, 'But his eyes say one thing, his silence another,' her head beside Hilaal's, hers pillowless, his on a pillow high as a throne. 'And please don't psychoanalyse us,' she had added.

Silent and withdrawn, yes. But your mind was busy, your tongue active. And you put a distance between yourself and the world. Your mind was busy and your tongue active throughout this period, because you read everything out loud, every bit of writing that came your way, you devoured every printed word you encountered. You read everything out loud so you would hear and not forget what you had read. You were excited in the manner of an Arab who has made a new friend. You were under the hypnosis of a newly found friend – the material you happened to be reading. And Salaado chose tales from *Khaliila wa Dimna* and you read it together, your voice hesitant, hers confident as a trickster's.

Alone in your bed at night, lonely in your room, the first few nights were disheartening. You wished you were allowed to share their room. You were frightened of the dogs that barked in a house not very far away, you wondered if they might jump over your fence and enter your room. Salaado was sufficiently sensitive to have given it a thought. One night, she smuggled a small radio into your room and you slept to its jabbering. The radio was to stay. Did it take Misra's place – Misra, whose voice regulated your sleeping rhythms? Maybe. Anyway, you slept to its jabbering as though it were talking to you and when you awoke in the morning, the large radio was on in the living-room, giving the news bulletin.

They took turns reading to you at night. Uncle Hilaal's favourite was Al-Macarri's *Letter of a Horse and a Mule*; Salaado's was *Khaliila wa Dimna*. You couldn't help comparing them to Misra; you couldn't help deciding that you adored all three. But you wouldn't tell them how you missed Misra. In short, you drew a curtain of silence round yourself. The question was, if this was merely a phase you were going through. 'What if this is all there is?' said Salaado.

'He'll speak,' predicted Hilaal. 'He's just like my sister, his mother.'

*

Then, one day, you gave to Uncle Hilaal your mother's journal. You never said why you had held it as your unshared secret, why you never mentioned you had it to anyone.

And the curtain dropped – there was sunshine and Salaado and Hilaal saw how much vigour you had in you, how active you were behind the artificial veil; and the noise coming from behind the clouds of your quietness was so deafening they were pleased, but at the same time a little apprehensive. You were, as Salaado put it, 'overtures in the human form of friendliness. He is *wonderful*.' Uncle Hilaal read your mother's journal, turning the pages with anxiety. You waited to be told what the gist of your mother's journal was. Instead – a question:

'What was Uncle Qorrax like?' he asked.

You remembered seeing his name occur in the journal a couple of times. Was he important to her? Was he vicious and nasty and wicked to her? You wished someone would tell you. But no one did. 'What was he like?'

'Did Uncle Qorrax abuse my mother's trust?' you asked.

Uncle Hilaal said, 'What makes you say that?'

You remembered the goings-on between him and Misra on the one hand, and Aw-Adan and Misra on the other. But you also sensed that Hilaal's interest in what Qorrax had been like was genuine. 'Did he rape my mother?' you asked. 'Did he want to marry her when news about my father's death came?'

'Go and rest awhile,' suggested Salaado.

'No,' you said and were aggressive.

There was a pause. Then: 'Then tell us what he was like,' said Hilaal.

And you abandoned yourself. You took a moment's breath, you paused, every now and then, as though a gag had suddenly been removed. You were a belated outpouring, you were heavy like overdue rain. And you shook as you spoke. But you spoke and spoke and spoke. What was Uncle Qorrax like? He was terrible, ruthless, a brute and he beat his wives and his children from sunup to sundown. You remembered (it was amazing, you thought, you remembered this – and you congratulated yourself, like an actor who had performed well) that you were fond of him only for a very brief period of time – when you loved his shoes. You gave him what was his due. He knew how to choose his shoes. There was no denying that. They delighted your sense of vision, when, as a crawling infant, you came anywhere near them, during that brief shoe-loving phase that all children go through.

You loved them so much you wanted to put them into your mouth. However, when you outgrew the shoe-loving phase, you began to hate him all the more. You distrusted him – that was it. You had no faith in him. Right from the very instant – you weren't even two days old – when, washed and clean, you were shown to him, you cried. Yes, you said to Uncle Hilaal and Salaado, you cried most furiously. You thought for a while, you reasoned, that you were allergic to his odour. But now you knew why you had nothing but a plethora of contempt for him. Apparently, it was atavistic – something you received in your mother's milk. She hated him.

'How do you know? You haven't read her journal, have you?' Hilaal asked you.

Uncle Hilaal and Salaado watched you as you sifted your ideas and sorted them out. You appeared desperate, like a man upon whom it has just dawned that a future is not possible without his disowned past. Then the river of your emotions flowed again. And you said (Uncle Hilaal will never forget this. Not only that, but he holds the view that you became another *person* speaking it, and that, unbeknownst to yourself these were your mother's precise words), 'The man has made others suffer, his children, his dependents, his wives, yes, he has made every one of them suffer when he himself does not know what the word "suffer" means. It is a tragedy.'

Being excitable, he let his emotions speak for him. Hilaal said, 'Now I see *the third*,' much in the same manner as you might have said, pointing at Misra, 'Here is the earth!' The child in him surfaced and you saw an aspect of him you were to love forever – his kindness. He touched you once, twice, thrice, encouraging you on, like a fan on a cyclist's road to victory slapping the saddle-seat of his idol, shouting joyously, 'Go on. K O!'

You did. You began from the beginning, a second time and a third time. Misra was the heroine of your tale now and you played only a minor supporting role. Which was just as well. You needed to tell 'Misra's story', obviously. A story has to be about someone else even if it is about the one telling it. You talked about your worries, about your inhibitions with regard to other people who mistrusted Misra. You spoke and your features thickened and you were enveloped in the darkness of moonless nights – and you were in her cuddle, you were her third leg or her third breast, and the two of you rolled upon each other in your sleep and each complained about the other who had kicked or taken the sheet away from the other. You were the stare in your eye. You focused it on her guilt. You were the stopper

141

of fights, the beginner of quarrels, of gossip, and it was about you that conversations with Misra easily started. You were most dependent on her. 'She's bewitched him,' people said. They said she fed you all kinds of herbs, that she had taken possession of your soul. 'Look at his eyes,' they said. 'They are wide open even when he is asleep.' Nor did you fail to mention the last breakfast, the one you were filling your empty viscera with when you left Kallafo.

You came to Aw-Adan. He was your teacher, you explained, and your rival for Misra's attentions. He invested his hate in his forearm when he caned you. She beat you only when she was in season. Then you became the charge of a kindly woman called Karin. A dream of a woman. 'Did you know,' you asked rhetorically, 'that when women miss their periods, they're not always pregnant?' Karin had gone past the age of having them. And when once Misra missed hers, they inserted herbs and things into her – to abort. But you took care not to mention anything about Misra's divining powers or the materials she used – water, blood or raw meat. You were worried this might impress Hilaal and Salaado wrongly. You wanted them to love her. When you finished, there was a long, long, long silence. Salaado then said, 'For you, life has been a war of sorts.'

And Hilaal, hugging you, said, 'We're in each other's life now. No more wars. We're a family. The three of us.'

That night, they talked it over and decided they would tell you their story, in the honesty and open-heartedness with which you had narrated yours. 'It is only fair,' said Salaado.

However, the telling of their story didn't take place until a month later. In the meantime, they had got a tutor by the name of Cusmaan to help you with your studies, specially your reading of maps. It was Hilaal who told it to you, the two of you alone in the car, he in the passenger's seat and you in the back. He told it naturally, as one might talk of one of those once-in-a-lifetime diseases one has had ages ago. He said, 'We owe you an explanation, Askar.'

It was Friday. The car in which you were sitting was parked in front of the Lido Club. Salaado had gone into the club to buy three ice-cream cones. It was late afternoon and you had spent the greater part of the afternoon swimming or sitting by the sea. You were slightly exhausted, your head was full of sea-water, your hair of unwashed sand.

'We owe you an explanation,' he repeated, and in silence the two of you watched birds perform their acrobatics exhibitionistically. You envied them their agility. He went on, 'For example,' grinningly looking over his left shoulder to talk to you in the back seat of the car. You thought his 'For example' had something complete about it. It seemed you didn't expect him to say anything after that. Then, like parents who've adopted children past a certain age, Hilaal's preliminaries contained such assurances as were needed to ensure that the child understands he is loved as though he were of their own blood and flesh. There was no need for him to say all that – you knew it and it was very obvious to you. Then he said, 'I don't like driving, for example. Salaado loves it. I drive only reluctantly. I hope you've noticed that.'

'Yes, I have.'

He wound up the window on his side of the car, shutting out the noise of the hawkers selling things or beggars asking for alms or displaying their physical disasters: an amputated arm, a sick baby at a milkless breast. Again, he began talking, but was waylaid by his 'For example' like one who has run into a friend who's asked one to take a drink and chat for a while. Uncle Hilaal shifted about in his seat, he looked ahead of himself in absent-minded concentration, looked at a noisy bunch of boys playing rough football. Then, 'I love cooking, for example. Salaado doesn't. Not only that. But she is a terrible cook. And she burns the bottom of pots, saucepans and the food in them; the water she boils vapours into thin air because she doesn't remember she has something on the stove. What she does, at times, is to over-indulge her rice with water so you have rice-porridge or something similar. Disaster after disaster. But I love cooking.'

You grew impatient because you didn't know where his dialogue was leading you, and wound down the window on your side of the car. The place was apparently overflowing with human chatter. You wound it up immediately as beggars and hawkers descended on you. That way you shut out the whole world except Hilaal's erratic breathing and his 'For example'. When you looked in his direction, you felt lost in the open space his crooked elbow had made, an elbow which, when he was gesticulating to make a point, was somehow arrested in mid-movement. Then, 'We have no children, Salaado and I,' he said. 'Or rather, we didn't have any before you joined us. That's right. We're not bothered by the fact that we didn't have any of our own. We love each other the way we are. The trouble is, others talk, they say terrible things about a woman who can't have children. There were complications. And Salaado had to undergo a serious operation in Europe. It was most painful and she suffered greatly. For example.'

You thought, they've probably arranged the moment in such a way Salaado will not return until he's finished saying whatever he is intending to say to me. He went on. Without 'for example' this time.

'A most obligatory, painful operation for Salaado. You probably won't know what ovaries are. That's what the doctors removed. When our relations on our side learnt that she cannot have children for me, they came and suggested I take another wife. No, I said. But they insisted. Still no, I said. Then I decided to have an operation called vasectomy. It renders men sterile but is not very painful. Anyway, I figured this country is over-populated – why have children?' He paused as though this might lessen the touch of anxiety in his voice. And, 'Anyway, she cannot have children, nor can I. Her operation was necessary. Mine was done because I chose to. But we have you now and we have no need for babies of our own flesh and blood. It's all very simple, no?' He paused, the upper part of his body rising a little higher, as if he were half-lifting his weight off the seat. You thought it was the way he spoke the question which suggested this, in particular the lifting of the final 'no'.

When he spoke next, he sounded as if his full weight were firmly on the seat. He said, 'It's not all that simple, to be truthful. Society doesn't approve of a man who loves a woman who doesn't bear him children, a woman who doesn't cook his food, mind his home, wash his underthings. A woman who sits behind the wheel of a car driving when the man is a passenger – to our society, this is unpardonable. It is sex, sooner or later. And there are the hierarchies which escort the notion of sex. Now ... for example. This is why you don't see many people coming to, and going away from, our house. My relations have boycotted me on account of my obstinate position. So, whenever you see someone visit us, you can be sure this person is either a good friend of ours or a relation of Salaado's.'

A cavalcade of ideas raced through your head the moment he fell silent. You wished to say that you actually loved them greatly. But Salaado saved the situation – she appeared and stood by your side of the car, holding out to you your cone of vanilla. You drove in bewitched silence.

[3]

You liked Salaado immensely, directly you saw her. You felt comfortable with the space around her and you followed her to places, your body close to hers. 'He is the egret, and Salaado the cattle,' a neighbour had commented. You had your trust in her. Often, you held on to her little finger. You sat at her feet as she told you a story. You touched the hem of her dress and, at times, to the amusement of Uncle Hilaal, you felt its silky smoothness against your cheeks. She became the only teacher you were willing to learn from, hers was the company you preferred to everyone else's. And she taught you, in a record two days, how to write your name in Somali, how to identify many of the sounds you made and how to write them down. All this time, however, Hilaal remained significantly on the periphery of your life. He cooked the meals, washed up and dried the dishes and put them away in their appropriate places; he pressed his own shirts and trousers, and helped you get used to becoming independent. At first, the reversal of male and female roles upset you a little, but you accepted them, in the end, and were all the happier because you felt as though you were a member of a unique set-up. You didn't know any two people to contrast them with, didn't know of any household as outstanding as the one destiny had driven you to, didn't know how fortunate you had been. You merely sensed they were heads above most men and most women.

She was beautiful. And she dressed well. She was tall and slim and wore no make-up. In you, she raised whirlwinds of a different kind – different from the one Misra used to draw out of you. Salaado made you work harder at being yourself. She would give you a map so you could identify where you were born and would insist that you saw yourself in that context – a young boy from the Ogaden, one whose world was in turmoil. And so, nailed next to the map which indicated where you were born, there was a calendar. There, if you wished, you could follow the progress of the war in the Ogaden. Nailed next to the calendar, there was a mirror. Here, you could register your bodily changes, see how much taller you were or fatter or whether you were losing weight by the day. Salaado was indubitably the most beautiful woman you had ever seen and you wished she were your mother, or that you could think of her or address her as one. In preference to calling her 'Aunt', you chose to refer to her as 'Teacher'. Which she was professionally. For she would leave home at about seven in the morning, she would drive herself in the car, parked at night in the car-shelter, and wouldn't return on most days until after four p.m. While she was away, you were supposed to study what she had assigned so you would not waste an academic year's worth doing nothing. If you had queries, you would knock at Uncle Hilaal's study, and he would grudgingly give you time and answer your questions. Otherwise, you could go and play with the children next door – although you didn't like their ideas about games that might entertain one. In the end, it was decided, since you preferred your solitary existence to their 'infantile' company, Uncle Hilaal would buy you a bicycle all your own. Again, it was Salaado who taught you how to keep balance while learning to ride it. Wonderful Salaado!

Uncle Hilaal was equally kind, when with you. His was a voice with a long reach – like a hand. You were always amazed at how comforting it was to listen to it; and, like a hand, it patted you on the head or the shoulders; it lifted you out of your dormant spirit when you were that way inclined. At its command, you would get up, eat the food you were about to push away; in short, you would do anything it ordered you to. As a result, his voice was always there, present in the back of your thoughts, a voice reassuring when your spirits were down, a censuring voice when they were wild and out of control; it was a voice from whose depth, as though it were a well, you could draw bucketfuls of sustenance. And you went to bed with its resonance echoing in your ears; you awoke, listening to the rise and fall of its music. When he was not there, the walls of your memory re-echoed its hypnotic quality, so much so that it assumed a life of its own, a life inseparable from your uncle's.

One day, when she was busy with marking examination papers, you asked Salaado to explain something to you. She was gentle, as usual, but said she was otherwise occupied and suggested you ask Uncle to teach you for that and the following two days.

'It is his voice,' you said.

She didn't quite understand. 'How do you mean? What is it about his voice that you don't like? Or does he frighten you? Tell me.'

You noted one thing in your brain – the fact that she didn't address you as Misra used to, didn't clothe her speeches with endearments, and yet you did not feel distanced from her, ever. Also, for whatever it was worth, you noted something else in your mind – the fact that *you* took a back seat, allowing others to take life's seats of prominence. You were not, in other words, the only one who existed, you were not the one around whom the sun, the moon, the stars, in short, the world, revolved.

'Answer me, Askar. What's it about Hilaal's voice that bothers you?' she said, holding your hands gently in hers.

You said, 'It does not allow me to concentrate on what he is saying.'

'I still do not understand,' she said.

You tried to express yourself better, but realized that you hadn't the courage to speak the thoughts which crossed your mind. It was years later that you told Salaado that, 'Just as the beauty of the world fades when compared with yours, all other voices and life's preoccupations are rendered inexistent when he speaks. His bodied voice appears before me as though it were another person. Looking at him, I find I cannot also concentrate what *the other*, i.e. the voice, is saying. Are you with me?'

'Yes,' she nodded, her voice almost failing her.

[4]

Nowadays, you can afford to laugh at the thought of yourself resisting the temptation to pull at Uncle Hilaal's nose – pull at it and squeeze it teasingly, as one might a cute baby's cheeks – since you always believed he had a nose small as an infant's fist with his fat face, very much like a child's. You suspected it was his voice which held you at bay, his voice which held you at arm's distance, his voice which was strong, almost baritone, varying in levels as it did in registers and which you stored away in the depository of your memory so you could make use of it in old age and remember what he said to you, as much as to anyone else – a voice which you could replay as often as you pleased.

Of course, you cannot put dates to events, nor can you recall precisely when Uncle Hilaal said it and to whom. Possibly, it was when the Somalis were still victorious and the 'Ethiopians' were in total disarray, fleeing 'homewards' and leaving behind them cities which were intact; when her infantry escaped, leaving behind unused cartridges of ammunition. And you think it was then that he said, 'The point is, who's an Ethiopian?'

Now what made you repeat to yourself the rhetorical question, 'The point is, who's an Ethiopian?' Weren't you repeating it to yourself because in those days it gave you immense pleasure to mimic Uncle Hilaal's voice? Salaado happened to be standing near by. You know how adults like answering children's questions? For although your question wasn't addressed to anybody in particular, Salaado answered it. You weren't displeased, but you were startled. Politely, you listened to her talk as she pointed out the difference between the country which Menelik named Ethiopia – meaning in Greek 'a person with a black face' (Salaado suspected it was a foreigner who named it Ethiopia) – and that which had been his power base until his army's occupation of the southern territories at the turn of the century. You were attentive and learning a great deal from Salaado when Uncle Hilaal joined you. He listened for a while before making his contribution.

Hilaal said, 'Ethiopia is the generic name of an unclassified mass of different peoples, professing different religions, claiming to have descended from different ancestors. Therefore, "Ethiopia" becomes that generic notion, expansive, inclusive. Somali, if we come to it, is specific. That is, you are either a Somali or you aren't. Not so with "Ethiopian", or for that matter not so with "Nigerian", "Kenyan", "Sudanese" or "Zaïroise". The name "Ethiopia" means the land of the dark race.'

'And Abyssinia?' asked (you think) Salaado.

Uncle Hilaal, disregarding the question, continued, 'Did you know that Zaïre is the Portuguese word for river – which was perhaps how a Portuguese traveller named the country he happened to have been in – although there's nothing "authentically national" about it, as Sesse Seko would have us believe. "Nigeria", did you know, was named such by Lugard's mistress, again after the river Niger, and Sudan after the Blacks whose country it is. Somalia is unique. It is named after Somalis, who share a common ancestor and who speak the same language – Somali.'

'I said, what about Abyssinia?' asked Salaado with a certain anxiety.

He said, 'Abyssinia, too, is a generic name, coming, as it does, from the Arabic word "Xabasha" – meaning Negro. Again, the country assumes a generic name – not specific. Before it became an empire, when it was but a small kingdom, it was called Abyssinia; later, when it expanded and became an empire, Ethiopia. Both names have generic qualities about them.'

'Now what are we to learn from these concepts? And what do they mean in terms of the war in the Horn?' she asked.

He thought for a long time. Then: 'What is at war are the generic and the specific as concepts – the Soviet Union, the USA, the African countries who are members of the OAU support the generic as opposed to the specific. Obviously, they themselves belong to the generic kind.'

'But the specific is winning the war?' she put in.

He predicted, 'Only temporarily.'

'How do you mean?'

Again he thought for a long time.

'The generification of Africa is a concept which the Ethiopian and other African governments whose peoples belong to different ethnic groupings and sources use, whenever it is challenged by secessionists and ethnic minorities living in their expansionist and inclusive boundaries. Only in logical propriety do Somalis win their case – the Somali, as a people, divided into two British Somalilands (one of them independent and now forming part of the Republic, the other at present known as Kenyan Somaliland); French Somaliland; Italian Somaliland (forming part of the present-day Republic – democratic or not!) and former French Somaliland (now the Republic of Djebouti). The Somali-speaking peoples have a case in wanting to form a state of their own nation . . . but . . . !' and, shrugging his shoulders, he fell silent.

'But what?' she wanted to know.

He smiled. 'That's it precisely.'

Tense, she said, 'But what?'

'It is the "but" which introduces an element of the uniqueness of the Somali case, as well as the generally accepted fear that if Somalis were allowed to get what they are after, then the Biafrans will want to try it again, the Masai will want their own republic, and the people of southern Sudan their own "generic" state. What escapes detractors of the great national dream is that Somalis have fought and will fight for the realization of their nationalist goals, but that the Masai haven't and aren't likely to; and that Somalis aren't the only ethnic minority in Ethiopia who are displeased with their low status in the Amharic-speaking people's Empire; or that the Somalis in Kenya, in the only British-held referendum, voted phenomenally highly, as a people deciding to be part, not of Kenya, but of the Republic. It is the "but" which stands in the way of the Somali.'

Naturally, you cannot imagine yourself pulling at the nose of someone whose life was an embodiment of ideas; whose voice was immensely larger than any mansion you had ever seen; and who lived in the contradictory roles of 'Mother' to you and Salaado. Didn't you both rest your heads drowsily on his chest? Misra, in her limited way, taught you to separate the body from the soul; Salaado, the person from the personable; and Uncle Hilaal helped you home in on *the other*.

Now, do you remember when you asked, 'But what do you do,

Uncle, locked up in your study, day in day out?' Do you remember what answer you got – and if you were at all satisfied with it?

[5]

Your uncle's study faced east and, in the mornings, when you looked out of the window, the sun's brightness blinded you, and when you looked inside, you saw nothing but books, some heavy, some light to carry, some with pictures and some without. At any given time, there were a number of them open and he consulted them with concentration. You learnt, much later, that he had been researching into the psychological disturbances the war had caused in the lives of children and women. He never appeared keen on asking you questions. He knew you would speak, sooner or later; that you would tell him the dreams which had left impressions on your growing self; that you would, eventually, if given the chance to express yourself, enable him to put together his findings into the appropriate research categories he had been working on. Very patiently, he listened to you talk about Misra, hardly interrupting you, at times taking notes and at times not.

One day, together in his study, when he was explaining to you something about the deliberate distortion of the sizes of the continents (a distortion which made an essential difference to the size of Europe and Africa), you surprised him, and yourself too, by shouting, 'Look, look!'

Uncle Hilaal saw a woman, visibly pregnant, chewing at something. 'She's eating earth,' you said. 'Just like I used to.'

He failed to make you see the difference between the 'earth' you used to eat mouthfuls of, and the cakes of clay which pregnant women nibble on. You turned on him and, with a suddenness which made him half laugh, you said, 'The reason why the continent of Africa is smaller is because the adult, as well as the small among us, eat its earth – which obviously makes it shrink in size. Could that be it?'

Again, with the patience worthy of a scholar addressing a potentially very intelligent pupil, Uncle Hilaal explained the reasons to you, giving you the political implications as well as the imperialist intentions of the cartographers. He was still on the subject when the tumult of excitement took you over and you were bubbling with enthralment.

Apparently, there was another revelation you wished to make. And he let you.

'Uncle, do you know what I did once?' you asked, pulling at his chin.

He said, 'Tell me.'

'I menstruated.'

He was crestfallen.

'I menstruated one night when I was asleep. Just like women do. Just like Misra used to. I could put the difference between my menstruation and a woman's to the fact that I felt no pain whatsoever before or after; and that it happened to me only once.'

In total disbelief, 'Only once?'

'Although, now and again, I have a strange feeling that there is *another* in me, one older than I – a woman. I have the conscious feeling of being spoken through, if you know what I mean. I feel as if I have allowed a woman older than I to live inside of me, and I speak not my words, my ideas, but hers. And during the time I'm spoken through, as it were, I am she – not I. And it pains to part with someone you've allowed to dwell inside of you, because they have no life of their own, because they died young or some unforeseen disaster has cut their life short. In a way, there is a faint sense of unease in that I feel as if my mother's death was my birth, or, if you prefer, her death gave birth to me.'

Your uncle got up from his chair and silently stood behind the window. Something claimed his attention and he moved away from you, disregarding all your attempts at reaching him. Until you started saying, 'I've never seen the woman of whom I speak thus, except once, and even then, I saw the back of her neck and no more. Although that has a striking similarity to the half-profiled photograph of the woman you say was my mother.'

He moved nervously about the room. 'How old are you?' he asked.

'Eight.'

He now had the look of one who had let go a whole universe's worth and more. He gathered his notes and let the pile lie under his hand as he thought what his next move was going to be. He opened a drawer and brought out a matchbox.

'Do you want to come with me to the garden?' he said to you.

'What are we going to do there?' you said.

He picked up the pile of papers he had gathered, saying, 'We're going to make a fire. You like fires, don't you?'

'I do,' you confessed.

He said, 'Well, let's make one then. What're you waiting for?'

And he burnt all his research papers and later said to Salaado that talking to you had made him unmistakably aware that he had been moving in the wrong direction all along. 'Wars,' he said, 'are rivers that burn.'

[6]

Who is to say whether you remembered hearing someone else speak the same words, 'Wars are rivers that burn' before?; who is to say if you registered the hesitation and dismay on Uncle Hilaal's face that day as he burnt a year's work?; that it was he who dwelled in a territory of pain, lying vertical, saying something peculiarly irrational: 'As long as I lie in bed, I don't think, can't think any thoughts, can't be bothered with thoughts any more'? Who is to say if you made the right inferences from various things which took place following the revelations?; who is to say if you *now* remember any of the stories told about your mother – Hilaal's younger sister? At no time were you aware of births and deaths as much as you became then. Possibly, it was then (or as a result of it?) that Uncle Hilaal told you why Salaado and he didn't have any children.

'To think that the one you love most will suffer pain after interminable pain in order to have a dead child! This was why we had to do something. Every time she would carry it for seven months or so, then the most painful labours and then she would emit a dead child, half in blood, a flood of blood really. It happened a number of times and we hoped, every time, not for death but birth and prayed and prayed and prayed; and sought out the best doctors. Finally, it had to occur. One of her ovaries had to be removed. That did it for me. My beautiful wife had suffered, I said. I too must. So I took myself off to the hospital. And had a vasectomy done. If she couldn't – well, so I too couldn't. But we love each other.'

Perhaps this was said much later – when you were already grown up, when you didn't have to look up the word 'vasectomy' in the dictionary, since you would agree there is no Somali word for that kind of operation. No? You will doubtless remember that Misra had had a breast removed – or rather that Uncle Hilaal said he had been told so. Maybe it was then that you made a most regrettable remark – something to do with Misra and Salaado's swapping bodies – and

152

if only this were possible, you were supposed to have said, then a child would have had a living mother with no organ partly mutilated or half removed! You don't remember any of this exchange either? No? What do you remember then?

It is understandable that you confuse dates, and that you cannot say precisely when the conversation centred on maimed bodies, amputated hands or removed organs. There was a great deal of talk in the press about these and related subjects in order to point accusatory fingers at the enemy who was a 'cannibal and most inhumane'. The newspapers carried photographs of maimed bodies; the same newspapers carried articles about an Islamic leader whose adherence to Islamic justice resulted in his insisting they cut off the arms of a man who had stolen a small item from a supermarket; the same newspapers carried pieces on ritual murder taking place in Nigeria where they were said to remove certain organs on a medicine-man's recommendation, if one wanted to win a seat at the Federal Assembly. You knew in person, and saw with your eyes, people who had lost a leg in the war; or an eye; or a son; or a daughter. Things that had been remote were brought nearer when talked about again and again until you could bring yourself to feeling, with the tip of your fingers, the dead nerve that had been cut in order to save a hand. No wonder, then, that you couldn't be certain when exactly your uncle spoke of his or Salaado's respective losses of parts of their bodies.

You listened to stories told of men who survived the fire of the enemy, by heroically walking, without blinking an eyelash, to get to where they wanted – the men who liberated towns like Jigjiga. You listened to others showing off about the medals of bullets which went through their shins, narrowly missing the bone, through their foreheads (you couldn't imagine anyone would live after that – but some did) or breaking the nose-bridge. You listened to stories about the penis of one dead soldier being stuck between the teeth of his living comrade who was to be shot (if both sides were so barbaric was there any point in telling the stories at all?). You heard stories of raped women; of pregnant women emptied of their as-yet-unborn issues. You wondered, as all these stories were being told, if the men had the necessary time to say a small prayer or two before the bullet struck them; or if they washed – that is, if they performed their ablutions before death hit them. Didn't Salaado always insist that you put on your cleanest underwear if you were being taken to see the doctor about something which made it a must that you undressed? In other words, did these men encounter death and then God, their creator, cleaner than the day they were born? Every one of these men, you were told, was a martyr whose soul would forever sit in the company of saints, prophets and Allah; every one of these raped women would avenge themselves in whichever way they liked; and every one of these children would be re-born all the wiser, happier – re-born to live longer.

Stories with fragmented bodies!

Bodies which told fragmented stories!

Tales about broken hearts and fractured souls!

In the end, who is to say, but you, what you wish to relegate to an unremembered past?; who is to say if a couple of paintings by naïve artists Hilaal introduced you to, when you showed interest in drawing, tug at the nerves of your memories?; who is to say if Picasso's *Guernica*, again shown to you by Hilaal, did the expected thing – remind you that wars are rivers that burn, rivers whose waters, rough as crags, distort reality? Yes, who is to say, but you, if you can actually be as precise as a compass's needle pointing its forehead in a northerly direction towards the pivot of repeatable exactnesses? Who but you?

CHAPTER EIGHT

[1]

Misra was in my thoughts a lot of the time during the early months. The war had been on then and the Somalis were winning it on the ground at least and I started talking of visiting Kallafo – meaning I was going to visit Misra. I even began writing letters to her, letters in which I told her of my intended visit. I doubted if she could've read them because she didn't read Somali orthography. Perhaps somebody would've helped her to. I never finished writing these letters. We spent a great deal of the time by the radio, listening to the latest news from the war front, listening to the conflicting reports coming from the Battle for Harar and Dire Dawa. We were proud and happy the Somalis were pushing on.

Then, one Wednesday, I came home with high fever. By Thursday morning, I was taken to see a doctor. On Friday, the doctor's diagnosis – malaria. I was dizzy most of the time, unable to raise my head. I resided in a land of dolorous mist, my body-temperature extraordinarily high, my lips dry as wood, my mouth red as though it were a fresh wound. I didn't know night from day, couldn't tell who was there and who wasn't and couldn't be bothered to eat. Every time I was helped to walk to the lavatory, I felt the earth tremble, I sensed my legs wobble. In point of fact, I could've sworn the earth had been shaking under my feet and wondered why no one else commented on it.

Anyway, that weekend entered the annals of Somali history as The Tragic Weekend. In it, the Soviet, Cuban and Adenese generals (with a little help from the Ethiopians) masterminded the decisive blow which returned the destiny of the Ogaden and its people to Ethiopian hands. And imagine, I was ill and in bed when this happened. While the nation mourned, I lay unconscious in a swamp of my own fever, my own rubble, my own stubble. Transported across mirages by the burning heat of my own blood, I discovered sheets were too hot to come anywhere near me, the mattress not level enough to keep my aching body in firm position. I asked for impossible things, I demanded that miracles be performed. These included studying the possibility of replacing my skin, because it was too hot, with another – cooler.

When the nation mourned the loss of the Ogaden, I was preoccupied with the state of my health, my body, my skin. I will never forget that.

I was the last to hear of the loss. By then, there was no point in crying over spilt milk. 'One has to be strong enough to accept defeat. But we'll return in maybe ten, maybe twenty years and put back the Ogaden where it belongs – in Somali hands.' I said this as I fed my then undernourished, frail body with the food Uncle Hilaal had prepared for me. Propped up against the wall supporting my back, with a spoon in my hand, my knees trembling under the sheets, I asked, 'What next? What do you think will happen now?'

He predicted, 'An influx of refugees. That's what defeat will mean.'

My expression told him that I didn't follow his argument. Whereupon, he remarked that if the Somalis had won the war, there wouldn't have been 'Somali' refugees, but Ethiopian refugees. In any case, he went on, for-exampling his way to the nerve of the matter, since Ethiopia had only military garrisons and no civilian population in the Ogaden (in Kallafo, there may have been a couple of hundred women who provided one service or another to the military garrison on the hill – and many never crossed the bridge separating the Ethiopians' side of the river from the civilian Somali population), yes, if the Ethiopians had lost the war, the men who fell into Somali hands would have become prisoners-of-war and not refugees.

'And if I hadn't come as early as I had done, if I hadn't come until after the Ogaden was reconquered by the generals from the Soviet, Cuban and Adenese armies – what then?'

'Every ethnic Somali is entitled to live in the Somali Republic. They may belong to any Somali-speaking territory, be it Kenyan, Ethiopian or even Djebouti. Every Somali has the constitutional birthright to reside anywhere in the Republic. The status of who *is* a refugee, however, points two fingers at two parallel issues – political and economic. If a Somali in Ethiopia or Kenya or Djebouti fears for his life, that Somali has the status of a political refugee, but doesn't need to declare himself as such unless he is in no position to look for and obtain a job and live practising his profession. If, however, the Somali from outside the Republic is not economically self-sufficient, or if his relations aren't well-off enough to support him, then they might declare themselves as "refugees". It is estimated that more than a third of the registered population in the Republic came over from the Ogaden or Djebouti long before the 1977 war. Many have joined the army. They form a large percentage of the soldiery as well as the officer corps. Many have joined schools and the university here, or the civil service or the government in one capacity or another, some holding very highly placed jobs as ministers, director-generals or else they have been recruited into the diplomatic corps.'

'And what will happen to those who do not flee the Ogaden?'

'For example, the Ethiopians poison their wells, rape their women and conscript their children into the Ethiopian army or the police force. They compel them to learn Amharic, force them to adopt the "Amharic" culture and dispossess them of their land.'

There was a pause. I took mouthfuls of the minestrone Uncle had dished out for me, having added salt, pepper and lime. He sat on the edge of the bed, his back unsupported, and I suspected the strain was affecting his lumbago. He touched his spine as though it were cold and he were rubbing blood into its circulatory system.

I asked, 'Are there any parallel situations you can think of anywhere?'

'How do you mean?' he said.

'Can you think of any other country where a person born in another may assume its nationality on the strength of ethnic origin?' I asked.

'Yes. An ethnic German is, by right, a national of the Federal Republic of Germany. Anyone born in East Germany after its creation is also a *bona fide* national of West Germany.'

He looked exhausted – and talked tiredly too – becoming long-winded as he spoke. I wondered if it was pain in his back causing strain on his nerves. I suggested he sit on a proper chair. He did. I? I felt weak – almost as weak as Misra when she aborted. I remembered her lying in bed for days. The loss of the Ogaden was greater, of course. But I could only view it as a personal loss so as to understand its dimensions. It was as if my whole blood had been drained out of me – that was how weak I felt. To me, that was how tremendous the loss had been.

'But they're not coming here, are they?' I said.

'They? They who?'

'The Ethiopians? They're not coming to Mogadiscio?' I said.

Uncle Hilaal reflected for a while, then, 'Menelik, the Emperor that gave the country its name, once claimed the boundaries of his country to include the whole of Somalia, parts of present-day Tanzania, a greater part of Kenya and Uganda including Lake Victoria and parts of the Sudan up to and including Khartoum because he was wanting to claim the Nile. He was after a littoral territory for a landlocked Abyssinia. Emperor Haile Selassie made similar access-to-the-sea claims as recently as 1953. In the end, Haile Selassie gave up his claim because Eritrea, which has access to the sea, was *given* him by the United Nations to administer. He annexed Eritrea.'

I said, 'We won't allow it. Mogadiscio is ours.'

'We won't,' he said. 'Now eat.'

After a pause, I said, 'I like Mogadiscio a lot.'

I accepted Mogadiscio as a provisional measure, loving its sandy beaches, swimming in its sea, disliking its mid-day heat but liking its enormous spaces and its reddish-brown earth in which my ideas flowered. It was understood that, come one day, I would leave it but perhaps to love it more. *I had a job to do*, as Armadio used to say. I had a home to return to and re-liberate, a mother to be reunited with. 'But before you leave . . . ,' I can hear Uncle Hilaal say; 'But before you leave us,' I can hear Salaado begin – I know! I knew I would've had to study harder, put in more hours of study, read more than the boys or the girls who didn't have the same sort of responsibilities as I, who didn't have a job to do, as I. I would sit with Hilaal or Salaado and things would be explained to me in great illustrated detail. Maps were shown to me; the psychology of warfare; why the Cubans dared not enter directly into war with the South African army in Angola; why they withdrew whenever the army of apartheid made belligerent incursions into the country in which twenty thousand of their soldiers were stationed. In the company of Salaado and Hilaal, the universe altered perspective, it shrunk into a tiny chessboard where the Africans weren't the kings, the queens, the bishops and not even the pawns – where we were part of the reserve; our land was nothing but a playfield; our wars were turned into weekend affairs, during which the Russians borrowed a West-German-manufactured tank code-named *Leopard* and sold it to Libya. The idea was to test if this sophisticated article of German warfare would stand the conditions and climate of the Ogaden. After the weekend job, *Leopard* was flown to Odessa and dismantled, western intelligence reports were quoted by Reuter and other agencies. A rat race faster than the arms race – and we're starving!

Mogadiscio – whose sand was white as the smoke of a fire just built. Mogadiscio – the most ancient city south of the Sahara, a city bombed by the Portuguese, looted by the Arabs, colonized by the Ottoman Turks, subdued by the Italians and bought, at the turn of the century, by a Zanzibari who paid for it a little more than Bombay had cost Britain or Haarlem the Dutch. The Sultan of Zanzibar sublet the territory to the Italians. I love its centre which sports a multiracial, multicultural heritage. I love it because it doesn't make me feel small looking up at very tall skyscrapers.

Mogadiscio – a place with dry laundry. This was how I saw it when I first entered it. I saw flags of clean clothes on washing-lines outside people's homes and in their courtyards. I saw flags of them waving welcoming messages to a frightened boy, me. And the first two things I noticed when I entered what became 'home' – shoes on a rack in the corridor and mirrors, many mirrors on the walls. It was explained to me later that Uncle Hilaal has to own many pairs because he walks a lot and his feet wear them out faster than anyone anybody has seen. His shoelaces break, the heels come off, he discards most pairs in a month, maximum two, Salaado had said. I noticed they were not of the best quality – not half as good as Uncle Qorrax's, I decided.

What else did I notice when I first got here? That it takes longer to become a grown-up person. It takes years before one is readily convinced that one is to acquire a wife if you are a man, or a husband if you are a woman. I remembered many girls getting married before their fifteenth birthday, and many boys before they were twenty. Not so in Mogadiscio. And girls and boys didn't look forward to getting married and having children, no. They dreamt of going abroad. Was it the smell of the sea that put this into their heads? Or the aromas of foreign foods in the air, foods suggesting other worlds, other cultures – Indian, Persian, Arab, Italian, Egyptian. In Mogadiscio, I thought I could read in people's faces the wish of remaining young and beautiful and slim forever, and middle-aged men and middle-aged women behaved as though they were in their early twenties.

No river rises in Mogadiscio, the sea does. It begins here, the sea. It feels as if it does. Blue as it is on the map in front of me, the sea is veined with noble waves, as alive as they are deadly; it is veined with tides which give one the time of day or night, tides which tell one if it is full moon or half moon. The sea has its drifts, moods and deceits; it gives gifts, it robs one of life, shows one where one's weaknesses are and the body where its pores are. The sea is the skirt the ships-with-goods wear, it is the necklace the gold lovers put on, it is the untaxed merchandise the smuggler brings into the land. The sea is a map: it tells those who are literate in its language where they are, it reveals, to those who are able to uncover secrets, where the treasures are. Haven't all the *daters* employed it, as they employed their intelligence and their map-reading facilities, their writing capabilities – haven't they crossed it to conquer, to subjugate, to colonize? 'Somalia's misfortune,' Uncle Hilaal once suggested, 'is that the "two colonizing powers" – I use this inadequate phrase for lack of a better one – who stand in the way of the Ogaden, join the Republic. Yes, these two "nations" are themselves non-European and neither has crossed oceans. Both are Somalia's neighbours. In other words, it is easier ridding yourself of a colonialist from beyond the seas than it is to oust an African one. Western Sahara is finding it tough going; Eritrea, in a very similar position, finds itself isolated and often friendless. Namibia is different. Whether we like it or not, the question of colour plays a significant role in today's politics – and Namibia has the advantage of being colonized, if that's the right word, by a "power" from beyond the seas.'

Mogadiscio! Salaado once asked Hilaal, 'What's it about Mogadiscio that seduces the visitor? Why, no one leaves it once they come.'

Uncle Hilaal explained the nature of neo-colonial governments and how these develop a couple of cities, leaving the hinterland to its own disastrous destiny.

'Yes, yes, but why?'

'Cities with obscure histories have no charming qualities about them. Mogadiscio's history is illumined like a manuscript. There are historical monuments that date from the ninth century; there are mosques, tombs which mark with bones the histories they illustrate. Maybe these keep them here?'

Mogadiscio – for me, you are a temporary haven. I will leave you but will always love you.

As predicted, Mogadiscio's seams broke with the influx of refugees a few months later. You couldn't go anywhere without seeing them in the streets, dusty and famished-looking as the earth they left behind. Those who had relations wealthy enough to put them up and feed them did so discreetly. But many had no one to go to. Or had relations who themselves couldn't manage on the little they had, considering the inflationary prices the war had brought about, for it was a very expensive war, claiming lots of lives and properties. After the war, the Somali shilling had to be devalued. Everything, except hunger, corruption and poverty, became scarce. People began to be unkind to one another and kindness became one of those rare commodities. Generosity met the same fate and was fed on by suspicion everyone harboured for everyone else. We, too, had numerous relations who came to stay for a while. Uncle Hilaal and Salaado filled their bellies with food and their fists with travel money and hoped they went on their own journeys of exploration. Some of these eventually added their names and histories to the statistics and headaches of UN-run relief agencies.

Then two things happened, more or less simultaneously. I cannot remember which took place first. Uncle Hilaal reported that his friend at the *Anagrafo del Municipio* – where every Somali national who is at school, seeking employ or wishes to join the civil service is registered – said the Mayor had signed my papers. These papers identified me as a dependant of Uncle Hilaal and Salaado. Also, I think it was during the same week, or maybe a couple of days earlier or later, that Salaado brought home the news that she had found Cusmaan. I am not sure about the dates. Cusmaan was a relation of hers and was a student at the National University of Somalia in an area related to sociolinguistics. If I remember correctly, his long essay was titled something like, 'The *Mispronouncing* of Non-native Speakers of Somali'. Although the title might or could've been 'The Misgendering of Non-native Speakers'. For non-native speakers of Somali have difficulties similar to those most foreign learners face when they learn German.

They were enjoying themselves, Hilaal and Salaado, I could see, although I didn't quite know why. Cusmaan's tutor was himself apparently a 'Misgenderer': a term indicating where the genders are confounded, the masculine third-person singular wrongly replaced or displaced by the female third-person singular. 'Cusmaan's is an ideal situation, having as his tutor someone who is one's best subject for study,' said Salaado.

They didn't like Cusmaan's tutor, apparently. He was a Somali from somewhere in East Africa, maybe Tanzania. He had a way of attaching himself to you, linking arms with you as though you were his female companion. I saw him from close quarters, I watched him when he came to our house once and helped himself to whatever was in the fridge without asking if he might, oblivious of the existence of others. He was said to be a traitor, he was said to have betrayed his friends and many people spoke ill of him. But he was respected greatly by foreigners. When this man lapsed into Somali, he reminded me of the Ethiopian soldiers whom I heard speaking Somali at the market-place, confounding their sexes, addressing the men as 'she', and the women as 'he'.

'For example,' said Uncle Hilaal in a voice which suggested two things – that the subject had been slightly changed, and that he was intending to make an original statement. 'In Wolof,' he said, 'did you know there is hardly any indicator of gender. A man who otherwise speaks faultless French might, when speaking about his wife who is right in front of you, and whom you can see display all her gender's paraphernalia, refer to her as "he". Likewise, the wife might refer to her husband as "she".'

Unbelieving, I asked, 'Is that true, Uncle?'

'Ask any Wolof speaker,' he said.

Salaado said, 'How shocking!'

Her voice said that we had exhausted the subject and perhaps it was time we moved on to other areas of common interest. Somehow, we couldn't help returning to the question of my identity papers. When would I get them? What psychological effect might they have on me? Would I consider settling in the Republic permanently? What were my chances of returning to the Ogaden or joining the Liberation Movement? In short, what did all this mean? And then I surprised even myself, asking: 'Is there any room for Misra in my identity papers?'

Hilaal said, his voice anaemic, so to speak, 'How do you mean?'

'You remember you've shown me yours,' I said – and then I saw how unhappy he looked and I thought I knew why, but I continued speaking nonetheless, this time with my look averted – 'and I see that in identity papers there is space allotted to biological parents and to guardians but none to somebody like Misra, who is neither a biological parent nor a guardian at present.'

All he said was, 'Of course,' but I bet he didn't know what he was talking about.

I was about to add that Misra meant a lot more to me than anyone else when Salaado excused herself and left the living-room altogether. We looked away from each other, Uncle Hilaal and I, and each waited for the other to say something. I sensed each knew what thought buzzed in the other's head, thoughts which were imprisoned in our heads like bees caught inside a bottle out of which they know not how to emerge. I had never seen him looking so sad, nor have I ever seen him appear so dejected, save on the other occasion, when there was an eclipse of the sun, but we'll come to that later. Suffice it to say, I resolved right there and then that I would never raise the subject again; that I wouldn't make references to my parents, to Misra and to Uncle Hilaal and Salaado in the same breath. Naturally, I remembered how evasive he had been when I asked him once to give me the salient points in my mother's journal. In those days, ugly thoughts often crossed my mind: that Uncle Qorrax had raped my mother and I was his son. From then on, my mother's journal didn't exist, except in so far as one entry proved that she died *after* I was born, an entry contradicting the view held by Misra – or am I confusing things? After a long, long silence, I said, 'The truth of the matter is, Misra, being Oromo as you've explained to me once, belongs to a peripheral people. Nor would anyone believe that the Oromo form over sixty per cent of Ethiopia's population, despite their occupying only a marginal position. And as such, the Oromo have either to assume Somali or Amhara identity. Thank God, my ethnic origin matches the papers with which I shall be issued,' I concluded.

I forget what he said, or whether he said anything. I remember him looking sort of relieved that we had come to the end of that round. So please keep this in mind if, during the course of this narrative, I make no overt or indirect references to my mother's journal or related topics.

[2]

A couple of days after this discussion, Uncle Hilaal entered the living-room where Salaado was helping me practise my writing. He walked in exalted, like a man who has discovered a most coveted treasure all by himself. Somehow, I didn't think it had anything to do with me, or that I might even get an unexpected gift. I sat where I was and let Salaado talk to him, let her find out what had so pleased him.

Salaado asked, 'What is it?'

He said, in a matter-of-fact way, 'Here it is.'

And he pulled out of his pocket a paper whose green, I thought, had faded a little, a paper with some writing on it, a paper folded up and, from what I could gather, cheaply printed, produced inexpensively and rather hurriedly, with my own photograph pasted on its top right-hand side and its spine bent unevenly.

He said, 'I said, take it,' and it was only then that I saw, as though for the first time, that he was looking at me. The thought that it was *I* and not somebody else that he was addressing and to whom he would give something did cross my mind, but I didn't speak it. I got to my feet in awe and extended out both my hands to receive it.

'It is your *carta d'identità*,' he declared.

From the way he gave it to me, you would've thought he was entrusting to me a brand-new 'life'. Here you are, he seemed to say, with another life all your own, one that you must take good care of, since it is of paper, produced by the hand of man, according to the laws of man. I held it tenderly but also firmly, the way you hold a sickly infant. While I was looking at it, Uncle Hilaal engaged Salaado in a solemn conversation, as if she were to be a witness at my being wed to myself.

'Open it,' he said. 'Come on. It won't break.'

I did as told.

'Read it,' he said.

I chose to read it to myself. I held it open before me as one would a book, and felt its uneven spine as one would a person with a hurt disc in the vertebral column. The paper gave my particulars – name, father's name and grandfather's, as well as mother's. There was a hyphen, I noticed, conveniently placed between my father's actual name and the nickname he had acquired by going to the Ogaden from a Xamar base. I was to commit to memory the number of the identity card and was not to lose it. Otherwise, the school wouldn't accept me. After all, I was not a refugee! Didn't Salaado say that I would need the card to be with them? Anyway, looking at the photograph and, under it, like a caption, my name, I began to see myself in images carved out of the letters which my name comprised. It meant that I had a *foglio famiglia* and that I wasn't just a refugee from the Ogaden. It is unfair, I thought to myself, that Misra wasn't even given a mention on my identity card. Now I discarded my earlier belief that this was because she was Oromo and I, Somali. Perhaps, I concluded, it was because our relationship dates back to before my coming to Mogadiscio and before – goes back to before I myself acquired the Somali identity in written form. I reminded myself that Misra belonged to my 'non-literate' past – by which I mean that she belonged to a past in which I spoke, but did not write or read in, Somali.

Then hurriedly, my thoughts moved to less controversial topics. And I remembered the day the photograph was taken; I remembered how much fuss was made about my clothes; I remembered being forced to change the shirt and trousers that had been my favourites, then – thinking it wasn't *I* who wore them but that *they* wore me. (Very often, I associate certain items of clothes with one person or the other. For instance, Salaado's necklace has an 'S' dangling down from it, so not only do I associate the letter with her but it is, for me, the same letter with which the notion of 'Somalia' comes.) And I wondered if it made any sense believing that passport-size photographs would help anyone identify a person? Are we merely faces? I mean

164

are faces the keys to our identity? What of a man, like Aw-Adan, with a wooden leg – would you know it from the photograph? What of a baby just born, a baby abandoned in a waste-bin, a baby, violent with betrayal – would you be able to tell who it was by wiping away the tear-stains and the mucus, would you know its begetter, would you trace it to its mother or father?

Alone, I studied the details of my new identity with the care with which one does such things – a tender care. I learnt how tall I was, how much I weighed, how my grandfather's name was spelt in a Somali script new to me. With nostalgia, I read the name of the town in the Ogaden in which I was born – Kallafo – and was happy to know that, professionally, I was a student. Then two questions came to my mind simultaneously: one, would Misra be given a Somali identity card if she came? If not, why not?

I confess, I did think that I was expected, from that moment onwards, to perceive myself in the identity created for me. Although there were other sorts of difficulties which I encountered head-on when a young man, unemployed and a relation of Salaado's, was hired to become my tutor. His name was Cusmaan. Now this young man insisted that he remind me who I was. 'Do you know who you are?' he would say. 'You are a refugee. You've fled from the war in the Ogaden and, whether the Somalis have lost this war or no, you will have to remember who you are and, when you grow up, you must return to the Ogaden as a fighter, as a liberator.' Salaado and Uncle Hilaal, however, took a different position – that of allowing me to live my life – of course, promising and trying as hard as they could to make living easier. As far as Cusmaan was concerned, I should be trained as a soldier. Not sent to the school as any normal Somali child, no. He argued if the Azanians had not been given the comforts of citizenship or refugee status, as they had in the front-line states, maybe they would've wielded their strong spirit into a greater force that the apartheid regime wouldn't be able to cope with. I confess that I had difficulty perceiving myself in Cusmaan's concepts, although I realized later that he made some sense. Salaado, however, told him, more than once, to stop preaching to me. 'No politics,' she said one day. 'Just teach him writing and reading.' Uncle Hilaal spoke at length, saying how writing and reading were as political as casting your vote, if you happen to live in a country where elections are held. 'Think of the Arabs imposing on our African language their alien thought; think of the staunch Somali nationalists giving us a script which was uneconomical and difficult to read. So what is more political than

165

writing? Or, for that matter, reading?' he said, turning to Salaado who had remained silent, apparently because she realized he had misunderstood her.

As I remembered all this, I gave the identity paper further scrutiny and it assumed a greater importance than what either Cusmaan, my tutor, or Uncle Hilaal had said. For I could decidedly see that, in front of the space of 'Nationality', there was, neatly typed in capital letters, the word 'Somali'. Did that mean that I was not to consider myself a refugee any more?

I put the question to Uncle Hilaal.

And while he was finding the right things to say, on this particular occasion, I began to study with appropriate seriousness the linguistic map of the continent as updated by researchers at the AIA, London.

[3]

'A Somali,' said Uncle Hilaal, 'is a man, woman or child whose mother tongue is Somali. Here, mother tongue is important, very important. Not what one looks like. That is, features have nothing to do with a Somali's Somaliness or no. True, Somalis are easily distinguishable from other people, but one might meet with foreseeable difficulty in telling an Eritrean, an Ethiopian or a northern Sudanese apart from a Somali, unless one were to consider the cultural difference. The Somali are a homogeneous people; they are homogeneous culturally speaking and speak the same language wherever they may be found. Now this is not true of the people who call themselves "Ethiopians", or "Sudanese" or "Eritreans", or Nigerians or Senegalese.'

A river of ideas, winding as were the Shebelle and the Juba in the map in front of me, poured into my brain. I felt calmed by his voice; I felt calm listening to the rise and fall of his beautiful rendering of his own ideas.

'Somali identity,' he went on, 'is one shared by all Somalis, no matter how many borders divide them, no matter what flag flies in the skies above them or what the bureaucratic language of the country is. Which is why one might say that the soul of a Somali is a meteor, shooting towards that commonly held national identity.'

I had a question. 'Yes?' he asked.

'If Misra were to apply, would she be entitled to be issued the nationality papers which would make her legally and forever a

Somali?' I said, and waited anxiously because I knew I had laboured the point.

'If her Somali is as good as yours, then I doubt if any bureaucratic clown would dare stand in her way or dare deny her what is hers by right. Remember this, Askar. For all we know, there is no ethnic difference which sets apart the Somali from the Ethiopian – the latter in inverted commas. What she might need is a couple of male witnesses to take an oath that they've known her all her life and that she is a Somali, etc., etc.; no more. And all they have to do is sign an affidavit, that is all.'

I had another question. 'What's it this time?' Uncle Hilaal said.

'How would you describe the differences which have been made to exist between the Somali in the Somali Republic and the Somali in either Kenya or in the Ethiopian-administered Ogaden?' I said, again feeling that I had expressed myself poorly.

He answered, 'The Somali in the Ogaden, the Somali in Kenya both, because they lack what makes the self strong and whole, are *unpersons.*'

Silence. Something made me not ask, 'But what is an unperson, Uncle?' Now, years later, I wish I had told him I didn't understand the concept. Years later, I find it appropriate to ask, 'Is Misra a Somali?' 'Am I a refugee?' 'Am I an unperson?' 'Is or will Misra be an unperson – if she comes to Mogadiscio?'

[4]

My tutor, Cusmaan, behaved as though he were the self-avowed conscience of the Somali nation. He came to the house daily, taking upon himself to remind me that unless people like myself returned to the Ogaden to fight for its liberation, the province would remain colonially subjected to foreign rule. I resolved not to report him to Salaado who, I was sure, would probably have told him to leave. One reason was because I liked him. The second reason was because he was willing to share with me the pornographic magazines he used to borrow from friends of his who had just come from Italy. I don't know if he was aware of the inherent contradictions in what he was doing – but I didn't mind. I thought it was fun to build a secret subway tunnel between my tutor and me, a tunnel to whose wide or narrow passage only he and I had access. Somehow, this secret knowledge enabled me to exert on him whatever pressures I chose. Whenever I didn't do my homework, whenever I was too lazy to study, I said so and we found a way of occupying ourselves. Then he would say, 'You must take your studies seriously so that, when you are a grown-up man, you will use your knowledge to liberate your people from the chains of colonialism.'

'And is that why I should learn to read and write Somali and also English?' I would ask.

'Yes.'

I remember, a couple of days or so later, putting the same or similar questions about written and oral traditions to Uncle Hilaal. And he explained that 'History has proven that whoever is supported by the written metaphysics of a tradition wins, in the long run, the fight to power.' And he went on speaking of a God – with capital G – backed by technology, however unadvanced the stage, and gods – with small g – who were not. 'That is, the Amharic-speaking people, because they had a written tradition, could spread their power over peoples of the oral tradition such as Somalis, the Arusas and even the Oromos, who form the largest single ethnic community in Ethiopia. The Amharic-speaking people were themselves conquered, at an earlier period of their history, by the Tigregna-speaking people – apparently a people with a script, namely Gaez.'

This made sense. It made sense to me the way a mother's encouraging a child to eat the soup laid before him, so he would grow up to be a strong man, might make sense to the child in question. And every letter became a sword – by pronouncing it, I sharpened it; by drawing it, I gave it a life of its own; all I had to do was to say 'Cut' and it would cut the enemy's head. Mind you, I knew that this was a highly personal interpretation of things, but it freed my imagination from any constraints. And that, I found, was not something to take lightly.

Nevertheless, my life was taking a different turn from what I had presumed. My tutor, balancing the dignified and the undignified ethos, would have the centrefold of *Playboy* in view and would also have our textbook open at the appropriate page. That was how I learnt my first English sentence. I can hear it today, I can feel my tongue wrestle with its sounds, I can sense my questioning the logic of why the first sentence of *Book One Oxford English* had to be 'This is a pen', and the second sentence, 'This is a book'.

I repeated these two sentences again and again until I was hypnotized by the sounds each word made and my head wove a tapestry from which I deciphered a divine design. From that emerged the first words the Archangel Gabriel dictated to the then illiterate Mohammed, thereafter Prophet – may his name be honoured! That is, I remembered the Koranic verse 'Read, read in the name of Allah who created you out of clots of blood, read!' I also had the calm of mind, and the composure, to remember another verse from the Sura, *The Pen*, a verse which goes: 'By the pen and what it writes, you are not mad!' Then my imagination cast its net further afield and I was younger and was in Kallafo with Misra.

And under a thatch roof, in Kallafo, I found a much smaller boy also named Askar, a boy in a woman's embrace, and the woman was asking this young boy to repeat after her – (she wasn't decently covered and his recently bathed body was in direct contact with hers) – she was telling him to repeat after her the sentences 'That is the sky' and 'This is the earth'.

A question to Uncle Hilaal, years later.

'What was I to make of all this? I wonder if the pastoralist nature of the Somali sees an inborn link between the child and its cosmology by having it learn the words "sky" and "earth"? First, the child is taught to identify its mother, then its father and there are a chorus of questions like "Who is this?" and, naturally, "Who is that?" or "What is this or that?" I suspect that the cosmology of the nomads comprehends, at a deeper psychical level, the metaphoric contents of the statements "This is the earth" and "That is the sky". Can this be interpreted to mean "God and the grave"? Or do you prefer "Rain and food"? In the latter, you identify or locate the source of life, as it were.'

Uncle Hilaal was silent, making no further observation. And I was hearing in my mind the child's answer 'This is the earth', although not pointing at the earth but touching Misra's bosomy chest, and she laughing and teasing him, pardon, me. By then – or after a little while – I was back with Hilaal who was saying, 'Now what about "This is a pen" and "That is a book", which are the first sentences that open the English world to a Somali or an East-African child?'

I wasn't sure if he expected me to answer, but he didn't, apparently. So I simply said, 'What about it?'

'An exploratory question. Let's start with one.'

I waited.

He said, 'Are we, in any manner, to see a link between "This is a book" and the Koranic command "Read in the name of God", addressed to a people who were, until that day, an illiterate people?

In other words, what are the ideas behind "pen" and "book"? It is my feeling that, plainly speaking, both suggest the notion of "power". The Arabs legitimized their empire by imposing "the word that was read" on those whom they conquered; the European God of technology was supported, to a great extent, by the power of the written word, be it man's or God's.'

He was silent again. I thought I had to make an intelligent contribution. So I said, 'That is why the Muslims refer to the Christians and the Jews as the "People of the Book", isn't it?'

'That's right.'

And he sat there, friendly, lovable – and fat. I thought that he was two balls screwed together: the top, his head, was round like a globe and it turned on its axis and travelled, returning every time it made a circle, to the point of reference upon which he pontificated; the middle, his chest, was the seat of his emotion – his paunch breathed like bellows when he laughed and his voice had a fiery fervour about it, setting ablaze, inside my head, a great many fires whose thought-flames burned the ground separating me from him.

'You might take pens and books,' he was saying when I turned to him, 'as metaphors of material and spiritual power. And the most powerful among us is the one who will insist that pens write his thoughts in the form of a letter of glory to posterity and that books record his good deeds.'

I thought – but didn't say – that the one who teaches one either the written or the oral word remains, for oneself, the most powerful among us. Hence the influence of Misra, Salaado, Cusmaan, Aw-Adan and finally Uncle Hilaal, on me. And suddenly, I had a most ingenious thought, 'What happens when a people with no written tradition invades a people with such a long history of it?'

I waited anxiously. I wondered if he would use the only example of such a conqueror I could think of. For an instant, I was trapped in the fear that I was off the mark.

'The Goths, a Teutonic people who were illiterate in the sense that they had no written culture, pillaged Rome and Southern Gaul as well as Spain. I am certain there are many others, such as the Mongol warriors.'

'And the view of history? How does history view such conquests?' I asked.

He said, 'History treats rather badly emperors who hail from a scattered nomadic warrior people – I'm thinking of Genghis Khan – and who reach the walls of such seats of scientific learning as Peking or Iran's Tabriz. Genghis Khan – the name means universal emperor – may have been at the head of a cavalry of master horsemen, but history portrays him as "barbaric" and accuses him of pillaging cities of learning and setting fire to libraries of tremendous worth.'

I was about to ask him another question when I acknowledged Salaado's entry into the living-room where we were. She said something about lunch being ready and could we both join her at the table and eat so that she could go back to the school where there was a meeting. I said to Uncle Hilaal, 'We know what conquerors with written traditions who occupy a land belonging to a people of the oral tradition do. We know they impose upon them a law which makes it unlawful to think of themselves as human. The European colonialists have done so. Can you think of a conquering people, whether nomadic or no, who didn't impose alien learning, language and culture upon those whom they conquered?'

He got to his feet and reflected.

I readied to follow him should he decide to sit at the dinner-table.

'I can think of one special case.'

I asked, 'Who?'

'The Fulanis.'

I said, coming closer, 'Who?'

He was silent until we reached the table, until we each picked up a paper serviette. He tucked his under his fat chin (I snickered every time he did that!) and I unfolded mine and laid it on my lap (thinking of the writings I used to scribble on my thighs and on every part of my body, when younger; thinking of Misra, who taught me Amharic in secret).

'The Fulanis of West Africa are the only conquering people I know of who adopted as their own language and culture the one of the people whom they conquered. I've never learnt why.'

Plates were passed to and fro. And I grieved at the thought that millions of us were conquered, and would remain forever conquered; millions of us who would remain a traditional people and an oral people at that. And I saw, abandoned, burning cities the Goths had set ablaze (I didn't know who the Goths were, but promised myself that I would find out). I saw, in my mind, the Mongol Emperor, and he was riding a horse and kicking his heels against the beast's ribs and setting fire to all the letters of the alphabet and more. I also saw abandoned dead bodies – those of men and women and children dead from napalm spray – and cursed the Russians and the Cubans and the Adenese. (I think this must have been after the Russians, the

Cubans, the Adenese and the Ethiopian soldiers defeated the unaided Somali army.) And I saw history books open at the page beginning with the encyclopaedic definition of the concept 'Civilization'.

The written metaphysics of a people is their 'civilization'.

So read, read in the name of 'civilization', I thought to myself. And write, write down your history in the name of the same 'civilization'. 'This is a pen.' 'This is a nib.' 'That is a book.' Power!

Once, long ago, I said to myself, Misra *was* my cosmos. She was good, she was kind, she was motherly and I loved her warmly, I cared about her tenderly. Now that cosmos has been made to disintegrate, and Misra has betrayed. What am I to do? I, who still love her!

[5]

'Wars disorient one,' said Uncle Hilaal the day we learnt that Misra would definitely call the following day. 'Wars make one do the unpardonable. And in any case, we don't know if she was the one who betrayed. I mean, we don't know for certain if she was the person who informed on the freedom fighters, we have no evidence.'

I hid my inner torment behind the silence I stood in – my hands behind my back, my body upright, my mind alert, my thoughts stirring within me echoes of conversations I had with Misra years ago, with Cusmaan who was my tutor some nine or so years ago, with Salaado – and with myself. Somehow, I felt I knew I had to betray one of them. I had to betray either Misra, who had been like a mother to me, or my mother country. However, part of me was worried – worried that a curse would be placed on my head by either. And I couldn't help remembering dreams in which I saw an old man with a girl's face and features, or another in which the dreamer, a young man who imagined he had envied a woman's menstruation, menstruated.

Many years have gone past since I last saw Misra; many months since she was accused of betraying a freedom fighters' camp in which six hundred men lost their lives – or were said to have done so; many since I was preached to and shown pornographic magazines by Cusmaan, my tutor, and I have, since then, for whatever it is worth, made my own friends – one of them a young woman, my age. And I know now what Misra and Aw-Adan were up to at night, in the dark. I also appreciate what grand sacrifices Uncle Hilaal has made and what a great 'receiver' Salaado has been. And here I stand at the crossroads. Shall I leave Salaado and Uncle Hilaal for a freedom fighters' camp in the Ogaden? Shall I register as a student at the university? And what must we do about Misra when she calls tomorrow?

Nothing was clear in my head. One moment, I was young and with Misra; the next moment, I was allowing a country to be born inside of my thoughts; then, I was being trusted with a new life by Uncle Hilaal, and Salaado was looking on as a witness to my being wed to 'myself'; and finally, I was being told about Misra's betraying secrets to the enemy. I was at a loss. I was very sad. Oh, Karin, my dear Karin – is it true?

I was unwell that day.

CHAPTER NINE

[1]

In the wake of the greater national loss: a personal one, equally as devastating. He felt terrible and this left a horrible taste in his mouth, something his tongue (i.e. his memory) couldn't give an appropriate name to. He became weak from want of energy, he walked about wooden as his soul. Again, he wouldn't eat, complaining that he was tasting blood in his saliva. His body united in itself two temperatures: one moment, he said he was feeling very hot, the following instant he was very cold as if he had 'ice circulating in my arteries and veins, not warm, living blood'. His eyes were bloodshot from sleeplessness. To the point of obsessiveness, his imagination 'heard' loud reports of guns being fired and he saw men, women and children falling, and dying under the fire power. Six hundred and three of them!

He mourned for the souls of the betrayed dead. The loss was so great, the tremor in his soul so distressing, that Askar behaved like a man watching a part of him slip away. He had been well when he was given the sad news – well, and alive to the detailed horrors which Karin offered. He remembered he had been ill and in bed when the Ogaden, in a *coup de grâce*, was returned to Ethiopian hands by the Soviets. He remembered someone commenting then, that what the British imperialists had put together wouldn't be pulled asunder by Somalis – the Soviets, themselves imperialists, wouldn't permit that to happen. But what could one say now? Misra, dearest Misra, why did you have to do this?

He was alone with Karin and she told it to him alone. In his room, with its maps and mirrors, radio and other items he had acquired, or was given as presents. Karin was served tea. She had aged slightly, her skin smooth as old leather, her chin sporting a longish Ho Chi Minh 'beard'. She gave him the latest news about Qorrax ('He is very chummy with the newly appointed governor, he is often with him. A traitor, no doubt about it. He always was'), about Aw-Adan ('An exceptional man. He is a legendary figure in the town's history. Bare-handed, he took on three of them and killed them. Just like that. As easily as a strong-armed man might behead a hen. They say his faith in the destiny of his people – he wasn't Somali, he was a Qotto, you knew that? – they say that was his strength, gave him confidence'), about Shahrawello ('She died, poor thing, leaving behind her a pool of blood, no more. She cut her throat. No one knows why. Some thought it was because she felt humiliated by Qorrax's treachery, others because all her sons had been killed in the massacre'), about Misra, what news about Misra?

'Why ask,' she had said, 'why bother about her?'

Indeed, why did he wait until the last minute to ask about her, he said to himself. He should've started with her. She was, after all, as close to his own beginnings as anyone is ever likely to be. 'Why not?' he said. 'What's become of her?'

Karin studied him and thought Askar looked more innocent now than he had been when younger. For one thing, his 'stare' had lost its sharpness; for another, the satanic mischievousness which used to light his eyes with lamps more powerful than any wick, this, too, wasn't there. She said, 'It means you haven't heard.'

For a moment, there was a flash, lasting barely a second – an outburst of flames in his look which reminded her of his younger self. It was an ambiguous look, transitory. Karin didn't know what to make of it. 'Heard what? Is she dead?'

'No. That she is not.'

He knew there was bad news coming. He didn't speak until after he had steeled himself against it. He hardened his body, he deadened his soul – he was ready to hear anything. Then, like somebody who derives courage from the certainty of death and who says, 'What're you waiting for? Kill me, shoot me, get on with it and quick too,' Askar said, 'Go on. Tell me the worst. What're you waiting for?'

'There is a young Ethiopian soldier who's taken Misra's fancy. She is said to be living with him. A dashing, handsome young man, the Prince Charming type, whom she's been wanting to meet all her life,' said Karin.

He wasn't troubled by what he heard. However, he was wise enough not to shrug his shoulders and say, 'So what? A woman has the right to fall in love with a man and I don't see why his nationality matters. After all, all "Ethiopians" are not enemies of all "Somalis". It is the cause that matters.' There returned to him a steadiness of the kind a confident person displays. He took a sip of tea (which she didn't touch), he crossed his legs, settling his body into the cosiness of an unexpected comfort. She said, 'But that's not all.'

Second deaths are more painful when you come to think of it, thought Askar. He was numb in soul and body. He knew the rest of the story. She needn't bother. Misra had fallen in love with a man from the enemy camp and she had betrayed. There were deaths. There was a massacre. Houses were razed to the ground. Wells poisoned. Newborns were bayoneted to death, their mothers raped and then killed, and their bodies savagely hacked to pieces, limb from limb. And children were rounded up, lectured to and then machine-gunned. He said, 'You can spare me the detailed horrors. Just give me the figure.'

She thought he was too far ahead of her. 'Then it means you've heard?' she said. 'Let me tell it to you if you haven't,' she added, and waited to hear his response.

'The trouble is,' and here his voice assumed an inordinate calmness which he had got from being close to Hilaal, 'in gruesomeness, massacres are all the same wherever in the world they occur. And at the centre of them all, there is a traitor. So just give me the figures, and spare me the details.'

He decided to watch her face intently for the slightest hesitation in her voice, the slightest tremor in the tone in which she spoke, as she said, 'Six hundred and three.'

He didn't know why, but he believed she was telling the truth as she knew it. Something convinced him she was. But he had a question. 'Why three? How does the figure three enter the picture? Why not six hundred and four or eight or nine?'

Again, there was no hesitation in her voice. 'Shahrawello's three sons, massacred later.'

Without being asked, she gave further details, not about the massacre, but about the 'dashing, handsome young Ethiopian officer in charge of security'. He was from the same village as Misra and he called her by a different name. 'Not Misra, which we all called her, no.'

He was intensely shocked. He mouthed, 'What? What's this?'

'He called her Misrat. Listen to it carefully. Misrat.'

Blood ran visibly up to and into his eyes. He stared at Karin questioningly, focussing on the furrowed wrinkles of her forehead and the bridge of her nose. He saw a 't' written there and remembered he had had difficulties pronouncing or distinguishing the Arabic letter *ta* from that of *tha* when he was a pupil at Aw-Adan's Koranic School, a fact no one else substantiated. 'Are you sure that there is a 't' in it now? Because you see, Misra is the Arabic name for "Egypt" and Somalis prefer it to their own corrupted form "Massar", which also gives you the Somali word for "headscarf". And when I asked Misra what her name meant in her language, I remember her saying that it meant "foundation", I think "the foundation of the earth" or something. Now what could Misrat mean?' He turned to Karin.

Karin thought he was more disturbed by the changes in Misra's name than about the massacre of which he had heard. She found this disturbing and was about to ask him about it when he said, 'What can that mean, the change in the name?'

'It can only mean one thing: treason.'

He said, 'I didn't mean that,' and she could see he was greatly upset. 'Not in that sense, no. Names mean something and to me, as a child, she was the cosmos.' He paused. 'Maybe, I shan't take note of the changes in her name. I am quite certain,' he was now talking to his face in the mirror, 'now that I think of it, that somebody who speaks Amharic has confirmed to Uncle Hilaal that "Misra" without a 't' means "the foundation of the earth". Or if you like, "the foundation of the universe". Personally, I prefer rendering it as "the foundation of the earth". But I am not certain. You have to ask someone who speaks that language, I don't any more.'

He was now at peace with himself. This was what Karin found weird. Also, he didn't offer her the chance to tell him more, or ask him further questions. He was up on his feet, his height towering above her, extending his hand for her to shake, making gestures that their conversation had come to an end. She prepared to leave and shouted, offering her address care of one of her daughters who, she said, worked in the Central Post Office, the one near Hotel Juba. 'You must come and see us,' she went on, as she formalized their parting by taking both his hands in hers. He wished he had the will to tell her that Bevin's portrait was still with him, and so was his fond memory of her kindness to him.

'God bless,' was apparently all he managed to say. Someone else saw her to the door, he couldn't say who. He was taken ill immediately he was alone – quick as bushfire. His temperature ran high, his saliva tasted of blood and his body broke with perspiration although he insisted he was feeling very cold.

[2]

He couldn't hold a thought in his head for two, three days. He walked in his sleep, a somnambulator roaming the darkened corridors of a past he couldn't recognize himself in. He behaved as though he were looking in one of the night's opaque corners for his missing half. No amount of talking would help him or make him lie down quietly and sleep. He was mortally mortified and sad at the thought that Misra was no longer worthy of his trust, his love. For the first time ever, Askar consented to talk at length about Misra's divining in blood, raw meat and water.

Hilaal said, 'In other words, she is a witch, a bitch, a whore and a traitor?'

Askar didn't say anything. Salaado interjected, 'He hasn't said that.'

Hilaal turned to Salaado, 'What did he say?'

Because Salaado wouldn't speak, Hilaal to Askar: 'What exactly did you say, Askar? Because if you say that Misra is a witch, a whore and a traitor, then you're not making an original statement.'

'Meaning?' asked Salaado.

Hilaal shifted in his chair, 'Women as whores, women as witches, women as traitors of their blood, women as lovers of men from the enemy camp – throughout history, men have blamed women for the ill luck they themselves have brought on their heads. Women are blamed for every misfortune which has befallen man from the first day of creation, including *his* fall from heaven. *Woman* is said to have betrayed *man* at the first opportunity. Throughout history, Askar.'

Salaado said, 'Let him be, please.'

'No, no, please,' said Askar to Salaado.

Hilaal continued, looking from Askar to Salaado, 'You've no proof, and you've asked for no proof. Men have always done that. They've condemned unjustly and asked for no evidence. What do you say to that?'

Askar sat silently, staring at his lap as though his ruined logic had fallen there. Would he be able to gather his broken pieces into his cupped hands and then respond? It seemed, however, that no sooner had he picked up a shattered piece than he discovered that he could only see a very little of a face (Misra's), an eye (his own, as though it were a mirror) and nothing else. He floated, poised between the earth and the sky. He dwelled in a no-man's-land, remaining suspended between numerous undefined states of reality and unreality; sandwiched between not-so-clearly defined selves. Dreaming (was he?), sleeping (was he?) or listening to a taped conversation between himself and Uncle Hilaal.

There was a silence akin to that which obtains when a radio is switched off suddenly. Hilaal was there, yes; Salaado was there as well; and the large radio in the living room wasn't on. Well?

A voice (most probably Hilaal's) telling a story:

A man. A woman. And a dog. The neighbours don't like the man, who doesn't like them either. They suspect, but they have no evidence, that he is a jealous husband. The woman is very beautiful, but quiet in an unassuming way, simple in her tastes, and loves her plainness. The dog? The dog is a German shepherd, large, handsome, costing the master a lot of money to feed, although the master doesn't seem to mind the expense. The dog is given liver for breakfast, meat for lunch and dinner. The gate, however, is locked day and night and is opened when someone is entering or leaving. On most days, it is opened only twice: when the husband is leaving in the morning and when he re-enters in the evening.

One day, a stranger arrives. Yes, into these convolutions walks, one noon, a man. The dog barks, bares its teeth, growls, but the man walks past it without so much as hesitating or pausing for a moment. For hands, the man has stumps – his hands, or so people say, having been amputated in Iran, because, again people say (and where they got their news only God knows) he had stolen money from a minor Ayatollah. The man, when he returns in the evening, stays indoors and so does the stranger, so do the wife and the dog. The stranger, the wife and the dog remain inside. The man, as usual, leaves in the morning and, as usual, doesn't return until evening. Now what does the man do? Nobody knows. Does he work for the government, is he self-employed? Nobody knows. But people don't say they don't. They make up their stories when they don't know what's what.

Who's the stranger? He is the younger brother of the man. People say he used to be a wicked man, who broke into houses, robbed banks. People also say that the house in which the man and his wife live is in his name, for he bought it from monies acquired through felonious methods. But nowadays, the stranger is as saintly as a mixraab. You won't see him without his rosary (he holds one end of the rosary between his toes and the other hangs, like a wrist-watch, on the healed scar of the stump), nor will you catch his lips idle.

For example, Askar. In this story just told, there are truths and half-truths. The husband is a very jealous man – that is true. But the wife is saintly and has never reciprocated the advances made by any man. She loves her lawful husband.

It is also true, for example, that the dog is a German shepherd, large

179

*as the largest among the breed and handsome too. But it is not at all fierce.
It bares its teeth, all right, and growls, and thus appears aggressive
but it is very timid, very shy. Its eyes are gentle, its anger wore out at
the edges when the intruder smiled, calling it 'Bruder', German,
meaning brother. Why was it given such a name? Nobody knows. But
people say that her Somali master inherited it from a Polish gentleman
who gave her the name. But surely, a Polish UN expert would know
enough German to know that bruder was brother, and wouldn't call a
female dog that?*

*The stranger? He is a relation of the man, that is true. In fact, he is
the first and only son. Not a younger brother. It would be too much to
expect two 'brothers' in the same story, wouldn't it? Two 'brothers' who
are not brothers themselves but who also are non-brothers. And where did
he get his hands amputated? In Iran. That much is true. But not because
he stole from a minor Ayatollah, no. He was working in a factory and a
moment of carelessness chopped off his hands. Yes, he is the one in whose
name the house is. Again, not because he bought it. The man registered
the house in his name, that's all.*

*No one visits these people. They have a dog who is fierce, a man who
is very jealous, a wife who is unfaithful, a stranger whose hands have been
amputated in Iran. Would they listen to you if you tried to enlighten them?
Would they hear you out if you tried to challenge their prejudices? Of
course not. Note, please, that the prejudice of the western press feeds the
acquired prejudices of the colonial and neo-colonial peoples, as much as it
misinforms the underinformed in Europe or North America. And note
also, that because the new Somali master didn't know the meaning of the
German word 'Bruder', the question why such a name was given to a
she-German shepherd never crossed his or other people's minds. Was the
Polish gentleman playing a Freudian game with his own or the dog's
unconscious, giving it 'Bruder' as a name?*

*Now, for example. An unremoved bullet might cause a man's death.
But you need more than undealt-with tetanus and the rigidification of the
muscles of the jaws for death to happen. Doctors, like the societies to which
they belong, diagnose their patients, drawing conclusions based on their (I
grant you here 'learned') prejudices. What I am trying to say, inarticulately,
all this time, is you need more than scientific evidence for you to disown
the woman who, for the first few years of your life, you called 'Mother'.
Think, Askar.*

Now he could hear the voice, now he couldn't. And his breathing was
slow and shallow and he lay tucked in bed, thinking and thinking and

*

thinking, remembering, unremembering and remembering. The result of his silent reflections, his quiet meditations, his discursive consultations with Hilaal and Salaado, the result: he decided that Misra's wraith in Askar had died a spiritual death. What good would it do if he asked her point-blank, did you betray? Are you a traitor? And, pray, what is your true name?

And the voice was in his ears, repeating to him Salaado and Hilaal's coalition of views. And someone was saying that Misra had been seen in Mogadiscio, that she was already here, looking for him – looking for Askar, 'my Askar, my son'.

'What will you do if you meet her?' someone asked.

Askar's answer, 'I don't know.'

The sun's light in the room was breaking into tiny particles the size of atoms and while he thought of what he would do if he were to meet her again, Askar studied the phenomenon in thoughtful silence. The sun's rays of atoms, his own shattered, fragmented selves.

'Misra, why did you have to do this to me? Why? Why?'

And he heard the voices of dawn and he felt cold, he felt hot, and curled into a foetal position, seeing himself young again, in Kallafo again. Then, suddenly, all this vanished and he was in Mogadiscio, in bed and Salaado was calling his name.

[3]

Misra grew smaller as she aged, he realized; he, bigger as he grew up. He told himself that her voice had thinned, the brightness in her eyes had faded a little too. And yet he couldn't stop wondering if her *other half* was hiding inside her and would somehow re-emerge and take over eventually, the way voices of one person speak in another's body, when under the powers of an exorcist. She was an actress without her props; she was a clown without paint. He saw her start – it was sudden as a hiccup, fast. He didn't know why. He moved about, measured of step, economical of gestures – he took his distance from her. It was enough that they had embraced, that was as far as he was willing to go. He had felt something run through his body as they hugged. That Uncle Hilaal and Salaado were there didn't help matters either. If anything, their presence made things worse for him. He might have been franker with her if they were alone, in a room, in

Mogadiscio, after God knows how many years of not meeting or being together; he might have told her openly why their physical contact gave him a sense of repugnance. And once they hugged, did he say anything? Or did she? What did he say? Did he welcome her? He looked from Salaado to Uncle Hilaal and then to Misra, and she was ugly as guilt, small and distant. He decided he would ask Salaado what things were said between them as they touched – maybe there was something he could learn about himself in this manner.

'How long have you been here?' he said to Misra.

She rearranged her tatters which were dust free, although she had come a long way, although the roads between Mogadiscio and Kallafo breathed the dust of travel all the way. He looked around for signs which, he hoped, would indicate if she had brought her baggage with her. Wouldn't her belongings be here, in the living-room, if she had brought them?

Her voice was thinner than he remembered. 'Where? Here?'

He stole a quiet glance in the direction of Uncle Hilaal. Askar told himself that he had been sadly mistaken in thinking that Uncle could have reminded him of Misra in the first place. In the second, there was a world's difference between their voices – one was rich and comforting, the other thin as though dressed in the cheapest of rags.

'Yes,' he said at last.

He waited to see if her 'missing half' would make itself useful somehow. Why, she was reduced to half her original size and he was certain there was something uncanny about it all. For a second or so, he couldn't trust his own memory, wondering if the woman in his uncle and Salaado's living-room was an imposter. He couldn't have known what she thought about him and the cold welcome offered her, but her pride in him was in her eyes and no matter how she tried, she couldn't help displaying it to all and sundry.

There was a long pause.

And he remembered a dream in which *he* was inside a woman who remained nameless in the dream and he was trying his best to give birth to himself. Ejected, he was in a pool of blood and he swam in it, washed in it and the blood blinded him; and his face wore a mask of blood; and the place crawled with insects and serpents. Like a blind man, he had his hands ahead of himself, his legs splayed, his palms open, feeling and touching things upon which he bestowed names as he encountered them in the dark, pushing some of these items out of the way because he couldn't give them names. And all this time, he was moving upwards, inside another woman, and he was travelling northerly, bearing slightly to the east, that is towards the sun, towards the ocean; and he cut corners, took short cuts, as he crawled towards the cavity from which emanated a voice, a human voice – his own! And he groaned, struggling against becoming his own coffin. Then the wish to be born whole, the wish to burst forth and *be* – this wish took on a life of its own and, for a while, lived its own separate existence. And he was shouting and screaming and kicking against the ribs of the woman who had caged him inside of her. And it was then that he heard the voice of yet another woman call him by name, a woman who was saying, 'Askar, wake up. Misra is here.' And he wouldn't wake because he believed his dream was dreaming a dream. And the woman repeated, 'Askar, where are you? Wake up, Askar. Misra is here.' The woman who had called his name – Salaado (he saw this directly he opened his eyes, in fact even before he did so, he recognized her voice, etc.); the woman who had called and who was probably in the living-room – Misra! Was this the reason why everything inspired uneasiness, why there was, in the air, something he considered wicked and uncanny?

Now Misra was saying, 'I've been in Xamar for three days.'

'And how did you get here?' he asked.

He noticed that neither Hilaal nor Salaado said anything. Indeed, they were uncomfortable and might have preferred to leave them alone together if they'd been sure he didn't mind. And Misra? She was explaining that somebody who knew someone knew a relation of Hilaal's – and that was how she finally traced them.

'You've been here for a couple of hours, have you?'

She nodded. With hindsight, he resolved that her being there during the time he was dreaming would explain his discomfort and sense of awe. Apparently, she wasn't in high spirits either. He would talk to her alone and find out. If she were in need of help, he was certain Salaado and Uncle Hilaal would offer her just that.

'And where are you putting up? Or rather with whom?' he said.

He resisted looking in the direction of Uncle Hilaal. But when he did, he discovered his face weary with concern. It wouldn't be long, thought Askar, before he was ready to take over the conversation and Salaado, he was sure, would come to his aid. The two of them would talk to her, ask her any questions they pleased. Misra, because she had never known them before, would feel at ease with them. At any rate, he didn't know how to put embarrassing questions to a woman who had once been like a mother to him.

Askar withdrew the instant he sensed Uncle Hilaal and Salaado were prepared to relieve him – that is, to replace him. He made a lame excuse to her. Saying to her, 'Welcome, Misra,' he took leave of them.

[4]

That her voice had lost its 'weight' whereas his had broken into a man's; that she had grown smaller, thinner and been reduced to half her original size, whereas he had grown taller, bigger and handsomer; that he had prepared to leave Uncle Hilaal and Salaado's solidly built home in order that he might fight for the liberation of the Ogaden whereas she had left the Ogaden, disguised as another, and come to a Mogadiscio with whose coastal winds she wasn't at all familiar, a Mogadiscio in which she was a refugee but feared to declare herself as one, 'because I am sure', she explained to Hilaal and Salaado when Askar wasn't even there, 'somebody from Kallafo is bound to recognize me. And I am afraid of what might happen to me.'

She spoke to them with disarming honesty.

Barren of voice, small of stature, she wept every time she mentioned the word 'traitor' – for she was thus described. She was not a traitor. She had not betrayed anyone, had sold no secrets, contacted no enemy. True, she spoke the enemy's language; true, she had spoken to a soldier. But they exchanged no such vital information. The two had talked about whether or not someone she knew would sell milk to the soldiers. She admitted to going round and buying milk for them. She said she reasoned it this way: the civilian populace in the Ogaden had need of money, not of milk which some had plenty of. In so far as she was concerned, she was doing something for 'her people'.

She stopped, appearing dismayed by her story, her destiny.

'The problem is, who are "my people"?' she said. 'For me, my people are Askar's people; my people are my former husband's people, the people I am most attached to. Those who were looking for a traitor and found one in me, rationalize that because I wasn't born one of them, I must be the one who betrayed. Besides, it is easier to suspect the foreigner amongst a community than one's own cousin or brother. But I swear upon Askar's life that I did not inform on the freedom fighters' movements or on their camp of sojourn.'

Salaado thought (and said later to Askar) that Misra had cut a tragic figure and she – Salaado – wept for her in her own heart. Hilaal thought (and said so later to Askar) that Misra was like a tree-stump you see in the far distance and which you mistake for a person. You had your own thoughts but chose not to share them with anybody.

'You see, Askar left when the Somalis were overrunning the Ogaden and the Ethiopian army of occupation in the Ogaden was in total disarray. Inside a year, however, the Russians had entered the war and reversed the situation, turning the Ethiopians into a victorious army literally overnight. Now this was hard to take. I mean, when you've been triumphant for over a year, you don't expect that a weekend's job deprives you of all that you've gained. And as a result of this, there was a great bitterness among Somalis everywhere. Many, I believe, were ready to do anything so that they might survive. One of these, I am sure, sold the information to the Ethiopians,' she said sadly, shaking her head.

After a pause, Hilaal asked, 'How many of the fighters were rounded up and killed, did you say?'

'The number is estimated to be between five and six hundred dead and about fifty taken alive, tortured and then executed because they wouldn't speak, wouldn't betray, wouldn't give the locations of the other freedom fighters' camps all over the Ogaden.' She spoke with convincing clarity, having, naturally, given it thought previously.

Again after another pause, Salaado asked, 'When you were accused of being a traitor, what exactly did they do to you?'

Misra reflected for a long time. To Salaado now, Misra was the infant who had crawled out of an adult's view into another room, somewhere in the same house, and she wanted so much to know what Misra was thinking, which thoughts she was intending to suppress and which to speak. 'They set fire to the part of the house I was living in.'

'But you weren't in the house then?' said Hilaal.

'I was not.'

'I am sorry – but was that all?' from Salaado.

Her voice failed her. And Salaado and Hilaal were indulgently silent. They had the appearance of conspirators trapping a foe. They were friendly, even in their silence, and they focussed on her, waiting for her to say something, to tell them something.

'I was raped,' she said.

Now that was hard to take. At first, neither knew what to say nor what kind of sigh of horror to utter. Then they looked at each other and communicated their sense of inner torment to one another. Salaado went and knelt beside her in prostrated quietness, saying nothing, doing nothing – but evidently apologetic. Salaado, holding out her hands to Misra, as though she were making an offering of some sort, said, 'Who raped you?'

'Someone arranged a dozen young men to rape me,' she said in a matter-of-fact manner. 'Two men followed me home one evening. They said Abdul-Ilah, Askar's uncle on his father's side, was waiting for me somewhere. I hadn't seen him for years and was pleased to be joined with him again, for I didn't know if he had survived the war. When I entered the hut they said he was in, several strong men sprang on me out of the dark and they raped me.'

'I hope you reported the incident to someone of your household,' said Salaado, her hands parted and clearly empty of the gift or offering they might have contained earlier. 'Did you?'

It was harder to take when she told them. 'The story these young men circulated (and everyone who believed that I was a traitor had no difficulty accepting it) was that I had been raped by baboons. Thank God, they said, they happened to be there, these young men, these gallant youths. Otherwise, I might have been fed on by lions. The baboons, said the poet amongst them (and one of them was a poet), smelt the beast in her and went for it; the baboons smelt her traitor's identity underneath the human skin and went for it again and again. Thank God, we were there to save her body since, as a traitor, she had ransomed her soul.'

Neither Salaado nor Hilaal could think of anything to say. As for her, she was too tired, and admitted she was when asked. Would she like to lie down in the guest-room? 'Yes,' she said.

[5]

Askar was most ruthless. He said, on hearing the tragic stories which had befallen Misra, that he wasn't at all moved. He accused her of showing to the world the brutal scars of a most ravenous war – that was all. Hadn't they seen, with their own eyes, men and women with amputated arms or legs? Hadn't they felt a sense of disgust when a beggar whom one had known for years suddenly appeared at the street-corner and displayed his knee couched in a wooden leg, claiming that he had lost a leg, a wife and a child in the war? He went on, 'We're not asking her to play the heroine in a tragic farce, no, we're not. We're asking her, if we're asking her anything at all, to prove that she didn't give away an essential secret. Prove.'

'Could you prove that it was she who had done it?' asked Salaado.

He pondered for a moment or two. And his face wore something as improvident as one who submits to being blinded before he is hanged. Clearly, he was in pain. He turned away from Salaado and the plates laid before him and concentrated on the distant corner in which Hilaal had been standing, thickening the gravy with a couple of spoonfuls of cornflour. (Misra felt disoriented when she learnt that Hilaal cooked most meals, spent a great many hours in the house whilst Salaado went out and returned with a bagful of shopping; disoriented because she had never been in a home where the man did the woman's job and the woman more or less the man's.)

'You remember I asked you once if a people can be said to be terribly mistaken? We were talking in reference to whether or not Somalis everywhere can be described as "terribly wrong" in view of their nationalist stand. Do you remember what you said?' He addressed his question as much to Salaado as he was addressing it to Hilaal. 'Do you?'

'I said, I think, that a people cannot be said to be terribly mistaken; that we can arguably challenge a person's views or a small community's rightness or wrongness. Not a nation.'

Because he remained silent, the room resounded with the relic of the wisdom just recalled and the three of them lived, for disparate moments, in separate mansions of memory. Salaado took this to mean that since the township of Kallafo accused Misra of being the traitor, no one was right in challenging their verdict. Hilaal was of a different opinion, although he hadn't the wish to express it then. Indeed, he belived that a people can be sadly mistaken about themselves, their own position *vis-à-vis* the ideas which concern them. Not only that, but they may not know how misinformed they are; they may never realize they are wrong. He thought of the American people; thought how uninformed the people of the Soviet Union were. *E comè!* he said to himself. Askar? He was pleased with what he had achieved and, like a mediocre player of chess, waited for the opponent to make any move. Salaado:

'Now what I cannot understand is how you can allow yourself, intelligent as you are, sensitive as you are, to be so irreverent towards a woman who had once been like a mother to you? Yes, so irreverent and so disrespectful, Askar.'

The blow was stronger than he had anticipated and it floored him. He hadn't expected she would make such an unforeseen move, one that would force him to look at himself afresh, take note of his own surroundings – and see Misra as a victim, first of his people and then of himself. He felt like one who was dropped into a deep well and whose ears were filled with water and therefore he couldn't hear anything, not even his own breathing. He was inexcusably silent. Salaado stared at him, as wrestlers stare at their rivals who take refuge in a corner while they catch their breath lost in a previous round. And because he wouldn't say anything, Salaado said, 'Do you know that she is staying with us?'

The shadows of the afternoon sun were drawn on his face, and Hilaal, who had joined them, carrying the gravy and the roast beef in his left hand and the salad in his right, couldn't determine if Askar was smiling or not. As he put down things on the table-mats, he said to Askar, 'We cannot understand how you can be so insensitive, so unkind to the woman who had been once a mother to you. We wondered if you're likely to disown us the day one of life's many misfortunes calls on us!'

He sat in shamefaced silence. Salaado:

'She says she dare not join one of the refugee camps. Not only because she fears the reprisals if someone from Kallafo were to recognize her, but also because she entered the country in disguise, bearing someone else's name and was registered as such at the border-post. It would be taking a great risk to tamper with the papers.'

Hilaal served Salaado and handed her plate over to her. He was serving Askar his portions when, exploiting the silent moment, he said, 'I've offered to register her as my dependent. In fact, I'll register her in our *foglio famiglia* as a relation. That means she will stay with us, be one of us, a member of our family.'

Salaado continued as the salad bowls were being passed around, 'She believes she is very sick and predicts she will die soon. Now that doesn't worry us. We think that, given the loving care she needs, she will recover. We'll take her to one of my cousins who's one of the best surgeons of this country and he will take care of her complaint. All her complaints. Today, before she went to sleep, she appeared distressed on account of a pain in her left breast.'

Askar's stare became so severe, it disturbed both Hilaal and Salaado and when they followed it, they could understand it. Apparently, Misra, quiet as an insect, had crept in on them. They fell silent for a second. Then Hilaal and Salaado's voices clashed clumsily, each giving up their seat, forgetting there was an untaken chair next to Askar. As she walked further in, looking a little rested, Hilaal and Salaado each offered her a portion of their meat. Askar pushed his towards the empty chair and said, 'You can have my share, since I don't want any of it, anyway.'

And before anyone spoke to him, he was gone.

[6]

The doctor said he could determine what ailed her only after she had undergone a thorough medical examination. But to Salaado and Hilaal he said he suspected the tumour in Misra's left breast was malignant and that the breast would have to be removed.

No one told her this. Which was why there was, in the air, a sense of uneasiness as soon as they returned to the house. Salaado's confiding the newly revealed secret to Askar (she spoke to him in Italian so Misra couldn't follow) complicated matters further. He sounded as though he were indifferent to the sad news. And this greatly upset both Salaado and Hilaal. To ease the tension, Salaado asked Misra, 'Is there anything you've always had a passion to see in, say, Mogadiscio? Something you've always had a wish to see before you ... er ... die as we all must when our day comes? Is there anything, Misra?'

Salaado registered Hilaal's hard stare, which wouldn't dissolve despite her quiet appeal. And Askar wasn't impervious to what was occurring after all. For it was he who intervened when, maybe preoccupied with the theme of death and the worries pertaining to it, Misra couldn't speak of any passion other than the one lodged in the centre of her heart – the passion to live! Maybe also Askar remembered the rule of their house in Kallafo – that no one should speak of death. He could forgive Salaado for doing so – but he had to set things right and quickly too. And: 'You've always had a passion to see the sea, no?' he addressed Misra, surprising himself not so much as he pleased Salaado and Hilaal. 'You've always had a passion to see the ocean.'

A little resigned, she said, 'That's true.'

'Then we shall go, all four of us, to Jezira, shall we?' Salaado said to Askar, meaning that she was sure she, Hilaal and Misra would definitely go, but would he?

And before he said, 'Let's', the necessary preparations were under way – Hilaal had entered the kitchen to slice bread and cheese for a possible picnic and Salaado had disappeared into their bedroom to bring out towels, swimming-trunks, etc. She returned after a while, reminding Askar he should bring his and two towels, one for himself and another for Misra. 'But she doesn't know how to swim,' he said, half-shouting.

She hushed him. 'Never mind,' she said, after a brief pause. 'Get something for her, it doesn't really matter. And let us get going so we can be at Jezira and return before it is dark.'

They went their separate ways and converged in the living-room. Hilaal had a carrier-bag in his hand and they knew what it contained. And Misra? She was standing against the furthest wall as though she were part of it, or as though she were a carpet, rolled up and standing against the wall. And she saw them as a threesome, she saw herself apart from them: she was sick, they were not; she wasn't a Somali and they were. Only after Askar went to her did she move away from the corner where she had been.

'Are you all right?' he said.

She nodded. Her eyes, Askar could see, were on his hands. Of what was she afraid? Of what was she suspicious? he thought to himself. He was much taller, much heftier – he was her cosmos, he said to himself. Just the way she used to be his when he was a great deal younger. He extended a friendly hand out to her. At first, she wouldn't take it. He looked over his right shoulder and saw Hilaal and Salaado nervously watching them, neither saying anything lest they disturbed them. 'Come on,' he said, this time extending to her only his little finger, as if to a child. And she took it.

They walked level for several paces. She was the child, he the adult. 'You do want to come to the ocean, don't you?' he asked, aware that he was addressing her like a child; aware there was a streak of condescension in his voice.

'Yes,' she said.

He said, 'I will teach you to swim if you wish.'

She nodded.

Again, he was addressing her like a child, 'Is there anything you wish passionately to see when we are at the sea? Anything else you've always wished to see?'

They were standing in front of Hilaal and Salaado. And they became conscious of how each spoke, how each responded. Now they were playing to an audience, they had to be careful. Consequently, there seeped into their voices an awareness of the outside world, of Salaado and Hilaal, an awareness of their own past together, an awareness of *the other* in each of them.

'I would very much like to see a shark,' she said.

Hilaal thought, what an impossible request to make. I wish I could make it happen. I wish I could take her to an aquarium – if only there were one in Mogadiscio. But why a shark? And Salaado thought, I like this woman's imagination, it is wide, it is encompassing, it is inclusive, it is larger than the world of which she isn't an integral part. Why a shark? Because she is dissatisfied with the little she's been offered and wants more, feels she is entitled to be given more and will do the best she can to acquire more. What an imagination! As for Askar, his thoughts led him away from the territory of reason to one in which he was a small child asking if it was possible for a boy to menstruate? Or if it was possible to meet 'death' face to face and survive? He saw in her request a yearning, a passion for a past long gone.

After a long pause, Salaado said, 'It is not every day one sees sharks in these parts. But we can go to behind the Xamar Slaughter House, the newly built one, and there we're likely to see a shark. In fact, the story goes that a woman swam while menstruating heavily and thus attracted a shark's passionate attentions and he made of her a morsel – that was all.'

Silence. When Askar looked at Misra, he found her quietly standing in another corner, sulking. She was like a rolled carpet tied with a rope at both ends, leaning against the wall. She stared ahead of herself, trembling a little, perhaps at the thought that she would be fed, as the menstruating woman (or rather as a sacrificial beast?) to the famished sharks behind the Xamar Slaughter House? She didn't say anything. She took the little finger offered her by Askar, whom she found to be friendly.

'Shall we go?' he said, his finger secure in Misra's grip.

'Let's,' said Hilaal.

And they were in a car in less than two minutes. Askar thought, I will teach Misra how to swim. Hilaal thought, I am glad she's beginning to trust Askar again and am glad Askar is lavishing on her his affectionate warmth, in which she will rediscover their old selves so they will be happy again together. Salaado thought, as you travel further from your home-base, the cosmos shrinks proportionately in size. Does Misra expect her seeing a shark will remind her of a larger cosmos, a much more aggressive universe, one in which blood is not a life-force but that of death and self-destruction?

Salaado drove the car. Hilaal sat beside her. Misra and Askar were in the back together, their bodies very close, their fingers entwined. In the rear mirror, Salaado saw, they were so engrossed in each other they didn't need to acknowledge the existence of the outside world. When alone, and at the beach, she reported what she suspected she saw to Hilaal. And he was happy.

PART THREE

Who shall deliver me from the body of this death?

Romans 7:24

CHAPTER TEN

[1]

You spent less time in your house now that Misra was also there. You entered it quiet as a trespasser, showered, changed into clean clothes only to get out again, saying, at times, where you would be ('I am at Riyo's place, we're studying geography together' – Riyo being a girl your age – a neighbour and classmate), and on occasion, you didn't bother giving indications as to whether you would return home and have a meal. One thing was obvious – Hilaal and Salaado were in some kind of a moral dilemma. Of course, when it came down to making choices, they would've preferred your presence to Misra's. Also, they thought it unkind to throw her out. What they did was to pray, together and separately, for a threshold of understanding to be reached. Otherwise, thought Hilaal, they would have to precipitate a mild confrontation between the two of you. With such a prospect in mind, Karin's name was dropped. Misra picked it up, as though Salaado had flung it in the mud, and dusted it clean with the edge of her newly washed robe. All she was said was, 'The worst enemy in the world is one who has been your dearest and most intimate friend half your life.' And from then on, no one dared pollute the air by mentioning Karin's name again. Nor did anybody get the chance to ask her about her uncovered identity, with her name ending with 't' and meaning something like 'foundation of the earth'. To dissolve the thickness of the tension in the room, somebody teased you. But Misra remained standing outside your acquired freehold territory, feeling she was barred from entering it.

To provoke you (or was this meant to tease you), Salaado, on this particular evening, said: 'You don't seem to us,' and she looked at Hilaal and Misra, this being as wide as the parenthesis could extend, 'as though you will leave for a war zone. Such a person gets rid of all extra burdens save a gun, say, a belt of ammunition or maybe two, perhaps the odd item such as binoculars, if they can be had and, who knows, a revolver. Why, I hope you don't mind my saying so, but you appear to me like a young man who has found a new love – Riyo what's-her-name – who, I hear, you're intending to take with you to the war front, God knows as what.'

Hilaal called Salaado's name – they all got his meaning!

'Are you saying, Salaado,' you began your self-defence with a newly acquired confidence, 'that I am the proverbial coward who is reported to have told every child and adult in his village that he was preparing for a fight and went into the forest, returning thence, burdened with so many clubs he couldn't even walk. When the villagers asked why he was carrying so many, in contrast to his opponent's one, the coward said, "I wish everybody to know that I, who can cut so many trees and carry so many clubs, can floor any number of contestants." Are you saying I am like that proverbial coward, Salaado?'

Hilaal appeared pleased with your robust state of mind. He was happy your enthusiasm was again ablaze with the same kind of informed argumentativeness as before and that you were like your old self again. He commented: 'I've never heard it told so elegantly. Or is this not Cigaal Shiidaad's story?'

By then, Salaado had risen from her seat and switched on the light; by then, Misra had discreetly asked Hilaal if it was true you were intending to travel to the war front with what's-her-name, Riyo. And when Misra wanted to comment, Hilaal raised his hand – *basta!* Silence. Salaado took her chair. You got up from yours. Misra half got up from hers, as if she were following you to wherever you were going. And Hilaal watched all of you behave in this nervous way with a certain disquiet.

Salaado, suspecting that you were about to go out of the house, said, 'Isn't it too late to go out for your shooting practice?'

You could hear Hilaal intone, '*Dio mio*, Salaado, don't you know when to let go, when to stop?' You looked up at the ceiling and your stare met the burning bulb's. 'Too late,' you said.

Again, you looked up at the bulb, like one who expected it to say something. You told yourself there was something upsetting about how Salaado was getting possessively interested in your movements, probing into your affairs, reading your notes and interrogating you whenever there was a chance. She didn't want you to leave for the war front, that much was apparent. But neither did Hilaal. Silent, you looked at the electric bulb, when, pop! And the bulb fell to the floor within a couple of inches of you, rendering your half of the room dark. You stood where you were for a moment, before you bent down to pick it up. You shook it gently, then a bit harshly, you brought it nearer your ears and listened to it. You certified it dead.

Hilaal said, 'Bulbs give so many light hours and then they go pop and are dead.'

Misra looked from him to you, then from you to Salaado and then back at you, for she knew, somehow, that you wouldn't let that go without a comment. You said, 'A man, however, doesn't have a set number of hours, days, months or years to live. Why do you think that is so?' And you addressed the question to no one in particular.

Hilaal was beyond himself with delight. You were well, your head was working, you were thinking and were not morose, silent, with-drawn. You were fun. As before. 'Tell us. Why.'

'Imperfections or perfections ... or if you prefer ... the absence or presence of ... er ... imperfections and perfections in the order of things. Man. Woman. God. Eh?'

Hilaal was clearly delighted that you had put the ball back into his side of the court. In his, there was light; in yours, darkness. You knew what he would say – or so you thought. But he didn't have the slightest idea where you might bounce from next. He said, 'Depends.'

'If one believes in God or no?'

He nodded his head. You made as though you would leave.

Salaado said, 'Where are you going, Askar?'

Hilaal to Salaado, '*Per amor di dio*, Salaado!'

But she disregarded his comment. She said to Askar, 'I'm asking because next door they are having a *mingis* ceremony tonight and I remember your telling me you wanted to attend it. Would you like to stay for dinner and then go later with whoever is coming?' And she spoke in such a gentle voice you couldn't bring yourself to refuse.

You nodded your head in the darkened half of the room and were not sure if anyone *saw* your answer. But it didn't matter. In an hour or so, you knew the kitchen would receive you all, the tables would seat you, the cutlery would feed you (unless Hilaal ate with his fingers) and Misra would be uneasy, sitting awkwardly at table, her knife every now and then ending in the wrong hand, her fork dropping to the floor. Hilaal would say, 'All this is nonsense. Eat with your fingers the way I am doing.'

Salaado would say, 'Chicken is best eaten with one's fingers,' although she herself might be using a fork and a knife. Something was happening to Salaado. Askar was unhappy about it.

Hilaal said, 'Let's go and cook.'

When chopping up onions, Salaado forgot an elementary principle Hilaal had taught her – that she should cut it in two halves and let them soak in water for a couple of minutes. Then she wouldn't drop tears as big as French onions, sniffing, onion-eyed and complaining, 'Oh, what must I do now?'

Hilaal gave her a napkin with which to wipe away the tears. As she was leaving the kitchen, he said, not so much for your benefit as for Misra's – Misra, who was standing near the sink, staring at the thawing meat – 'When two persons have been living together for over a decade, they tend not to listen to each other's advice. I've told her time and again, perhaps a million times.'

But what was he thinking, staring at Misra? Was he thinking ill of her? It wasn't something he said. It was the way he kept looking at her as she looked furtively at the meat thawing in the kitchen sink. The trouble was, you were wrong. It seemed your prejudice bred monstrous ideas. In fact, he was saying amicably, 'And you, Misra? What would you like to do?'

She didn't know what to say.

'I suggest you season the meat,' he said. 'You did it so handsomely well, the other day, it *ate* superbly.' However, he stopped in mid-thought, like a man who discovers a richer diamond deposit than the iron-ore he has been mining all this time. 'Why don't I leave the two of you together? I'll join Salaado and help her pick the rice clean. Is that all right?'

For a long time, neither you nor she spoke. Then you both filled the emptiness with conversation equally uncontroversial and empty of real substance. She talked of how much she liked the kitchen you were in. She touched the washing-machine which was standing next to the fridge, one switch bright red and on, the other dull and not on. Karin's name, Qorrax's, Aw-Adan's were not mentioned. Nor was any reference made to herself or to the lieutenant whom she had befriended. You were saying something as agreeably pleasant and banal as, 'When I see a woman carrying on her head firewood, on her back a child and in front, hugging to her chest, the day's shopping, my heart bleeds in sympathy for such a martyr.'

Suddenly, you appeared relieved – like a husband who warmly welcomes an unexpected guest, arriving just at the instant when his wife is about to put an embarrassing question to him – because Cusmaan, your former tutor, had arrived. You introduced them to each other. They displayed the pleasant surprise of each indicating that he/she imagined the other to look not exactly as 'I had imagined'.

In a friendly way, Misra said, 'Perhaps Askar has misled you.'

'No, no,' said Cusmaan. 'I've misconstructed images of you which apparently do not match the reality. It is all my fault,' and they shook hands again.

'He's certainly misinformed me,' said Misra, still in her consistently friendly manner.

'He overpraised me. He always does.'

Misra said, 'On the contrary.'

'He underpraised me?'

Misra nodded her head.

Cusmaan remained charmingly polite and exchanged a few more niceties with Misra. Then he gave you a booklet which was to give you the basics of how to repair a car. You opened the book with obvious excitement and saw a highway of technical signs which you didn't know how to read, and then glanced at the glossary offering explanatory footnotes to the jargon of motor mechanics. 'Once you've understood what this booklet says, you are on your way to becoming a potential repairer of vehicles appropriated from the enemy.'

You knew things were not as easy as all that. But you were glad he had come. His arrival had injected new blood into everybody and there was a great deal of excited movement. You were all in the kitchen, milling round one another. Hilaal then offered to finish cooking the food whilst you talked to Cusmaan.

By chance, your gaze fell on Misra. She was pressing the inside of her forearm against her chest – a gesture breast-feeding mothers make when they are full of unsucked milk. You guessed, correctly, that her breasts were aching. Also, when she saw Hilaal, Salaado and Cusmaan's look home in on her too, Misra's arm ceased moving and there occurred something similar to the transformations caused by a whirlwind turning over dust, earth, etc., only to leave everything, a moment later, in the hands of gravity, trusting it to restore to the elements the balance they had lost. You came closer to her. And you smelled her.

True. She had started her period at the very instant you looked at her.

'If you went?' said Salaado; and looked in your direction.

All five of you were at table, all five, including Misra. You thought that either Misra's body's habits had undergone surprising changes or you didn't have your facts right. Although at this moment in time, that wasn't your main worry. You were attentively listening to a point Cusmaan was making, Cusmaan, who had become an expert at spinning a tapestry of controversies, having learnt the trade from Hilaal. The gist of what he was saying wasn't vivid even to himself, you could see, but it was touching on a topic which interested you, namely the relationship between 'high' literature and 'scripts'. He quoted two instances: Amharic, although a written language for centuries, with little or, he said, no 'exceptional' literary figures to speak of; Somali, a language that had no orthography until October 1972, with 'exceptional' poets, gifted orators and highly talented wordsmiths. The question, he argued, was not a case of one of oral literature against a written one, no. It was a language (i.e. Somali) with phenomenally sophisticated literature, against another (Amharic) served poorly by her poets and prose writers.

Cusmaan's point became clearer in the brief silence between the moment he stopped talking and the instant Hilaal picked its loose threads, adding a couple of his balls of cotton-threads and weaving out of them a plait of conclusions, with its own web of yarns, warps and wefts.

'No, no, no, you don't get my point,' argued Cusmaan.

Hilaal said, 'I do. I do.'

'You don't.'

Salaado said, 'You are saying the same thing, Cusmaan.'

Hilaal was saying, 'But this is a dangerous point Cusmaan is making. You don't know enough about Ethiopian literature to compare it fairly with Somali literature. For example.'

'Please no for examples. Listen to me.'

The women communicated secretly (Misra was in her seasonal pain and Salaado decided to be with her) and left the men to determine how best to rule the world. In the meantime, Hilaal got caught in the intricacies of his ideas. In his spiral thinking he went up and up the entwining stairway, reaching such great heights as would justify his encroaching on historical as well as literary theories, in and outside the Horn of Africa. At some point, when he got to a landing, he paused. Leaning against a ramshackle railing, his hands open in the shape of brackets, he commented on the political and literary activities of Sayyid Mohamed Abdulle Hassan, the Somali peoples' greatest warrior-poet to date and Menelik, his contemporary, the architect of the Ethiopian empire. Suddenly, however, Hilaal's eyes narrowed and he appeared ill at ease, as though the flight of stairs leading up to the summit of his climb would give way if he tried to ascend them. Another pause, this time of a more pedestrian kind. He looked up and saw that Salaado had returned alone. 'What is the matter with Misra?'

'She is a woman,' said Salaado.

A briefer pause, and he was moving round his spiral thinking, ascending now, descending now, describing vividly the poetic feud which involved the Sayyid and a number of detractors including one unheard-of English poet who entered the feud with a contribution 'veined as the romantic arm extended out to the victim who must be cajoled before he is dealt the final blow. For example.'

And there came a chorus of complaints. 'Wait, wait.'

You heard drumming. You thought of the *mingis* ceremony. Salaado nodded her head in your direction and said, 'She's resting for a while, but she says she will come with you.'

Cusmaan was saying, 'Ethiopia, let me for-example you, Hilaal, has never been colonized. Her national language, although spoken by a minority, has had a script from long before Christ. And yet, how is it that this country, that has been independent all through the ages of documented history, this Ethiopia whose population is ten times that of Somalia's; this Ethiopia, with a script from long before Christ – how is it that Ethiopia has not produced one poet, ancient or contemporary, relying either on the oral or the written form, one single Ethiopian genius of a poet, who is comparable to Somalia's hundreds of major poets that Somalis can field?'

'Don't be ethnocentric. That's all I say. Of course, being independent for a hundred years didn't get Liberia into the same bracket as Ethiopia. No one can explain these things. How, for example, does it happen that two-thirds of Somalia's major poets come from the Ogaden and the Haud?'

Silence. And the voice of the master of *mingis* ceremony singing, right in the heart of Mogadiscio, in a language definitely not Somali – this fact alone deserved a body of study and research work. The masters or mistresses of these ceremonies chant in the language the spirits understand – and that language is not Somali. It is Boran. Just as voodoo ceremonies in Haiti are conducted in Yoruba and not in the language of the island, Creole.

'Let's go,' Misra said to you.

[4]

You were admitted into a large room and there were many people and there was a great deal of toing and froing, with a stream of men and women entering or leaving. The neighbour's wife had been ill for some time. According to the shamanistic prescription, the woman would have the spirits in her influenced for the better, and they would leave her, if a white-tailed sheep was slaughtered; if the blood was smeared all over her body; and if she submitted herself trustfully to the incantantory rite of dancing and singing for three solid days and nights. The neighbour, an Xamari, was very wealthy and he loved his wife, who was his youngest. He didn't mind the expense. He agreed to pay the priest-doctor a handsome fee and would probably buy him an air ticket to and from Mecca. Also, the man refused to analyse or comment on the religious and philosophical contradictions surrounding his activities. He was a colleague of Salaado's, he was, by anybody's standards, a knowledgeable man, and was the son of a well-to-do Xamari family.

You and Misra, on being invited, went and watched the dance as you might have watched any theatrical performance – no more. But you didn't understand the language in which they sang, you couldn't decipher the chant. The language was definitely not Somali. Did Misra understand? You were surprised how much she was able to comprehend. And the woman-patient danced and danced and danced; and the priest-doctor challenged the spirits, asking that they name themselves – at least identify themselves, at least say whether they were human or jinn – and she danced and danced and danced.

'What's the name of the woman?' asked Misra.

His voice, loud, overpowered the drumming and he said, 'Waliima Sheikh.'

Impatient, the priest-doctor beckoned to the drummers to beat softer, slower. And he took the woman's hand, then held her by the shoulders and he started shaking her and shouting, 'Tell us who you are. Are you jinn or human? And what do you want?'

The woman danced and danced and danced.

The priest-doctor asked, 'Now, who are you? We haven't much time nor patience. We'll deliver you from the diabolical demands of the evil spirits who've apparently taken residence in you. So who are you?'

And the woman stopped dancing altogether. The drumming ceased too.

As if exhausted, the woman-patient began to speak, but her voice wasn't loud enough and nothing save the first part of the sentence could be heard clearly. But the 'I am ... I am', which evidently was heard by everybody, did generate a great deal of interest and hope in the hearts and minds of the audience. The priest-doctor concentrated intensely on the forehead of his patient as though his powers would drill through to her brain cells and this would help him, in the end, to solve the shamanistic riddle of what jinn or human could be so obstinate as to have withstood his probing for forty-eight hours. Presently, he signalled to the drummers to resume their drumming and they did as instructed. As more dancers encircled the woman-patient, the priest-doctor left the floor for his throne on the left-hand side of what was once the wife's living-room. But he rose again immediately as if he sat on thorns, and he was moving in the direction of his patient and saying, 'I will punish you severely if you don't tell us who you are,' and was shaking her body as though fruits, small as jinns or large as human eyeballs, would drop to the floor and he would just pick them up and make a gift of them to the patient's husband who was seated in another corner, on the right-hand side of the room.

You were not sure 'who' the priest-doctor was addressing; you were not sure 'who' he would punish severely – the woman-as-human or the spirit in the woman. After all, you knew the woman's name and you hoped the priest-doctor knew her human name too, or even if he didn't, the husband was there to remind him, or one of the neighbours. But then, what confounded you more was that he was now whipping her and was repeating loudly, again and again, the sentence, 'Just tell the congregation your name, address and, if possible, your profession. Are you a man, are you a woman or are you a child? Are you human or jinn?'

She stopped dancing and her head dropped to her chin – the way toys' heads do when the springs which hold them fail or snap. The drumming stopped. Everybody listened.

'Your name, sex, profession and address?' repeated the priest-doctor.

The woman finally said, 'I am Deeqo Amin.'

'And where do you live?' said the priest-doctor.

Silence. Meantime, the congregation repeated, in various manners, the name the patient mentioned. Somebody cursed 'Deeqo', another wished her hell, here and in the hereafter, but many waited before they pronounced their verdict. 'Where do you live?'

You remembered the *cuudis* ceremony in Kallafo, the one in which Karin gave a name different from her real one, and her identity as that of a man. *Mingis! Cuudis!* And you thought about the Egyptian *Zaar* and about the Mogadiscian's *Beebe* and *Booran.* You asked yourself, But who are we? Are we the jinn who dwell inside 'us' from time to time? Or are we always the human beings that we claim to be? What proportions of us are human and what jinn? Now the woman was shouting, 'I live in the Medina quarter of Xamar,' a statement she repeated thrice.

The priest-doctor waited for that to sink in. Then, 'And how many children have you?'

'I have none.' The members of the audience mumbled something to one another.

He repeated the question louder and expected the patient would repeat her answer louder too. 'I said, I have no children.' (And someone shouted, 'A bad eye.')

'What's the name of your husband, the full name please?'

The woman answered, 'I am a widow. My husband died in the Ogaden war.'

'And you have no children?' repeated the shaman.

The woman-patient said, 'That's right.'

You could tell from his voice that he was pleased his patient spoke somebody's name; that she claimed to be somebody else with a name and an address; that he had convinced all those present of his expertise. 'Please tell the congregation here, why you've chosen to "take residence" in Waliima Sheikh? Do you know her? Have you ever met, you and Waliima? Are you envious of her, her children and life style?'

'You might say that I've known Waliima Sheikh from when we played house-and-family together as girls and you would be right if you assumed that I've coveted her her marriage, her wealth, her children and her good looks. I married badly, she well; I left school early, she finished at hers and did well by it.'

He put more and more questions to the woman-patient until it became obvious *another* was speaking through her; *another*, with a different name and address; another, whose voice interfered with the proceedings, for it emanated from a different *other*. Could a good person live in an utterly bad one? you ask yourself, your imagination overwhelmed by the thought that this was possible. Could Misra hide in you? Could *another* dwell in her?

The world of the unknown had greater potentials, you thought, and lost interest in the mundanities of what the priest-doctor was saying or what wicked actions the audience was prescribing as punishment for the woman who, out of jealousy, 'took residence' in *another*.

Do you remember?

[5]

There was a flood.

And you floated. You floated, heavy as a corpse, asleep to the end of the world. You floated easterly, towards the sea. You remember someone saying there would no longer be any more rebirths, or renewals of any sort. Millions of people had lost their lives and property in the flood, but then everyone agreed this didn't matter, for this was the end of the world and the flood was to mark the end-of-the-world's beginning. And when a woman who had floated beside you for days asked what you were doing, you responded that you had come to bury yourself in the water. You said you would blow out the light and, in the total darkness surrounding you, you would expire. You prophesied that a heavy downpour of successive floods would fall from the heavens, joining the earth and the sky, obliterating from everybody's memory all the dreamt dreams, and there would be no past, no present and no future. Then you turned to the woman who had earlier asked you why you were there and you inquired of her why she too was there. She said, 'My husband and I are in the business of building tombs on seabeds.' You took a fresher look at the woman. And you put a name to her face.

You were spat by the flood, as though you were an uprooted weed on the bank of a river, green with young foliage – foliage whose chaotic message you couldn't follow. There, you were met by an old man who, in a big way, reminded you of Aw-Adan, but also, in a small way, looked like your younger tutor, Cusmaan. Suddenly, the heavens darkened and all you could see was the man's grey hair, bushy and also silvery. Then the man put his hand into his pocket and he gave you a knife. You dared not ask the man what you were supposed to do with the knife, but you said, surprising even yourself, 'But why the flood?' And the old man with the white head said, 'Floods are a product of a common bad.' Now do you remember, or have you chosen, as usual, to remember only the good things, deciding to forget the bad?

Anyway!

You were surrounded by darkness. You were surrounded by multitudinous water. Inside the water, you passed more water, your own water that is, as though you were expected to make a contribution, however small. And there shone in the sky a fairly young moon, beautiful as a maiden's face. The sea was green as the silver of a mirror and you could see your own shadow on the tinier crests your body's movements created. You had bloodshot eyes, but you didn't know because you couldn't see it yourself. You were alone, but you didn't think about it and you didn't feel at all lonely. You would dive every now and then, and reach the bottom of the deep, deep sea, and whenever you came out to take another lungful of fresh air, you felt as if you were an entirely different person. Tired from swimming alone, you went to sit by a sand-dune near the sea.

It was light already – dawn had broken.

And there was a young boy, barely ten, who was meditatively busy washing clean a skull. He was performing his task with absolute devotion – you could tell from the way he breathed, you could see the concentration on his face, you could sense, without touching him, the tension in his own body. The skull was that of a human. But you couldn't determine, even when you held it in your hands, whether it had belonged to a small person or a heavily built man or woman. You could decide, without taking undue risk, that it had been there for years. For one thing, plants had begun to sprout in it. For another, the colour had worn off its cheekbone, which had grown a shade browner.

You watched in reverent silence.

The young boy dipped it wholly in the water, removing the grains of sand which had been lodging in there. He shook it a little too roughly, emptying it of life. As he held it away from himself, the young boy watched, with utter amazement (or was it amusement?) as the insects moved, in a fury of fright and frenzy, as they scattered here and there – like a cinema crowd running confusedly down the exit stairway because the safety-curtain had caught fire. When he was satisfied that he had emptied it of life of all forms, he dipped it again

in water, soaped it again and again until it was as white as the foams
the sea frothed at his feet. From where you stood, you could read the
letter 'M' tattooed on the skull in blue. And you provided the missing
letters of that name – just as you had earlier put a name to a face you
had seen.

Do you remember any of that?

You don't? How very weird!

You asked the young boy why he was washing the skull clean. As
if in response to you, he dipped it in water and drank from it. You
stared at him in total bewilderment.

He said, 'There is life in death, there is death in life.'

Not only that he said nothing original, but the fact that you didn't
ask him anything – this, perhaps, made you stare at him in a hostile
manner. Then he explained, 'This skull belonged to a man who raped
his own daughter. He died in old age, a hated man, a man without
friends, a man alienated from his own community. For years, he saw
dreams in which he wore a young girl's face. He died in a tempestuous
flood.'

At least, admit you remember this.

You don't?

Your memory, dare I say? is very selective!

[6]

You swam through the gate of purgatory and washed clean your doubts
in the waters of certainty. You were penurious in your comments, but,
once it was suggested by Uncle, you agreed to call at the hospital
where Misra had undergone an operation in which she lost a breast.
(Her state of mind was such that she couldn't determine how she
'felt'. 'Perhaps more like a man,' she said, half-laughing, 'now that I
have to have the chest bandaged forever.') She lay in hospital, pained.
You called on her, doubtful of your own reactions. You sat by her
and held her hand in yours – you hardly knew what to say. Your
conversations, needless to say, were replete with empty silences,
unfilled spaces, incomplete dots, and inconsistent holding on to, or
letting go of, certain consonants, before you pronounced the vowels
preceding them clearly and accurately.

You remembered that, in the hospital corridor just before you
entered her private ward, you had seen a young boy, aged five, walk

into the Ladies', escorted by his mother. You remembered thinking how, in sex, age mattered greatly. The women in the hospital's Ladies', you suspected, didn't mind having amongst them a *Homo sapiens* of the male gender so long as he was small and as yet underdeveloped in so far as the male ego was concerned. And neither did Misra bother about you, when you were such a small boy yourself. Now, you could see how self-conscious she was, how prudent in her self-preservation, how cautious in her mannerisms, how womanly aware of the man in you. If you were honest with yourself, you would've requested that she showed you how much of the breast the doctor had removed – and you almost did so. Which was how you knew she couldn't tell whether it was the left or the right the surgeon's knife had eaten into. Should she make a display of it in the way those returning from the Ogaden war had exhibited the stump of the leg, the grazed forehead or the broken nose-joint? Should she, or should she not blame it on the war as everybody had blamed every misfortune or misdeed that befell him or her?

You said, your hand resting near her kneecap, 'And how have things been with you?'

She spoke of what worried her: that she thought the nurse attending to her was related to someone from Kallafo and that she was mortally worried that the nurse might report on her or poison her food or mix wrongly, but deliberately (although it might appear innocently) all her medicines so she would take them and die of the poisonous mixture. But how was she certain that the nurse knew of her background? Because of the way she asked questions about Kallafo 'without my ever mentioning the name of that accursed town, without my ever saying that I came from that wretched place'. This was what made her think that a woman with whom the nurse had spoken amicably was related to a male patient in an adjacent ward, a man who had come from the war in the Ogaden 'without his manhood, for a bomb had blown off his testicles. And what use can a man make of a penis without testicles?' she asked, underlining, in her voice, the words 'penis' and 'testicles'.

Should I not tell that the nurse knew she was from Kallafo because Uncle Hilaal was the one who had filled in the form and that he had been told he might, in the end, persuade the hospital authorities to give a deduction on the basis of the patient's coming from Kallafo? you thought to yourself.

'You believe that I am paranoid?' she asked.

You said, 'Of course not.'

Would you help her if she were in terrible need? she inquired of you. Would you keep watch on the movements of people if this became absolutely necessary? Would you spill your own blood to save her? Would you kill those who were plotting to do her in? Of course you would. You wouldn't take them to court or anything, but you would use the knife they had used to kill her in order to take vengeance? But you caught your breath with a view to slowing down the pace of the conversation and you asked why it mattered whether you would take her murderers to court or kill them yourself with your own hands and with the same weapon as they had used? She reasoned that almost all the courts in Somalia would set the culprits free because they had killed, on suspicion, a woman who was not Somali herself and whose innocence was harder to believe or even to account for.

'Be truthful,' you began to say, deliberately slowly. 'Be truthful and tell me what I must know if I must take vengeance. Did you or did you not do it? Be truthful.'

She shifted in her bed and you let go her hand. You could sense she had moved into that undefined space between a smile and a cry. She held her head up lest her nose dripped, lest her eyes emptied themselves of the tears welled up in them. She remained motionless but tense, the way one might when one is anticipating one's system to emit a storm of a sneeze when one is in respectable company without a clean handkerchief.

'To think that you might suspect me of betraying . . .' she said, once she could speak. 'I would have thought myself incapable of doing any such wicked thing until somebody said I had done it.'

You didn't say anything.

'To think that you could even suspect me of betraying . . .' And then she burst into tears, shaking a little. You held her hand tighter in yours, for you could feel the tremor in her body, you could sense the torment in her pained soul.

After a pause, you said, 'Who was it that accused you of being a traitor?'

'That most wretched, most wicked man,' she swore.

'What's his name?'

You could see how it hurt when she said, 'That most sinful man.'

'His name?'

Again, she tilted her head forward so her chest wouldn't pain her most awfully, you thought. And her body emitted a tremor that was total, like an earthquake's. You were both in a room, somewhere in Kallafo, and it was you who was taking your body's pained measurements, your body's space, as the guide in your dealings with other people, for it was you who had been in pain.

She said, 'I had trusted him, how I trusted him.'

'His name?' you said, speaking like one who would kill.

She finally said, 'Aw-Adan.'

There was suddenly a power cut. The room became hot and stuffy and you couldn't think of anything to say. Neither could she.

[7]

A week later, when she was still in hospital, you showed Uncle Hilaal and Salaado your first completed drawing, because you thought you were satisfied with it. In it, there is a man of about sixty, with a loin-cloth for a wrapper, and he has, sitting on his lap, a hen. The man's features clearly indicate his origin – he's an Adenese. Behind him, there is a guava orchard and, standing purposelessly about, there are a few young boys, aged between ten and fifteen. It is obvious that the boys are waiting for something. But they are all looking up – some, evidently, at the blue sky, a sky peaceful as it is inviting; others at a hill upon whose most northern point is hoisted a mast flying a white flag.

To the left of the Adenese-looking man with the pointed features, there is a woman, larger than a quarter of the canvas. The woman's body is divided into four squares and in each square, the artist manages to place an appropriate image. In one, a horseman is dropped to the floor and the horse rides the wind, eastwards; in another, a man in priestly robes is counting money, and re-counting it so he will at least get that right; in a third, there is an infant cradled in innocence and his stare dissolves in tears – but one can see where his stare is focused – at the huge woman; and in the furthest square, that is the fourth, the infant has grown bigger and is lying down on his chest and is learning to shoot a rifle. His eyes are now fixed on the hill above him.

To the east of the woman, the ocean. And at its shores, a festive crowd, shouting slogans of victory. Everybody here is looking at the sky. The day is bright with light but there is a solitary star and it is displaying only three of its five points. Is every member of this festive crowd wondering why all the star's points aren't there, why they have been amputated and by whom?

Further east but northerly, there is a young man posed in quiet elegance. He is big now. Slung round his shoulders, a gun. And beside him lies a woman who is in pain. To her left, blood. To her right, a knife, stained with caked blood.

[8]

A few days later, you did something you had never done before. You brought a girl home with you and took her to your room. The girl's name was Riyo. She was a classmate of yours. Often, you went to her place. But today, you came to yours because her parents' house was busy with people coming and going, for some event was taking place there and she didn't have to attend it. Riyo was a year younger than you but you liked her a lot because she hardly ever asked you questions and you were gentle with each other. She helped you with your English, which she spoke almost like a native. She had been born in Britain, where her father had done his higher education. She was weak in maths and physics and you drew her maps for her when your geography teacher assigned one as your homework.

Riyo was delightfully surprised to see your collection of maps and books. She also envied you the space you had in the house – a room all to yourself. She had known of these before, but confessed she didn't believe them to be true. She suspected you made them all up just as some other boys she had met at school or elsewhere invented the stories they narrated to city girls who were impressionable. Of course, you were honest with her. As expected, you told her that you were likely to leave for the war front if called up. Her only comment was, 'But aren't wars dangerous? I've seen films in which people get killed. You won't die, will you?' She was sweet and had an innocent look and her face wore a smile, as though forever. There was something worshipful about her eyes when she stared at you, listening to you pontificate on a subject you had discussed with either Hilaal or Salaado. Her face reminded you of a girl you saw in a dream the day you crossed the *de facto* border at Feer-Feer. She was the kind of girl you could trust, the kind that you could have as a companion and as a wife if you went on a sabotage mission or had a job to do. It was with her that you left your manuals from which you learnt how to dismantle a revolver or start a car without the proper ignition keys. Once, you left in her care a couple of *Playboy*-like magazines. She

211

kept them for days without even opening them. And when you showed her your paintings, she confessed she didn't understand what they were about, but imagined she would love them if she did. She said, 'You are indeed talented.' And you were very pleased.

Then you told her about Misra. She said, 'Poor thing. I am sorry for her, I really am.'

'She is in hospital,' you said, 'and I am going to visit her. Perhaps today.' But you didn't tell her why she was in hospital and neither did she ask. And you said, 'Would you like to come with me?'

'I don't like hospitals very much, but if you like, I will come,' she said.

CHAPTER ELEVEN

[1]

I was eating, with great relish, a slice of the sky and it was most delicious. It was blue – as steaks are brown when well done – and it lay in great heaps in front of me, with a star crowning it as though it were some sort of icing, a star already partly eaten. I was unhappy that I couldn't determine how many points the star had had in the first place and how many it had now. I knew I could have had the clouds for my dessert if I chose to. I also knew I was sitting on a water mattress in the shape of a water-bottle, which was why I sat unevenly, swaying every now and then, whenever I changed position or had a mouthful.

I wasn't alone in the hall. That I could tell from the din of voices which served as background to my silent thinking. For instance, among the voices which I could easily identify were those of Uncle Hilaal, Salaado, Aw-Adan, my tutor Cusmaan – but not Misra's. Also, there were a number of my own peers and some had grown taller than I, some thinner, some weightier. But their experiences were nothing compared to mine, their mental reach definitely not as wealthy and varied as mine. I didn't know what to say to them. Their conversations with one another placed them in the geography of infancy whose maps and contours meant very little to them. I noticed there were no soul-searching questions asked, and that their lives centred on material acquisitions and on who owned what and how much this or that item cost. Not I!

The hall was very bright and I could see and identify every face I knew. Naturally, I looked for Misra – if only to ask her how she was; if only to apologize for my not calling on her of late. I thought I had seen her earlier, when not particularly looking for her. Now I went to the same spot. And there was something strange – I felt stupid when I realized that I had been talking to Misra's dress though she wasn't there herself. I cannot remember what I said. Now, I stared at the shadow the dress had made and I was more furious with myself. Then I heard the clamour created by a group of teenagers who had just arrived. Because I couldn't make them stop their annoying chatter, I walked out of the hall myself.

When outside, I thought to myself that things had to be different from this moment on. You cannot eat the sky as you do steaks, have the clouds as your dessert and expect the universe to turn on its axis, lightening the days with its thundery storms, brightening them with its suns, darkening the night with its dusky hours. I discovered that, although there were hundreds of thousands of men and women partaking of the meal in which slices of the heavens were being served as the first course and the clouds as dessert, we had no common language in which to exchange views, or even communicate our suspicions or fears of this new reality – a reality in which God was but absent; one in which somebody might have had him as his meal. How blasphemous, I thought, and ceased thinking altogether. What? I had a slice of the sky as my first meal, did you say? You must be mad, somebody was bound to say. How could you? And you say you had 'God Almighty' as your aperitif. You blasphemous fool. Get out of my sight before I lynch you. Surely, I said to myself, somebody was bound to be infuriated by these blasphemous pronouncements.

I stood by the window, which was open. The curtain blew in my face and teased it. Then I felt a drop of water on my forehead. I touched the spot with my dry index finger. Another drop and a third. These tasted of salt water. Did it mean that I was near a great body of water? I walked in the direction from where the smell of the ocean came. I walked through a field of ripe Indian corn. I plucked as I went. I plucked the shapeliest of them; I plucked the overgrown ripe corns and threw them aside. I trampled on anything that was in my path. I went on, treading blindly, my hands outstretched ahead of myself as though gathering, or receiving alms. My mind was bent on reaching the ocean whose smell grew less pungent the nearer I got to it. Finally, I could sense the grains of sand in my sandals. Although I couldn't tell why I couldn't smell the ocean in the blowing breeze.

And there *it* was, my feet in it, my cupped hands bringing its salty water so I might take a sip of it, taste it, feel at home in it. There it was for me to swim in and be received by it – large as a womb, warm as life, comforting as a friend.

And there *she* was too – Misra, I mean. She stood in the shallows and fishes came to her, playful fishes, going between her legs, the curve of her elbow; small and big fishes, and on occasion even a shark, timid as a lamb. She didn't see me. She was busy feeding the fishes with her blood, the flow of her period. She was busy tending to the sickly among the fishes, feeding them with motherly care.

I was utterly in love with her.

I couldn't comprehend how anyone could've accused her of betrayal.

Then I looked up at the sky. I resolved that we couldn't have eaten it all. All was peaceful. And I wished I were a fish – wouldn't she feed me? I thought to myself. She had fed me, had cared for me, loved me, brought me up on a body of ideas all her own. How could I bring myself to suspect her of any wrongdoing, how could I?

She was saying, as she attended to a sickly baby fish, 'They came to my ward last night and threateningly said they would kill me – those people from Kallafo. And it frightens me.'

'I doubt it if they will,' I said. 'They dare not.'

She said, 'If and when that happens and I am dead and no more, please take note of what I say to you now – I have not betrayed. I am innocent of the crime. You are the one person I care about so much that I want you to know the honest truth. The rest may go where they please or believe whatever they will. I don't care.'

The sea wore its blue gown. The sky had no hiatus. There were clouds in the heavens. And the moon was reflected in the water. And so was our shadow – Misra's and mine – as we embraced.

No, I do not remember anything else!

I remember no flood!

I recall nothing else either!

[2]

The following morning, I awoke and there was a taste of blood in my mouth. I found it odd that, although my tongue scoured the area surrounding the palate and the floor of the mouth, I could not account for it. Had I drunk drunk blood when asleep? I brushed my teeth a number of times. My saliva was as clear as sperm. I sensed no pain anywhere in my mouth. I confess it caused me some concern. And I couldn't help recalling the day I 'menstruated'. But what could the reason be?

I was torn between sharing the secret with Uncle Hilaal and Salaado and a wish to keep it all to myself, since I didn't tell it to Misra the first time this happened in Kallafo. I decided to make myself busy so I would occupy my thoughts with grander notions and I began to re-draw my map of the Horn of Africa. (In my map, the Ogaden was always an integral part of Somalia.) Anyway, no sooner had I completed the first draft than I heard a knock on the door and I answered, 'Please come in. It is open.' Uncle Hilaal entered, holding in his tight grip a teacup he had brought for me.

'Good morning,' he greeted.

I said, 'Good morning,' and thanked him for the tea.

My uncle stared at the map for a long, long time, piercing it with his severe concentration. I wondered if he did so because he noticed that my map didn't have a generic name, but a specific categorization, in that I had scribbled not 'The Ogaden' but simply 'Western Somalia', thereby, in a sense, making The Ogaden lose its specific identity, only to gain one of a generic kind. I was surprised that his imagination had taken him to a destination very different from the one I had considered. He said, 'Tell me, Askar. Do you find truth in the maps you draw?'

My mind became the blotted paper one had covered worthless writings with, but it took me nowhere, it mapped nothing, indicating no pathway to follow. I repeated the question aloud to myself as if to be sure, 'Do I find truth in the maps I draw?' and waited to see if the coarse ink on the blotted brain would dry, and if I would be able to visualize a clearer image, of which I could make better sense myself. All I could see was a beam of dust the sun had stirred nearer the window. I remained silent.

Uncle Hilaal clarified his point more. 'Do you carve out of your soul the invented truth of the maps you draw? Or does the daily truth match, for you, the reality you draw and the maps others draw?'

Now, I walked the pathways of my thoughts cautiously. I was an old man negotiating with his feet (he was nearly blind – longsighted as well as shortsighted – you may as well ask, how can that be? but he was!) the hazardous, slippery staircase of a condemned building, ancient as himself. I was sure everything would collapse on my head before long. With the confidence of one who's regained possession of a mislaid identity: 'Sometimes,' I began to say, 'I identify *a* truth in the maps which I draw. When I identify *this* truth, I label it as such, pickle it as though I were to share it with you, and Salaado. I hope, as dreamers do, that the dreamt dream will match the dreamt reality – that is, the invented truth of one's imagination. My maps invent nothing. They copy a given reality, they map out the roads a dreamer has walked, they identify a notional truth.'

Either he was dissatisfied with my reaction to his question or he didn't understand it. After he had allowed me time to take a sip of the tea he had just brought in for me, he said, 'The question is, does *truth* change?'

'Or do we? Do we, men and women and children, change? Or does truth?'

He said, coming closer, 'Better still, who or what is more important: the truth or its finder? You look at a map, of the British colonies in Africa, say, a map whose pinkish portions competed in terms of size and imagination with the green which represented the portions of the continent under the French. Now compare the situation today with its ghostly past and someone may think that a great deal of change has taken place and that names of a number of countries have been altered to accommodate the nationalist wishes of the people of these areas. But has the more basic truth undergone a change? Or have we?'

In the meantime, I picked up an old atlas: Somalia Italiana, British Somaliland, French Somaliland, the Northern Frontier District (which was then a protectorate, administered separately from the rest of Kenya) and a larger Ogaden. And I remembered seeing a map a German cartographer had drawn as his country invaded and conquered more and more of Europe. In my mind, I compared this 'temporary truth' of the German's redrawn map with Somalia's remapping the Ogaden as an integral part of the Republic when it held it for a few months. I compared them as 'truths', not as analogous points of rationalization. For in my view, there was a substantial difference – the Germans had no 'truthful' right to reassign territories, redesign maps just because they overran these lands and subjected the inhabitants to their tyrannical regimentation, but I believed the Somalis had a 'truthful' right to the Ogaden and, in a 'just' world, wouldn't have had to reconquer it.

Uncle Hilaal asked if I had heard of the name of Arno Peters? And of Eduard Kremer?

I said I had.

'And did you know that Eduard Kremer, who was the drawer of the 1567 map, introduced numerous distortions, thereby altering our notion of the world and its size, did you? Africa, in Kremer's map, is smaller than Greenland. These maps, which bear in mind the European's prejudices, are the maps we used at school when I was young and, I am afraid to say, are still being reprinted year after year and used in schools in Africa. Arno Peters's map, drawn four hundred years later, gives more accurate proportions of the continents: Europe is smaller, Africa larger.'

He had laid his finger on the map, tracing the African continent's projections from its Cape Guardafui in the Somali Peninsula down to the raped Cape in the South, up to North Africa, which once formed part of a Mediterranean world of values. The 'truth' was, I thought to myself, that Africa had little or no place in the anciently mapped thoughts of a mini-world. And what was he doing? He was staring at the map and then at me. And I saw in his stare an ambivalence of a kind I had difficulty interpreting. His finger, however, lay on the Somali Peninsula – his finger, skeletal, feeble and without energy.

Then he spoke at length and gave me a richer background, addressing himself to the Mercator projections of the world map and the image the cartographers imprinted on the imagination of billions of school-going populations anywhere in the world. He added, 'There is truth in maps. The Ogaden, as Somali, is truth. To the Ethiopian map-maker, the Ogaden, as Somali, is untruth.'

Silence. My stare presently dwelled on the cup of tea, whose brim was mapped with a whiter, unskimmed milk, which, to both of us, indicated its undrinkability. As he took it away, he stopped, like one who just then remembered why he had come in the first place. He massaged his forehead and finally spoke. 'I meant to ask you if you wanted to come with me because I am calling on Misra. Do you?'

I thought for a minute or two. 'Give me five minutes,' I said.

'You have ten,' he said.

[3]

The sky lay, like an afterbirth, in the secundine of the sea's womb, it having been expelled in the act of parturition. And Uncle and I sat in the car, with the wipers going *flik-flaag*, one of them fast, the other limply slow and half-broken, and it poured very, very heavily with rain. I couldn't tell why we were where we were, there was no reason I could give why Uncle Hilaal had decided to go in that direction. Could it be that we were both upset by the news that Misra had disappeared from her hospital bed? Perhaps 'disappeared' is not the right word. Perhaps 'taken away' is the right expression. But you have to know something in order to express it well, you have to have evidence so that you may describe things well or know what to do, or, for that matter, decide whether to think badly of someone, or a group of persons. Could it be, for instance, that she was kidnapped by the people whom she thought ill of, because she believed that they suspected her of betrayal?

'But what is one to do?' he would say every now and then, when we were both sadly silent for a long time. His look in my direction read like pages of appeal to me and it wasn't difficult to decipher it. It read, 'Since you've known her longest, since you know her a lot better than I, please tell me what to do.' In other words, he wanted me to be his guide in this.

However, it didn't take long for it to come out that I didn't know under what name she had entered the country and hadn't bothered to ask her who her own contacts in Mogadiscio were. It was only then that one began to regret; that one said what should've been done in the first place; how I should've been kinder, more sensitive, more understanding; that Uncle should've been more inquisitive and, in a sense, tougher in his dealings with her and if need be more bureaucratically minded. And Salaado? Uncle and I appeared lost without her. It occurred to me that he was most definitely unhappy because she wasn't with him to suggest what next course of action to take. We had driven around for quite a while looking for her. We had been to our house at least three times. We had called at the school where she taught and the principal said she had gone shopping. Since we didn't know what she was buying, we didn't know what market to go to when searching for her. As a matter of fact, while driving around, Uncle suggested I keep my eyes wide open just in case 'she' was also walking amongst other people, in one direction or another. The 'she' my eyes were intent on spotting was not 'Salaado' but 'Misra'. Although I thought things might have been eased a great deal once we saw Salaado. How we needed her, Uncle and I!

At the hospital, they said, three men had come and 'taken her away' because 'they' argued 'she' wanted to go. When asked, Misra gave the response, herself, in the affirmative to the nurse. Did she look threatened, tortured, did she appear at all frightened? had inquired Uncle Hilaal. The nurse wondered why she should have. Why should a woman leaving hospital of her own accord appear frightened? the nurse had argued. Of course not. 'She was, to me, a woman ready to go for a quick dip in the sea,' said the nurse. 'The three men were carrying towels – or something like towels anyway, and they were dressed in casual clothes and were addressing her in a friendly manner, each teasing the other and she, in turn, teasing them too.' (I wished I could've asked the nurse what language Misra and the men had communicated in, but I thought better of it because it might not have made any sense to her.) When did she leave the hospital grounds and how? No one knew in what – maybe a taxi, maybe a private car. The time recorded by the nurse on duty was precise to the second – eight thirty-five in the morning. Before the ward's doctor made the rounds.

'What are we to do?' Uncle said.

We were still in the car and it was pouring with the heaviest of downpours I had seen in years. I thought he had looked, not in my direction, but at the sea when asking the question and I wondered why!

'Suppose they kidnapped her?' I said.

He was suddenly conscious of one thing – that perhaps there was nothing we could do – and he looked most unhappy. 'Well, in that case, we'll have to revise our strategy, won't we? We must find out how best we can save her life. That is most essential. Save her life.'

'How?' I said.

He was relieved that it began to rain less heavily. He switched off the noisy wipers and sighed loudly. He drummed on the dashboard of the car, staring away from me, in silent concentration. 'We could go to the National Security and ask that they intervene. I have some friends. I can tell them the whole truth, tell them it is a matter of life and death. In the meantime, we inquire around, see if we know anyone who might know anyone from Kallafo who might know the kidnappers.'

I was about to say something in disagreement when, suddenly, I tasted blood in my mouth again. I rubbed my tongue against the front of my teeth, down and under them too and tasted my saliva which, in my mind, was white, as spittle generally is. Without giving due thought to the consequences, I placed my cupped hands in front of me and spat into them, only to see that the saliva was actually not affected by the taste in my mouth. My uncle was puzzled. I wouldn't help him at first. I spat out again. And saw, to my great relief, that it wasn't red as blood.

'What are you doing?' he finally said, when he realized that I had repeated the process a number of times. 'Are you all right?'

I said, 'I don't know.'

My tongue, in the meantime, was busy working the mouth and tasting the saliva, which the rubbing act had produced. 'There is the taste of blood in my mouth,' I told him.

'Blood?'

'Yes, blood.'

'In your saliva, there is the taste of blood?' he asked, worried.

He seemed anxious about finding a link between the taste in my mouth and Misra's disappearance. He reflected for a long time. He had an exuberance of expression, one moment delighted at discovering a link in his head; the following moment, unhappy because he couldn't pursue the idea any further. He said, 'Is this the first time ever?'

And he didn't let me answer him. He held me by the chin, saying, 'Open your mouth and let me see,' and was breathing heavily into my face, making me feel ill at ease. 'Move your tongue around,' he said. I did as requested. 'But it is white,' he suggested. 'Your saliva is white. How can you taste blood in it?' he challenged.

I sensed in Uncle's voice a helplessness, but I remained silent. It made me sad that I couldn't explain to him the workings of my own body, that I couldn't give him the reason why this most illogical of occurrences had taken place. Could I claim to know Misra better than anyone else when I didn't know my own body, when I couldn't determine what made me taste, in my white saliva, the redness of blood? I was sad that I couldn't say, 'This is I. This is my body. Let me explain how it works, why it behaves the way it does.' Or had I underestimated my body? Was it seceding from me, making its own autonomous decisions, was my body forming its own government, was it working on its own, independent of my brain, of *my* soul? Did we have to go to an arbitrator, say, a doctor, a psychoanalyst, who would determine why it was I had tasted blood in my saliva that day, in Kallafo, many years ago, at the same time as I jumped up in glee because Misra had seen and foretold a future, my future. Was my future *in* blood? Would I kill? Would I avenge the martyred warriors of Kallafo and therefore 'drink' the blood of the one I kill?

Uncle Hilaal sat back, resigned. He said, 'What do we do?'

'Let's go back to Salaado,' I suggested.

At the mention of her name, he appeared animated with life. He was like one who had found the right road to self-confidence. He started the engine of the car and, clumsily, didn't coordinate the clutch and gear shifts so the vehicle jumped and the ignition went off. Then the car wouldn't start because he flooded the carburettor. Finally we got out. 'Let's take a taxi home to Salaado,' he said. 'She'll come and drive the car home herself.'

We walked away from the car in subdued silence. We walked for a long time and were unable to find a taxi. Which was just as well, for we had the opportunity to talk and think.

I said to Uncle Hilaal that instead of thinking about Misra's disappearance, I started becoming obsessed with 'bodies' – human bodies,
that is, my body, Misra's, etc. I admitted that I could find an even
subterranean link between bodies and Misra's disappearance. This
gave Hilaal a golden chance and he talked about Freud, Jung, Lévi-
Strauss, Marx and Fraser, men, he said, 'who've divided up the
universe of thought amongst themselves, leaving little for us to
contribute'. I think he quoted passages from each of these. I think he
threw in other twentieth-century figures – poets like Eliot and Neruda,
and 'body poetesses' like Sylvia Plath and Anne Sexton, and 'body
novelists' like Toni Morrison and Günter Grass. He for-exampled
me for what appeared like a long time and then we entered the tunnel
leading to my subconscious. I don't know precisely where, but I
abandoned him in a dark corner in 'my subconscious', digging for
psychoanalytical evidence. As if this would illumine an obscure section,
he mentioned the names of Otto Rank, Wilhelm Reich, William James
and Adler too.

At the thought that I had to read and know thoroughly everything
these 'men' had written about one's relationship with one's body,
mind, sub- or unconscious, I said, 'No, thank you. Millions of people
live happily, believing that knowing more will not help them, but will
rather stand in the way of enjoying themselves.'

'Nonsense,' he said.

'I understand it is in your material and intellectual interest to
promote these names, for you to teach psychology at the university
and to teach these thinkers' findings to your students, yes – but . . . !'

'For example.'

I don't remember what he said after this. I only remember my
questions – queries which have become part of me in the way wrinkles
are an integral part of somebody's face, inseparable from it. It seems
to me, when I look back on this conversation, that Hilaal, as though
he were hard of hearing, gave his answers to questions I didn't put
to him. I didn't let him get away with it, I thought I shouldn't. I said,
among other things, that I am a question to myself – and my body
asked the first question. Was it salvaged from the corpse of my mother?
What's a body for? To worship God? To have sex, have children? Has
anybody known a man who menstruated? What is it that is in the
'mind' of a man's *uff* that makes it 'rise' to the naked body of a
woman? What's in the touch of a woman's breasts or thighs?

'Sooner or later, sex,' said Hilaal. What did he mean by that?

'No story is complete without sex; no story can be considered well told unless sex runs in its veins like blood in a living being. If sex is not present, then its absence indicates inhibitions, unless the symbols, motifs and metaphors that make the tale work, are such they narrate the story in a veiled manner. For example, Abul-cualaail Macarri's *Letter of a Horse and a Mule.* What's more, no family can be happy without sex. And the sex of a child – a boy or a girl. Sex as honour. Good sex. Bad sex. Sooner or later, everything is sex. Religion organizes sex. That's why society frowns upon and punishes unauthorized sex. The economics of non-industrial societies consider cattle and women as chattles, as properties that change hands. And sex costs money. To marry, you pay dowry, you give so many heads of cattle in exchange for what? For a hand? No. For sex. I keep asking myself if the Adenese in your story, the one who raped hens and small boys, was simply stingy or was he beastly?'

'I don't understand.'

He said, 'Sex between the higher and the lower animals (that is between human beings and beasts) is taboo in all societies. I won't go into the politics of apartheid in South Africa which essentially denies the humanity of the African. Nevertheless, there is an element of superiority and inferiority relationships in sex. The master has access to his servant/slave – Qorrax and Misra is a case in point – the teacher to his pupil – Aw-Adan and Misra. But when the Adenese copulates with his hen, he does something more than break a taboo. For this is substantially different from the one he breaks when he mates with small, non-consenting boys. The small boys belong to the higher-animal category and society frowns upon sex between two beings belonging to the higher-animal category. Sex between men (who are, in all traditional, i.e. male-dominated, societies, placed higher than women) and women is okay. Sex between Misra and her rapists, who themselves assumed the identity of baboons – is this sex between higher and lower animals?'

He scoured the area, looking for a taxi. None. He went on, 'For example. In almost all these relationships, the woman occupies the lower rung. In bed, she is the one below, the one being made love to. Sex, sooner or later. God is male. All the prophets are male. And it is no accident that Prophet Mohammed worked for a woman who, in the end, he married and subdued. It is significant that he was an *ummi* – the Arabic word suggesting, at one and the same time, that he was illiterate and that he was a man of his mother's people. You can deduce whatever Freudian conclusions you please. Sooner or later, at any rate, sex.'

Again, he fell into his 'for-exampling' euphoria, talking about boys who because their rudimentary nipples grow visibly larger than other boys', refuse to shower in the company of their peers. These boys are so obsessed with their bodies, they wonder if they are girls underneath the skin. Women who grow beards or moustaches early in their lives tend to worry about this too. But when a girl plays with boys and enjoys (with a certain immodesty, and, it must be said, panache) taking part in one tomfoolery or another, it is the parents who are preoccupied.

Suddenly, just when I was about to start wondering why he was talking nervously and continuously, he paused. I thought he, too, was anxious about Misra's disappearance and this was why he was talking non-stop. But he surprised me. I knew, from the twinkle in his eye, that he had thought of something funny or wise. He said, 'Do you know why sex bothers me, why I give it much thought?'

I said I didn't.

He laughed. Then, 'Because you *come* when you are not ready to *go*,' and he laughed at his own joke. I retraced his steps to before his first laugh. Oh what I fool, I thought to myself, when I got the joke. But I couldn't laugh to my heart's content because he had already moved on further afield, picking ripe fruits off trees older than the one planted by Misra the day I was born. How did I know that he had picked tasty fruits? Because he was tasting his 'thoughts' like a peasant pouring a quarter of a pound of sugar into a mug of tea, one who is plainly after the sweetness of the hot, brown water, not the nicotine content of the beverage. However, he was speaking slowly, moving relaxedly in the spaciousness of his ideas, although he appeared to be full of mistrust, like a baby born with its bottom first because it is sure someone will do an untoward thing to its sight.

His concluding remark was, 'Truth is body.'

I stared at him questioningly. I didn't understand him.

'Look at a man who is after a woman,' he said. 'For example.'

'Yes?'

'The blood warms up, his thing rises, he loses his head, his concentration on any other aspect of life is nil. Watch him sneak into bed with her, spy on him courting her, listen to him tell lies to the woman, his victim – what have we here? A body that rules the mind – I almost said, the man. Religion forbids that we subordinate the "thinking" faculties to that of lust. Why? Because, when one is making love, one doesn't think about God, at least I don't. Take a look at lovers together, look at the way they concentrate on each other's demands, offering to each other bodies of sacrifice. To them, the world does not exist. God doesn't. They do.'

A congenial smile. A taxi came into view. He waited. I flagged it down. No luck. It was hot and dusty. We stood in the shade of a tree. We were both thirsty and hungry. But he was still talking – afraid of silence, I thought, keeping my mind and his busy with ideas so neither would think about Misra's disappearance.

'Good sex. Bad sex. Adultery is a complicated science in Islam. To prove it, you must swear that a needle, not a camel, a needle, wouldn't have found sufficient space between the bodies of the man and the woman and that his member was inside her. It's not enough that the man and the woman were naked or that they were together, alone, in a room, no. It's very unIslamic to give a man so many lashes on the strength of suspicions. So?'

This time, he looked at me as though I were a latter-day Ayatollah, giving adulterous men sixty or so lashes and stoning adulteresses. In any case, what did the 'So!' ending in the ascending tone mean? Possibly, he was making a point, subtly – that I had no evidence that Misra made love to either Uncle Qorrax or Aw-Adan? And neither did Karin have proof? After allowing him time in which he indulged his vanity, I decided to return to the topic of 'bodies', making certain we kept Misra out of it. I said, 'What irritates me about the human body is, you just don't walk into a shop and say to a salesperson, "Look, I don't like my foot, I want it replaced. What's the cheapest you've got?" You just don't do that sort of thing, you cannot.'

He fell for the trap. He said, 'But you can. People in industrialized societies have begun making such demands on science.'

'You mean, replace the limb you don't like any more with its plastic equivalent?' I asked, egging him on.

'You can have the extra fat in your body reduced, your pot-belly removed, your nose altered, you can have lots of things done. You can change most parts.'

'And the cost?'

'Well, you know!'

'Why, it costs more to replace a part than what one has paid for the whole. A part more expensive than the whole?' I argued.

He laughed. 'How much did you pay for your body?'

The whole? The part? Uncle then found the tunnel in whose dark corners he had earlier discovered the pathways leading to my subconscious – and the tunnel led us finally to Misra. Had I not said that a part of me had died when I learnt that Misra had betrayed our trust? At last, we hailed a taxi whose driver recognized Uncle. He gave us a lift home.

Salaado asked, 'Where's the car?'

I told her what happened.

'Useless men,' she said and hopped into the same taxi to bring the car home. 'The carburettor is flooded, can you imagine?' she was saying to the taxi driver, 'and they just lock it up and walk away. Useless men.'

Vapour and dust and smoking piston-rings of the taxi.

[5]

When Salaado returned, I was in my room, busy drawing (how did she put it) space-in-space-out-of-space, but was, at that point in time, in a mood to be interrupted – which she did. She looked me over. I wondered why and learnt, to my pleasant surprise, that Riyo and Salaado had met and that she had brought greetings from her. 'And where did you meet?'

'She was going out of our house when I saw her.'

I said, 'But why didn't you ask her to wait?'

'Maybe she didn't want to disturb you.'

There was a set pattern – I visited her and she came to see me only once. Had she heard about Misra's disappearance and come to hear what news we had of her? 'We talked a little,' volunteered Salaado. 'Naturally, about you.'

'Yes?'

'She said, for instance, that she finds something elegant, something ... er ... how did she put it ... gallant about your gaze – gentle, formal, sweet, but gallant.'

I said, 'It's very kind of her.'

She said, 'I told her about Misra.'

'What do you mean? Do you know any more than we do?'

She shook her head. 'No, I meant how she menstruated the first moment she met your stare when you were God knows how many hours old. And I agreed with her that you make women lose their hold on themselves, you disarm them with your look,' she said, and then stopped suddenly like one who wasn't sure whether to continue or not. 'Riyo says she feels a small girl making passes at a boy not at all interested in her.'

Quick as a flash, I had to think of something that would make her change the subject, or at least go off it. I said, mimicking Hilaal's voice, 'Sex, sooner or later.'

After a pause, she was apologetic. 'I am sorry to disturb you,' she said.

Much in the same way a polite guest might insinuate the idea that if no one else is having the portion of meat still left in the serving dish . . . , I said something polite, 'No, you're not.'

She opened the door as if to go out and the odour of the garlic in the *champignon provençale* entered the room. The scent of the meal was so powerful, we both went and joined him in the kitchen.

At table, Salaado told the story of a schoolmate of hers who once said, in the presence of at least a dozen of his classmates, that he was going to commit suicide. He gave the precise day, date and minute when he would. The boy was in love with a girl, but she wasn't in love with him. He said goodbye to each and every one of them and begged that they pray for his soul. 'A month and a day later guess what happened?'

'The girl committed suicide?'

Salaado shook her head, no.

'He returned home alive?'

'Precisely.'

Hilaal remained silent. So I said, 'A coward.'

'You must hear why he returned home alive.'

Hilaal's only contribution, 'Why?'

'The boy said, touching his body all over, that what we saw when we looked at him was "just body". His body was here with us, he said, but not his soul. We used to fall silent whenever he joined our groups. Little by little, however, it became apparent that there was something in what he had said – the boy had undergone very noticeable changes. Not only did he appear pale, bloodless, a man with no spine, a man with no fight in him, but there was external bodily evidence that he had changed. In the end, he wore away like the garments he had on. He wore away from underuse of brain and body as well. He's still alive, all right. In fact, I saw him today, driving back from the hospital. Do you know what he was doing? He was walking the streets of his madness.'

I moistened my lips and felt anxious. Why did she tell us this story? There must be a reason, I thought, remembering the conversation

Hilaal and I had had earlier on in the day. Then, just in time, I saw my fork dripping with red juice – the beetroot's. Salaado took in all that and then said, 'You are wondering why I've told you this horror of a story?'

I nodded my head; Hilaal, his.

She said, 'Expressing regret, Misra told me (I don't know why she chose to confide in me and not Askar or you, Hilaal, but there we are – perhaps because I am a woman and you're not – who knows!) anyway ...'

Hilaal said, 'What did she tell you?' and he was anxious.

'She told me that she had lived with a man, in Kallafo, an "Ethiopian", please do not forget the inverted commas. He was a lieutenant, handsome, as Karin had accurately described him. Also, he came from the village that Misra was born in. The two of them had shared a similar beginning – he was the "boy" the Amhara nobleman had been searching for, the issue of a *damoz* union between the nobleman and the boy's mother. As happens, generally in Indian films, they didn't know of their beginnings until after they had fallen in love and lived together for nearly two years. Misra explained that she had withheld from him her origins and had given him the name of a different village right from the start. He was younger than her by a few years, was an Addis city boy, one who had attended the cosmopolitan city's best schools – which was why, naturally, he was interested in his starting point. The story is much more complicated ...' and she took a break from talking and looked from one to the other.

'Naturally. Incest is complicated and complex,' said Hilaal.

'You see, a number of things began to occur to her following your departure, Askar. One positive thing was that her periods were no longer escorted by excruciating pains as before. Nobody could tell her why. Another was, she had plenty of time, suddenly, and didn't know what to do with it. That was when she met this young man.'

'The Romeo of Juliet, a dashing, handsome young man,' said Hilaal.

'He was seen entering or leaving her compound. She was seen with him in public. He was known to be a cruel man, insisting that they raze to the ground villages harbouring pro-Somali saboteurs. Defeat had already created disharmony among the Kallafo townspeople. And so, when the massacre took place, Misra said, she became the primary suspect. People said she had led him and his men to the hiding-place of the martyred WSLF warriors. But she swore on Askar's life that she didn't.'

Suddenly, the beetroot in my mouth tasted bitter. Not only was its

colour red, but it tasted of blood, too. I was worried I might bring it
up if I opened my mouth or tried to say something.

Hilaal asked, 'Is her version different from Karin's?'

'Not different in substance but different in their conclusions.'

Hilaal continued, 'She says she wasn't there when the massacre
took place and wasn't the one who had led her Romeo to the hiding-
place of the Liberation Front fighters?'

'Obviously,' said Salaado.

'We won't know, will we?'

'I am afraid, no.'

There was a long silence. I rushed into the nearest toilet and found
a basin. I was sick, but not for long. I lay in bed, flanked by Hilaal
and Salaado. He was telling the story of man's beginning-point –
incest.

'If you believe in the Adam-Eve story in the Koran or the Bible,
well, then there's an aspect of it.' And his face darkened in wrinkled
concentration. 'I don't know if it is Islamic or Somali, but there is the
myth that Eve gave birth only to twins, a boy and a girl in quick
succession, in order to populate the earth. Now the twins born together, it is said, swapped the boys and girls with the sets immediately
after them. But the day came when one of the twins, namely Cain,
fell in love with his co-twin, whose stars had predicted was to become
Abel's wife. Cain didn't want to swap. To marry her, he killed,
committing the first murder, but not the first incest.'

'And that's where we all began?' asked Salaado.

'Yes. If you consider Adam "giving birth" to Eve, in a manner of
speaking. After all, she was created from his rib, flesh and blood – in
him, her beginning. Adam's beginnings are in the command (i.e. the
Word): Be! And he *became*. He *was*.'

I yawned. They left the room.

[6]

I couldn't help thinking that Salaado was inwardly happy that Misra
had disappeared, although she hoped nothing bad would happen to
her. To me, she was indulgently sweet, making no comments or
references to my intended departure and no allusions to my romance
with Riyo. As a matter of fact, it was Salaado who had the foresight
to suggest that we leave our doors open. And she literally meant that

– keep all doors wide open, just in case Misra returned when we were asleep. Misra pervaded our thoughts. This reminded me of my infant days – then I was deeply attached to her; then, our doors were left open. Nothing else meant anything: Maps; the Ogaden itself was reduced to a past so far away it occupied no space in my mind. Only Misra! All because she disappeared and because we didn't know what had happened to her.

It transpired that we didn't have her particulars. To the bewilderment of Hilaal and Salaado, it became obvious I didn't know her father's name. I knew the name of the Jigjigaawi man who raised her, then married her and who, in the end, she murdered. Surely, she couldn't have used his name as her father's! Then someone remembered that she had entered the country in disguise, under another name. What name was that? The one I knew her by, spelt as Misra or variations of it? Or the one Karin gave me? Even if we wanted, we had no name to report to the police as a 'Missing Person', nor did we have one to release to the press. Misra? Massar? Masrat? Massarat? What name can we find you under and where?

Sadly, I concluded I didn't know Misra. I said so.

'No, wait,' Uncle said. But his voice had undergone a frightening change – it was like a person cut in two halves – you would want to look for the missing half. He added, 'Let us not despair. Let us think.'

We were clumsy in the views we offered, we were helpless and misguided in our predictions. Salaado, at one time, set the dinner-table for four while Hilaal prepared the meal. We sat and waited, our eyes downcast as though we were saying grace. The wind spoke to us; the wind knocked on our doors which were not even shut, the wind made us go to the windows behind which we stood, our eyes, this time, scouring the space ahead of us, our minds attentive to any changing shadows, expectantly waiting for Misra to turn up and say, 'I am sorry, I meant to tell you that I was going to call on a friend.' Each of us prophesied what would happen, but in each, she was alive and was well; in each she complained of a small irritant pain in the legs or the area surrounding the removed breast or her groin. Never did any of us suggest that she had died, or tell a story predicting that she might have been killed.

Suddenly, with a fury I had never associated with her, Salaado said, 'We cannot be sitting here and speculating about the poor woman. We must do something.'

'What?' asked Uncle Hilaal.

Salaado was up on her feet and saying, 'We'll go to the police station.'

'And report Misra's disappearance?'

Salaado very determinedly said, 'Why not!'

'Too early. The police will say it is too early, that we'll have to wait for a couple of days or more. You can't report someone as missing until after a reasonable period of time,' Uncle Hilaal said, his voice sounding emaciated.

Salaado wouldn't be persuaded. The woman, she argued, didn't know anybody else in Mogadiscio and was our guest. She was not well and couldn't be said to have decided to go out for a walk or for a rendezvous with someone, she was in no position to do either. Three men, unknown to her, forced their way to her private ward, for which we were paying, and they frog-marched her out of the hospital.

'Two things,' said Uncle Hilaal, raising his fingers in a V-shape.

Salaado said, 'One?'

'You don't know whether she knew the three men, nor whether they frog-marched her out of the hospital. You haven't enough information to go by,' he said, and waited for her to indicate that she was ready for the second point.

She said, 'Two?'

'Will you tell the police the whole story? Will you tell them about her background? Will you talk about the suspicions, however unfounded, that she led the Ethiopian security forces to the WSLF warriors' hiding-place in Kallafo? Will you tell them this and more?' he challenged.

I didn't know why then, but I found it odd that they both looked at me as if taking note of my presence for the first time. I acknowledged their stare by becoming more self-conscious than ever.

Salaado said, 'He'll be the principal witness, won't he?'

Uncle Hilaal nodded.

She sighed sadly and said, 'I wish there was something we could do, short of pointing suspicious fingers at Askar or making life difficult for everyone. I wish she would just turn up, just like that.' She snapped her fingers. 'I like her very much. She is a strong woman and I'm sure she'll survive this and many more difficulties. Something tells me she will.'

'Yes, she was a likeable, strong woman,' said Uncle Hilaal.

The taste of blood in my mouth dominated my mind and I cut myself a slice of bread and chewed it. I took a sip of water to chase it down my dry throat. My thoughts led me to a familiar territory – I was younger again, I was with Misra, and she was my universe, she was the one who determined the circumferences of my cosmos, her body was an extension of mine, my body her third leg as we slept and snored away time, my head her third breast as she rolled away from the sheet which had covered her earlier on. I wished I could find answers to the meaning of the taste of blood in my mouth; I wished I knew what her disappearance meant.

'Do you think the Western Somali Liberation Front has something to do with her disappearance?' I asked, naturally worried about what I might do if it had.

In unison, they both said, 'Oh no, no, no.'

For four solid days, we waited to hear news of Misra.

CHAPTER TWELVE

[1]

Two days later.

The eclipse was total – there was nearly eight minutes of primeval darkness. During this brief period, people sought one another's company or tried to find refuge in the spacious word of the Almighty, a word inside whose letters some discovered a shelter, a word in whose womb others obtained the required warmth, blood and love. The mosques began to fill with worshippers; the wealthy among the community of Muslims opened their gates to beggars whom they fed generously; those who were in love but had not yet decided when to marry proposed matrimony immediately their frightened souls were no longer depressed by the hour of trial, the hour of darkness; those who had planned to commit wicked perfidies undid the knots of their conspiracies, repenting the regretful time spent away from their Creator. In short, the streets of Mogadiscio were empty of strollers, the markets of buyers or sellers, and the mosques filled with men, the homes with women. And dogs barked unceasingly, afraid for their canine souls, donkeys brayed in fright whilst horses were seen running, as though mad, in the streets of the virtually empty centre of the city. 'The apocalypse, now as always,' said Hilaal, himself falling into a dark of depression, 'sooner or later, sex!'

And Askar looked up at the heavens and saw the moon's shadow obscuring the sun's light. It was a most unique experience – a darkness gathering like dust, a rim of faint light, the sky dark as the eclipsed pathway, the moon moving, its shadow racing across the earth from one horizon to the other. He was indeed fascinated by all this, which he thought he would never forget, like one doesn't forget a most distinct personality one has encountered only once. Askar would preserve the memory of this moment, forever, in his head, a thought treasured among his most memorable thoughts, an event amongst the events to be remembered forever and after, like the stare Misra held 'preserved' in her vision of him the day she found him, the 'stare' which focussed on the centre of her guilt and made her 'come' in blood. 'Sex, sooner or later.'

However, it pained him immensely to see Uncle Hilaal looking so unwell, silent and depressed. (Salaado had gone out to do the week's shopping and hadn't returned as yet.) It seemed as though Hilaal had suddenly aged. He walked about as old people do, looking straight ahead of himself, attentive, as seniles are, to the space surrounding his body, his feet firmly on the ground, his back a little too stooped, his gait shufflingly slow and predictable, his gaze absent-mindedly dwelling on the items of furniture in his peripheral vision. 'I am depressed, like a woman in season,' he said. 'It's the eclipse, I'm afraid.'

Depressed, Hilaal's voice had undergone substantial changes. For one thing, it lost its charm; for another, it had thinned. But why should an eclipse have such an effect on Hilaal's psychology? Why should it play havoc on his bodily constitution? Why should his migraine be so acute as to create an imbalance in him, upsetting his view of the universe, impairing his sight, imposing a vertiginous view-point on every thought he had, distorting his perception of realities, why? He found no analogous cases in his annals with which to compare Hilaal's state, save his memory of Misra in season. Her body ached, her hands pressed the kernels of her breasts, she sat for one second, only to rise a second later, remaining restless all the time, losing her temper often. Hilaal dropped into a black hole, deep as Misra's depressions – Hilaal, whom he had never known to be unwell.

Presently, Hilaal walked fast past Askar without acknowledging his presence. A moment later, he walked past him a second time, but slowly, like somebody carrying a wobbly weight whose body leans forward on account of the burden. But he didn't speak to Askar. And when he did, which was later, he pointed at things, he stared blankly at items as though he had forgotten what they were called. For instance, he touched his stomach, then made motions suggesting it was running. A little later, he tapped on his forehead and Askar wasn't sure if he meant to say his head ached or that he had gone mad.

Askar was not affected by vertigo nor did his stomach run nor did his head ache. He retained his water intake, his body repelled nothing, his bladder expelled no liquid of any colour, unnecessarily. He went back and forth, making himself useful, offering assistance when he could, now a towel, now a glass of water, now a word of consolation, of assurance, now moral support and now physical support as Hilaal walked back from the toilet for the nth time. Askar thought he was as efficient as Karin, remembering how she plied the road between a woman in season and an old husband who lay on his back, disabled, invalid.

When it seemed Hilaal was feeling a little better, towards early afternoon (roughly siesta-time), Askar asked him how he was. Hilaal confirmed he was feeling better. Then, 'I wonder how she is,' said Askar, without identifying the person to whom he was referring.

'Who?' said Hilaal, saying the word so fast he spat it out, as though it were hot and bitter at the same time.

Askar (was it deliberate or no, no one could tell) disregarded the question and went on, 'And if she is well.'

'Who?' repeated Hilaal forcefully, his voice hoarse, his dry throat making a grating sound – something between a cough and the clearing of a throat. Askar wondered if, together with his intellectual sobriety, Hilaal had misplaced or been deprived of his memory too. Just at the moment Askar was remembering Misra's depressive seasonals, Hilaal started. It was as if (Askar thought) Hilaal were a woman whose advanced pregnancy had given her a kick in the ribs. No, no, thought Askar. It was as if he was one of those robots which, before speaking, made hiccupping sounds, alerting their audience so they kept themselves ready for their messages. Hilaal said, 'Do you mean Salaado?'

For a long time, Askar had been wanting to pass water but he hadn't the will to. Also, he thought Hilaal might need him for something or other. So instead of saying, 'No', because he was referring to Misra and not to Salaado, he said, 'Yes'.

Hilaal was disappointed. Would mentioning code-name 'Misra' have lifted Hilaal momentarily out of his depression? Where was Misra anyway? Or how was she? If she were here, who knows, she might have suggested that blood-letting would do Hilaal a lot of good. Askar said, 'I hope Misra, too, is all right.'

At the mention of Misra's name, Hilaal stirred involuntarily. Then, 'Yes, where the hell is she?' said Hilaal.

Askar rushed to the toilet before he wet himself.

[2]

He was in a garden which was lush with foliage and plants with memories of their own. And he recognized the tree that had the same birthday as himself, he sat in its shade which was sweet, ate what he could of its ripe fruits. Then, in a revelatory moment such as that which accompanies the unexpected recall of a forgotten name belonging to somebody who had once been one's most intimate friend,

Askar remembered who had planted the tree – Misra. His tongue lay in a mess of blood; his head began to whirl about, giddy, his eyes red like dried blood, a mouthful of which had already turned his mouth bitter – as bitter as guilt! What began as a reunion of rejoicing with a recalled Misra, ended in anomolous bodily behaviour. Where did the mess of blood in his mouth originate? Why this giddiness? Or the cakes of blood which he tasted in his guilt?

Then the scene changed. He was standing at the centre of the garden's clearing and was giving the appropriate names to the trees and plants just as Adam might have done on the first day of creation. There was no tension in him. No memory of Misra. No bitterness, no taste of blood or guilt in his mouth. If anything, he was happy. He was wrapped in the skin of a goat whose meat he was sure he had eaten. He could not remember the names of the two women who had fed him the goat's meat. But the skin was mapped with routes which led him back to his past, a map which took him back to his own beginnings, a map showing earth roads, the rivers which rise in the region, a map whose scales followed a logic known only to himself.

And he was being entertained. There was a vulture, gamey, playful, with a vicious look when it displayed its anger, indicating that it wasn't happy with the fresh alterations in the rules of play. There was a she-dog, one Askar remembered as belonging to a jealous neighbour, and named Bruder. The game consisted of a piece of meat being dropped from a given height. The vulture and the dog would start from the same point, marked on the earth with red chalk; obviously the dog on the ground, the vulture above it. A shot would sound (Askar couldn't tell where the shot was coming from or who was firing it), the piece of meat would emanate from on high like birds in flight, dropping faeces of fright. Six out of ten, the dog got the meat. The crowd applauded loudly. But what did it all mean? he asked himself.

As if to answer, the Adenese and Uncle Qorrax came into view. The Adenese had a shoe in his mouth and he was biting it hard. There was a heavy man riding his back, and this man gave him a kick in the ribs every time he sensed he was about to let the shoe drop. Walking behind them, as though on a promenade, Uncle Qorrax, who was barefoot. And the sand was hot and it pained him to walk without shoes. Which was why he couldn't catch up with the Adenese who had a shoe in his mouth. In all probability, he would've accepted the offer of a single shoe if he were given it. After all, his feet were sore and the earth had begun to enter and fill the cuts in his bleeding soles.

Before the procession ended, there appeared – sitting on a throne, majestically, rested-looking, like somebody at the end of all suffering, somebody who can only expect things to improve – Misra. She waved to Askar. He waved back. She alighted. He joined her. She was happy to see him again. They hugged. But her gaze was as distant as the nether heavens. Was she longing to return from whence she came? She was the ruler of this land of games, of maps telling one's past and future, of vultures fighting a duel against dogs. A man approached. He was an old man and was holding his back, which perhaps pained him. From the small distance separating them, Askar could tell the man was hard of hearing. The man reminded him of another to whom he put a question about time, pointing at his wrist-watch. Obviously, either the man didn't get the question or he deliberately heard it wrongly. For he began talking about a blood-pressure complaint and said to Askar, 'Are you a doctor by any chance?' What did he (Askar) want?

The man spoke toothlessly, saying the same things over and over again. But what on earth was he saying? Apparently, he was Karin's husband and he recognized Misra and wanted to greet her, and, if others hadn't said so before him, he wished to thank her on behalf of the community of Kallafo for the good things she had done for young Askar.

And horses neighed in the distance. And dogs barked nervously. And dust stirred. And a horse dropped its rider. And from behind the dust emerged a young girl riding a black horse with white nostrils. And it was night. Then it was day. And ghosts came. And ghosts went. And a host of ghosts replaced one another. At times, said the young girl becoming old, I was one of these ghosts, leaving your doors open, allowing yesterday's experiences to enter and mingle with today's, and for the past and the present to encounter in your head – the dreamer. Like the sun's rays and the season's dust mixing in a room facing east. Some of the ghosts had large hips and they carried you; some fed you; some told you stories. At times, I knocked on your doors of sleep and woke you up. But now I am dead and you are alive and that's all I hope to be able to do – knock on your doors of sleep, enter into bed and be with you until your eyes open and the door of sleep is shut.

Misra said, 'All that one hopes to remain of one is a memory dwelling in someone's head. In whose will I reside? Those who brought about my death, or yours?'

'But do these notions, I mean those of death and a memory of me, do these two notions come together in your head like keys come with locks in our thoughts?' he asked.

Alas, no answer. Somebody knocked on his door of sleep – Hilaal.

[3]

Her body was prepared for burial and Askar was not present. They buried Misra and he was not at the funeral. That night, when he was taken ill suddenly, he resisted being admitted to hospital. Indeed, it came to pass that he and Misra were in the same hospital – he in the men's ward, she in the sexless ward – the mortuary – but in the very wing he spent the night in, although she was in the basement and he in a private room on the third floor. He was alive and she dead; he, very hot, because of his high temperature, whereas she was in a freezer and therefore ice-cold. He, who had known of her lying in state in the mortuary in the basement, saw her in his dream and she was a queen, on a throne, leading a procession of sorts, an event of a kind. Did Misra see him in her dream? Do the dead dream?

Told about the burial and the funeral, he asked, 'Why did you not shake me out of my fever?'

Hilaal said, 'We were worried.'

'Worried?' and as he looked up he saw Salaado enter. She, always longer coming, always arrived later, because she had had to find parking-space in the hospital yard, or out of it. She kissed him lightly on the forehead and smelt of smoke, as though she was the MC at a cremation.

'How's he?' she asked Hilaal, as though he were not present or couldn't understand Somali or was hard of hearing or was deaf. The conversation, in fact, went on like this for a while.

Gently, Hilaal said, 'He's asking questions.'

'Why he wasn't told of the burial?'

'And of the funeral too.'

Salaado began, 'Well, he wasn't in a . . .' and then stopped, realizing he was there, right in front of her, propped up in bed, with a book in hand, using his index finger as a page marker.

Hilaal said, 'Speak to him.'

She felt awkward, like somebody gossiping about a person – imagine that person turning up and hearing everything said about him. The lump of embarrassment in her throat didn't clear for a long time.

Then, 'We were worried, let's face it,' and she addressed herself to Hilaal, primarily to Hilaal, who looked away and at Askar. 'The slightest tremors shake you. You're like moist earth at the centre – soft. We were worried what you might do if you saw her mutilated body and what that might do to you for the rest of your life.'

Askar looked at Hilaal. Did he want Uncle to confirm what Salaado had said? Hilaal remained silent, like a husband whose cues have been taken by his wife. 'Mutilated? Her body was mutilated?'

Salaado nodded, yes.

'But you said not even sharks touched her?' he said to Salaado. Then to Hilaal, 'You were there when she said that. The day of the eclipse. The day she prayed, and you fell ill, and I was well.'

Hilaal reiterated Salaado's worry. 'Yes, we were worried. For example. You were taken ill during the tragic weekend when the Ethiopians, helped by their Cuban, Adenese and Soviet allies, reoccupied the Ogaden. The slightest earth tremor shakes you, the slightest gives you the shock of an earthquake, your temperature runs high, your blood pressure goes up, your eyes become bloodshot – and we don't know what to do.' And he hugged Salaado and when their bodies had the shape of a bracket, one of them took his right hand, the other his left and the three of them formed a circle.

As they retook their respective seats, Askar said, 'Tell me how her body was mutilated? Tell me all. What was missing? Why? Tell me all. Tell me everything you know.'

They consulted discreetly. Salaado was the first to speak. Hilaal would stay directly behind her and would help, confirming her story if need be, changing it slightly if necessary. 'We suspect there may have been foul play of a wicked kind,' said she, her voice shaken, like someone regretting he had said more than he intended. A pause. She turned to Hilaal. It was obvious she was seeking his assistance. 'Please,' she said, taking his hand.

Hilaal took over. 'The heart was missing. For example.' And he unclasped his hand from Salaado's grip. 'We suspect *they* performed a ritual murder on her body. Perhaps we are wrong. We haven't the evidence. But the removal of the heart took place *before* she was tossed into the ocean – already dead. That is, if we're to take our suspicions very seriously.'

Askar knew that when one of them talked, the other kept an eye on him. His expressions were under scrutiny, his movements, his gestures were being studied for clues as to what he might do. He was all right. He could prove to them that he was. He asked, 'What did they say at the mortuary?'

Hilaal said, 'For example. In view of the complications involved, not knowing how not to have you go through the traumatic experience of court cases, police interrogations and other related bureaucratic tortures, we decided – in view of the political trapdoors which would open, let you in but keep us locked out or vice versa – in view of all this, we decided not to raise the issue of ritual murder, or a missing heart or a mutilated corpse. But we could not deny that she existed, that she was who she was . . . er . . . to you, that she became whom . . . er . . . you had suspected her to have become and that you are to us . . . er . . . who you've been – a son. In view of this, for example, we decided, Salaado and I, that is, as though we believed we had your consent too – we decided, we would not raise these burning questions or ask for an investigation team to be appointed and a case opened – no. It pained our conscience, for instance, but we committed an unforgivable felony.'

Askar asked, 'What's that?'

'We bribed the technicians at the mortuary to silence them,' he said, his tone sad, adding, 'You might well ask why we did all this? We did it so that the healing wounds in your soul won't get festered again. In other words, we did this for the good of all concerned. Considering, as I said before, for example, the bureaucratic, political and other complications. And conscience too.'

Salaado agreed, 'Yes,' and looked up as though she were reading the transcript of Hilaal's aforespoken statement. 'We talked about it, yes. It pained our conscience, but that was the best we could do, we thought.'

'That's right,' said Hilaal, who was in a supporting role, agreeing with Salaado in turn. Askar wondered – had they rehearsed all this before they called on him?

'Do we know who *they* are?' he asked, speaking soberly.

Salaado said, 'Not any more than you know.'

'I don't,' he said.

'Neither do we,' said Hilaal.

And then Askar said to Salaado, following a brief pause, 'I don't recall. Possibly you've told it and I've forgotten it. But how did you know that her body was at the mortuary?'

Salaado was overcome by a sense of despair, for there was a gap between what she knew to be true and what she suspected he would think she knew. In other words, she didn't think he would believe her. 'I was in a shop when . . .' but then she shrugged her shoulders, saying, 'What's the point, you won't believe a word I say.'

He said, 'Why not?'

Like someone turning in his tormented sleep, Salaado uttered an indistinct sound, one between noises made by some people who talk in their sleep and others who speak to their interlocutors in their dreams.

Askar asked, 'Are you hiding something from me?'

'No.'

'Well. Tell it then.'

She said, 'When I told him, Hilaal didn't believe my story.'

Askar said, 'Who am I? Hilaal?'

And Salaado pulled herself together at once. She appeared sufficiently apologetic and wished he hadn't pushed her thus far. They both sought Hilaal's comment – they understood he was determined to stay out of it. She then spoke, slowly, 'I was in this so-called supermarket, when I overheard two women, both nurses working at the general hospital known as *Digfar*, talk about what one of them described as "the corpse of a woman, black as dead shark". At first, I took no interest, save the gentle curiosity which the description stirred in my otherwise indifferent mind, and I half-listened to what she was saying. But the more I heard the more certain I became it was Misra they were discussing. What decided it for me was the mention of a mastectomy operation, a recent one, in which one of the woman's breasts had been removed. How I gained the few paces separating me from them, I cannot tell. What words I used to talk to the nurses, I cannot remember. I rushed straight to the hospital, found a doctor I knew and went, with him, to the mortuary. It was Misra – a corpse no one claimed. She had been reduced to that.'

He said, 'And you claimed her body?'

'I had her removed from the section of "unclaimed corpses" to one in which a daily fee is paid. There's a difference between the rich and the poor, even when dead. The poor stink,' she said, disgusted at remembering the state of filth and stench the 'Unclaimed Corpses Section' had been in. She went on, 'I was sick. I couldn't come home straight, I didn't want to infect you with the sickness which had come upon me. I was telling the story of my disgust and despair, the story above all of Misra's death, when the eclipse happened. I joined everyone else in prayer. I'm afraid I couldn't remember the text of the *Faatixa*, let alone any other verse of the Koran. I put this down to my mental state – but I wouldn't be able to remember any even now. Can you believe it? *I*, Salaado, prayed, together with everyone else. I was true to my name – Salaado, meaning prayer or devotions.'

Silence. No questions from Askar, nothing. His back straight, appearing in great discomfort, his Adam's apple moving up and down, gulping, sending down his throat the taste of blood, the saliva of his guilt. 'Are you all right?' from Hilaal.

'I am,' he said.

But he was, and also seemed, very upset.

'What's wrong, Askar?' and Salaado touched him gently on the knee. A gesture of supplication? Why?

He said, 'Do you remember what verse of the Koran, what chapter was read by the Sheikh who presided over the rituals of Misra's funeral?' addressing it this time to Hilaal.

'What verse, did you say?' he said, half-looking at Salaado as well, with eyes which turned on the axis of the repeated query. 'Verse, did you ask, Askar?'

'Yes.'

'Why?'

'Do you remember the verses the priest supervising over Misra's *janaaza* read over her corpse?'

'No.'

'Could we ask him?'

'We don't know ... er ... didn't know who the priest was. Someone suggested him. He came, he did his thing and left. We didn't spend any thought on that aspect of the *janaaza*, we're sorry,' said Salaado.

'What's all this, Askar?'

He reflected for a moment. Then, 'Because I might have suggested a couple of verses. If you had come and shaken me out of my fever.'

Almost indifferent, Hilaal asked, 'Like what?'

'Verses fourteen, fifteen and sixteen of Sura Luqmaan.'

No one was in any mood to speak for a while. Salaado and Hilaal apologized to him profusely. All three joined hands and they hugged, wrapped in one another's bodies and clothes, half-struggling, like a crowd upon whom a tarpaulin had collapsed.

[4]

He was back – in his room, at home. He was back to the warm space between his thoughts – warm as the space between the sheets covering him. He was back to his unread books, back to his unstudied maps on the wall in his room – at home. He was back to his mirrors, also on the walls, mirrors reflecting only the present, but not good enough to travel to a past beyond the tin amalgam plating their backs. He was back to the unplanned future – a future without a Misra; back also to the unfilled, unsubmitted forms from the Western Somalia Liberation Front and that of the National University of Somalia. The empty space of the twenty-one-odd questions stared back at him, preventing his brain from dealing with them, scattering his memory, like dust in a whirlwind, to the seven horizons of the cosmos – a world without a Misra!

He was standing before a mirror. He saw an unhappy face – his. It 'wore' like a mask. He thought there was something absurd about a sadness confined only to the face, a sadness which wouldn't spread to the rest of his body; something absurd about a face whose features had become as overwhelming as a spider's abdomen, a spider with virtually no visible shanks and whose large belly spins webs – and fables with morals. So, he asked, who was *Misra*? A woman, or more than just a woman? Did she exist as I remember her? Or have I rolled into a great many other persons, spun from the thread leading back to my own beginnings, incorporating with those taking one back to other beginnings, other lives? Misra? Masra? Misrat? Massar? Now with a 't', now without!

He now studied the map as reflected faithfully in the mirror before him. So many hundred kilometres to Kallafo, so many to Jigjiga; so many from Jigjiga to Hargeisa; and from Hargeisa to Mogadiscio; so many from Mogadiscio to Marsabet in the Somali-speaking part of Kenya. Maps. Truth. A mind travels across the graded map, and the eye allots the appropriate colours to the different continents. The body takes longer to make the same journey. Decimal grids, according to Arno Peters, are vastly different from Mercator's map, in existence since the middle of the sixteenth century. And there is a big, painful difference, thought Askar, between the Somali situation today and that of the early 1940s when all the Somali-speaking territories, save Djebouti, were under one administration. And so it was again, for a brief period in 1977–8, when the Ogaden was in Somali hands. But the Somalis, government and people, were busy fighting a war on the ground and in the corridors of diplomatic power and no one released an authorized map of the reconquered territory. Truth. Maps.

He heard footsteps approaching but didn't turn to see who it was. Two faces entered the mirror's background – Salaado in Hilaal's jellaba, he in her caftan. They had been having their afternoon siesta but hadn't been away for long.

'Would you like to come with us?' asked Salaado.

'Where are you going?'

Hilaal said, 'We'll buy a goat.'

'What for?'

Salaado said, 'As an expression of thanks to the gods that protect us. We, too, like all the Mogadiscians, have decided to slaughter a goat as sacrifice.'

Hilaal added, 'There are other reasons. For example.'

'Like?'

Salaado said, 'Sac-ri-fice. It does cover a large area – the notion of sacrifice, I mean. Hilaal and I have talked it over and he, too, thinks so.'

There was no doubt about it, she had become religious.

He repeated the word to himself, like a blind man touching the items surrounding him, a man familiarizing the senses of his body with what his mind already knows. And he *saw*. He *saw* Misra divine, he *saw* her stare at the freshly slaughtered goat's meat, and he *saw* her tell a future when the meat quivered. The scene changed. Now he *saw* her open a chicken, he *saw* her give him an egg which she had salvaged from the dead fowl's inside and he *saw* her talk of a future of travels, departures and arrivals. Again the scene changed. And he *saw* a horse drop its rider, he *saw* a girl kidnapped, he *saw* the girl grow into a woman ripe as corn, he *saw* the hand that had watered the corn pluck it, then eat it – he *saw* the man-of-the-watering-hand murdered. Sac-ri-fice! For Misra – a mastectomy; Hilaal – a vasectomy; Salaado – removal of the ovaries; Qorrax – exaction of blood, so many ounces a-bleeding; Karin – a life of sacrifices; Arla and Cali-Xamari – his parents – their lives; the Somali people – their sons, their daughters and the country's economy. In short, life *as* sacrifice. In short, life *is* blood, and the shedding of one's blood for a cause and for one's country; in short, life is the drinking of enemy blood and vengeance. Life is love too. Salaado and Hilaal are love. Arla – the earth; Qorrax – the sun in its masculine manifestations; Hilaal – the moon; Salaado – solemnity, prayers, etc.; Misra*t* – foundation of the earth; Karin – a hill in the east, humps on backs; Cali-Xamari – a return to a beginning; and Riyo – dreams dreaming dreams!

Now he saw faces, now he didn't see them; now he saw shades – like larvae under a microscope, these moved in the mirror. He started.

When he calmed again, he took an unperturbed look. Hilaal and Salaado were in the doorway. They had changed into decent clothes to go out in. 'Are you coming with us or aren't you?' Hilaal asked.

'I have one question to answer before I set foot out of this house,' said Askar. He fell silent and couldn't help feeling they were studying his movements with some concern.

Salaado said, 'What is the question?'

'Who *is* Askar?'

The question made sense to its audience a minute or so later. No one said or did anything for a long time, as though in deference to the question which had been posed. In any case, there fell the kind of silence a coffin imposes upon those whom it encounters during its journey to the cemetery. And the sun entered the room they were in, in silence, then a slight breeze, smelling of the sea, entered in its wake, whereupon the dust and the rays merged, like ideas, and these were, like faces bright with smiles, reflected in the mirror. Askar was about to break the silence when he noticed that clouds, dark as migrating shadows, swooped down upon the rays of dust in the mirror, like vultures going for a meaty catch. Tagged on to the tail-end of the clouds, travelling at the speed of a vehicle being towed, the moon. Then ... !

Then two other shadows fell across and obliterated the clouds and Askar was in no doubt that the men, to whom these belonged, one tall and ugly, the other short and handsome, were in police uniform. It was the tall one who spoke first. He said, 'Which of you,' looking from Hilaal to Askar, 'answers to the name of Askar?'

There was no time to indulge in metaphysical evasions, no time to consider the rhetorical aspects of one's answering to a name. Without looking at Hilaal or Salaado, whose lips were already astir with prayers, Askar: 'It is I.' And after a pause, 'Why?'

It was the short one's turn to speak. He said, 'We are from the police station nearby, *Giardino*. We have questions to put to you. Please come with us.'

Hilaal moved nearer the short constable. He asked, 'What questions? And in what connection, pray?'

The tall one, who was probably senior in rank and age, said, 'Do the names Misra*t*, Aw-Adan, Qorrax and Karin mean anything to Askar? This is the question,' and he went nearer Hilaal. 'I suppose you are Hilaal and that is Salaado?'

Everyone was quiet. In the meantime, the short constable bent down (maybe to lace his boots) but Askar felt as if the man was digging out of the earth roots of shadows, short as shrubs. The constable's body shot up suddenly, his back straightened and the room was awash with sunshine. Hilaal said, his voice thin and tense, 'What are we waiting for? Let's go.'

Giardino was half a kilometre away and they walked, Askar, Hilaal and Salaado ahead, and following them, like jailers prisoners, the two police officers. Above them, an umbrella of clouds, reassuring as haloes, and on their faces, shadows long and crooked like question marks. The tall constable, who took upon himself to lead the last ten metres of the walk, wore an anklet of shadows round his feet, treading on stirred memories of (Askar's?) dust. They entered the station in silence.

A third police constable, sitting behind a typewriter, asked Askar, 'What is your name?'

'Askar Cali-Xamari.'

And that was how it began – the story of (Misra/Misrat/Masarat and) Askar. First, he told it plainly and without embellishment, answering the police officer's questions; then he told it to men in gowns, men resembling ravens with white skulls. And time grew on Askar's face, as he told the story yet again, time grew like a tree, with more branches and far more falling leaves than the tree which is on the face of the moon. In the process, he became the defendant. He was, at one and the same time, the plaintiff and the juror. Finally, allowing for his different personae to act as judge, as audience and as witness, Askar told it to himself.

PANTHEON MODERN WRITERS ORIGINALS

THE VICE-CONSUL

by Marguerite Duras, translated from the French by Eileen Ellenbogen

The first American edition ever of the novel Marguerite Duras considers her best—a tale of passion and desperation set in India and Southeast Asia.

"A masterful novel."—*Chicago Tribune*

0-394-55898-7 cloth, $10.95   0-394-75026-8 paper, $6.95

MAPS

by Nuruddin Farah

The unforgettable story of one man's coming of age in the turmoil of modern Africa.

"A true and rich work of art. . . .. [by] one of the finest contemporary African writers."
—Salman Rushdie

0-394-56325-5 cloth, $11.95   0-394-75548-0 paper, $7.95

DREAMING JUNGLES

by Michel Rio, translated from the French by William Carlson

A brilliant, hypnotic novel about an elegant French scientist who sets off to study chimpanzees in turn-of-the-century Africa, and his shattering confrontation with the jungle, passion, and at last, himself.

"Very beautiful and very witty."—Mark Strand

0-394-55661-5 cloth, $10.95   0-394-75035-7 paper, $6.95

BURNING PATIENCE

by Antonio Skármeta, translated from the Spanish by Katherine Silver

A charming story about the friendship that develops between Pablo Neruda, Latin America's greatest poet, and the postman who stops to receive his advice about love.

"The mix of the fictional and the real is masterful, and . . . gives the book its special appeal and brilliance."   —*Christian Science Monitor*

0-394-55576-7 cloth, $10.95   0-394-75033-0 paper, $6.95

YOU CAN'T GET LOST IN CAPE TOWN

by Zoë Wicomb

Nine short stories powerfully evoke a young black woman's upbringing in South Africa.

"A superb first collection."—*The New York Times Book Review*

0-394-56030-2 cloth, $10.95   0-394-75309-7 paper, $6.95

PART ONE

No children for me. Give me grown-ups.

Charles Dickens

Living begins when you start doubting
everything that came before you.

Socrates

ACKNOWLEDGEMENTS

The germs of *Maps* developed in the soil of my mind as germs generally do, although as a necessary ingredient of its culture, I introduced various organisms from other bacteria grown in other brains, other earths. Obviously, it is an impossible task to name all my sources. However, prominent among these are *The Wise Wound* by Peter Redgrove and Penelope Shuttle (Routledge & Kegan Paul Ltd) and *The Epic in Africa* by Isidore Okpewho (Columbia University Press).

I would also like to take this opportunity to thank the Dean of the Faculty of Arts, University of Jos, Nigeria, from whom I received much help and encouragement when, for two academic years, 1981–3, I was attached to the Department of English as Visiting Reader. It was during this period that I wrote not only a full-length play but also the first version of *Maps*. However, when doing this final version, I was given generous moral and material assistance from my good friends Lenrie Peters, Liz D., Hewit, and Dr Ogba – to whom, my thanks.

Nuruddin Farah
1985

To Muxammad
my eldest brother
and trusted counsellor